Life of Pi

YANN
MARTEL

About the author

Yann Martel was born in Spain but currently lives in Montreal. He is the highly acclaimed[1] author of *Self*, a novel, and of the story collection[2] *The Facts Behind the Helsinki Roccamatios*[3]. *Life of Pi* is his third book and was shortlisted[4] for the Governor General Award[5], the Commonwealth Writers Prize[6] and was the winner of the 2002 Man Booker Prize[7].

1. unanimement salué par la critique

2. recueil de nouvelles

3. « L'Histoire de la famille Roccamatios à Helsinki », paru sous le titre « Paul en Finlande »

4. sélectionné

5. Prix du gouverneur général du Canada

6. Prix des écrivains du Commonwealth

7. [prestigieux prix accordé à des écrivains du Commonwealth ou de la République d'Irlande]

DIRECTION DE LA PUBLICATION : Carine Girac-Marinier

DIRECTION ÉDITORIALE : Claude Nimmo

NOTES EN MARGE : Émilie Bourdarot

RÉVISION DES NOTES : Giovanni Picci

RELECTURE : Joëlle Narjollet

INFORMATIQUE ÉDITORIALE : Marie-Noëlle Tilliette

CONCEPTION GRAPHIQUE : Uli Meindl

MISE EN PAGES : Cynthia Savage

FABRICATION : Rebecca Dubois

Mot de l'Éditeur

Vous aimeriez lire en langue originale, mais le vocabulaire, les expressions figurées ou la syntaxe vous arrêtent parfois ?

Cette collection est faite pour vous !

Vous trouverez en effet, en note dans la marge, une traduction de certains mots et expressions qui vous permettra d'avancer facilement dans votre lecture.

Nous n'avons pas cherché à vous donner une traduction littéraire de l'ouvrage et nous nous sommes parfois écartés du sens littéral pour vous fournir celui qui convient le mieux à l'histoire. Aussi les mots sont-ils traduits dans le contexte du texte original.

Les expressions figées anglaises sont, bien entendu, rendues par une expression équivalente en français.

Les allusions à des réalités culturelles du monde anglo-saxon sont expliquées également dans la marge, pour vous aider à mieux comprendre la trame de l'histoire.

Vous aurez ainsi, en regard du texte original, tout le savoir-faire d'un dictionnaire rien que pour vous et adapté à ce livre !

Notre objectif est de vous mener jusqu'au mot FIN en vous donnant les clés nécessaires à la compréhension du récit.

Laissez-vous gagner par l'angoisse, l'humour et le suspense qui règnent chez les maîtres de la littérature anglo-saxonne.

Lire en VO ? You can indeed!

À mes parents et à mon frère

AUTHOR'S NOTE

This book was born as I was hungry. Let me explain. In the spring of 1996, my second book, a novel, came out[1] in Canada. It didn't fare well.[2] Reviewers[3] were puzzled[4], or damned it with faint praise[5]. Then readers ignored it. Despite[6] my best efforts at playing the clown or the trapeze artist, the media circus[7] made no difference. The book did not move.[8] Books lined the shelves of bookstores like kids standing in a row[9] to play baseball or soccer[10], and mine was the gangly[11], unathletic kid that no one wanted on their team. It vanished[12] quickly and quietly.

The fiasco did not affect me too much. I had already moved on to another story, a novel set in Portugal in 1939. Only I was feeling restless.[13] And I had a little money.

So I flew to Bombay. This is not so illogical if you realize three things: that a stint[14] in India will beat the restlessness out of any living creature; that a little money can go a long way[15] there; and that a novel set in Portugal in 1939 may have very little to do with Portugal in 1939.

I had been to India before, in the north, for five months. On that first trip[16] I had come to the subcontinent[17] completely unprepared. Actually, I had a preparation of one word. When I told a friend who knew the country well of my travel plans, he said casually[18], "They speak a funny English in India. They like words like bamboozle[19]." I remembered his words as my plane started its descent towards Delhi, so the word bamboozle was my one preparation for the rich, noisy, functioning madness of India. I used the word on occasion, and truth be told[20], it served me well[21]. To a clerk[22] at a train station I said, "I didn't think the fare[23] would be so expensive. You're not trying to bamboozle me, are you?" He smiled and chanted[24], "No sir! There is no bamboozlement[25] here. I have quoted you the correct fare[26]."

1. a été publié
2. Il n'a pas connu beaucoup de succès.
3. Les critiques
4. perplexes
5. se sont montrés peu élogieux
6. Malgré
7. cirque médiatique
8. Les ventes du livre ne progressaient pas.
9. en rang
10. football
11. dégingandé
12. Il a disparu des étagères
13. Mais j'avais envie de voyager.
14. séjour
15. permet de tenir longtemps
16. voyage
17. sous-continent indien
18. négligemment
19. embobiner
20. à vrai dire
21. il m'a été bien utile
22. guichetier
23. billet
24. entonna
25. embobinage
26. prix

This second time to India I knew better what to expect and I knew what I wanted: I would settle[1] in a hill station[2] and write my novel. I had visions of myself[3] sitting at a table on a large veranda, my notes spread out[4] in front of me next to a steaming[5] cup of tea. Green hills heavy with mists[6] would lie at my feet and the shrill[7] cries of monkeys would fill[8] my ears. The weather would be just right, requiring a light sweater[9] mornings and evenings, and something short-sleeved[10] midday. Thus set up, pen in hand, for the sake of[11] greater truth, I would turn Portugal into a fiction. That's what fiction is about, isn't it, the selective transforming of reality? The twisting of it to bring out[12] its essence? What need did I have to go to Portugal?

The lady who ran the place would tell me stories about the struggle to boot the British out[13]. We would agree on what I was to have for lunch and supper the next day. After my writing day was over, I would go for walks in the rolling hills[14] of the tea estates[15].

Unfortunately, the novel sputtered[16], coughed[17] and died. It happened in Matheran, not far from Bombay, a small hill station with some monkeys but no tea estates. It's a misery[18] peculiar to[19] would-be writers[20]. Your theme is good, as are your sentences. Your characters are so ruddy with life[21] they practically need birth certificates[22]. The plot[23] you've mapped out for them is grand[24], simple and gripping[25]. You've done your research, gathering[26] the facts—historical, social, climatic, culinary—that will give your story its feel of authenticity[27]. The dialogue zips along[28], crackling with tension. The descriptions burst with colour, contrast and telling[29] detail. Really, your story can only be great. But it all adds up to nothing[30]. In spite of the obvious, shining promise of it, there comes a moment when you realize that the whisper[31] that has been pestering you all along[32] from the back of your mind is speaking the flat, awful truth: it won't work[33]. An element is missing, that spark[34] that brings to life a real story, regardless of wheth-

er the history or the food is right[1]. *Your story is emotionally dead, that's the crux of it*[2]. *The discovery is something soul-destroying*[3], *I tell you. It leaves you with an aching hunger*[4].

From Matheran I mailed the notes of my failed novel. I mailed them to a fictitious address in Siberia, with a return address, equally fictitious, in Bolivia. After the clerk[5] had stamped[6] the envelope and thrown it into a sorting bin[7], I sat down, glum and disheartened[8]. "What now, Tolstoy? What other bright ideas do you have for your life?" I asked myself.

Well, I still had a little money and I was still feeling restless. I got up and walked out of the post office to explore the south of India.

I would have liked to say, "I'm a doctor", to those who asked me what I did, doctors being the current purveyors of magic and miracle. But I'm sure we would have had a bus accident around the next bend[9], and with all eyes fixed on me I would have to explain, amidst the crying and moaning[10] of victims, that I meant in law[11]; then, to their appeal to help them sue[12] the government over the mishap[13], I would have to confess that as a matter of fact[14] it was a Bachelor's[15] in philosophy; next, to the shouts of what meaning such a bloody tragedy could have, I would have to admit that I had hardly[16] touched Kierkegaard; and so on[17]. I stuck to[18] the humble, bruised[19] truth.

Along the way[20], here and there, I got the response, "A writer? Is that so?[21] I have a story for you." Most times the stories were little more than anecdotes, short of breath and short of life[22].

I arrived in the town of Pondicherry, a tiny self-governing Union Territory[23] south of Madras, on the coast of Tamil Nadu. In population and size it is an inconsequent[24] part of India—by comparison, Prince Edward Island is a giant within Canada—but history has set it apart[25]. For[26] Pondicherry was once the capital of that most modest of colonial empires, French India. The French would have liked to rival[27] the British, very much so, but the only Raj[28] they

1. quelle que soit la qualité de l'histoire ou des recettes
2. le nœud du problème
3. démoralisante
4. un terrible manque
5. employé de la poste
6. a eu timbré
7. boîte de tri
8. morose et découragé
9. au prochain virage
10. au milieu des cris et lamentations
11. en droit
12. poursuivre en justice
13. accident
14. en fait
15. licence
16. à peine
17. et ainsi de suite
18. Je m'en suis tenu à
19. douloureuse
20. Au fil du temps
21. Vraiment ?
22. qui manquaient de souffle et de vie
23. un minuscule territoire autonome de l'Union indienne
24. sans importance
25. l'histoire lui a donné un statut particulier
26. Car
27. égaler
28. empire

1. poignée
2. Ils s'y sont accrochés
3. de larges rues perpendiculaires les unes aux autres
4. plafond
5. Des ventilateurs tournent
6. rempli de
7. quiconque
8. du pain perdu
9. Il y est facile d'engager la conversation.
10. un homme d'un certain âge, fringant, aux yeux pétillants
11. et à la tignasse blanche comme neige
12. en effet
13. et ainsi de suite
14. routards
15. Il a eu l'air surpris et a hoché la tête quand il a appris ma profession.
16. addition
17. méfiant
18. Témoin de Jéhovah
19. qui frappait à ma porte
20. au fin fond de
21. il y a quelques années
22. ravi

managed to get was a handful[1] of small ports. *They clung to these[2] for nearly three hundred years. They left Pondicherry in 1954, leaving behind nice white buildings, broad streets at right angles to each other[3], street names such as rue de la Marine and rue Saint-Louis, and kepis, caps, for the policemen.*

I was at the Indian Coffee House, on Nehru Street. It's one big room with green walls and a high ceiling[4]. Fans whirl[5] above you to keep the warm, humid air moving. The place is furnished to capacity with[6] identical square tables, each with its complement of four chairs. You sit where you can, with whoever[7] is at a table. The coffee is good and they serve French toast[8]. Conversation is easy to come by.[9] And so, a spry, bright-eyed elderly man[10] with great shocks of pure white hair[11] was talking to me. I confirmed to him that Canada was cold and that French was indeed[12] spoken in parts of it and that I liked India and so on and so forth[13]— the usual light talk between friendly, curious Indians and foreign backpackers[14]. He took in my line of work with a widening of the eyes and a nodding of the head.[15] It was time to go. I had my hand up, trying to catch my waiter's eye to get the bill[16].

Then the elderly man said, "I have a story that will make you believe in God."

I stopped waving my hand. But I was suspicious[17]. Was this a Jehovah's Witness[18] knocking at my door[19]? "Does your story take place two thousand years ago in a remote corner of[20] the Roman Empire?" I asked.

"No."

Was he some sort of Muslim evangelist? "Does it take place in seventh-century Arabia?"

"No, no. It starts right here in Pondicherry just a few years back[21] and it ends, I am delighted[22] to tell you, in the very country you come from."

"And it will make me believe in God?"

"Yes."

"That's a tall order[1]."

"Not so tall that you can't reach[2]."

My waiter appeared. I hesitated for a moment. I ordered two coffees. We introduced ourselves.[3] His name was Francis Adirubasamy. "Please tell me your story", I said.

"You must pay proper attention[4]", he replied.

"I will." I brought out[5] pen and notepad[6].

"Tell me, have you been to the botanical garden?" he asked.

"I went yesterday."

"Did you notice the toy train tracks[7]?"

"Yes, I did."

"A train still runs on Sundays for the amusement of the children. But it used to run[8] twice an hour[9] every day. Did you take note of[10] the names of the stations?"

"One is called Roseville. It's right next to the rose garden."

"That's right. And the other?"

"I don't remember."

"The sign was taken down.[11] The other station was once called Zootown. The toy train had two stops: Roseville and Zootown. Once upon a time[12] there was a zoo in the Pondicherry Botanical Garden."

He went on. I took notes, the elements of the story. "You must talk to him", he said, of the main character[13]. "I knew him very, very well. He's a grown man[14] now. You must ask him all the questions you want."

Later, in Toronto, among nine columns[15] of Patels in the phone book[16], I found him, the main character. My heart pounded[17] as I dialed[18] his phone number. The voice that answered had an Indian lilt[19] to its Canadian accent, light but unmistakable[20], like a trace of incense[21] in the air. "That was a very long time ago", he said. Yet[22] he agreed to meet. We met many times. He showed me the diary[23] he kept during the events. He showed me the yellowed newspaper clippings[24] that made him briefly, obscurely famous. He told me his story. All the while[25] I took notes. Nearly a year lat-

1. vraie gageure

2. y arriver

3. Nous nous sommes présentés.

4. Il va falloir être très attentif

5. J'ai sorti

6. carnet

7. les rails du petit train

8. autrefois, il roulait

9. toutes les demi-heures

10. Avez-vous remarqué

11. Le panneau a été enlevé.

12. Il fut un temps où

13. personnage principal

14. adulte

15. colonnes

16. annuaire

17. battait la chamade

18. je composais

19. intonation

20. caractéristique

21. encens

22. Cependant,

23. journal intime

24. les coupures de journaux jaunies

25. Pendant tout ce temps

er, after considerable difficulties, I received a tape[1] and a report[2] from the Japanese Ministry of Transport. It was as I listened to that tape that I agreed with Mr. Adirubasamy that this was, indeed, a story to make you believe in God.

It seemed natural that Mr. Patel's story should be told mostly in the first person—in his voice and through his eyes. But any inaccuracies[3] or mistakes are mine.

I have a few[4] people to thank. I am most obviously indebted to[5] Mr. Patel. My gratitude to him is as boundless as[6] the Pacific Ocean and I hope that my telling of his tale does not disappoint him[7]. For getting me started on the story, I have Mr. Adirubasamy to thank. For helping me complete it, I am grateful to[8] three officials[9] of exemplary professionalism: Mr. Kazuhiko Oda, lately[10] of the Japanese Embassy[11] in Ottawa; Mr. Hiroshi Watanabe, of Oika Shipping Company[12]; and, especially, Mr. Tomohiro Okamoto, of the Japanese Ministry of Transport, now retired[13]. As for[14] the spark of life[15], I owe it to[16] Mr. Moacyr Scliar. Lastly, I would like to express my sincere gratitude to that great institution, the Canada Council for the Arts[17], without whose grant[18] I could not have brought together this story[19] that has nothing to do with Portugal in 1939. If we, citizens, do not support our artists, then we sacrifice our imagination on the altar of crude reality[20] and we end up believing in nothing[21] and having worthless[22] dreams.

1. cassette
2. rapport
3. inexactitudes
4. quelques
5. Je suis bien entendu particulièrement redevable à
6. aussi vaste que
7. ne le décevra pas
8. reconnaissant envers
9. représentants officiels
10. récemment
11. ambassade
12. de la société de transport maritime Oika
13. à présent à la retraite
14. Quant à
15. l'étincelle de vie
16. je la dois à
17. le Conseil des arts du Canada
18. sans la bourse duquel
19. je n'aurais pas pu rassembler les éléments de cette histoire
20. sur l'autel de la dure réalité
21. nous finissons par ne plus croire à rien
22. insignifiants

Coup de pouce pour vous aider à bien comprendre le début de l'histoire...

Nous sommes au Canada. Piscine Molitor Patel (Pi), le protagoniste de cette histoire, commence à raconter ses études universitaires à Toronto et sa double spécialisation : les études religieuses et la zoologie.

Dans ses toutes premières pages, Pi se livre à une description détaillée du comportement du *paresseux à trois orteils*, un mammifère arboricole de l'Amérique tropicale, calme, pacifique, au sourire bienveillant, parfait pour apaiser ses souffrances. De quelles souffrances s'agit-il ? Qu'y a-t-il eu de si bouleversant dans sa vie ?

Retour en arrière, en Inde, où l'incroyable histoire de Pi commence... c'est le début des années 1970, à Pondichéry, dans le zoo dirigé par son père...

PART ONE

Toronto and Pondicherry

CHAPTER 1

My suffering[1] left me sad and gloomy[2].

Academic study[3] and the steady, mindful practice[4] of religion slowly brought me back to life. I have kept up[5] what some people would consider my strange religious practices. After one year of high school[6], I attended[7] the University of Toronto and *took a double-major Bachelors degree*[8]. My majors[9] were religious studies and zoology. My fourth-year thesis[10] for religious studies concerned certain aspects of the cosmogony theory of Isaac Luria, the great sixteenth-century Kabbalist from Safed[11]. My zoology thesis was a functional analysis of the thyroid gland of the three-toed sloth[12]. I chose the sloth because its demeanour[13]—calm, quiet and introspective—did something to soothe my shattered self[14].

There are two-toed sloths and there are three-toed sloths, the case being determined by the fore-paws[15] of the animals, since all sloths have three claws[16] on their hind paws[17]. I had the great luck one summer of studying the three-toed sloth *in situ* in the equatorial jungles of Brazil. It is a highly intriguing[18] creature. Its only real habit is indolence. It sleeps or rests[19] on average[20] twenty hours a day. Our team tested the sleep habits of five wild three-toed sloths by placing on their heads, in the early evening after they had fallen asleep, bright red plastic dishes filled with water[21]. We found them still in place late the next morning, the water of the dishes swarming with insects[22]. The sloth is at its

1. Mes souffrances

2. sombre

3. Les études

4. la pratique régulière et consciencieuse

5. J'ai conservé

6. lycée

7. je me suis inscrit à

8. j'ai fait des études de licence avec une double spécialisation

9. Mes matières principales

10. Le mémoire que j'ai écrit en quatrième année

11. [l'école kabbalistique]

12. du paresseux à trois orteils

13. comportement

14. apaiser mon moi brisé

15. pattes avant

16. griffes

17. pattes arrière

18. tout à fait fascinante

19. se repose

20. en moyenne

21. des assiettes en plastique rouge vif remplies d'eau

22. grouillant d'insectes

busiest at sunset[1], using the word *busy* here in the most relaxed sense. It moves along the bough of a tree[2] in its characteristic upside-down position[3] at the speed of roughly 400 metres an hour[4]. On the ground, it crawls[5] to its next tree at the rate of[6] 250 metres an hour, when motivated, which is 440 times slower than a motivated cheetah[7]. Unmotivated, it covers[8] four to five metres in an hour.

The three-toed sloth is not well informed about the outside world. On a scale of 2 to 10, where 2 represents unusual dullness[9] and 10 extreme acuity, Beebe (1926) gave the sloth's senses of taste, touch, sight and hearing a rating of 2[10], and its sense of smell a rating of 3. If you come upon a sleeping three-toed sloth in the wild, two or three nudges[11] should suffice to awaken it; it will then look sleepily in every direction but[12] yours. Why it should look about is uncertain since the sloth sees everything in a Magoo-like blur[13]. As for hearing, the sloth is not so much deaf as uninterested in sound. Beebe reported that firing guns[14] next to sleeping or feeding[15] sloths elicited little reaction[16]. And the sloth's slightly better sense of smell should not be overestimated. They are said to be able to sniff[17] and avoid decayed[18] branches, but Bullock (1968) reported that sloths fall to the ground clinging to[19] decayed branches "often".

How does it survive, you might ask.

Precisely by being so slow. Sleepiness and slothfulness keep it out of harm's way[20], away from the notice of jaguars, ocelots, harpy eagles[21] and anacondas. A sloth's hairs shelter an algae[22] that is brown during the dry season and green during the wet season, so the animal blends in with the surrounding moss and foliage[23] and looks like a nest of white ants or of squirrels[1], or like nothing at all but[2] part of a tree.

The three-toed sloth lives a peaceful, vegetarian life in perfect harmony with its environment. "A good-natured[3] smile is forever on its lips", reported Tirler (1966). I have seen that smile with my own eyes. I am not one given to[4] projecting human traits and emotions onto animals, but many a time[5] during that month in Brazil, looking up at sloths in repose, I felt I was in the presence of upside-down yogis deep in meditation[6] or hermits[7] deep in prayer, wise beings[8] whose intense imaginative lives were beyond the reach of my scientific probing[9].

Sometimes I got my majors mixed up[10]. A number of my fellow[11] religious-studies students—muddled[12] agnostics who didn't know which way was up[13], who were in the thrall of reason[14], that fool's gold for the bright[15]—reminded me of the three-toed sloth; and the three-toed sloth, such a beautiful example of the miracle of life, reminded me of God.

I never had problems with my fellow scientists[16]. Scientists are a friendly, atheistic, hard-working, beer-drinking lot whose minds are preoccupied with sex, chess[17] and baseball when they are not preoccupied with science.

I was a very good student, if I may say so myself[18]. I was tops[19] at St. Michael's College four years in a row[20]. I got every possible student award[21] from the Department of Zoology. If I got none from the Department of Religious Studies, it is simply because there are no student awards in this department (the rewards[22] of religious study are not in mortal hands, we all know that). I would have received the Governor General's Academic Medal, the University of Toronto's highest undergraduate[23] award,

1. un nid de termites ou d'écureuils

2. rien d'autre que

3. bon enfant

4. Je ne suis pas du genre à

5. souvent

6. en pleine méditation

7. ermites

8. des sages

9. échappaient à mes investigations scientifiques

10. je mélangeais mes spécialités

11. Un certain nombre des autres

12. à l'esprit embrouillé

13. complètement désorientés

14. esclaves de leur raison

15. le miroir aux alouettes des gens intelligents

16. les autres scientifiques

17. les échecs

18. si je peux me permettre de le dire moi-même

19. parmi les meilleurs

20. d'affilée

21. prix

22. récompenses

23. du premier cycle universitaire

of which no small number of illustrious Canadians have been recipients[1], were it not for[2] a beef-eating pink boy with a neck like a tree trunk and a temperament of unbearable good cheer[3].

I still smart a little at the slight.[4] When you've suffered a great deal in life, each additional pain is both unbearable and trifling[5]. My life is like a memento mori painting[6] from European art: there is always a grinning skull[7] at my side to remind me of the folly of human ambition. I mock[8] this skull. I look at it and I say, "You've got the wrong fellow.[9] You may not believe in life, but I don't believe in death. Move on![10]" The skull snickers[11] and moves ever closer, but that doesn't surprise me. The reason death sticks so closely[12] to life isn't biological necessity—it's envy. Life is so beautiful that death has fallen in love with it, a jealous, possessive love that grabs at[13] what it can. But life leaps over oblivion lightly[14], losing only a thing or two of no importance, and gloom is but the passing shadow of a cloud[15]. The pink boy also got the nod from[16] the Rhodes Scholarship committee. I love him and I hope his time at Oxford was a rich experience. If Lakshmi, goddess of wealth[17], one day favours me bountifully[18], Oxford is fifth on the list of cities I would like to visit before I pass on[19], after Mecca, Varanasi, Jerusalem and Paris.

I have nothing to say of my working life, only that a tie is a noose[20], and inverted though it is[21], it will hang a man nonetheless[22] if he's not careful.

I love Canada. I miss the heat of India, the food, the house lizards on the walls, the musicals on the silver screen[23], the cows wandering[24] the streets, the crows cawing[25], even the talk of cricket matches, but I love Canada. It is a great country much too cold for good sense, inhabited by compassionate[1], intelligent people with bad hairdos[2]. Anyway, I have nothing to go home to[3] in Pondicherry.

Richard Parker has stayed with me. I've never forgotten him. Dare I say I miss him?[4] I do. I miss him. I still see him in my dreams. They are nightmares mostly, but nightmares tinged[5] with love. Such is the strangeness of the human heart. I still cannot understand how he could abandon me so unceremoniously, without any sort of goodbye, without looking back even once. That pain is like an axe that chops at my heart[6].

The doctors and nurses at the hospital in Mexico were incredibly kind to me. And the patients, too. Victims of cancer or car accidents, once they heard my story, they hobbled and wheeled over to see me[7], they and their families, though none of them spoke English and I spoke no Spanish. They smiled at me, shook my hand, patted me[8] on the head, left gifts of food and clothing[9] on my bed. They moved me to uncontrollable fits of laughing and crying[10].

Within a couple of days I could stand[11], even make two, three steps, despite nausea, dizziness[12] and general weakness. Blood tests revealed that I was anemic, and that my level of sodium was very high and my potassium low. My body retained fluids and my legs swelled up tremendously[13]. I looked as if I had been grafted with[14] a pair of elephant legs. My urine was a deep, dark yellow going on to brown. After a week or so, I could walk just about normally and I could wear shoes if I didn't lace them up[15]. My skin healed[16], though I still have scars on my shoulders and back[17].

The first time I turned a tap on[18], its noisy, wasteful, superabundant gush[19] was such a shock that I became incoherent and my legs collapsed beneath me and I fainted[20] in the arms of a nurse.

1. charitables
2. des coiffures affreuses
3. je n'ai pas d'attaches
4. Oserais-je dire qu'il me manque ?
5. empreints
6. une hache qui me fend le cœur
7. ils sont venus vers moi, en boitillant ou en fauteuil roulant
8. m'ont donné des petites tapes
9. m'ont fait cadeau de nourriture et de vêtements
10. des crises de rire ou de larmes
11. tenir debout
12. les étourdissements
13. gonflaient terriblement
14. On aurait dit qu'on m'avait greffé
15. si je ne faisais pas les lacets
16. a guéri
17. des cicatrices sur mes épaules et mon dos
18. j'ai ouvert un robinet
19. le jet d'eau bruyant, excessif et surabondant qui en est sorti
20. je me suis évanoui

The first time I went to an Indian restaurant in Canada I used my fingers. The waiter looked at me critically[1] and said, "Fresh off the boat, are you?[2]" I blanched[3]. My fingers, which a second before had been taste buds[4] savouring the food a little ahead of[5] my mouth, became dirty under his gaze[6]. They froze like criminals caught in the act.[7] I didn't dare lick them.[8] I wiped them guiltily[9] on my napkin[10]. He had no idea how deeply those words wounded me[11]. They were like nails being driven[12] into my flesh. I picked up the knife and fork. I had hardly ever used[13] such instruments. My hands trembled. My sambar[14] lost its taste.

CHAPTER 2

He lives in Scarborough. He's a small, slim man—no more than five foot five[15]. Dark hair, dark eyes. Hair greying at the temples[16]. Can't be older than forty. Pleasing coffee-coloured complexion[17]. Mild fall weather, yet[18] puts on a big winter parka with fur-lined, hood[19] for the walk to the diner[20]. Expressive face. Speaks quickly, hands flitting about[21]. No small talk.[22] He launches forth.[23]

CHAPTER 3

I was named after a swimming pool. Quite peculiar considering my parents never took to water[24]. One of my father's earliest business contacts was Francis Adirubasamy. He became a good friend of the family. I called him Mamaji, *mama* being the Tamil word for *uncle* and *ji* being a suffix used in India to indicate respect and affection. When he was a young man, long before I was born[1], Mamaji was a champion competitive swimmer[2], the champion of all South India. He looked the part[3] his whole life. My brother Ravi once told me that when Mamaji was born he didn't want to give up on[4] breathing water and so the doctor, to save his life, had to take him by the feet and swing him above his head round and round[5].

"It did the trick![6]" said Ravi, wildly spinning his hand above his head. "He coughed out water and started breathing air, but it forced all his flesh and blood to his upper body[7]. That's why his chest is so thick[8] and his legs are so skinny[9]."

I believed him. (Ravi was a merciless teaser.[10] The first time he called Mamaji "Mr. Fish" to my face I left a banana peel[11] in his bed.) Even in his sixties[12], when he was a little stooped[13] and a lifetime of counter-obstetric gravity[14] had begun to nudge his flesh downwards[15], Mamaji swam thirty lengths[16] every morning at the pool[17] of the Aurobindo Ashram.

He tried to teach my parents to swim, but he never got them to go beyond wading up to their knees[18] at the beach and making ludicrous round motions[19] with their arms, which, if they were practising the breaststroke[20], made them look as if they were walking through a jungle, spreading the tall grass[21] ahead of them, or, if it was the front crawl, as if they were running down a hill and flailing their arms so as not to fall[22]. Ravi was just as unenthusiastic.

Mamaji had to wait until I came into the picture[23] to find a willing disciple[24]. The day I came of swimming age, which, to Mother's distress[25], Mamaji claimed was seven, he brought me down to the

1. longtemps avant ma naissance
2. nageur de compétition
3. Il en a eu le physique
4. s'arrêter de
5. le faire tourner plusieurs fois au-dessus de sa tête
6. Ça a marché !
7. vers le haut de son corps
8. son torse est si épais
9. maigres
10. Ravi adorait taquiner
11. peau de banane
12. à l'âge de 60 ans
13. voûté
14. alors que les effets conjugués de la gravité et du temps
15. ramollir son corps
16. longueurs
17. piscine
18. patauger avec de l'eau jusqu'aux genoux
19. des mouvements circulaires ridicules
20. brasse
21. écartant les herbes hautes
22. en agitant les bras pour ne pas tomber
23. ma naissance
24. un disciple fervent
25. désarroi

beach, spread his arms seaward[1] and said, "This is my gift to you."

"And then he nearly drowned you[2]", claimed Mother.

I remained faithful[3] to my aquatic guru. Under his watchful[4] eye I lay on the beach and fluttered my legs[5] and scratched away at the sand[6] with my hands, turning my head at every stroke[7] to breathe. I must have looked like a child throwing a peculiar, slow-motion tantrum[8]. In the water, as he held me at the surface, I tried my best to swim. It was much more difficult than on land. But Mamaji was patient and encouraging.

When he felt that I had progressed sufficiently, we turned our backs on the laughing and the shouting[9], the running and the splashing, the blue-green waves and the bubbly surf[10], and headed for[11] the proper rectangularity and the formal flatness[12] (and the paying admission[13]) of the ashram swimming pool.

I went there with him three times a week through-out[14] my childhood, a Monday, Wednesday, Friday early morning ritual with the clockwork regularity of a good front-crawl stroke[15]. I have vivid[16] memories of this dignified old man stripping down to nakedness[17] next to me, his body slowly emerging as he neatly disposed of each item of clothing[18], decency being salvaged[19] at the very end by a slight turning away[20] and a magnificent pair of imported athletic bathing trunks[21]. He stood straight and he was ready. It had an epic simplicity. Swimming instruction, which in time became swimming practice, was gruelling[22], but there was the deep pleasure of doing a stroke with increasing ease and speed, over and over, till hypnosis practically, the water turning from molten lead[23] to liquid light.

It was on my own[1], a guilty[2] pleasure, that I returned to the sea, beckoned by the mighty waves[3] that crashed down and reached for me in humble tidal ripples[4], gentle lassos that caught their willing Indian boy[5].

My gift to Mamaji one birthday, I must have been thirteen or so, was two full lengths of credible butterfly[6]. I finished so spent[7] I could hardly wave to him[8].

Beyond the activity of swimming, there was the talk of it. It was the talk that Father loved. The more vigorously he resisted[9] actually swimming, the more he fancied it[10]. Swim lore[11] was his vacation talk from the workaday talk of running a zoo[12]. Water without a hippopotamus was so much more manageable than[13] water with one.

Mamaji studied in Paris for two years, thanks to the colonial administration. He had the time of his life.[14] This was in the early 1930s[15], when the French were still trying to make Pondicherry as Gallic as the British were trying to make the rest of India Britannic. I don't recall[16] exactly what Mamaji studied. Something commercial, I suppose. He was a great storyteller[17], but forget about his studies or the Eiffel Tower or the Louvre or the cafés of the Champs-Elysées. All his stories had to do with swimming pools and swimming competitions. For example, there was the Piscine Deligny, the city's oldest pool, dating back to 1796, an open-air barge moored to the[18] Quai d'Orsay and the venue[19] for the swimming events of the 1900 Olympics. But none of the times were recognized by the International Swimming Federation because the pool was six metres too long. The water in the pool came straight[20] from the Seine, unfiltered and unheated[21]. "It was cold and dirty", said Mamaji.

1. seul
2. coupable
3. salué par les imposantes vagues
4. qui s'écrasaient pour m'atteindre sous la forme d'humbles ondulations
5. un petit Indien qui ne s'y opposait pas
6. brasse papillon
7. épuisé
8. lui faire signe de la main
9. Plus il résistait vigoureusement à
10. plus il aimait en parler
11. Discuter de natation
12. le changeait de ses conversations de tous les jours sur la gestion d'un zoo
13. était beaucoup plus facile à gérer que
14. Il y a passé des moments inoubliables.
15. au début des années 1930
16. Je ne me souviens pas
17. un merveilleux conteur
18. une péniche à ciel ouvert amarrée au
19. lieu
20. directement
21. non chauffée

"The water, having crossed all of Paris, came in foul enough[1]. Then people at the pool made it utterly disgusting[2]." In conspiratorial whispers[3], with shocking details to back up his claim[4], he assured us that the French had very low standards of personal hygiene[5]. "Deligny was bad enough. Bain Royal, another latrine on the Seine, was worse. At least at Deligny they scooped out the dead fish[6]." Nevertheless, an Olympic pool is an Olympic pool, touched by immortal glory. Though it was a cesspool[7], Mamaji spoke of Deligny with a fond[8] smile.

One was better off[9] at the Piscines Château-Landon, Rouvet or du boulevard de la Gare. They were indoor pools with roofs[10], on land and open year-round[11]. Their water was supplied by the condensation from steam engines[12] from nearby factories[13] and so was cleaner and warmer. But these pools were still a bit dingy[14] and tended to be crowded[15]. "There was so much gob and spit[16] floating in the water, I thought I was swimming through jellyfish[17]", chuckled[18] Mamaji.

The Piscines Hébert, Ledru-Rollin and Butte-aux-Cailles were bright, modern, spacious pools fed by artesian wells[19]. They set the standard for excellence in municipal swimming pools. There was the Piscine des Tourelles, of course, the city's other great Olympic pool, inaugurated during the second Paris games, of 1924. And there were still others, many of them.

But no swimming pool in Mamaji's eyes matched the glory of[20] the Piscine Molitor. It was the crowning aquatic glory[21] of Paris, indeed, of the entire civilized world.

"It was a pool the gods would have delighted to swim in[22]. Molitor had the best competitive swimming club in Paris. There were two pools, an in-

1. était déjà assez nauséabonde

2. parfaitement répugnante

3. En chuchotant de manière complice

4. soutenir ses propos

5. avaient une hygiène corporelle déplorable

6. ils enlevaient les poissons morts

7. cloaque

8. tendre

9. mieux loti

10. des piscines couvertes

11. toute l'année

12. machines à vapeur

13. usines situées à proximité

14. crasseuses

15. bondées

16. crachats

17. méduses

18. gloussait

19. puits artésiens

20. n'était aussi splendide que

21. le chef-d'œuvre aquatique

22. dans laquelle les dieux auraient été ravis de nager

door and an outdoor. Both were as big as small oceans. The indoor pool always had two lanes[1] reserved for swimmers who wanted to do lengths. The water was so clean and clear you could have used it to make your morning coffee. Wooden changing cabins[2], blue and white, surrounded the pool on two floors. You could look down and see everyone and everything. The porters who marked your cabin door with chalk[3] to show that it was occupied were limping[4] old men, friendly in an ill-tempered way[5]. No amount of shouting and tomfoolery[6] ever ruffled them[7]. The showers gushed hot, soothing water.[8] There was a steam room[9] and an exercise room. The outside pool became a skating rink[10] in winter. There was a bar, a cafeteria, a large sunning deck[11], even two small beaches with real sand. Every bit of tile, brass and wood gleamed.[12] It was—it was…"

It was the only pool that made Mamaji fall silent, his memory making too many lengths to mention[13].

Mamaji remembered, Father dreamed.

That is how I got my name when I entered this world, a last, welcome addition to my family, three years after Ravi: Piscine Molitor Patel.

CHAPTER 4

Our good old nation was just seven years old as a republic when it became bigger by a small territory[14]. Pondicherry entered the Union of India on November 1, 1954. One civic achievement[15] called for another[16]. A portion of the grounds of the Pondicherry Botanical Garden was made available rent-free[17] for an exciting business opportunity and—lo

1. couloirs
2. Des vestiaires en bois
3. craie
4. boiteux
5. sympathiques et grincheux
6. pitreries
7. ne les troublaient jamais
8. De l'eau chaude, réconfortante, jaillissait des douches.
9. bain de vapeur
10. patinoire
11. solarium
12. Chaque parcelle de carreau, cuivre et bois brillait.
13. faisait trop de longueurs pour qu'il ait le loisir d'en parler
14. elle a été agrandie d'un petit territoire
15. prouesse
16. en a appelé une autre
17. mise à disposition gratuitement

1. voilà
2. tout neuf
3. sur le plan biologique
4. qui s'étendait sur
5. il tient
6. inondé de soleil et de couleurs vives
7. Il y a toujours une multitude de fleurs.
8. des arbustes et des plantes grimpantes
9. des figuiers des pagodes, des flamboyants, des flammes de la forêt, des bombax, des jacarandas, des manguiers, des jacquiers
10. des bancs
11. étendus
12. se jettent timidement des regards furtifs
13. s'agitent dans les airs
14. se touchant parfois
15. surpris
16. accès de fureur
17. singes
18. seulement dépassé par les cris stridents
19. tourniquet
20. distraitement
21. une fosse peu profonde
22. puissants
23. depuis le début
24. étang

and behold[1]—India had a brand new[2] zoo, designed and run according to the most modern, biologically sound[3] principles.

It was a huge zoo, spread over[4] numberless acres, big enough to require a train to explore it, though it seemed to get smaller as I grew older, train included. Now it's so small it fits[5] in my head. You must imagine a hot and humid place, bathed in sunshine and bright colours[6]. The riot of flowers is incessant.[7] There are trees, shrubs and climbing plants[8] in profusion—peepuls, gulmohurs, flames of the forest, red silk cottons, jacarandas, mangoes, jackfruits[9] and many others that would remain unknown to you if they didn't have neat labels at their feet. There are benches[10]. On these benches you see men sleeping, stretched out[11], or couples sitting, young couples, who steal glances at each other shyly[12] and whose hands flutter in the air[13], happening to touch[14]. Suddenly, amidst the tall and slim trees up ahead, you notice two giraffes quietly observing you. The sight is not the last of your surprises. The next moment you are startled[15] by a furious outburst[16] coming from a great troupe of monkeys[17], only outdone in volume by the shrill cries[18] of strange birds. You come to a turnstile[19]. You distractedly[20] pay a small sum of money. You move on. You see a low wall. What can you expect beyond a low wall? Certainly not a shallow pit[21] with two mighty[22] Indian rhinoceros. But that is what you find. And when you turn your head you see the elephant that was there all along[23], so big you didn't notice it. And in the pond[24] you realize those are hippopotamuses floating in the water. The more you look, the more you see. You are in Zootown!

Before moving to Pondicherry, Father ran a large hotel in Madras. An abiding[1] interest in animals led him to the zoo business. A natural transition, you might think, from hotelkeeping to zookeeping. Not so. In many ways, running a zoo is a hotelkeeper's worst nightmare. Consider[2]: the guests[3] never leave their rooms; they expect not only lodging but full board[4]; they receive a constant flow of visitors[5], some of whom are noisy and unruly[6]. One has to wait until they saunter to their balconies[7], so to speak[8], before one can clean their rooms, and then one has to wait until they tire of the view[9] and return to their rooms before one can clean their balconies; and there is much cleaning to do, for the guests are as unhygienic as[10] alcoholics. Each guest is very particular about his or her diet[11], constantly complains about the slowness of the service[12], and never, ever tips[13]. To speak frankly, many are sexual deviants[14], either terribly repressed[15] and subject to explosions of frenzied lasciviousness[16] or openly depraved, in either case regularly affronting management[17] with gross[18] outrages of free sex and incest. Are these the sorts of guests you would want to welcome to your inn[19]? The Pondicherry Zoo was the source of some pleasure and many headaches[20] for Mr. Santosh Patel, founder, owner[21], director, head of a staff of fifty-three[22], and my father.

To me, it was paradise on earth. I have nothing but the fondest memories[23] of growing up in a zoo. I lived the life of a prince. What maharaja's son had such vast, luxuriant grounds to play about? What palace had such a menagerie? My alarm clock during my childhood was a pride of[24] lions. They were no Swiss clocks, but the lions could be counted upon to roar their heads off[25]

1. vif
2. Jugez plutôt
3. hôtes
4. non seulement le logement, mais aussi la pension complète
5. ils reçoivent constamment des visiteurs
6. bruyants et turbulents
7. ils se rendent tranquillement sur leur balcon
8. pour ainsi dire
9. ils se lassent du paysage
10. ont une hygiène aussi déplorable que
11. a des exigences particulières en matière de nourriture
12. se plaint de la lenteur du service
13. ne donne jamais de pourboire
14. pervers
15. inhibés
16. lascivité déchaînée
17. offensant la direction
18. vulgaires
19. auberge
20. maux de tête
21. fondateur, propriétaire
22. patron de 53 employés
23. Je n'ai que de très bons souvenirs
24. une troupe de
25. rugir férocement

1. des singes hurleurs, des mainates religieux et des cacatoès à huppe rouge
2. regard bienveillant
3. loutres
4. costauds
5. qui bâillaient
6. pour éviter que les paons ne me fassent dessus
7. roussettes
8. piaillements et jacassements
9. des casoars unicaronculés
10. des colombes diamant, des choucadors à épaulettes rouges, des perruches nanday, des inséparables rosegorges ou des conures à front rouge
11. phoques
12. actifs
13. les cerfs
14. mangoustes
15. la gueule irisée
16. majestueux
17. un ara qui escaladait un grillage en s'aidant des griffes et du bec
18. un bec-en-sabot du Nil qui faisait claquer son bec pour me saluer
19. lubrique
20. en toute tranquillité

between five-thirty and six every morning. Breakfast was punctuated by the shrieks and cries of howler monkeys, hill mynahs and Moluccan cockatoos[1]. I left for school under the benevolent gaze[2] not only of Mother but also of bright-eyed otters[3] and burly[4] American bison and stretching and yawning[5] orang-utans. I looked up as I ran under some trees, otherwise peafowl might excrete on me[6]. Better to go by the trees that sheltered the large colonies of fruit bats[7]; the only assault there at that early hour was the bats' discordant concerts of squeaking and chattering[8]. On my way out I might stop by the terraria to look at some shiny frogs glazed bright, bright green, or yellow and deep blue, or brown and pale green. Or it might be birds that caught my attention: pink flamingoes or black swans or one-wattled cassowaries[9], or something smaller, silver diamond doves, Cape glossy starlings, peach-faced lovebirds, Nanday conures, orange-fronted parakeets[10]. Not likely that the elephants, the seals[11], the big cats or the bears would be up and doing[12], but the baboons, the macaques, the mangabeys, the gibbons, the deer[13], the tapirs, the llamas, the giraffes, the mongooses[14] were early risers. Every morning before I was out the main gate I had one last impression that was both ordinary and unforgettable: a pyramid of turtles; the iridescent snout[15] of a mandrill; the stately[16] silence of a giraffe; the obese, yellow open mouth of a hippo; the beak-and-claw climbing of a macaw parrot up a wire fence[17]; the greeting claps of a shoebill's bill[18]; the senile, lecherous[19] expression of a camel. And all these riches were had quickly, as I hurried to school. It was after school that I discovered in a leisurely way[20] what it's like to have an elephant search your clothes in the friendly hope of finding a hidden nut, or an orang-utan pick through your hair for tick snacks[1], its wheeze of disappointment[2] at what an empty pantry[3] your head is. I wish I could convey[4] the perfection of a seal slipping[5] into water or a spider monkey swinging[6] from point to point or a lion merely turning its head. But language founders[7] in such seas. Better to picture it in your head[8] if you want to feel it.

In zoos, as in nature, the best times to visit are sunrise[9] and sunset. That is when most animals come to life. They stir[10] and leave their shelter and tiptoe to the water's edge[11]. They show their raiments[12]. They sing their songs. They turn to each other and perform their rites. The reward for the watching eye and the listening ear is great. I spent more hours than I can count a quiet witness[13] to the highly mannered, manifold[14] expressions of life that grace our planet. It is something so bright, loud, weird[15] and delicate as to stupefy the senses.

I have heard nearly as much nonsense[16] about zoos as I have about God and religion. Well-meaning but misinformed people[17] think animals in the wild are "happy" because they are "free." These people usually have a large, handsome predator in mind, a lion or a cheetah (the life of a gnu or of an aardvark is rarely exalted[18]). They imagine this wild animal roaming[19] about the savannah on digestive walks after eating a prey[20] that accepted its lot piously[21], or going for callisthenic runs[22] to stay slim after overindulging[23]. They imagine this animal overseeing its offspring proudly[24] and tenderly, the whole family watching the setting of the sun from the limbs[25] of trees with sighs[26] of pleasure. The life of the wild animal is simple, noble and meaningful[27], they imagine. Then it is captured by

1. qui fouillait vos cheveux à la recherche de tiques
2. sifflement de déception
3. garde-manger
4. bien rendre
5. se glissant
6. s'élançant
7. échoue
8. l'imaginer
9. le lever du soleil
10. Ils se réveillent
11. ils s'avancent doucement vers les points d'eau
12. parures
13. témoin
14. multiples et sophistiquées
15. étrange
16. absurdités
17. Des gens bien intentionnés mais mal informés
18. la vie d'un gnou ou d'un oryctérope du Cap est rarement glorifiée
19. errant
20. proie
21. qui a accepté son sort pieusement
22. des petits footings
23. après avoir trop mangé
24. surveiller sa progéniture avec fierté
25. branches
26. des soupirs
27. sensée

wicked[1] men and thrown into tiny jails[2]. Its "happiness" is dashed[3]. It yearns mightily for[4] "freedom" and does all it can to escape. Being denied[5] its "freedom" for too long, the animal becomes a shadow of itself, its spirit broken. So some people imagine.

This is not the way it is.

Animals in the wild[6] lead lives of compulsion and necessity within an unforgiving[7] social hierarchy in an environment where the supply of fear is high and the supply of food low[8] and where territory must constantly be defended and parasites forever endured[9]. What is the meaning of freedom in such a context? Animals in the wild are, in practice, free neither in space nor in time, nor in their personal relations. In theory—that is, as a simple physical possibility—an animal could pick up and go[10], flaunting[11] all the social conventions and boundaries proper to its species. But such an event is less likely to happen[12] than for a member of our own species, say a shopkeeper[13] with all the usual ties[14]—to family, to friends, to society—to drop[15] everything and walk away from his life with only the spare change[16] in his pockets and the clothes on his frame[17]. If a man, boldest[18] and most intelligent of creatures, won't wander from place to place[19], a stranger to all, beholden to none[20], why would an animal, which is by temperament far more conservative? For that is what animals are, conservative, one might even say reactionary. The smallest changes can upset them[21]. They want things to be just so, day after day, month after month. Surprises are highly disagreeable to them. You see this in their spatial relations. An animal inhabits its space, whether in a zoo or in the wild, in the same way chess pieces move about a chessboard[22]—significantly. There is no more happenstance[1], no more "freedom", involved in the whereabouts of a lizard[2] or a bear or a deer than in the location of a knight[3] on a chessboard. Both speak of pattern and purpose[4]. In the wild, animals stick to the same paths[5] for the same pressing[6] reasons, season after season. In a zoo, if an animal is not in its normal place in its regular[7] posture at the usual hour, it means something. It may be the reflection of nothing more than a minor change[8] in the environment. A coiled hose[9] left out by a keeper has made a menacing impression. A puddle[10] has formed that bothers[11] the animal. A ladder[12] is making a shadow. But it could mean something more. At its worst[13], it could be that most dreaded thing to a zoo director[14]: a *symptom*, a herald[15] of trouble to come, a reason to inspect the dung[16], to cross-examine[17] the keeper, to summon the vet[18]. All this because a stork[19] is not standing where it usually stands!

But let me pursue for a moment only one aspect of the question.

If you went to a home, kicked down the front door[20], chased[21] the people who lived there out into the street and said, "Go! You are free! Free as a bird! Go! Go!"—do you think they would shout and dance for joy? They wouldn't. Birds are not free. The people you've just evicted[22] would sputter[23], "With what right do you throw us out? This is our home. We own it. We have lived here for years. We're calling the police, you scoundrel[24]."

Don't we say, "There's no place like home[25]?" That's certainly what animals feel. Animals are territorial. That is the key to their minds. Only a familiar territory will allow them to fulfill[26] the two relentless imperatives[27] of the wild: the avoidance of enemies[28] and the getting of food and water. A

1. hasard
2. qui détermine le lieu où se trouve un lézard
3. cavalier
4. de modèles et de buts
5. continuent d'emprunter les mêmes trajectoires
6. pressantes
7. habituelle
8. changement mineur
9. Un tuyau d'arrosage enroulé
10. flaque
11. gêne
12. échelle
13. Dans le pire des cas
14. ce qu'un directeur de zoo redoute le plus
15. signe annonciateur
16. les excréments
17. interroger
18. faire venir le véto
19. cigogne
20. vous enfonciez la porte d'entrée à coups de pied
21. vous chassiez
22. expulsés
23. diraient en bredouillant
24. scélérat
25. On n'est jamais mieux que chez soi
26. satisfaire
27. exigences vitales
28. éviter les ennemis

biologically sound zoo enclosure[1]—whether[2] cage, pit[3], moated island[4], corral, terrarium, aviary or aquarium—is just another territory, peculiar only in its size and in its proximity to human territory. That it is so much smaller than what it would be in nature stands to reason[5]. Territories in the wild are large not as a matter of taste but of necessity[6]. In a zoo, we do for animals what we have done for ourselves with houses: we bring together in a small space what in the wild is spread out[7]. Whereas[8] before for us the cave[9] was here, the river over there, the hunting grounds[10] a mile[11] that way, the lookout[12] next to it, the berries[13] somewhere else—all of them infested with lions, snakes, ants, leeches and poison ivy[14]—now the river flows through taps at hand's reach[15] and we can wash next to where we sleep, we can eat where we have cooked, and we can surround[16] the whole with a protective wall and keep it clean and warm. A house is a compressed[17] territory where our basic needs can be fulfilled close by[18] and safely. A sound zoo enclosure is the equivalent for an animal (with the noteworthy[19] absence of a fireplace or the like[20], present in every human habitation). Finding within it all the places it needs—a lookout[21], a place for resting, for eating and drinking, for bathing, for grooming[22], etc.—and finding that there is no need to go hunting, food appearing six days a week, an animal will take possession of its zoo space in the same way it would lay claim to[23] a new space in the wild, exploring it and marking it out in the normal ways of its species, with sprays[24] of urine perhaps. Once this moving-in ritual[25] is done and the animal has settled, it will not feel like a nervous tenant[26], and even less like a prisoner, but rather like a landholder[27], and it will behave in the same way within its enclosure as it would in its territory in the wild, including defending it tooth and nail[1] should it be invaded[2]. Such an enclosure is subjectively neither better nor worse for an animal than its condition in the wild; so long as[3] it fulfills the animal's needs, a territory, natural or constructed, simply *is*, without judgment, a given[4], like the spots[5] on a leopard. One might even argue[6] that if an animal could choose with intelligence, it would opt for living in a zoo, since the major difference between a zoo and the wild is the absence of parasites and enemies and the abundance of food in the first, and their respective abundance and scarcity[7] in the second. Think about it yourself. Would you rather be put up[8] at the Ritz with free room service[9] and unlimited access to a doctor or be homeless[10] without a soul to care for you[11]? But animals are incapable of such discernment. Within the limits of their nature, they make do with what they have[12].

A good zoo is a place of carefully worked-out coincidence: exactly where an animal says to us, "Stay out![13]" with its urine or other secretion, we say to it, "Stay in![14]" with our barriers. Under such conditions of diplomatic peace, all animals are content and we can relax and have a look at each other.

In the literature[15] can be found legions of examples of animals that could escape but did not, or did and returned. There is the case of the chimpanzee whose cage door was left unlocked[16] and had swung open[17]. Increasingly anxious, the chimp began to shriek and to slam the door shut[18] repeatedly—with a deafening clang[19] each time—until the keeper, notified[20] by a visitor, hurried over to remedy the situation. A herd of roe-deer[21] in a European zoo stepped out of their corral

1. bec et ongles
2. s'il était envahi
3. du moment que
4. une évidence
5. taches
6. On peut même penser
7. rareté
8. Préféreriez-vous être hébergé
9. service en chambre
10. sans domicile fixe
11. sans personne pour s'occuper de vous
12. ils font avec ce qu'ils ont
13. Interdiction d'entrer !
14. Interdiction de sortir !
15. Dans les livres sur le sujet
16. n'avait pas été fermée à clé
17. s'était ouverte d'un coup
18. claquer la porte
19. bruit métallique assourdissant
20. informé
21. Un troupeau de chevreuils

when the gate was left open. Frightened by visitors, the deer bolted for[1] the nearby forest, which had its own herd of wild roe-deer and could support more. Nonetheless, the zoo roe-deer quickly returned to their corral. In another zoo a worker was walking to his work site at an early hour, carrying planks[2] of wood, when, to his horror, a bear emerged from the morning mist[3], heading straight for[4] him at a confident pace[5]. The man dropped the planks and ran for his life[6]. The zoo staff immediately started searching for the escaped bear. They found it back in its enclosure, having climbed down into[7] its pit the way it had climbed out[8], by way of[9] a tree that had fallen over. It was thought that the noise of the planks of wood falling to the ground had frightened it.

But I don't insist. I don't mean to defend zoos. Close them all down if you want (and let us hope that what wildlife remains[10] can survive in what is left of the natural world). I know zoos are no longer in people's good graces[11]. Religion faces the same problem. Certain illusions about freedom plague them both[12].

The Pondicherry Zoo doesn't exist any more. Its pits are filled in[13], the cages torn down[14]. I explore it now in the only place left for it, my memory.

CHAPTER 5

My name isn't the end of the story about my name. When your name is Bob no one asks you, "How do you spell that?" Not so with Piscine Molitor Patel.

Marginal glosses:

1. ont filé vers
2. des planches
3. brume
4. se dirigeant droit sur
5. d'un pas confiant
6. a pris ses jambes à son cou
7. étant retourné dans
8. comme il en était sorti
9. grâce à
10. les quelques animaux sauvages qui restent
11. ne sont plus bien vus
12. nuisent aux deux
13. rebouchées
14. détruites

Some thought it was P. Singh and that I was a Sikh, and they wondered[1] why I wasn't wearing a turban.

In my university days I visited Montreal once with some friends. It fell to me to order pizzas[2] one night. I couldn't bear[3] to have yet another French speaker guffawing[4] at my name, so when the man on the phone asked, "Can I 'ave your name?" I said, "I am who I am.[5]" Half an hour later[6] two pizzas arrived for "Ian Hoolihan".

It is true that those we meet can change us, sometimes so profoundly that we are not the same afterwards, even unto[7] our names. Witness[8] Simon who is called Peter[9], Matthew[10] also known as Levi, Nathaniel who is also Bartholomew, Judas, not Iscariot, who took the name[11] Thaddeus, Simeon who went by[12] Niger, Saul who became Paul.

My Roman soldier[13] stood in the schoolyard[14] one morning when I was twelve. I had just arrived. He saw me and a flash of evil genius lit up his dull mind[15]. He raised his arm, pointed at me[16] and shouted, "It's *Pissing* Patel!"

In a second everyone was laughing. It fell away[17] as we filed[18] into the class. I walked in last[19], wearing my crown of thorns[20].

The cruelty[21] of children comes as news to no one[22]. The words would waft across the yard[23] to my ears, unprovoked, uncalled for[24]: "Where's Pissing? I've got to go." Or: "You're facing the wall. Are you Pissing?" Or something of the sort[25]. I would freeze[26] or, the contrary, pursue my activity, pretending not to have heard. The sound would disappear, but the hurt would linger[27], like the smell of piss long after it has evaporated.

1. ils se demandaient
2. C'était à mon tour de commander des pizzas
3. Je ne pouvais pas supporter l'idée
4. s'esclaffer
5. je suis qui je suis.
6. Une demi-heure plus tard,
7. jusqu'à
8. Voyez
9. Pierre
10. Matthieu
11. pas Judas Iscariote, qui a pris le nom de
12. Siméon qui était surnommé
13. Mon soldat romain
14. cour de l'école
15. un éclair de mauvais génie a traversé son esprit engourdi
16. m'a montré du doigt
17. C'est retombé
18. quand nous sommes rentrés en file
19. Je suis rentré le dernier
20. ma couronne d'épines
21. cruauté
22. n'est une nouveauté pour personne
23. flottaient à travers la cour
24. injustifiés
25. du même genre
26. Je me figeais
27. la blessure restait

Teachers started doing it too. It was the heat. As the day wore on[1], the geography lesson, which in the morning had been as compact as an oasis, started to stretch out[2] like the Thar Desert; the history lesson, so alive when the day was young, became parched and dusty[3]; the mathematics lesson, so precise at first, became muddled[4]. In their afternoon fatigue, as they wiped their foreheads and the backs of their necks[5] with their handkerchiefs[6], without meaning to offend or get a laugh[7], even teachers forgot the fresh aquatic promise of my name and distorted it in a shameful way[8]. By nearly imperceptible modulations I could hear the change. It was as if their tongues[9] were charioteers[10] driving wild horses. They could manage well enough the first syllable, the *Pea*, but eventually the heat was too much and they lost control of their frothy-mouthed steeds[11] and could no longer rein them in for the climb[12] to the second syllable, the *seen*. Instead they plunged hell-bent[13] into *sing*, and next time round[14], all was lost. My hand would be up[15] to give an answer and it would be acknowledged with a "Yes, Pissing". Often the teacher wouldn't realize what he had just called me. He would look at me wearily[16] after a moment, wondering why I wasn't coming out with the answer[17]. And sometimes the class, as beaten down[18] by the heat as he was, wouldn't react either. Not a snicker[19] or a smile. But I always heard the slur[20].

I spent my last year at St. Joseph's School feeling like the persecuted prophet Muhammad in Mecca[21], peace be upon him[22]. But just as he planned his flight to Medina[23], the Hejira[24] that would mark the beginning of Muslim time, I planned my escape and the beginning of a new time for me.

After St. Joseph's, I went to Petit Séminaire, the best private English-medium secondary school[1] in Pondicherry. Ravi was already there, and like all younger brothers, I would suffer from following in the footsteps[2] of a popular older sibling[3]. He was the athlete of his generation at Petit Séminaire, a fearsome bowler[4] and a powerful batter[5], the captain of the town's best cricket team, our very own Kapil Dev. That I was a swimmer made no waves; it seems to be a law of human nature that those who live by the sea are suspicious[6] of swimmers, just as those who live in the mountains are suspicious of mountain climbers[7]. But following in someone's shadow wasn't my escape, though I would have taken any name over[8] "Pissing", even "Ravi's brother". I had a better plan than that.

I put it to execution on the very first day of school, in the very first class. Around me were other alumni[9] of St. Joseph's. The class started the way all new classes start, with the stating of names[10]. We called them out from our desks[11] in the order in which we happened to be sitting.

"Ganapathy Kumar", said Ganapathy Kumar.

"Vipin Nath", said Vipin Nath.

"Shamshool Hudha", said Shamshool Hudha.

"Peter Dharmaraj", said Peter Dharmaraj.

Each name elicited a tick on a list[12] and a brief mnemonic stare from the teacher[13]. I was terribly nervous.

"Ajith Giadson", said Ajith Giadson, four desks away[14]…

"Sampath Saroja", said Sampath Saroja, three away…

"Stanley Kumar", said Stanley Kumar, two away…

---

1. établissement privé du secondaire en langue anglaise

2. marcher sur les traces

3. aîné populaire

4. un redoutable lanceur

5. batteur

6. se méfient

7. alpinistes

8. plutôt que

9. élèves

10. la présentation des noms

11. Nous les criions depuis nos bureaux

12. était coché sur la liste

13. le professeur fixait ensuite brièvement chaque visage pour le mémoriser

14. à quatre bureaux de moi

"Sylvester Naveen", said Sylvester Naveen, right in front of me[1].

It was my turn[2]. Time to put down[3] Satan. Medina, here I come[4].

I got up from my desk and hurried to the blackboard. Before the teacher could say a word, I picked up a piece of chalk[5] and said as I wrote:

My name is
Piscine Molitor Patel,
known to all as

—I double underlined[6] the first two letters of my given name—

Pi Patel

For good measure[7] I added

$$\Pi = 3.14$$

and I drew[8] a large circle, which I then sliced in two[9] with a diameter, to evoke that basic lesson of geometry.

There was silence. The teacher was staring at the board. I was holding my breath.[10] Then he said, "Very well, Pi. Sit down. Next time you will ask permission before leaving your desk."

"Yes, sir."

He ticked my name off.[11] And looked at the next boy.

"Mansoor Ahamad", said Mansoor Ahamad.

I was saved.

"Gautham Selvaraj", said Gautham Selvaraj.

1. juste devant moi
2. mon tour
3. neutraliser
4. me voilà
5. un bâton de craie
6. j'ai souligné de deux traits
7. Pour faire bonne mesure
8. j'ai tracé
9. j'ai ensuite divisé en deux
10. Je retenais mon souffle.
11. Il a coché mon nom.

I could breathe.

"Arun Annaji", said Arun Annaji.

A new beginning.

I repeated the stunt[1] with every teacher. Repetition is important in the training[2] not only of animals but also of humans. Between one commonly named boy and the next, I rushed forward[3] and emblazoned[4], sometimes with a terrible screech[5], the details of my rebirth[6]. It got to be that after a few times the boys sang along with me, a crescendo that climaxed[7], after a quick intake of air[8] while I underlined the proper note, with such a rousing rendition of my new name[9] that it would have been the delight of any choirmaster[10]. A few boys followed up with a whispered[11], urgent "Three! Point! One! Four!" as I wrote as fast as I could, and I ended the concert by slicing[12] the circle with such vigour that bits of chalk went flying[13].

When I put my hand up that day, which I did every chance I had[14], teachers granted me the right to speak with a single syllable that was music to my ears[15]. Students followed suit[16]. Even the St. Joseph's devils[17]. In fact, the name caught on[18]. Truly we are a nation of aspiring engineers[19]: shortly after, there was a boy named Omprakash who was calling himself Omega, and another who was passing himself off as Upsilon, and for a while there was a Gamma, a Lambda and a Delta. But I was the first and the most enduring[20] of the Greeks at Petit Séminaire. Even my brother, the captain of the cricket team, that local god, approved. He took me aside[21] the next week.

"What's this I hear about a nickname[22] you have?" he said.

I kept silent. Because whatever mocking was to come[23], it was to come. There was no avoiding it.[24]

1. combine
2. apprentissage
3. je me précipitais vers le tableau
4. j'inscrivais
5. crissement
6. renaissance
7. qui atteignait son point culminant
8. inspiration
9. avec un cri si passionné de mon nom
10. cela aurait fait les délices de n'importe quel chef de chœur
11. chuchoté
12. en partageant
13. des bouts de craie s'envolaient
14. dès que j'en avais l'opportunité
15. un régal pour mes oreilles
16. leur ont emboîté le pas
17. petits monstres
18. est devenu populaire
19. futurs ingénieurs
20. tenace
21. Il m'a pris à part
22. surnom
23. quelle que soit la raillerie qui allait venir
24. Il n'y avait aucun moyen d'y échapper.

"I didn't realize you liked the colour yellow so much."

The colour yellow? I looked around[1]. No one must hear what he was about to say, especially not one of his lackeys[2]. "Ravi, what do you mean?" I whispered.

"It's all right with me[3], brother. Anything's better than 'Pissing'. Even 'Lemon Pie[4].'"

As he sauntered away[5] he smiled and said, "You look a bit red in the face.[6]"

But he held his peace[7].

And so, in that Greek letter that looks like a shack[8] with a corrugated tin roof[9], in that elusive[10], irrational number with which scientists try to understand the universe, I found refuge.

CHAPTER 6

He's an excellent cook[11]. His overheated[12] house is always smelling of something delicious. His spice rack[13] looks like an apothecary's shop[14]. When he opens his refrigerator or his cupboards[15], there are many brand names[16] I don't recognize; in fact, I can't even tell what language they're in[17]. We are in India. But he handles Western dishes equally well[18]. He makes me the most zesty[19] yet subtle macaroni and cheese I've ever had. And his vegetarian tacos would be the envy of all Mexico.

I notice something else: his cupboards are jam-packed[20]. Behind every door, on every shelf[21], stand mountains of neatly stacked cans and packages[22]. A reserve of food to last the siege of Leningrad[23].

CHAPTER 7

It was my luck to have a few good teachers in my youth, men and women who came into my dark head and lit a match[1]. One of these was Mr. Satish Kumar, my biology teacher at Petit Séminaire and an active Communist who was always hoping Tamil Nadu would stop electing movie stars and go the way of Kerala[2]. He had a most peculiar[3] appearance. The top of his head was bald and pointy[4], yet he had the most impressive jowls I have ever seen[5], and his narrow[6] shoulders gave way to a massive stomach[7] that looked like the base of a mountain, except that the mountain stood in thin air[8], for it stopped abruptly and disappeared horizontally into his pants[9]. It's a mystery to me how his stick-like legs[10] supported the weight[11] above them, but they did, though they moved in surprising ways at times, as if his knees could bend in any direction[12]. His construction was geometric: he looked like two triangles, a small one and a larger one, balanced on[13] two parallel lines. But organic, quite warty actually[14], and with sprigs[15] of black hair sticking out[16] of his ears. And friendly. His smile seemed to take up the whole base of his triangular head.

Mr. Kumar was the first avowed atheist[17] I ever met. I discovered this not in the classroom but at the zoo. He was a regular visitor[18] who read the labels and descriptive notices in their entirety[19] and approved of[20] every animal he saw. Each to him was a triumph of logic and mechanics, and nature as a whole was an exceptionally fine illustration of science. To his ears, when an animal felt the urge to mate[21], it said "Gregor Mendel", recalling the father of genetics[22], and when it was time to show

1. y ont allumé une allumette
2. suivre l'exemple du Kerala [État indien ayant élu démocratiquement un régime communiste en 1957]
3. très étrange
4. chauve et pointu
5. les mâchoires les plus impressionnantes que j'aie jamais vues
6. étroites
7. surmontaient un ventre énorme
8. dans le vide
9. son pantalon
10. ses jambes comme des allumettes
11. poids
12. se plier dans n'importe quelle direction
13. en équilibre sur
14. couverts de verrues en fait
15. des touffes
16. sortant
17. la première personne qui se proclamait athée
18. un habitué
19. entièrement
20. trouvait formidable
21. avait un besoin urgent de procréer
22. évoquant le père de la génétique

1. courage
2. ce que nous prenions pour des bêlements, des grognements, des sifflements, des ébrouements
3. des rugissements, des grondements, des hurlements, des gazouillis ou des cris perçants
4. n'était que de forts accents étrangers
5. prendre le pouls
6. revigoré
7. qui chancelait à l'intérieur du zoo
8. je n'ai pas osé
9. Même si je l'appréciais
10. sujet
11. chèvres
12. de moins en moins
13. À titre provisoire
14. s'habituer à
15. précieux
16. la mare boueuse
17. Ce mode de vie
18. une main accrochée à la balustrade
19. s'agitant
20. il m'a fait signe de m'approcher de lui

its mettle[1], "Charles Darwin", the father of natural selection, and what we took to be bleating, grunting, hissing, snorting[2], roaring, growling, howling, chirping and screeching[3] were but the thick accents of foreigners[4]. When Mr. Kumar visited the zoo, it was to take the pulse[5] of the universe, and his stethoscopic mind always confirmed to him that everything was in order, that everything *was* order. He left the zoo feeling scientifically refreshed[6].

The first time I saw his triangular form teetering and tottering about the zoo[7], I was shy[8] to approach him. As much as I liked him[9] as a teacher, he was a figure of authority, and I, a subject[10]. I was a little afraid of him. I observed him at a distance. He had just come to the rhinoceros pit. The two Indian rhinos were great attractions at the zoo because of the goats[11]. Rhinos are social animals, and when we got Peak, a young wild male, he was showing signs of suffering from isolation and he was eating less and less[12]. As a stopgap measure[13], while he searched for a female, Father thought of seeing if Peak couldn't be accustomed to[14] living with goats. If it worked, it would save a valuable[15] animal. If it didn't, it would only cost a few goats. It worked marvellously. Peak and the herd of goats became inseparable, even when Summit arrived. Now, when the rhinos bathed, the goats stood around the muddy pool[16], and when the goats ate in their corner, Peak and Summit stood next to them like guards. The living arrangement[17] was very popular with the public.

Mr. Kumar looked up and saw me. He smiled and, one hand holding onto the railing[18], the other waving[19], signalled me to come over[20].

"Hello, Pi", he said.

"Hello, sir. It's good of you to come to the zoo."

"I come here all the time. One might say it's my temple. This is interesting…" He was indicating the pit. "If we had politicians like these goats and rhinos we'd have fewer problems[1] in our country. Unfortunately[2] we have a prime minister who has the armour plating of[3] a rhinoceros without any of its good sense[4]."

I didn't know much about politics. Father and Mother complained[5] regularly about Mrs. Gandhi, but it meant little to me[6]. She lived far away in the north, not at the zoo and not in Pondicherry. But I felt I had to say something.

"Religion will save us", I said. Since when I could remember, religion had been very close to my heart[7].

"Religion?" Mr. Kumar grinned broadly[8]. "I don't believe in religion. Religion is darkness[9]."

Darkness? I was puzzled[10]. I thought, Darkness is the last thing that religion is. Religion is light. Was he testing me? Was he saying, "Religion is darkness", the way he sometimes said in class things like "Mammals lay eggs[11]", to see if someone would correct him? ("Only platypuses[12], sir.")

"There are no grounds[13] for going beyond[14] a scientific explanation of reality and no sound reason[15] for believing anything but our sense experience[16]. A clear intellect[17], close attention to detail[18] and a little scientific knowledge will expose religion as superstitious bosh[19]. God does not exist."

Did he say that? Or am I remembering the lines of later atheists[20]? At any rate[21], it was something of the sort. I had never heard such words.

"Why tolerate darkness? Everything is here and clear, if only we look carefully[22]."

1. moins de problèmes
2. Malheureusement
3. blindé comme
4. bon sens
5. se plaignaient
6. cela ne voulait pas dire grand-chose pour moi
7. m'avait toujours tenu à cœur
8. avait un grand sourire
9. les ténèbres
10. perplexe
11. Les mammifères pondent des œufs
12. les ornithorynques
13. motif
14. au-delà
15. pas de raison sérieuse
16. l'expérience de nos sens
17. Un esprit clair
18. une attention particulière portée aux détails
19. démontrent que la religion n'est qu'un ensemble de superstitions absurdes
20. les paroles d'autres athées, rencontrés plus tard
21. En tout cas
22. attentivement

47

He was pointing at Peak. Now though I had great admiration for Peak, I had never thought of a rhinoceros as a light bulb[1].

He spoke again. "Some people say God died during the Partition in 1947[2]. He may have died in 1971 during the war. Or he may have died yesterday here in Pondicherry in an orphanage[3]. That's what some people say, Pi. When I was your age, I lived in bed, racked with polio[4]. I asked myself every day, 'Where is God? Where is God? Where is God?' God never came. It wasn't God who saved me—it was medicine. Reason is my prophet and it tells me that as a watch stops, so we die[5]. It's the end. If the watch doesn't work properly, it must be fixed here and now by us[6]. One day we will take hold[7] of the means of production and there will be justice on earth."

This was all a bit much for me. The tone was right—loving and brave[8]—but the details seemed bleak[9]. I said nothing. It wasn't for fear of angering[10] Mr. Kumar. I was more afraid that in a few words thrown out[11] he might destroy something that I loved. What if his words had the effect of polio on me? What a terrible disease[12] that must be if it could kill God in a man.

He walked off, pitching and rolling[13] in the wild sea that was the steady ground[14]. "Don't forget the test on Tuesday. Study hard, 3.14!"

"Yes, Mr. Kumar."

He became my favourite teacher at Petit Séminaire and the reason I studied zoology at the University of Toronto. I felt a kinship[15] with him. It was my first clue[16] that atheists are my brothers and sisters of a different faith[17], and every word they speak speaks of faith. Like me, they go as far

---

1. ampoule

2. [La partition de l'Inde en 1947 a abouti à la création de deux États indépendants : le Pakistan, à majorité musulmane et l'Union indienne, à majorité hindoue.]

3. orphelinat

4. ravagé par la polio

5. nous mourrons comme une montre s'arrête

6. c'est nous qui devons la réparer, là, tout de suite

7. nous prendrons possession

8. courageux

9. peu réjouissants

10. mettre en colère

11. en jetant quelques mots

12. maladie

13. tanguant et roulant

14. la terre ferme

15. parenté

16. indice

17. foi

as the legs of reason will carry them—and then they leap[1].

I'll be honest about it. It is not atheists who get stuck in my craw[2], but agnostics. Doubt is useful for a while. We must all pass through the garden of Gethsemane. If Christ played with doubt, so must we[3]. If Christ spent an anguished night in prayer, if He burst out from the Cross[4], "My God, my God, why have you forsaken me[5]?" then surely we are also permitted doubt. But we must move on[6]. To choose doubt as a philosophy of life is akin to[7] choosing immobility as a means of transportation.

CHAPTER 8

We commonly say in the trade[8] that the most dangerous animal in a zoo is Man. In a general way we mean how our species' excessive predatoriness[9] has made the entire planet our prey[10]. More specifically, we have in mind the people who feed fishhooks to the otters[11], razors to the bears, apples with small nails[12] in them to the elephants and hardware variations on the theme[13]: ballpoint pens, paper clips, safety pins, rubber bands, combs, coffee spoons, horseshoes[14], pieces of broken glass, rings, brooches[15] and other jewellery (and not just cheap plastic bangles[16]: gold wedding bands[17], too), drinking straws, plastic cutlery[18], ping-pong balls, tennis balls and so on. The obituary[19] of zoo animals that have died from being fed foreign bodies[20] would include gorillas, bison, storks, rheas, ostriches[21], seals, sea lions, big cats, bears, camels, elephants, monkeys, and most every variety of deer, ruminant and songbird. Among zookeepers, Gol-

1. ils sautent
2. qui me restent en travers de la gorge
3. nous devons faire de même
4. il a crié depuis la Croix
5. pourquoi m'as-tu abandonné
6. avancer
7. revient à
8. dans la profession
9. le comportement excessivement prédateur de notre espèce
10. proie
11. qui donnent à manger des hameçons aux loutres
12. clous
13. toute une quincaillerie du même genre
14. des stylos à bille, des trombones, des épingles à nourrice, des élastiques, des peignes, des cuillères à café, des fers à cheval
15. des broches
16. bracelets
17. des alliances
18. des pailles, des couverts en plastique
19. La notice nécrologique
20. parce qu'on leur a donné à manger des corps étrangers
21. des nandous, des autruches

1. hémorragie
2. le bec fracassé avec un marteau
3. orignal
4. après qu'il l'a tendu pour attraper les noix qu'on lui offrait
5. les bois d'un cerf attaqués à la scie à métaux
6. ayant reçu un coup d'épée
7. des épingles à cheveux, des aiguilles à tricoter, des ciseaux et que sais-je encore
8. dans le but de
9. des onanistes qui s'excitent sur
10. un fanatique religieux
11. a tranché la tête d'un serpent
12. d'un élan
13. nous avons plutôt eu de la chance
14. Nous avons échappé aux
15. qui sévissent dans
16. notre gerbille de Mongolie a disparu
17. des faisans, des paons
18. des plumes
19. avides
20. enclos
21. le démon
22. [un des écrits fondamentaux de la mythologie hindoue]
23. épouse
24. a été pris en train de

iath's death is famous; he was a bull elephant seal, a great big venerable beast of two tons, star of his European zoo, loved by all visitors. He died of internal bleeding[1] after someone fed him a broken beer bottle.

The cruelty is often more active and direct. The literature contains reports on the many torments inflicted upon zoo animals: a shoebill dying of shock after having its beak smashed with a hammer[2]; a moose stag[3] losing its beard, along with a strip of flesh the size of an index finger, to a visitor's knife (this same moose was poisoned six months later); a monkey's arm broken after reaching out for proffered nuts[4]; a deer's antlers attacked with a hacksaw[5]; a zebra stabbed with a sword[6]; and other assaults on other animals, with walking sticks, umbrellas, hairpins, knitting needles, scissors and whatnot[7], often with an aim to[8] taking an eye out or to injuring sexual parts. Animals are also poisoned. And there are indecencies even more bizarre: onanists breaking a sweat on[9] monkeys, ponies, birds; a religious freak[10] who cut a snake's head off[11]; a deranged man who took to urinating in an elk's[12] mouth.

At Pondicherry we were relatively fortunate[13]. We were spared[14] the sadists who plied[15] European and American zoos. Nonetheless, our golden agouti vanished[16], stolen by someone who ate it, Father suspected. Various birds—pheasants, peacocks[17], macaws—lost feathers[18] to people greedy[19] for their beauty. We caught a man with a knife climbing into the pen[20] for mouse deer; he said he was going to punish evil[21] Ravana (who in the Ramayana[22] took the form of a deer when he kidnapped Sita, Rama's consort[23]). Another man was nabbed in the process of[24] stealing a cobra. He was a snake charm-

50

er whose own snake had died. Both were saved: the cobra from a life of servitude and bad music, and the man from a possible death bite[1]. We had to deal on occasion with stone throwers, who found the animals too placid and wanted a reaction. And we had the lady whose sari was caught by a lion. She spun[2] like a yo-yo, choosing mortal embarrassment over mortal end. The thing was, it wasn't even an accident. She had leaned over, thrust her hand[3] in the cage and waved the end of her sari in the lion's face, with what intent we never figured out[4]. She was not injured; there were many fascinated men who came to her assistance. Her flustered[5] explanation to Father was, "Whoever heard[6] of a lion eating a cotton sari? I thought lions were carnivores." Our worst troublemakers[7] were the visitors who gave food to the animals. Despite our vigilance, Dr. Atal, the zoo veterinarian, could tell by the number of animals with digestive disturbances[8] which had been the busy days at the zoo. He called "tidbit-itis[9]" the cases of enteritis or gastritis due to too many carbohydrates, especially sugar. Sometimes we wished people had stuck to sweets[10]. People have a notion that animals can eat anything without the least consequence to their health. Not so. One of our sloth bears[11] became seriously ill with severe hemorrhagic enteritis after being given fish that had gone putrid by a man who was convinced he was doing a good deed[12].

Just beyond the ticket booth[13] Father had painted on a wall in bright red letters the question: DO YOU KNOW WHICH IS THE MOST DANGEROUS ANIMAL IN THE ZOO? An arrow[14] pointed to a small curtain[15]. There were so many eager[16], curious hands that pulled at[17] the curtain that we had to replace it regularly. Behind it was a mirror.

1. morsure mortelle

2. Elle a tourné

3. Elle s'était penchée en avant, avait introduit la main

4. nous n'avons jamais compris pourquoi

5. agacée

6. Qui a jamais entendu parler

7. fauteurs de troubles

8. problèmes

9. friand-ite

10. en soient restés aux bonbons

11. ours paresseux

12. action

13. Juste après le guichet

14. Une flèche

15. rideau

16. impatientes

17. ouvraient

1. à mes dépens

2. mignon
3. dévoué
4. joyeux
5. compréhensif
6. se tiennent en embuscade
7. dans tous les magasins de jouets
8. D'innombrables histoires
9. assoiffés de sang
10. courroux
11. qui passent leur colère sur eux
12. fléau
13. éloigné de nous
14. a déclenché un signal d'alarme
15. J'ai rapidement consulté
16. en paix
17. avoir des ennuis
18. les soins apportés aux animaux
19. la culpabilité

But I learned at my expense[1] that Father believed there was another animal even more dangerous than us, and one that was extremely common, too, found on every continent, in every habitat: the redoubtable species *Animalus anthropomorphicus*, the animal as seen through human eyes. We've all met one, perhaps even owned one. It is an animal that is "cute[2]", "friendly", "loving", "devoted[3]", "merry[4]", "understanding[5]". These animals lie in ambush[6] in every toy store[7] and children's zoo. Countless stories[8] are told of them. They are the pendants of those "vicious", "bloodthirsty[9]", "depraved" animals that inflame the ire[10] of the maniacs I have just mentioned, who vent their spite on them[11] with walking sticks and umbrellas. In both cases we look at an animal and see a mirror. The obsession with putting ourselves at the centre of everything is the bane[12] not only of theologians but also of zoologists.

I learned the lesson that an animal is an animal, essentially and practically removed from us[13], twice: once with Father and once with Richard Parker.

It was on a Sunday morning. I was quietly playing on my own. Father called out.

"Children, come here."

Something was wrong. His tone of voice set off a small alarm bell[14] in my head. I quickly reviewed[15] my conscience. It was clear[16]. Ravi must be in trouble[17] again. I wondered what he had done this time. I walked into the living room. Mother was there. That was unusual. The disciplining of children, like the tending of animals[18], was generally left to Father. Ravi walked in last, guilt[19] written all over his criminal face.

"Ravi, Piscine, I have a very important lesson for you today."

"Oh really, is this necessary?" interrupted Mother. Her face was flushed[1].

I swallowed.[2] If Mother, normally so unruffled[3], so calm, was worried, even upset[4], it meant we were in serious trouble[5]. I exchanged glances with Ravi.

"Yes, it is", said Father, annoyed. "It may very well save their lives."

Save our lives! It was no longer a small alarm bell that was ringing in my head—they were big bells[6] now, like the ones we heard from Sacred Heart of Jesus Church, not far from the zoo.

"But Piscine? He's only eight", Mother insisted.

"He's the one who worries me the most."

"I'm innocent!" I burst out[7]. "It's Ravi's fault, whatever it is[8]. He did it!"

"What?" said Ravi. "I haven't done anything wrong." He gave me the evil eye.[9]

"Shush![10]" said Father, raising his hand. He was looking at Mother. "Gita, you've seen Piscine. He's at that age when boys run around and poke their noses[11] everywhere."

Me? A run-arounder?[12] An everywhere-nose-poker?[13] Not so, not so! Defend me, Mother, defend me, I implored in my heart. But she only sighed and nodded[14], a signal that the terrible business could proceed[15].

"Come with me", said Father.

We set out[16] like prisoners off to their execution.

We left the house, went through the gate[17], entered the zoo. It was early and the zoo hadn't opened yet to the public. Animal keepers and groundskeepers[18] were going about their work. I noticed Sitaram, who oversaw[19] the orang-utans, my favourite keeper. He paused to watch us go by[20]. We passed

1. rouge
2. J'ai avalé ma salive.
3. imperturbable
4. très inquiète
5. dans un sacré pétrin

6. de grosses cloches

7. ai-je crié
8. quoi qu'il se soit passé
9. Il m'a lancé un regard furieux.
10. Chut !
11. mettent leur nez
12. Quelqu'un qui court partout ?
13. Quelqu'un qui met son nez partout ?
14. elle a seulement soupiré et hoché la tête
15. se poursuivre
16. Nous nous sommes mis en route
17. portail
18. les gens chargés de l'entretien du zoo
19. surveillait
20. nous regarder passer

birds, bears, apes[1], monkeys, ungulates[2], the terrarium house, the rhinos, the elephants, the giraffes.

We came to the big cats, our tigers, lions and leopards. Babu, their keeper, was waiting for us. We went round and down the path, and he unlocked[3] the door to the cat house, which was at the centre of a moated island[4]. We entered. It was a vast and dim[5] cement cavern, circular in shape, warm and humid, and smelling of cat urine. All around were great big cages divided up by thick, green, iron bars[6]. A yellowish light filtered down from the skylights[7]. Through the cage exits we could see the vegetation of the surrounding island, flooded with sunlight[8]. The cages were empty—save one[9]: Mahisha, our Bengal tiger patriarch, a lanky, hulking beast of 550 pounds[10], had been detained[11]. As soon as we stepped in[12], he loped up to[13] the bars of his cage and set off a full-throated snarl[14], ears flat[15] against his skull and round eyes fixed on Babu. The sound was so loud and fierce[16] it seemed to shake the whole cat house. My knees started quaking[17]. I got close to Mother. She was trembling, too. Even Father seemed to pause and steady himself[18]. Only Babu was indifferent to the outburst[19] and to the searing stare that bored into him like a drill[20]. He had a tested trust[21] in iron bars. Mahisha started pacing to and fro against the limits of his cage[22].

Father turned to us. "What animal is this?" he bellowed above Mahisha's snarling[23].

"It's a tiger", Ravi and I answered in unison, obediently pointing out the blindingly obvious[24].

"Are tigers dangerous?"

"Yes, Father, tigers are dangerous."

"Tigers are *very* dangerous", Father shouted. "I want you to understand that you are never[25]—under any circumstances[1]—to touch a tiger, to pet[2] a tiger, to put your hands through the bars of a cage, even to get close[3] to a cage. Is that clear? Ravi?"

Ravi nodded vigorously.

"Piscine?"

I nodded even more vigorously.

He kept his eyes on me.

I nodded so hard I'm surprised my neck didn't snap[4] and my head fall to the floor.

I would like to say in my own defence that though I may have anthropomorphized the animals till they spoke fluent[5] English, the pheasants complaining in uppity[6] British accents of their tea being cold and the baboons planning their bank robbery getaway[7] in the flat, menacing tones of American gangsters, the fancy was always conscious[8]. I quite deliberately dressed wild animals in tame costumes[9] of my imagination. But I never deluded myself as to[10] the real nature of my playmates[11]. My poking nose[12] had more sense than that. I don't know where Father got the idea that his youngest son was itching to step into[13] a cage with a ferocious carnivore. But wherever the strange worry came from—and Father was a worrier[14]—he was clearly determined to rid himself of it[15] that very morning.

"I'm going to show you how dangerous tigers are", he continued. "I want you to remember this lesson for the rest of your lives."

He turned to Babu and nodded. Babu left. Mahisha's eyes followed him and did not move from the door he disappeared through. He returned a few seconds later carrying a goat with its legs tied[16]. Mother gripped me[17] from behind. Mahisha's snarl turned into a growl deep in the throat[18].

Babu unlocked, opened, entered, closed and locked a cage next to the tiger's cage. Bars and a

1. quelles que soient les circonstances

2. caresser

3. vous approcher

4. que mon cou ne se soit pas détaché

5. couramment

6. snobs

7. planifiant leur fuite après un cambriolage de banque

8. j'avais conscience que ce n'était que le produit de mon imagination

9. Je revêtais délibérément les animaux sauvages de costumes domestiques

10. je n'ai jamais eu d'illusions quant à

11. compagnons de jeu

12. Mon nez fouineur

13. brûlait d'envie d'entrer dans

14. avait tendance à se faire facilement du souci

15. s'en débarrasser

16. attachées

17. m'a attrapé

18. un profond grognement

1. trappe
2. était tout contre les barreaux
3. et les frappait de la patte
4. ouaf
5. ses flancs se soulevaient
6. roulaient
7. Il a détaché
8. s'est levée
9. est sorti de
10. au même niveau que nous
11. un mètre
12. s'est précipitée
13. qui ne s'intéressait plus à
14. a également changé de niveau
15. Il s'est ramassé sur lui-même et n'a plus bougé
16. queue
17. d'un air sombre
18. bêlement
19. mon cœur qui battait fort
20. bruits aigus
21. hors de lui
22. faire voler les barreaux en éclats
23. hors de portée
24. niveau inférieur
25. plus loin
26. Elle faisait des bonds d'une hauteur incroyable.
27. lisse

trapdoor[1] separated the two. Immediately Mahisha was up against the dividing bars[2], pawing them[3]. To his growling he now added explosive, arrested *woofs*[4]. Babu placed the goat on the floor; its flanks were heaving[5] violently, its tongue hung from its mouth, and its eyes were spinning orbs[6]. He untied[7] its legs. The goat got to its feet[8]. Babu exited[9] the cage in the same careful way he had entered it. The cage had two floors, one level with us[10], the other at the back, higher by about three feet[11], that led outside to the island. The goat scrambled[12] to this second level. Mahisha, now unconcerned with[13] Babu, paralleled the move[14] in his cage in a fluid, effortless motion. He crouched and lay still[15], his slowly moving tail[16] the only sign of tension.

Babu stepped up to the trapdoor between the cages and started pulling it open. In anticipation of satisfaction, Mahisha fell silent. I heard two things at that moment: Father saying "Never forget this lesson" as he looked on grimly[17]; and the bleating[18] of the goat. It must have been bleating all along, only we couldn't hear it before.

I could feel Mother's hand pressed against my pounding heart[19].

The trapdoor resisted with sharp cries[20]. Mahisha was beside himself[21]—he looked as if he were about to burst through the bars[22]. He seemed to hesitate between staying where he was, at the place where his prey was closest but most certainly out of reach[23], and moving to the ground level[24], further away[25] but where the trapdoor was located. He raised himself and started snarling again.

The goat started to jump. It jumped to amazing heights.[26] I had no idea a goat could jump so high. But the back of the cage was a high and smooth[27] cement wall.

With sudden ease the trapdoor slid open[1]. Silence fell again, except for bleating and the click-click of the goat's hooves[2] against the floor.

A streak of black and orange flowed[3] from one cage to the next.

Normally the big cats were not given food one day a week, to simulate conditions in the wild. We found out[4] later that Father had ordered that Mahisha not be fed[5] for three days.

I don't know if I saw blood before turning into Mother's arms or if I daubed it on[6] later, in my memory, with a big brush[7]. But I heard. It was enough to scare the living vegetarian daylights out of me[8]. Mother bundled us out.[9] We were in hysterics.[10] She was incensed[11].

"How could you, Santosh? They're children! They'll be scarred[12] for the rest of their lives."

Her voice was hot and tremulous[13]. I could see she had tears in her eyes. I felt better.

"Gita, my bird, it's for their sake. What if Piscine had stuck his hand[14] through the bars of the cage one day to touch the pretty orange fur[15]? Better a goat than him, no?"

His voice was soft, nearly a whisper[16]. He looked contrite. He never called her "my bird" in front of us.

We were huddled[17] around her. He joined us. But the lesson was not over[18], though it was gentler after that.

Father led us to the lions and leopards.

"Once there was a madman in Australia who was a black belt[19] in karate. He wanted to prove himself against the lions[20]. He lost. Badly. The keepers found only half his body in the morning."

"Yes, Father."

The Himalayan bears and the sloth bears.

1.	s'est ouverte
2.	les claquements des sabots de la chèvre
3.	Un éclair noir et orange est passé
4.	Nous avons appris
5.	ne soit pas nourri
6.	je l'ai ajouté
7.	pinceau
8.	terrifier le petit végétarien que j'étais
9.	Maman nous a pris dans ses bras et entraînés dehors.
10.	Nous avions une crise de nerfs.
11.	furieuse
12.	traumatisés
13.	tremblante
14.	avait glissé la main
15.	fourrure
16.	murmure
17.	Nous nous étions blottis
18.	terminée
19.	ceinture noire
20.	se mesurer aux lions

1. *Un coup de griffes*
2. *de la part de ces grosses peluches*
3. *vos entrailles seront vidées et éparpillées sur le sol*
4. *molles et flasques*
5. *ils réduiront votre corps en purée*
6. *courir plus vite que vous*
7. *Les plus puissantes mâchoires*
8. *lâches*
9. *de la charogne*
10. *des brindilles*
11. *des animaux de compagnie*
12. *adultes*
13. *imprévisibles*
14. *L'autruche a l'air craintive et stupide, n'est-ce pas ?*
15. *coup de patte*
16. *écrasé*
17. *Le cerf axis.*
18. *il vous fonce dessus*
19. *bois*
20. *poignards*
21. *Une morsure baveuse*
22. *un gros morceau de chair*

"One strike of the claws[1] from these cuddly creatures[2] and your innards will be scooped out and splattered all over the ground[3]."

"Yes, Father."

The hippos.

"With those soft, flabby[4] mouths of theirs they'll crush your body to a bloody pulp[5]. On land they can outrun you[6]."

"Yes, Father."

The hyenas.

"The strongest jaws[7] in nature. Don't think that they're cowardly[8] or that they only eat carrion[9]. They're not and they don't! They'll start eating you while you're still alive."

"Yes, Father."

The orang-utans.

"As strong as ten men. They'll break your bones as if they were twigs[10]. I know some of them were once pets[11] and you played with them when they were small. But now they're grown-up[12] and wild and unpredictable[13]."

"Yes, Father."

The ostrich.

"Looks flustered and silly, doesn't it?[14] Listen up: it's one of the most dangerous animals in a zoo. Just one kick[15] and your back is broken or your torso is crushed[16]."

"Yes, Father."

The spotted deer.[17]

"So pretty, aren't they? If the male feels he has to, he'll charge you[18] and those short little antlers[19] will pierce you like daggers[20]."

"Yes, Father."

The Arabian camel.

"One slobbering bite[21] and you've lost a chunk of flesh[22]."

"Yes, Father."

The black swans.

"With their beaks they'll crack your skull[1]. With their wings they'll break your arms."

"Yes, Father."

The smaller birds.

"They'll cut through[2] your fingers with their beaks as if they were butter."

"Yes, Father."

The elephants.

"The most dangerous animal of all. More keepers and visitors are killed by elephants than by any other animal in a zoo. A young elephant will most likely dismember you and trample your body parts flat[3]. That's what happened to one poor lost soul[4] in a European zoo who got into the elephant house through a window. An older, more patient animal will squeeze you[5] against a wall or sit on you. Sounds funny—but think about it!"

"Yes, Father."

"There are animals we haven't stopped by. Don't think they're harmless[6]. Life will defend itself no matter how small it is. Every animal is ferocious and dangerous. It may not kill you, but it will certainly injure you. It will scratch you[7] and bite you, and you can look forward to[8] a swollen, pus-filled[9] infection, a high fever[10] and a ten-day stay in the hospital[11]."

"Yes, Father."

We came to the guinea pigs[12], the only other animals besides Mahisha to have been starved at Father's orders[13], having been denied their previous evening's meal[14]. Father unlocked the cage. He brought out a bag of feed[15] from his pocket and emptied it on the floor.

"You see these guinea pigs?"

1. crâne

2. Ils perceront

3. vous démembrera et piétinera vos membres

4. âme en peine

5. vous écrasera

6. inoffensifs

7. Il vous griffera

8. vous pouvez vous attendre à

9. enflée et purulente

10. forte fièvre

11. dix jours d'hospitalisation

12. cochons d'Inde

13. affamés sous l'ordre de Papa

14. puisqu'on les avait privés de leur repas de la veille au soir

15. nourriture

1. faiblesse
2. tandis qu'elles grignotaient frénétiquement leurs petites graines
3. en a ramassé un
4. se sont dispersés
5. qui couinait
6. Il voulait terminer sur une note plus légère.
7. est resté immobile, tendu, dans mes bras
8. je l'ai déposé doucement
9. Il s'est précipité vers sa mère.
10. ne mordaient ni ne griffaient jusqu'au sang
11. attraper
12. nues
13. saisir un couteau par la lame
14. Ravi et moi avons fait la tête
15. et nous sommes restés en froid avec Papa
16. j'ai eu l'impression que les rhinos baissaient la tête
17. perte
18. j'avais signé mon arrêt de mort
19. Dans les années qui ont suivi
20. il avait envie

"Yes, Father."

The creatures were trembling with weakness[1] as they frantically nibbled their kernels of corn[2].

"Well…" He leaned down and scooped one up[3]. "They're not dangerous." The other guinea pigs scattered[4] instantly.

Father laughed. He handed me the squealing[5] guinea pig. He meant to end on a light note.[6]

The guinea pig rested in my arms tensely[7]. It was a young one. I went to the cage and carefully lowered it[8] to the floor. It rushed to its mother's side.[9] The only reason these guinea pigs weren't dangerous—didn't draw blood with their teeth and claws[10]—was that they were practically domesticated. Otherwise, to grab[11] a wild guinea pig with your bare[12] hands would be like taking hold of a knife by the blade[13].

The lesson was over. Ravi and I sulked[14] and gave Father the cold shoulder[15] for a week. Mother ignored him too. When I went by the rhinoceros pit I fancied the rhinos' heads were hung low[16] with sadness over the loss[17] of one of their dear companions.

But what can you do when you love your father? Life goes on and you don't touch tigers. Except that now, for having accused Ravi of an unspecified crime he hadn't committed, I was as good as dead[18]. In years subsequent[19], when he was in the mood[20] to terrorize me, he would whisper to me, "Just wait till we're alone. *You're the next goat!*"

CHAPTER 9

Getting animals used to the presence of humans is at the heart of the art and science of zookeeping.

The key aim[1] is to diminish an animal's flight distance[2], which is the minimum distance at which an animal wants to keep a perceived enemy. A flamingo in the wild won't mind you[3] if you stay more than three hundred yards away[4]. Cross[5] that limit and it becomes tense[6]. Get even closer and you trigger[7] a flight reaction from which the bird will not cease until the three-hundred-yard limit is set again, or until heart and lungs fail[8]. Different animals have different flight distances and they gauge them[9] in different ways. Cats look, deer listen, bears smell. Giraffes will allow you to come to within thirty yards of them[10] if you are in a motor car[11], but will run if you are 150 yards away[12] on foot. Fiddler crabs scurry[13] when you're ten yards away[14]; howler monkeys stir[15] in their branches when you're at twenty; African buffaloes react at seventy-five.

Our tools[16] for diminishing flight distance are the knowledge we have of an animal, the food and shelter we provide, the protection we afford. When it works, the result is an emotionally stable, stress-free wild animal that not only stays put[17], but is healthy, lives a very long time, eats without fuss[18], behaves and socializes[19] in natural ways and—the best sign—reproduces. I won't say that our zoo compared to the zoos of San Diego or Toronto or Berlin or Singapore, but you can't keep a good zoo-keeper down[20]. Father was a natural[21]. He made up for a lack of formal training[22] with an intuitive gift and a keen eye[23]. He had a knack[24] for looking at an animal and guessing what was on its mind. He was attentive to his charges[25], and they, in return, multiplied, some to excess.

1. Le but principal
2. la distance de fuite d'un animal
3. Vous ne dérangerez pas un flamant rose sauvage
4. à plus de 300 m
5. Si vous dépassez
6. il se crispera
7. vous déclencherez
8. son cœur et ses poumons ne suivent plus
9. ils les établissent
10. vous approcher à moins de 30 m
11. voiture
12. à 150 m
13. Les crabes violonistes détalent
14. à 10 m
15. commencent à bouger
16. Nos moyens
17. ne bouge pas
18. sans rechigner
19. se comporte et interagit
20. on ne peut pas empêcher un bon gardien de zoo de faire du bon travail
21. avait son métier dans le sang
22. Il a compensé son manque de formation
23. un œil attentif
24. le don
25. animaux dont il avait la charge

CHAPTER 10

Yet there will always be animals that seek to escape[1] from zoos. Animals that are kept in unsuitable[2] enclosures are the most obvious example. Every animal has particular habitat needs that must be met[3]. If its enclosure is too sunny or too wet or too empty, if its perch[4] is too high or too exposed, if the ground is too sandy[5], if there are too few[6] branches to make a nest[7], if the food trough is too low[8], if there is not enough mud to wallow in[9]— and so many other ifs—then the animal will not be at peace. It is not so much a question of constructing an imitation of conditions in the wild as of getting to the *essence* of these conditions. Everything in an enclosure must be just right[10]—in other words, within the limits of the animal's capacity to adapt. A plague upon[11] bad zoos with bad enclosures! They bring all zoos into disrepute.[12]

Wild animals that are captured when they are fully mature[13] are another example of escape-prone[14] animals; often they are too set in their ways[15] to reconstruct their subjective worlds and adapt to a new environment.

But even animals that were bred[16] in zoos and have never known the wild, that are perfectly adapted to their enclosures and feel no tension in the presence of humans, will have moments of excitement that push them to seek to escape. All living things contain a measure of madness[17] that moves them in strange, sometimes inexplicable ways[18]. This madness can be saving[19]; it is part and parcel of[20] the ability to adapt. Without it, no species would survive.

Whatever[21] the reason for wanting to escape, sane or insane[22], zoo detractors should realize that animals don't escape *to somewhere* but *from something*.

Something within their territory has frightened them—the intrusion of an enemy, the assault of a dominant animal, a startling noise[1]—and set off[2] a flight reaction. The animal flees[3], or tries to. I was surprised to read at the Toronto Zoo—a very fine zoo, I might add[4]—that leopards can jump eighteen feet straight up[5]. Our leopard enclosure in Pondicherry had a wall *sixteen* feet high at the back; I surmise[6] that Rosie and Copycat never jumped out not because of constitutional weakness but simply because they had no reason to. Animals that escape go from the known into the unknown—and if there is one thing an animal hates above all else, it is the unknown. Escaping animals usually hide in the very first place they find that gives them a sense of security, and they are dangerous only to those who happen to get between them and their reckoned safe spot[7].

CHAPTER 11

Consider the case of[8] the female black leopard that escaped from the Zurich Zoo in the winter of 1933. She was new to the zoo and seemed to get along[9] with the male leopard. But various paw injuries[10] hinted at matrimonial strife[11]. Before any decision could be taken about what to do, she squeezed through a break in the roof bars[12] of her cage and vanished[13] in the night. The discovery that a wild carnivore was free in their midst[14] created an uproar[15] among the citizens[16] of Zurich. Traps were set[17] and hunting dogs were let loose[18]. They only rid[19] the canton of its few half-wild[20] dogs. Not a trace of the leopard was found for *ten weeks*. Final-

1. un bruit effarouchant
2. a entraîné
3. fuit
4. d'ailleurs
5. peuvent faire des bonds de 6 m de haut
6. Je suppose
7. ce qu'ils considèrent comme un endroit sûr
8. Prenons le cas de
9. elle semblait s'entendre
10. blessures aux pattes
11. laissaient entendre qu'il y avait des disputes conjugales
12. elle s'est glissée dans une brèche entre les barreaux du toit
13. a disparu
14. au beau milieu de leur ville
15. tollé
16. citoyens
17. Des pièges ont été installés
18. des chiens de chasse ont été lâchés
19. Ils ont seulement débarrassé
20. semi-sauvages

ly, a casual labourer came upon it[1] under a barn twenty-five miles away[2] and shot it[3]. Remains[4] of roe-deer were found nearby. That a big, black, tropical cat managed to survive for more than two months in a Swiss winter without being seen by anyone, let alone[5] attacking anyone, speaks plainly to the fact that[6] escaped zoo animals are not dangerous absconding[7] criminals but simply wild creatures seeking to fit in[8].

And this case is just one among many. If you took the city of Tokyo and turned it upside down[9] and shook it, you would be amazed at the animals that would fall out. It would pour[10] more than cats and dogs, I tell you. Boa constrictors, Komodo dragons[11], crocodiles, piranhas, ostriches, wolves, lynx, wallabies, manatees, porcupines[12], orang-utans, wild boar[13]—that's the sort of rainfall[14] you could expect on your umbrella[15]. And they expected to find—ha! In the middle of a Mexican tropical jungle, imagine! Ha! Ha! It's laughable[16], simply laughable. What were they thinking?

CHAPTER 12

At times he gets agitated. It's nothing I say (I say very little[17]). It's his own story that does it. Memory is an ocean and he bobs[18] on its surface. I worry that he'll want to stop. But he wants to tell me his story. He goes on. After all these years, Richard Parker still preys on his mind[19].

He's a sweet man. Every time I visit he prepares a South Indian vegetarian feast[20]. I told him I like spicy food[21]. I don't know why I said such a stupid thing. It's a complete lie.[22] I add dollop of yogurt after dol-

lop of yogurt.[1] Nothing doing.[2] Each time it's the same: my taste buds shrivel up[3] and die, my skin goes beet red[4], my eyes well up with tears[5], my head feels like a house on fire, and my digestive tract starts to twist and groan[6] in agony like a boa constrictor that has swallowed a lawn mower[7].

CHAPTER 13

So you see, if you fall into a lion's pit, the reason the lion will tear you to pieces[8] is not because it's hungry—be assured, zoo animals are amply fed[9]—or because it's bloodthirsty, but because you've invaded its territory.

As an aside[10], that is why a circus trainer must always enter the lion ring[11] first, and in full sight of the lions[12]. In doing so, he establishes that the ring is *his* territory, not theirs, a notion that he reinforces by shouting, by stomping about[13], by snapping his whip[14]. The lions are impressed. Their disadvantage weighs[15] heavily on them. Notice how they come in: mighty predators though they are[16], "kings of beasts", they crawl in[17] with their tails low and they keep to the edges of[18] the ring, which is always round so that they have nowhere to hide. They are in the presence of a strongly dominant male, a super-alpha male[19], and they must submit to his dominance rituals. So they open their jaws[20] wide, they sit up, they jump through paper-covered hoops[21], they crawl through tubes, they walk backwards, they roll over[22]. "He's a queer one[23]", they think dimly[24]. "Never seen a top lion like him. But he runs a good pride[25]. The

1. J'ajoute sans arrêt du yaourt.
2. Rien n'y fait.
3. mes papilles se rabougrissent
4. prend un teint de betterave rouge
5. les larmes me montent aux yeux
6. se tordre et à grogner
7. qui aurait avalé une tondeuse à gazon
8. vous mettra en pièces
9. reçoivent suffisamment de nourriture
10. Entre parenthèses
11. l'arène
12. de manière à ce que les lions le voient
13. en tapant du pied
14. en faisant claquer son fouet
15. pèse
16. ils ont beau être de puissants prédateurs
17. ils entrent en rampant
18. ils restent au bord de
19. un mâle dont la domination est indiscutable
20. gueule
21. des cerceaux
22. ils roulent sur le côté
23. Il est bizarre
24. vaguement
25. il a fière allure

larder[1]'s always full and—let's be honest, mates[2]—his antics[3] keep us busy. Napping[4] all the time does get a bit boring. At least we're not riding bicycles like the brown bears or catching flying plates like the chimps."

Only the trainer better make sure he always remains super alpha. He will pay dearly[5] if he unwittingly slips to beta[6]. Much hostile and aggressive behaviour among animals is the expression of social insecurity. The animal in front of you must know where it stands, whether above you or below you. Social rank is central to how it leads its life. Rank determines whom it can associate with and how; where and when it can eat; where it can rest; where it can drink; and so on. Until it knows its rank for certain[7], the animal lives a life of unbearable[8] anarchy. It remains nervous, jumpy[9], dangerous. Luckily for the circus trainer, decisions about social rank among higher animals are not always based on brute force. Hediger (1950) says, "When two creatures meet, the one that is able to intimidate its opponent[10] is recognized as socially superior, so that a social decision does not always depend on a fight; an encounter[11] in some circumstances may be enough." Words of a wise animal man. Mr. Hediger was for many years a zoo director, first of the Basel Zoo and then of the Zurich Zoo. He was a man well versed in the ways of animals[12].

It's a question of brain over brawn.[13] The nature of the circus trainer's ascendancy is psychological. Foreign surroundings[14], the trainer's erect posture[15], calm demeanour[16], steady gaze[17], fearless step forward[18], strange roar (for example, the snapping of a whip or the blowing of a whistle[19])—

these are so many factors that will fill the animal's mind with doubt and fear, and make clear to it where it stands, the very thing it wants to know. Satisfied, Number Two will back down[1] and Number One can turn to the audience[2] and shout, "Let the show go on! And now, ladies and gentlemen, through hoops of *real* fire..."

1. *cédera*
2. *public*

CHAPTER 14

It is interesting to note that the lion that is the most amenable to the circus trainer's tricks[3] is the one with the lowest social standing in the pride[4], the omega animal. It has the most to gain[5] from a close relationship[6] with the super-alpha trainer. It is not only a matter of extra treats[7]. A close relationship will also mean protection from the other members of the pride. It is this compliant[8] animal, to the public no different from the others in size and apparent ferocity, that will be the star of the show, while the trainer leaves the beta and gamma lions, more cantankerous subordinates[9], sitting on their colourful barrels[10] on the edge of the ring.

The same is true of[11] other circus animals and is also seen in zoos. Socially inferior animals are the ones that make the most strenuous, resourceful efforts[12] to get to know their keepers. They prove to be[13] the ones most faithful to them, most in need of[14] their company, least likely to challenge them[15] or be difficult. The phenomenon has been observed with big cats, bison, deer, wild sheep, monkeys and many other animals. It is a fact commonly known in the trade.

3. *qui se soumet le plus facilement aux tours du dompteur*

4. *le statut social le moins élevé dans le groupe*

5. *C'est lui qui a le plus à gagner*

6. *d'une certaine proximité*

7. *friandises supplémentaires*

8. *docile*

9. *des subordonnés plus revêches*

10. *tonneaux*

11. *Il en va de même pour*

12. *qui font les efforts les plus importants et les plus ingénieux*

13. *Ils s'avèrent*

14. *ceux qui ont le plus besoin de*

15. *ceux qui sont les moins susceptibles de les défier*

CHAPTER 15

His house is a temple. In the entrance hall hangs a framed[1] picture of Ganesha, he of the elephant head[2]. He sits facing out[3]—rosy-coloured, pot-bellied, crowned[4] and smiling—three hands holding various objects, the fourth held palm out[5] in blessing and in greeting[6]. He is the lord overcomer of obstacles[7], the god of good luck, the god of wisdom[8], the patron of learning. Simpatico in the highest.[9] He brings a smile to my lips. At his feet is an attentive rat. His vehicle. Because when Lord Ganesha travels, he travels atop a rat[10]. On the wall opposite the picture is a plain wooden Cross[11].

In the living room, on a table next to the sofa, there is a small framed picture of the Virgin Mary of Guadalupe[12], flowers tumbling from her open mantle[13]. Next to it is a framed photo of the black-robed Kaaba, holiest sanctum of Islam[14], surrounded by a ten-thousandfold swirl of the faithful[15]. On the television set is a brass[16] statue of Shiva as Nataraja, the cosmic lord of the dance, who controls the motions[17] of the universe and the flow[18] of time. He dances on the demon of ignorance, his four arms held out in choreographic gesture[19], one foot on the demon's back, the other lifted in the air. When Nataraja brings this foot down[20], they say time will stop.

There is a shrine[21] in the kitchen. It is set in a cupboard[22] whose door he has replaced with a fretwork arch[23]. The arch partly hides the yellow light bulb that in the evenings lights up[24] the shrine. Two pictures rest behind a small altar: to the side, Ganesha again, and in the centre, in a larger frame, smiling and blue-skinned[25], Krishna playing the flute. Both have smears[26] of red and yellow powder on the glass over their foreheads. In a copper[27] dish on the altar are three silver murtis, representations. He identifies them for me with a pointed finger: Lakshmi; Shakti, the mother goddess, in the form of Parvati; and Krishna, this time as a playful baby crawling on all fours[1]. In between the goddesses is a stone Shiva yoni linga[2], which looks like half an avocado with a phallic stump rising from its centre[3], a Hindu symbol representing the male and female energies of the universe. To one side of the dish is a small conch shell set on a pedestal[4]; to the other, a small silver handbell[5]. Grains of rice lie about, as well as a flower just beginning to wilt[6]. Many of these items[7] are anointed with dabs of yellow and red[8].

On the shelf below are various articles of devotion: a beaker[9] full of water; a copper spoon; a lamp with a wick coiled in oil[10]; sticks of incense; and small bowls full of red powder, yellow powder, grains of rice and lumps[11] of sugar.

There is another Virgin Mary in the dining room.

Upstairs in his office there is a brass Ganesha sitting cross-legged[12] next to the computer, a wooden Christ on the Cross from Brazil on a wall, and a green prayer rug[13] in a corner. The Christ is expressive—He suffers. The prayer rug lies in its own clear space. Next to it, on a low bookstand[14], is a book covered by a cloth[15]. At the centre of the cloth is a single Arabic word, intricately woven[16], four letters: an alif, two lams and a ha. The word God in Arabic.

The book on the bedside table[17] is a Bible.

CHAPTER 16

We are all born like Catholics, aren't we—in limbo[18], without religion, until some figure introduces

1. à quatre pattes

2. un Shiva lingam en pierre sur un yoni

3. une protubérance phallique érigée au centre d'une moitié d'avocat

4. une petite conque posée sur un piédestal

5. clochette

6. faner

7. objets

8. sont oints de jaune et de rouge

9. gobelet

10. une mèche enroulée dans de l'huile

11. morceaux

12. en tailleur

13. tapis de prière

14. étagère

15. morceau de tissu

16. étroitement tissé

17. sur la table de chevet

18. dans les limbes

us to God? After that meeting the matter ends for most of us. If there is a change, it is usually for the lesser rather than the greater[1]; many people seem to lose God along life's way[2]. That was not my case. The figure in question for me was an older sister of Mother's, of a more traditional mind, who brought me to a temple when I was a small baby. Auntie[3] Rohini was delighted[4] to meet her newborn neph-ew[5] and thought she would include Mother God-dess in the delight. "It will be his symbolic first out-ing[6]", she said. "It's a samskara!" Symbolic indeed. We were in Madurai; I was the fresh veteran of a seven-hour train journey[7]. No matter.[8] Off we went[9] on this Hindu rite of passage, Mother carrying me, Auntie propelling her[10]. I have no conscious mem-ory of this first go-around[11] in a temple, but some smell of incense, some play of light and shadow, some flame, some burst[12] of colour, something of the sultriness[13] and mystery of the place must have stayed with me. A germ of religious exaltation, no bigger than a mustard seed[14], was sown in me and left to germinate[15]. It has never stopped growing since that day.

I am a Hindu because of sculptured cones of red kumkum powder[16] and baskets of yellow turmeric nuggets[17], because of garlands[18] of flowers and piec-es of broken coconut[19], because of the clanging of bells[20] to announce one's arrival to God, because of the whine of the reedy nadaswaram[21] and the beat-ing of drums[22], because of the patter of bare feet[23] against stone floors down dark corridors pierced by shafts of sunlight[24], because of the fragrance[25] of incense, because of flames of arati lamps circling[26] in the darkness, because of bhajans being sweet-ly sung, because of elephants standing around to bless, because of colourful murals[27] telling colourful[1] stories, because of foreheads carrying, variously signified, the same word—*faith*. I became loyal to these sense impressions[2] even before I knew what they meant or what they were for. It is my heart that commands me so. I feel at home in a Hindu temple. I am aware of[3] Presence, not personal the way we usually feel presence, but something larger. My heart still skips a beat[4] when I catch sight of[5] the murti, of God Residing, in the inner sanctum[6] of a temple. Truly I am in a sacred cosmic womb[7], a place where everything is born, and it is my sweet luck to behold its living core[8]. My hands naturally come together in reverent worship[9]. I hunger for[10] prasad, that sugary offering[11] to God that comes back to us as a sanctified treat[12]. My palms need to feel the heat of a hallowed[13] flame whose blessing I bring[14] to my eyes and forehead.

But religion is more than rite and ritual. There is what the rite and ritual stand for. Here too I am a Hindu. The universe makes sense to me through Hindu eyes. There is Brahman, the world soul, the sustaining frame[15] upon which is woven[16], warp and weft[17], the cloth of being[18], with all its decorative elements of space and time. There is Brahman nirguna, without qualities, which lies beyond understanding, beyond description, beyond approach[19]; with our poor words we sew a suit for it[20]—One, Truth, Unity, Absolute, Ultimate Reality, Ground of Being—and try to make it fit[21], but Brahman nirguna always bursts the seams[22]. We are left speechless[23]. But there is also Brahman saguna, with qualities, where the suit fits[24]. Now we call it Shiva, Krishna, Shakti, Ganesha; we can approach it with some understanding[25]; we can discern[26] certain attributes—loving, merciful[27], frightening—and we feel the gentle pull[28] of relationship.

1. mouvementées
2. impressions des sens
3. Je perçois
4. fait un bond
5. J'aperçois
6. sanctuaire
7. matrice
8. c'est un bonheur intense que d'en contempler le cœur vivant
9. en signe de prière
10. J'ai terriblement envie de
11. offrande sucrée
12. friandise sanctifiée
13. sanctifiée
14. dont je porte la bénédiction
15. canevas
16. est tissé
17. en chaîne et trame
18. le tissu de l'être
19. qui ne peut être compris, décrit ou approché
20. nous lui cousons un costume
21. l'ajuster
22. fait éclater les coutures
23. sans voix
24. convient
25. nous le comprenons un peu
26. nous percevons
27. miséricordieux
28. attraction

Brahman saguna is Brahman made manifest to our limited senses, Brahman expressed not only in gods but in humans, animals, trees, in a handful[1] of earth, for everything has a trace of the divine in it. The truth of life is that Brahman is no different from atman, the spiritual force within us, what you might call the soul. The individual soul touches upon the world soul like a well[2] reaches for the water table. That which sustains the universe beyond thought and language, and that which is at the core of us and struggles for expression[3], is the same thing. The finite[4] within the infinite, the infinite within the finite. If you ask me how Brahman and atman relate precisely[5], I would say in the same way the Father, the Son and the Holy Spirit[6] relate: mysteriously. But one thing is clear: atman seeks to realize Brahman, to be united with the Absolute, and it travels in this life on a pilgrimage[7] where it is born and dies, and is born again and dies again, and again, and again, until it manages to shed the sheaths that imprison it here below[8]. The paths to liberation[9] are numerous[10], but the bank[11] along the way is always the same, the Bank of Karma, where the liberation account[12] of each of us is credited or debited depending on[13] our actions.

This, in a holy nutshell[14], is Hinduism, and I have been a Hindu all my life. With its notions in mind I see my place in the universe.

But we should not cling[15]! A plague upon fundamentalists and literalists! I am reminded of a story of Lord Krishna when he was a cowherd[16]. Every night he invites the milkmaids[17] to dance with him in the forest. They come and they dance. The night is dark, the fire in their midst roars and crackles[18], the beat of the music gets ever faster[19]—the girls dance and dance and dance with their sweet lord,

1. poignée
2. puits
3. cherche à s'exprimer
4. fini
5. quelle est précisément la relation du Brahman et de l'atman
6. l'Esprit saint
7. pèlerinage
8. se débarrasser de la gaine qui l'emprisonne ici-bas
9. Les chemins qui mènent à la libération
10. nombreux
11. banque
12. compte de libération
13. selon
14. en un mot sacré
15. nous ne devrions pas nous agripper trop fermement à nos croyances
16. vacher
17. trayeuses de vaches
18. gronde et crépite
19. le rythme de la musique s'accélère toujours plus

who has made himself so abundant[1] as to be in the arms of each and every girl. But the moment the girls become possessive, the moment each one imagines that Krishna is her partner alone, he vanishes. So it is that we should not be jealous with God.

I know a woman here in Toronto who is very dear to my heart[2]. She was my foster mother[3]. I call her Auntieji and she likes that. She is Québécoise. Though she has lived in Toronto for over thirty years[4], her French-speaking mind still slips on occasion[5] on the understanding of English sounds. And so, when she first heard of Hare Krishnas, she didn't hear right. She heard "Hairless[6] Christians", and that is what they were to her for many years. When I corrected her, I told her that in fact she was not so wrong; that Hindus, in their capacity for love, are indeed hairless Christians, just as Muslims, in the way they see God in everything, are bearded[7] Hindus, and Christians, in their devotion to God, are hat-wearing[8] Muslims.

CHAPTER 17

First wonder goes deepest[9]; wonder after that fits in the impression made by the first[10]. I owe[11] to Hinduism the original landscape[12] of my religious imagination, those towns and rivers, battlefields[13] and forests, holy mountains and deep seas where gods, saints, villains[14] and ordinary people rub shoulders[15], and, in doing so[16], define who and why we are. I first heard[17] of the tremendous, cosmic might of loving kindness[18] in this Hindu land. It was Lord Krishna speaking. I heard him, and I followed him. And in his wisdom and perfect love, Lord Krishna

1. qui s'est multiplié tellement de fois
2. qui m'est très chère
3. mère adoptive
4. elle vit à Toronto depuis plus de trente ans
5. trébuche parfois
6. sans cheveux, sans poils
7. barbus
8. porteurs de chapeaux
9. Les premiers émerveillements sont les plus profonds
10. ils façonnent les suivants
11. Je dois
12. paysage
13. ces champs de bataille
14. les manants
15. se côtoient
16. ce faisant
17. J'ai entendu parler pour la première fois
18. de la force prodigieuse de l'amour bienveillant

led me to meet one man.

I was fourteen years old—and a well-content[1] Hindu on a holiday—when I met Jesus Christ.

It was not often that Father took time off[2] from the zoo, but one of the times he did we went to Munnar, just over in Kerala. Munnar is a small hill station[3] surrounded by some of the highest tea estates in the world. It was early May and the monsoon[4] hadn't come yet. The plains of Tamil Nadu were beastly[5] hot. We made it to Munnar after a winding, five-hour car ride[6] from Madurai. The coolness[7] was as pleasing as having mint[8] in your mouth. We did the tourist thing. We visited a Tata tea factory[9]. We enjoyed a boat ride[10] on a lake. We toured a cattle-breeding centre.[11] We fed salt[12] to some Nilgiri tahrs—a species of wild goat—in a national park. ("We have some in our zoo. You should come to Pondicherry", said Father to some Swiss tourists.) Ravi and I went for walks in the tea estates near town. It was all an excuse to keep our lethargy a little busy[13]. By late afternoon Father and Mother were as settled in the tea room of our comfortable hotel as two cats sunning themselves[14] at a window. Mother read while Father chatted with fellow guests[15].

There are three hills within Munnar. They don't bear comparison[16] with the tall hills—mountains, you might call them—that surround the town, but I noticed the first morning, as we were having breakfast, that they did stand out[17] in one way: on each stood a Godhouse. The hill on the right, across the river[18] from the hotel, had a Hindu temple high on its side; the hill in the middle, further away[19], held up a mosque; while the hill on the left was crowned with a Christian church.

1. satisfait
2. prenait des congés
3. une petite station sur une colline
4. mousson
5. horriblement
6. cinq heures de trajet sur une route sinueuse
7. fraîcheur
8. de la menthe
9. usine de thé
10. Nous avons fait une promenade en bateau
11. Nous avons visité un centre d'élevage bovin.
12. Nous avons donné du sel
13. nous sortir un peu de notre léthargie
14. prenant le soleil
15. discutait avec d'autres clients de l'hôtel
16. On ne peut pas les comparer
17. elles se distinguaient tout de même
18. de l'autre côté de la rivière
19. plus éloignée

On our fourth day in Munnar, as the afternoon was coming to an end[1], I stood on the hill on the left. Despite attending a nominally Christian school[2], I had not yet been inside a church—and I wasn't about to dare the deed[3] now. I knew very little about the religion. It had a reputation for few gods and great violence. But good schools. I walked around the church. It was a building unremittingly unrevealing of what it held inside[4], with thick, featureless[5] walls pale blue in colour and high, narrow[6] windows impossible to look in through. A fortress.

I came upon the rectory[7]. The door was open. I hid around a corner to look upon the scene. To the left of the door was a small board[8] with the words *Parish Priest*[9] and *Assistant Priest*[10] on it. Next to each was a small sliding[11] block. Both the priest and his assistant were IN[12], the board informed me in gold letters, which I could plainly see. One priest was working in his office, his back turned to the bay windows[13], while the other was seated on a bench[14] at a round table in the large vestibule that evidently functioned as a room for receiving visitors. He sat facing the door and the windows, a book in his hands, a Bible I presumed. He read a little, looked up[15], read a little more, looked up again. It was done in a way that was leisurely[16], yet alert and composed[17]. After some minutes, he closed the book and put it aside[18]. He folded his hands together[19] on the table and sat there, his expression serene, showing neither expectation nor resignation.

The vestibule had clean, white walls; the table and benches were of dark wood; and the priest was dressed in a white cassock[20]—it was all neat, plain[21], simple. I was filled with a sense of peace.

1. touchait à sa fin
2. une école au nom chrétien
3. je n'étais pas prêt à oser le faire
4. qui ne révélait rien de son intérieur
5. sans ornements
6. étroites
7. presbytère
8. panneau
9. Prêtre de la paroisse
10. Vicaire
11. coulissant
12. PRÉSENTS
13. baies vitrées
14. banc
15. a levé les yeux
16. nonchalante
17. attentive et tranquille
18. l'a mis de côté
19. Il a joint les mains
20. soutane
21. bien ordonné, sobre

But more than the setting[1], what arrested me[2] was my intuitive understanding that he was there—open, patient—in case someone, anyone, should want to talk to him; a problem of the soul, a heaviness of the heart[3], a darkness of the conscience[4], he would listen with love. He was a man whose profession it was to love, and he would offer comfort and guidance to the best of his ability[5].

I was moved. What I had before my eyes stole into my heart and thrilled me[6].

He got up. I thought he might slide his block over[7], but he didn't. He retreated further into the rectory[8], that's all, leaving the door between the vestibule and the next room as open as the outside door. I noted this, how both doors were wide open. Clearly, he and his colleague were still available[9].

I walked away and I dared[10]. I entered the church. My stomach was in knots.[11] I was terrified I would meet a Christian who would shout at me, "What are you doing here? How dare you enter this sacred place, you defiler[12]? Get out, right now!"

There was no one. And little to be understood[13]. I advanced and observed the inner sanctum[14]. There was a painting. Was this the murti[15]? Something about a human sacrifice. An angry god who had to be appeased with[16] blood. Dazed[17] women staring up in the air[18] and fat babies with tiny wings[19] flying about[20]. A charismatic bird. Which one was the god? To the side of the sanctum was a painted wooden sculpture. The victim again, bruised and bleeding in bold colours[21]. I stared at his knees. They were badly scraped[22]. The pink skin was peeled back[23] and looked like the petals of a flower, revealing kneecaps[24] that were fire-engine[25] red. It was hard to connect this torture scene with the priest in the rectory.

The next day, at around the same time, I let myself IN.

Catholics have a reputation for severity, for judgment that comes down heavily[1]. My experience with Father Martin was not at all like that. He was very kind. He served me tea and biscuits in a tea set that tinkled and rattled[2] at every touch; he treated me like a grown-up[3]; and he told me a story. Or rather, since Christians are so fond of capital letters[4], a Story.

And what a story. The first thing that drew me in[5] was disbelief[6]. What? Humanity sins[7] but it's God's Son who pays the price? I tried to imagine Father saying to me, "Piscine, a lion slipped into[8] the llama pen[9] today and killed two llamas. Yesterday another one killed a black buck[10]. Last week two of them ate the camel. The week before it was painted storks[11] and grey herons[12]. And who's to say for sure who snacked on our golden agouti[13]? The situation has become intolerable. Something must be done. I have decided that the only way the lions can atone for their sins[14] is if I feed you to them[15]."

"Yes, Father, that would be the right and logical thing to do. Give me a moment to wash up[16]."

"Hallelujah, my son."

"Hallelujah, Father."

What a downright weird story.[17] What peculiar psychology.

I asked for another story, one that I might find more satisfying. Surely this religion had more than one story in its bag—religions abound with stories[18]. But Father Martin made me understand that the stories that came before it—and there were many—were simply prologue to the Christians. Their religion had one Story, and to it they came

1. ont la réputation d'être sévères, d'émettre des jugements tranchés

2. un service à thé qui tintait et cliquetait

3. adulte

4. aiment tellement les majuscules

5. m'a amené à m'y intéresser

6. scepticisme

7. pèche

8. s'est introduit dans

9. enclos

10. daim

11. des tantales indiens

12. hérons

13. qui a grignoté notre Gerbille de Mongolie

14. la seule façon qu'ont les lions d'expier leurs péchés

15. c'est de te manger

16. me débarbouiller

17. Quelle drôle d'histoire !

18. regorgent d'histoires

1. constamment

2. Cette histoire leur suffisait.

3. faire face à

4. sont confrontés à bon nombre de voleurs, tyrans, ravisseurs et usurpateurs

5. Des revirements de situation

6. Des trahisons

7. entièrement déshabillé, fouetté, ridiculisé, traîné dans les rues

8. pour couronner le tout

9. simples humains

10. par-dessus le marché

11. n'admettait pas la mort

12. par millions

13. La matière aussi disparaissait.

14. anéantie

15. en partie

16. Cela revient à

17. simulé

18. feignant

19. ressuscité

20. souillée

21. puanteur

22. gâcher

back again and again, over and over[1]. It was story enough for them.[2]

I was quiet that evening at the hotel.

That a god should put up with[3] adversity, I could understand. The gods of Hinduism face their fair share of thieves, bullies, kidnappers and usurpers[4]. What is the Ramayana but the account of one long, bad day for Rama? Adversity, yes. Reversals of fortune[5], yes. Treachery[6], yes. But *humiliation*? *Death*? I couldn't imagine Lord Krishna consenting to be stripped naked, whipped, mocked, dragged through the streets[7] and, to top it off[8], crucified— and at the hands of mere humans[9], to boot[10]. I'd never heard of a Hindu god dying. Brahman Revealed did not go for death[11]. Devils and monsters did, as did mortals, by the thousands and millions[12]—that's what they were there for. Matter, too, fell away.[13] But divinity should not be blighted[14] by death. It's wrong. The world soul cannot die, even in one contained part of it[15]. It was wrong of this Christian God to let His avatar die. That is tantamount to[16] letting a part of Himself die. For if the Son is to die, it cannot be fake[17]. If God on the Cross is God shamming[18] a human tragedy, it turns the Passion of Christ into the Farce of Christ. The death of the Son must be real. Father Martin assured me that it was. But once a dead God, always a dead God, even resurrected[19]. The Son must have the taste of death forever in His mouth. The Trinity must be tainted[20] by it; there must be a certain stench[21] at the right hand of God the Father. The horror must be real. Why would God wish that upon Himself? Why not leave death to the mortals? Why make dirty what is beautiful, spoil[22] what is perfect?

Love. That was Father Martin's answer.

And what about this Son's deportment[1]? There is the story of baby Krishna, wrongly accused[2] by his friends of eating a bit of dirt[3]. His foster mother[4], Yashoda, comes up to him with a wagging finger[5]. "You shouldn't eat dirt, you naughty boy[6]", she scolds him[7]. "But I haven't", says the unchallenged[8] lord of all and everything, in sport disguised[9] as a frightened human child. "Tut! Tut! Open your mouth", orders Yashoda. Krishna does as he is told. He opens his mouth. Yashoda gasps[10]. She sees in Krishna's mouth the whole complete entire timeless universe, all the stars and planets of space and the distance between them, all the lands and seas of the earth and the life in them; she sees all the days of yesterday and all the days of tomorrow; she sees all ideas and all emotions, all pity and all hope, and the three strands of matter[11]; not a pebble[12], candle[13], creature, village or galaxy is missing[14], including herself and every bit of dirt in its truthful[15] place. "My Lord, you can close your mouth", she says reverently[16].

There is the story of Vishnu incarnated as Vamana the dwarf[17]. He asks of demon king Bali only as much land as he can cover in three strides[18]. Bali laughs at this runt of a suitor[19] and his puny request[20]. He consents. Immediately Vishnu takes on his full cosmic size[21]. With one stride he covers the earth, with the second the heavens[22], and with the third he boots Bali into the netherworld[23].

Even Rama, that most human of avatars, who had to be reminded of his divinity when he grew long-faced over the struggle[24] to get Sita, his wife, back from Ravana, evil king of Lanka, was no slouch[25]. No spindly cross[26] would have kept him down. When push came to shove[27], he transcended his

1. comportement
2. accusé à tort
3. un peu de terre
4. mère adoptive
5. en faisant non de l'index
6. tu es un vilain garçon
7. gronde-t-elle
8. incontesté
9. qui pour plaisanter s'est déguisé
10. en a le souffle coupé
11. les trois qualités de la matière
12. caillou
13. bougie
14. ne manque
15. véritable
16. respectueusement
17. nain
18. parcourir en trois enjambées
19. cet avorton
20. sa demande dérisoire
21. reprend sa taille cosmique réelle
22. les cieux
23. il envoie Bali aux Enfers d'un coup de pied
24. quand il a fait grise mine devant la perspective de devoir se battre
25. tire-au-flanc
26. petite croix
27. Au moment décisif

limited human frame with strength no man could have and weapons no man could handle[1].

That is God as God should be. With shine[2] and power and might[3]. Such as can rescue[4] and save and put down[5] evil.

This Son, on the other hand, who goes hungry, who suffers from thirst[6], who gets tired, who is sad, who is anxious, who is heckled and harassed[7], who has to put up with followers who don't get it[8] and opponents who don't respect Him—what kind of a god is that? It's a god on too human a scale, that's what. There are miracles, yes, mostly of a medical nature, a few to satisfy hungry stomachs; at best a storm is tempered[9], water is briefly walked upon. If that is magic, it is minor magic, on the order of card tricks[10]. Any Hindu god can do a hundred times better. This Son is a god who spent most of His time telling stories, *talking*. This Son is a god who walked, a pedestrian[11] god—and in a hot place, at that[12]—with a stride like any human stride, the sandal reaching just above the rocks along the way; and when He splurged on transportation[13], it was a regular donkey[14]. This Son is a god who died in three hours, with moans, gasps and laments[15]. What kind of a god is that? What is there to inspire in this Son?

Love, said Father Martin.

And this Son appears only once, long ago, far away? Among an obscure tribe in a backwater[16] of West Asia on the confines of a long-vanished empire[17]? Is done away with[18] before He has a single grey hair on His head? Leaves not a single descendant, only scattered, partial testimony[19], His complete works doodles[20] in the dirt? Wait a minute. This is more than Brahman with a serious case of stage fright[21]. This is Brahman selfish[22]. This is

Brahman ungenerous and unfair[1]. This is Brahman practically unmanifest[2]. If Brahman is to have only one son, He must be as abundant as[3] Krishna with the milkmaids[4], no? What could justify such divine stinginess[5]?

Love, repeated Father Martin.

I'll stick to[6] my Krishna, thank you very much. I find his divinity utterly compelling[7]. You can keep your sweaty[8], chatty[9] Son to yourself.

That was how I met that troublesome rabbi[10] of long ago: with disbelief and annoyance[11].

I had tea with Father Martin three days in a row[12]. Each time, as teacup rattled against saucer[13], as spoon tinkled against edge[14] of cup, I asked questions.

The answer was always the same.

He bothered me[15], this Son. Every day I burned with greater indignation against Him, found more flaws[16] to Him.

He's *petulant*[17]! It's morning in Bethany and God is hungry; God wants His breakfast. He comes to a fig tree[18]. It's not the season for figs, so the tree has no figs. God is peeved[19]. The Son mutters, "May you never bear fruit again[20]", and instantly the fig tree withers[21]. So says Matthew, backed up by Mark.[22]

I ask you, is it the fig tree's fault that it's not the season for figs? What kind of a thing is that to do to an innocent fig tree, wither it instantly?

I couldn't get Him out of my head. Still can't. I spent three solid[23] days thinking about Him. The more He bothered me, the less[24] I could forget Him. And the more I learned about Him, the less I wanted to leave Him.

On our last day, a few hours before we were to leave Munnar, I hurried up[25] the hill on the left. It strikes me now[26] as a typically Christian scene.

1. radin et injuste
2. invisible
3. il doit être aussi fécond que
4. vachères
5. avarice
6. Je vais rester fidèle à
7. tout à fait irrésistible
8. en sueur
9. bavard
10. pénible rabbin
11. agacement
12. d'affilée
13. la tasse et la soucoupe s'entrecho-quaient
14. le bord
15. Il me préoccupait
16. défauts
17. irascible
18. figuier
19. irrité
20. Jamais plus tu ne porteras de fruits
21. dépérit
22. C'est ce que dit Matthieu, et ce que confirme Marc.
23. entiers
24. Plus il me préoccupait, moins
25. je suis monté en courant sur
26. Cela m'apparaît à présent

Christianity is a religion in a rush[1]. Look at the world created in seven days. Even on a symbolic level, that's creation in a frenzy[2]. To one born in a religion where the battle for a single soul can be a relay race[3] run over many centuries[4], with innumerable[5] generations passing along the baton[6], the quick resolution of Christianity has a dizzying effect[7]. If Hinduism flows placidly like the Ganges[8], then Christianity bustles like Toronto at rush hour[9]. It is a religion as swift as a swallow[10], as urgent as an ambulance. It turns on a dime[11], expresses itself in the instant. In a moment you are lost or saved. Christianity stretches back through the ages[12], but in essence it exists only at one time: right now.

I booted up that hill. Though Father Martin was not IN—alas[13], his block was slid over—thank God he was in.

Short of breath[14] I said, "Father, I would like to be a Christian, please."

He smiled. "You already are, Piscine—in your heart. Whoever meets Christ in good faith[15] is a Christian. Here in Munnar you met Christ."

He patted me on the head.[16] It was more of a thump[17], actually. His hand went BOOM BOOM BOOM on my head.

I thought I would explode with joy.

"When you come back, we'll have tea again, my son."

"Yes, Father."

It was a good smile he gave me. The smile of Christ.

I entered the church, without fear this time, for it was now my house too. I offered prayers to Christ, who is alive. Then I raced down[18] the hill on the left and raced up[19] the hill on the right—to offer thanks to Lord Krishna for having put Jesus of Nazareth, whose humanity I found so compelling[1], in my way.

CHAPTER 18

Islam followed right behind, hardly[2] a year later. I was fifteen years old and I was exploring my hometown[3]. The Muslim quarter wasn't far from the zoo. A small, quiet neighbourhood[4] with Arabic writing and crescent moons[5] inscribed on the facades of the houses.

I came to Mullah Street. I had a peek at[6] the Jamia Masjid, the Great Mosque, being careful to stay on the outside, of course. Islam had a reputation worse than Christianity's—fewer gods, greater violence, and I had never heard anyone say good things about Muslim schools—so I wasn't about to step in[7], empty though the place was[8]. The building, clean and white except for various edges[9] painted green, was an open construction unfolding around an empty central room. Long straw mats[10] covered the floor everywhere. Above, two slim, fluted[11] minarets rose[12] in the air before a background of soaring coconut trees[13]. There was nothing evidently religious or, for that matter[14], interesting about the place, but it was pleasant and quiet.

I moved on. Just beyond the mosque was a series of attached single-storey dwellings[15] with small shaded[16] porches. They were rundown[17] and poor, their stucco walls a faded green[18]. One of the dwellings was a small shop. I noticed a rack of dusty bottles of Thums Up[19] and four transparent plastic jars half-full of candies[20]. But the main ware[21] was something else, something flat, roundish[22] and

1. fascinant
2. à peine
3. ville natale
4. quartier
5. des croissants de lune
6. J'ai jeté un coup d'œil à
7. y entrer
8. même si elle était vide
9. bordures
10. nattes de paille
11. striés
12. s'élevaient
13. sur fond de grands cocotiers
14. d'ailleurs
15. une rangée de maisons mitoyennes à un étage
16. ombragés
17. délabrées
18. leurs murs étaient couverts de crépi d'un vert passé
19. des bouteilles poussiéreuses de Thums Up [cola indien] sur un présentoir
20. pots en plastique transparents à moitié remplis de bonbons
21. marchandise
22. arrondi

white. I got close.[1] It seemed to be some sort of unleavened[2] bread. I poked at one.[3] It flipped up stiffly.[4] They looked like three-day-old nans. Who would eat these, I wondered. I picked one up and wagged it[5] to see if it would break.

A voice said, "Would you like to taste one?"

I nearly jumped out of my skin.[6] It's happened to all of us: there's sunlight and shade[7], spots and patterns of colour[8], your mind is elsewhere—so you don't make out[9] what is right in front of you.

Not four feet away[10], sitting cross-legged before his breads, was a man. I was so startled my hands flew up and the bread went sailing halfway across the street[11]. It landed on a pat of fresh cow dung.[12]

"I'm so sorry, sir. I didn't see you!" I burst out. I was just about ready to run away.

"Don't worry", he said calmly. "It will feed a cow.[13] Have another one."

He tore one in two. We ate it together. It was tough and rubbery[14], real work for the teeth, but filling[15]. I calmed down.

"So you make these", I said, to make conversation.

"Yes. Here, let me show you how." He got off his platform[16] and waved me into[17] his house.

It was a two-room hovel[18]. The larger room, dominated by an oven[19], was the bakery[20], and the other, separated by a flimsy curtain[21], was his bedroom. The bottom of the oven was covered with smooth pebbles[22]. He was explaining to me how the bread baked on these heated[23] pebbles when the nasal call[24] of the muezzin wafted through the air from the mosque. I knew it was the call to prayer[25], but I didn't know what it entailed[26]. I imagined it beckoned[27] the Muslim faithful to the mosque, much like bells summoned[28] us Christians to church. Not so.[29] The baker interrupted himself mid-sentence[1] and said, "Excuse me." He ducked[2] into the next room for a minute and returned with a rolled-up carpet[3], which he unfurled[4] on the floor of his bakery, throwing up a small storm of flour[5]. And right there before me, in the midst of his workplace, he prayed. It was incongruous, but it was I who felt out of place[6]. Luckily, he prayed with his eyes closed.

He stood straight. He muttered in Arabic.[7] He brought his hands next to his ears, thumbs[8] touching the lobes, looking as if he were straining[9] to hear Allah replying. He bent forward. He stood straight again. He fell to his knees[10] and brought his hands and forehead to the floor. He sat up. He fell forward again. He stood. He started the whole thing again.

Why[11], Islam is nothing but an easy sort of exercise, I thought. Hot-weather yoga for the Bedouins. Asanas[12] without sweat[13], heaven without strain[14].

He went through the cycle four times, muttering throughout[15]. When he had finished—with a right-left turning of the head and a short bout[16] of meditation—he opened his eyes, smiled, stepped off[17] his carpet and rolled it up with a flick of the hand[18] that spoke of old habit[19]. He returned it to its spot in the next room. He came back to me. "What was I saying?" he asked.

So it went[20] the first time I saw a Muslim pray—quick, necessary, physical, muttered, striking[21]. Next time I was praying in church—on my knees, immobile, silent before Christ on the Cross—the image of this callisthenic[22] communion with God in the middle of bags of flour kept coming to my mind.

1. au milieu d'une phrase

2. Il s'est éclipsé

3. un tapis enroulé

4. qu'il a déroulé

5. un nuage de farine

6. qui ne me sentais pas à ma place

7. Il murmurait en arabe.

8. les pouces

9. il s'efforçait

10. Il s'est agenouillé

11. Tiens

12. Des postures de yoga

13. transpiration

14. effort

15. marmonnant du début jusqu'à la fin

16. période

17. s'est levé de

18. l'a enroulé sous l'impulsion d'une petite chiquenaude

19. qui suggérait qu'il s'agissait d'un geste coutumier

20. C'est ainsi que s'est passé

21. frappant

22. sportive

CHAPTER 19

I went to see him again.

"What's your religion about?" I asked.

His eyes lit up[1]. "It is about the Beloved[2]", he replied.

I challenge anyone[3] to understand Islam, its spirit, and not to love it. It is a beautiful religion of brotherhood[4] and devotion.

The mosque was truly an open construction, to God and to breeze[5]. We sat cross-legged listening to the imam until the time came to pray. Then the random pattern of sitters disappeared[6] as we stood and arranged ourselves shoulder to shoulder[7] in rows[8], every space ahead being filled by someone from behind until every line was solid and we were row after row of worshippers[9]. It felt good to bring my forehead to the ground. Immediately it felt like a deeply religious contact.

CHAPTER 20

He was a Sufi[10], a Muslim mystic. He sought[11] fana, union with God, and his relationship with God was personal and loving. "If you take two steps towards[12] God", he used to tell me, "God runs to you!"

He was a very plain-featured man[13], with nothing in his looks or in his dress[14] that made memory cry hark[15]. I'm not surprised I didn't see him the first time we met. Even when I knew him very well, encounter after encounter[16], I had difficulty[17] recognizing him. His name was Satish Kumar. These are common names in Tamil Nadu, so the coinci-

1. se sont illuminés
2. Bien-Aimé
3. Je défie quiconque
4. fraternité
5. était vraiment un bâtiment ouvert, à Dieu et à la brise
6. les regroupements fortuits de gens assis se défaisaient
7. coude à coude
8. en rangs
9. fidèles
10. soufi
11. recherchait
12. Si tu fais deux pas en direction de
13. Il avait des traits tout à fait ordinaires
14. vêtements
15. qui reste gravé dans la mémoire
16. après plusieurs rencontres
17. j'avais du mal à

dence is not so remarkable. Still[1], it pleased me that this pious[2] baker, as plain as a shadow[3] and of solid health, and the Communist biology teacher and science devotee[4], the walking mountain on stilts[5], sadly afflicted with polio in his childhood, carried the same name. Mr. and Mr. Kumar taught me[6] biology and Islam. Mr. and Mr. Kumar led me to study zoology and religious studies at the University of Toronto. Mr. and Mr. Kumar were the prophets of my Indian youth[7].

We prayed together and we practised dhikr, the recitation of the ninety-nine revealed names of God. He was a hafiz, one who knows the Qur'an by heart[8], and he sang it in a slow, simple chant. My Arabic was never very good, but I loved its sound. The guttural eruptions and long flowing[9] vowels rolled just beneath my comprehension like a beautiful brook[10]. I gazed into this brook for long spells[11] of time. It was not wide, just one man's voice, but it was as deep as the universe.

I described Mr. Kumar's place as a hovel. Yet no mosque, church or temple ever felt so sacred to me. I sometimes came out of that bakery feeling heavy with glory. I would climb onto my bicycle and pedal that glory through the air[12].

One such time I left town and on my way back[13], at a point where the land was high and I could see the sea to my left and down the road a long ways[14], I suddenly felt I was in heaven. The spot was in fact no different from when I had passed it not long before, but my way of seeing it had changed. The feeling, a paradoxical mix of pulsing energy[15] and profound peace, was intense and blissful[16]. Whereas before[17] the road, the sea, the trees, the air, the sun all spoke differently to me, now they spoke

1. Malgré tout

2. pieux

3. aussi discret qu'une ombre

4. adepte de la science

5. sur des échasses

6. m'ensei-gnaient

7. jeunesse

8. connaît le Coran par cœur

9. fluides

10. ruisseau

11. périodes

12. j'emportais cette gloire avec moi

13. sur le chemin du retour

14. au loin

15. une grande énergie

16. merveilleux

17. Alors qu'auparavant

one language of unity. Tree took account of[1] road, which was aware of[2] air, which was mindful of[3] sea, which shared things with sun. Every element lived in harmonious relation with its neighbour, and all was kith and kin[4]. I knelt a mortal[5]; I rose[6] an immortal. I felt like the centre of a all circle coinciding with the centre of a much larger one. Atman met Allah.

One other time I felt God come so close to me. It was in Canada, much later. I was visiting friends in the country. It was winter. I was out alone on a walk on their large property and returning to the house. It was a clear, sunny day after a night of snowfall[7]. All nature was blanketed in white[8]. As I was coming up to the house, I turned my head. There was a wood and in that wood, a small clearing[9]. A breeze, or perhaps it was an animal, had shaken a branch. Fine snow was falling through the air, glittering[10] in the sunlight. In that falling golden dust[11] in that sun-splashed[12] clearing, I saw the Virgin Mary. Why her, I don't know. My devotion to Mary was secondary. But it was her. Her skin was pale. She was wearing a white dress and a blue cloak[13]; I remember being struck by their pleats and folds[14]. When I say I *saw* her, I don't quite mean it literally, though she did have body and colour. I *felt* I saw her, a vision beyond vision. I stopped and squinted[15]. She looked beautiful and supremely regal[16]. She was smiling at me with loving kindness. After some seconds she left me. My heart beat with fear and joy.

The presence of God is the finest of rewards[17].

---

1. tenait compte de
2. avait conscience de
3. attentif à
4. tout faisait partie d'une même famille
5. J'étais un mortel quand je me suis agenouillé
6. je me suis levé
7. une nuit enneigée
8. couverte de blanc
9. clairière
10. et étincelait
11. poussière dorée
12. inondée de soleil
13. manteau
14. frappé par leurs nombreux plis
15. j'ai plissé les yeux
16. majestueuse
17. la plus belle des récompenses

CHAPTER 21

I am sitting in a downtown[1] café, after, thinking. I have just spent most of an afternoon with him. Our encounters always leave me weary of the glum contentment[2] that characterizes my life. What were those words he used that struck me? Ah, yes: "dry, yeastless factuality[3]" "the better story." I take pen and paper out and write:

> *Words of divine consciousness: moral exaltation; lasting[4] feelings of elevation, elation[5], joy; a quickening[6] of the moral sense, which strikes one as more important than an intellectual understanding of things; an alignment of the universe along moral lines, not intellectual ones; a realization that the founding[7] principle of existence is what we call love, which works itself out[8] sometimes not clearly, not cleanly, not immediately, nonetheless ineluctably[9].*

I pause. What of[10] God's silence? I think it over.[11] I add:

> *An intellect confounded[12] yet a trusting[13] sense of presence and of ultimate purpose.*

CHAPTER 22

I can well imagine an atheist's last words: "White, white! L-L-Love! My God!"—and the deathbed leap of faith[14]. Whereas the agnostic, if he stays true to[15]

---

1. du centre-ville
2. las du contentement morose
3. la réalité sèche, sans levain
4. durables
5. allégresse
6. stimulation
7. fondateur
8. se manifeste
9. mais néanmoins de manière inéluctable
10. Qu'en est-il du
11. J'y réfléchis.
12. confus
13. confiant
14. le saut de la foi sur le lit de mort
15. fidèle à

his reasonable self, if he stays beholden to[1] dry, yeastless factuality, might try to explain the warm light bathing him[2] by saying, "Possibly a f-f-failing[3] oxygenation of the b-b-brain", and, to the very end[4], lack imagination[5] and miss[6] the better story.

CHAPTER 23

Alas, the sense of community that a common faith brings to a people spelled trouble for me[7]. In time[8], my religious doings[9] went from the notice of those to whom it didn't matter and only amused, to[10] that of those to whom it did matter—and they were not amused.

"What is your son doing going to temple?" asked the priest.

"Your son was seen in church crossing himself[11]", said the imam.

"Your son has gone Muslim", said the pandit.

Yes, it was all forcefully brought to the attention of[12] my bemused[13] parents. You see, they didn't know. They didn't know that I was a practising Hindu, Christian and Muslim. Teenagers always hide a few things from their parents, isn't that so? All sixteen-year-olds have secrets, don't they? But fate[14] decided that my parents and I and the three wise men[15], as I shall call them, should meet one day on the Goubert Salai seaside esplanade[16] and that my secret should be outed[17]. It was a lovely, breezy, hot Sunday afternoon and the Bay of Bengal glittered[18] under a blue sky. Townspeople were out for a stroll.[19] Children screamed and laughed. Coloured balloons floated in the air. Ice cream sales were brisk.[20] Why think of business on such a day,

I ask? Why couldn't they have just walked by with a nod[1] and a smile? It was not to be. We were to meet not just one wise man but all three, and not one after another[2] but at the same time, and each would decide upon seeing us that right then was the golden occasion[3] to meet that Pondicherry notable, the zoo director, he of the model devout son[4]. When I saw the first, I smiled; by the time I had laid eyes on[5] the third, my smile had frozen[6] into a mask of horror. When it was clear that all three were converging on us, my heart jumped before sinking very low[7].

The wise men seemed annoyed when they realized that all three of them were approaching the same people. Each must have assumed[8] that the others were there for some business other than pastoral and had rudely chosen[9] that moment to deal with it. Glances of displeasure were exchanged.[10]

My parents looked puzzled to have their way gently blocked by three broadly smiling[11] religious strangers. I should explain that my family was anything but orthodox. Father saw himself as part of the New India—rich, modern and as secular[12] as ice cream. He didn't have a religious bone in his body. He was a businessman[13], pronounced *busy-nessman*[14] in his case, a hardworking, earthbound[15] professional, more concerned with inbreeding[16] among the lions than any overarching moral or existential scheme[17]. It's true that he had all new animals blessed[18] by a priest and there were two small shrines[19] at the zoo, one to Lord Ganesha and one to Hanuman, gods likely to please a zoo director, what with the first having the head of an elephant and the second being a monkey, but Father's calculation[20] was that this was good for business, not good for his soul, a matter of public relations ra-

1. hochement de tête

2. l'un après l'autre

3. une occasion en or

4. dont le fils était un modèle de dévotion

5. en voyant

6. s'était figé

7. a fait un bond, puis s'est serré fortement

8. supposer

9. avaient eu l'impolitesse de choisir

10. Ils se sont échangé des regards mécontents.

11. arborant un large sourire

12. profane

13. un homme d'affaires

14. un homme affairé

15. travailleur et prosaïque

16. consanguinité

17. un quelconque schéma moral ou existentiel supérieur

18. il faisait bénir tous les nouveaux animaux

19. sanctuaires

20. calcul

1. salut
2. Les inquiétudes spirituelles lui étaient étrangères
3. le troublaient
4. Une épidémie parmi les animaux du zoo
5. nous finirons dans la rue, au milieu d'une équipe de casseurs de cailloux
6. silencieuse
7. éducation
8. s'étaient annulées réciproquement
9. sur le plan de la religion
10. impie
11. opinion
12. les bandes dessinées
13. lisait beaucoup
14. fourré
15. grivois
16. arbitre
17. qu'il s'y connaissait un peu en matière de bowling
18. il aurait peut-être montré un intérêt quelconque pour la religion
19. son intérêt restait en sommeil
20. gêné
21. de la fierté
22. chorale
23. Vous devez faire erreur.
24. sans faute
25. s'améliore de jour en jour

ther than personal salvation[1]. Spiritual worry was alien to him[2]; it was financial worry that rocked his being[3]. "One epidemic in the collection[4]", he used to say, "and we'll end up in a road crew breaking up stones[5]." Mother was mum[6], bored and neutral on the subject. A Hindu upbringing[7] and a Baptist education had precisely cancelled each other out[8] as far as religion was concerned[9] and had left her serenely impious[10]. I suspect she suspected that I had a different take[11] on the matter, but she never said anything when as a child I devoured the comic books[12] of the Ramayana and the Mahabharata and an illustrated children's Bible and other stories of the gods. She herself was a big reader[13]. She was pleased to see me with my nose buried[14] in a book, any book, so long as it wasn't naughty[15]. As for Ravi, if Lord Krishna had held a cricket bat rather than a flute, if Christ had appeared more plainly to him as an umpire[16], if the prophet Muhammad, peace be upon him, had shown some notions of bowling[17], he might have lifted a religious eyelid[18], but they didn't, and so he slumbered[19].

After the "Hellos" and the "Good days", there was an awkward[20] silence. The priest broke it when he said, with pride[21] in his voice, "Piscine is a good Christian boy. I hope to see him join our choir[22] soon."

My parents, the pandit and the imam looked surprised.

"You must be mistaken.[23] He's a good Muslim boy. He comes without fail[24] to Friday prayer, and his knowledge of the Holy Qur'an is coming along nicely[25]." So said the imam.

My parents, the priest and the pandit looked incredulous.

92

The pandit spoke. "You're both wrong. He's a good Hindu boy. I see him all the time at the temple coming for darshan[1] and performing puja[2]."

My parents, the imam and the priest looked astounded[3].

"There is no mistake", said the priest. "I know this boy. He is Piscine Molitor Patel and he's a Christian."

"I know him too, and I tell you he's a Muslim", asserted the imam.

"Nonsense![4]" cried the pandit. "Piscine was born a Hindu, lives a Hindu and will die a Hindu!"

The three wise men stared at each other, breathless and disbelieving[5].

Lord, avert[6] their eyes from me, I whispered in my soul.

All eyes fell upon me[7].

"Piscine, can this be true?" asked the imam earnestly[8]. "Hindus and Christians are idolaters. They have many gods."

"And Muslims have many wives", responded the pandit.

The priest looked askance at both of them[9]. "Piscine", he nearly whispered, "there is salvation only in Jesus."

"Balderdash![10] Christians know nothing about religion", said the pandit.

"They strayed long ago[11] from God's path", said the imam.

"Where's God in your religion?" snapped[12] the priest. "You don't have a single miracle to show for it. What kind of religion is that, without miracles?"

"It isn't a circus with dead people jumping out of tombs all the time, that's what[13]! We Muslims stick to the essential miracle of existence. Birds fly-

1. [sorte de communion]

2. le rituel des offrandes

3. stupéfaits

4. Foutaises !

5. incrédules

6. détourne

7. se sont tournés vers moi

8. gravement

9. les a tous les deux regardés de travers

10. Balivernes !

11. Ils se sont écartés depuis longtemps

12. a rétorqué

13. voilà tout

ing, rain falling, crops growing[1]—these are miracles enough for us."

"Feathers[2] and rain are all very nice, but we like to know that God is truly with us."

"Is that so? Well, a whole lot of good it did God to be with you—you tried to kill him! You banged him to a cross with great big nails[3]. Is that a civilized way to treat a prophet? The prophet Muhammad—peace be upon him—brought us the word of God without any undignified nonsense[4] and died at a ripe old age[5]."

"The word of God? To that illiterate[6] merchant of yours in the middle of the desert? Those were drooling epileptic fits[7] brought on by the swaying[8] of his camel, not divine revelation. That, or the sun frying his brains[9]!"

"If the Prophet—p.b.u.h.[10]—were alive, he would have choice words for you[11]", replied the imam, with narrowed[12] eyes.

"Well, he's not! Christ is alive, while your old 'p.b.u.h.' is dead, dead, dead!"

The pandit interrupted them quietly. In Tamil he said, "The real question is, why is Piscine dallying with[13] these *foreign* religions?"

The eyes of the priest and the imam properly popped out of their heads[14]. They were both native Tamils[15].

"God is universal", spluttered[16] the priest.

The imam nodded strong approval[17]. "There is only one God."

"And with their one god Muslims are always causing troubles and provoking riots[18]. The proof of how bad Islam is, is how uncivilized Muslims are", pronounced the pandit.

"Says the slave-driver[1] of the caste system", huffed[2] the imam. "Hindus enslave people[3] and worship dressed-up dolls[4]."

"They are golden calf lovers.[5] They kneel before cows", the priest chimed in[6].

"While Christians kneel before a white man! They are the flunkies[7] of a foreign god. They are the nightmare of all non-white people."

"And they eat pigs and are cannibals", added the imam for good measure.

"What it comes down to[8]", the priest put out with cool rage, "is whether[9] Piscine wants *real* religion—or myths from a cartoon strip[10]."

"God—or idols", intoned[11] the imam gravely.

"Our gods—or colonial gods", hissed[12] the pandit.

It was hard to tell whose face was more inflamed. It looked as if they might come to blows[13].

Father raised his hands. "Gentlemen, gentlemen, please!" he interjected[14]. "I would like to remind you there is freedom of practice in this country."

Three apoplectic faces turned to him.

"Yes! Prac*tice*—singular!" the wise men screamed in unison. Three index fingers, like punctuation marks[15], jumped to attention[16] in the air to emphasize their point[17].

They were not pleased at the unintended choral effect[18] or the spontaneous unity of their gestures. Their fingers came down quickly, and they sighed[19] and groaned[20] each on his own[21]. Father and Mother stared on[22], at a loss for words[23].

The pandit spoke first. "Mr. Patel, Piscine's piety is admirable. In these troubled times[24] it's good to see a boy so keen on God[25]. We all agree on that." The imam and the priest nodded. "But he can't be a Hindu, a Christian *and* a Muslim. It's impossible. He must choose."

1. l'esclavagiste
2. a grommelé
3. réduisent des gens à l'esclavage
4. vénèrent des poupées costumées
5. Ils adorent le veau d'or.
6. a renchéri
7. laquais
8. L'essentiel, en définitive
9. c'est de savoir si
10. sortis d'une bande dessinée
11. a entonné
12. a sifflé
13. ils allaient en venir aux mains
14. a-t-il lancé
15. des points d'exclamation
16. se sont mis au garde-à-vous
17. souligner leur argument
18. l'effet d'écho involontaire
19. ont poussé un soupir
20. ont ronchonné
21. chacun de leur côté
22. continuaient à regarder la scène les yeux écarquillés
23. ne sachant que dire
24. Dans cette période de troubles
25. si croyant

1. vous avez raison

2. en direction des cieux

3. d'où

4. Un silence pesant s'est formé autour de moi.

5. m'a donné un coup de coude

6. ai-je laissé échapper

7. Un bâton à la main

8. espiègle

9. les yeux pétillants

10. J'imagine

11. s'est éclairci la voix

12. qui n'avait pas mis les pieds dans

13. dans un but religieux

14. cela a eu l'air de marcher

15. se sont éloignés

16. en arborant des sourires figés et réticents

17. s'est ravisé

18. s'est dirigé vers le vendeur de glaces le plus proche

19. interreligieux

"I don't think it's a crime, but I suppose you're right[1]", Father replied.

The three murmured agreement and looked heavenward[2], as did Father, whence[3] they felt the decision must come. Mother looked at me.

A silence fell heavily on my shoulders.[4]

"Hmmm, Piscine?" Mother nudged me[5]. "How do you feel about the question?"

"Bapu Gandhi said, 'All religions are true.' I just want to love God", I blurted out[6], and looked down, red in the face.

My embarrassment was contagious. No one said anything. It happened that we were not far from the statue of Gandhi on the esplanade. Stick in hand[7], an impish[8] smile on his lips, a twinkle in his eyes[9], the Mahatma walked. I fancy[10] that he heard our conversation, but that he paid even greater attention to my heart. Father cleared his throat[11] and said in a half-voice, "I suppose that's what we're all trying to do—love God."

I thought it very funny that he should say that, he who hadn't stepped into[12] a temple with a serious intent[13] since I had had the faculty of memory. But it seemed to do the trick[14]. You can't reprimand a boy for wanting to love God. The three wise men pulled away[15] with stiff, grudging smiles on their faces[16].

Father looked at me for a second, as if to speak, then thought better[17], said, "Ice cream, anyone?" and headed for the closest ice cream wallah[18] before we could answer. Mother gazed at me a little longer, with an expression that was both tender and perplexed.

That was my introduction to interfaith[19] dialogue. Father bought three ice cream sandwiches. We ate them in unusual silence as we continued on our Sunday walk.

CHAPTER 24

Ravi had a field day of it[1] when he found out[2].

"So, Swami[3] Jesus, will you go on the hajj[4] this year?" he said, bringing the palms of his hands together[5] in front of his face in a reverent namaskar[6]. "Does Mecca beckon?[7]" He crossed himself. "Or will it be to Rome for your coronation as the next Pope Pius[8]?" He drew in the air a Greek letter, making clear the spelling[9] of his mockery. "Have you found time yet to get the end of your pecker cut off[10] and become a Jew[11]? At the rate you're going[12], if you go to temple on Thursday, mosque on Friday, synagogue on Saturday and church on Sunday, you only need to convert to three more religions to be on holiday for the rest of your life."

And other lampoonery of such kind[13].

CHAPTER 25

And that wasn't the end of it. There are always those who take it upon themselves to[14] defend God, as if Ultimate Reality, as if the sustaining frame of existence, were something weak and helpless[15]. These people walk by a widow deformed by leprosy[16] begging for a few paise[17], walk by children dressed in rags[18] living in the street, and they think, "Business as usual.[19]" But if they perceive a slight[20] against God, it is a different story. Their faces go red, their chests heave mightily[21], they sputter[22] an-

1. s'en est donné à cœur joie
2. il a appris ce qui s'était passé
3. maître spirituel
4. en pèlerinage à La Mecque
5. joignant les mains
6. en signe de salutation révérencieuse
7. Est-ce que La Mecque t'appelle ?
8. ton couronnement en tant que prochain pape Pie
9. l'orthographe
10. de te faire couper le bout du zizi
11. juif
12. Au rythme où tu vas
13. moqueries du même genre
14. se donnent pour mission de
15. faible et impuissant
16. veuve rendue difforme par la lèpre
17. quémandant quelques petites pièces
18. en haillons
19. Les affaires continuent.
20. offense
21. leurs poitrines se soulèvent violemment
22. ils bafouillent

gry words. The degree of their indignation is astonishing. Their resolve[1] is frightening.

These people fail to realize[2] that it is on the inside that God must be defended, not on the outside. They should direct their anger at themselves[3]. For evil in the open[4] is but evil from within that has been let out[5]. The main battlefield[6] for good is not the open ground of the public arena but the small clearing[7] of each heart. Meanwhile, the lot of widows and homeless children[8] is very hard, and it is to their defence, not God's, that the self-righteous should rush[9].

Once an oaf[10] chased me away from the Great Mosque. When I went to church the priest glared at me[11] so that I could not feel the peace of Christ. A Brahmin sometimes shooed me away from darshan[12]. My religious doings were reported to[13] my parents in the hushed, urgent tones of treason revealed[14].

As if this small-mindedness did God any good.[15]

To me, religion is about our dignity, not our depravity.

I stopped attending Mass[16] at Our Lady of Immaculate Conception and went instead to Our Lady of Angels. I no longer lingered[17] after Friday prayer among my brethren[18]. I went to temple at crowded times[19] when the Brahmins were too distracted to come between God and me.

CHAPTER 26

A few days after the meeting on the esplanade, I took my courage into my hands[20] and went to see

Father at his office.

"Father?"

"Yes, Piscine."

"I would like to be baptized[1] and I would like a prayer rug[2]."

My words intruded slowly.[3] He looked up from his papers after some seconds.

"A what? What?"

"I would like to pray outside without getting my pants dirty[4]. And I'm attending a Christian school without having received the proper baptism of Christ."

"Why do you want to pray outside? In fact, why do you want to pray at all?"

"Because I love God."

"Aha.[5]" He seemed taken aback[6] by my answer, nearly embarrassed by it. There was a pause. I thought he was going to offer me ice cream again. "Well, Petit Séminaire is Christian only in name[7]. There are many Hindu boys there who aren't Christians. You'll get just as good an education without being baptized. Praying to Allah won't make any difference, either[8]."

"But I want to pray to Allah. I want to be a Christian."

"You can't be both. You must be either one or the other[9]."

"Why can't I be both?"

"They're separate religions! They have nothing in common."

"That's not what they say! They both claim Abraham as theirs. Muslims say the God of the Hebrews[10] and Christians is the same as the God of the Muslims. They recognize David, Moses[11] and Jesus as prophets."

1. me faire baptiser

2. un tapis de prière

3. Il a lentement saisi le sens de mes mots.

4. sans me salir le pantalon

5. Ah, ah!

6. déconcerté

7. n'a de chrétien que le nom

8. ne fera aucune différence non plus

9. l'un ou l'autre

10. juifs

11. Moïse

1. Quel rapport avec nous

2. est enterré au Cachemire

3. les sourcils froncés

4. Vraiment ?

5. Elle a posé son livre.

6. a senti un souffle d'air froid sur sa nuque

7. l'étagère

8. Elle avait déjà tendu le bras

9. s'est déplacé vers la gauche

10. a pivoté vers

11. Elle s'est rassise sur sa chaise

12. on voyait bien qu'elle ne résistait que pour la forme

13. ce qui voulait dire qu'il me fallait attaquer férocement aux bons endroits

14. Elle a remis un coussin en place.

15. zèle

"What does this have to do with us[1], Piscine? We're *Indians*!"

"There have been Christians and Muslims in India for centuries! Some people say Jesus is buried in Kashmir[2]."

He said nothing, only looked at me, his brow furrowed[3]. Suddenly business called.

"Talk to Mother about it."

She was reading.

"Mother?"

"Yes, darling."

"I would like to be baptized and I would like a prayer rug."

"Talk to Father about it."

"I did. He told me to talk to you about it."

"Did he?[4]" She laid her book down.[5] She looked out in the direction of the zoo. At that moment I'm sure Father felt a blow of chill air against the back of his neck[6]. She turned to the bookshelf[7]. "I have a book here that you'll like." She already had her arm out[8], reaching for a volume. It was Robert Louis Stevenson. This was her usual tactic.

"I've already read that, Mother. Three times."

"Oh." Her arm hovered to the left[9].

"The same with Conan Doyle", I said.

Her arm swung to[10] the right. "R. K. Narayan? You can't possibly have read all of Narayan?"

"These matters are important to me, Mother."

"*Robinson Crusoe!*"

"Mother!"

"But Piscine!" she said. She settled back into her chair[11], a path-of-least-resistance look on her face[12], which meant I had to put up a stiff fight in precisely the right spots[13]. She adjusted a cushion.[14] "Father and I find your religious zeal[15] a bit of a mystery."

"It is a Mystery."

"Hmmm. I don't mean it that way. Listen, my darling, if you're going to be religious[1], you must be either a Hindu, a Christian or a Muslim. You heard what they said on the esplanade."

"I don't see why I can't be all three. Mamaji has two passports. He's Indian and French. Why can't I be a Hindu, a Christian and a Muslim?"

"That's different. France and India are nations on earth."

"How many nations are there in the sky?"

She thought for a second. "One. That's the point. One nation, one passport."

"One nation in the sky?"

"Yes. Or none. There's that option too, you know. These are terribly old-fashioned things you've taken to.[2]"

"If there's only one nation in the sky, shouldn't all passports be valid for it?"

A cloud of uncertainty came over her face.[3]

"Bapu Gandhi said—"

"Yes, I know what Bapu Gandhi said." She brought a hand to her forehead[4]. She had a weary look, Mother did[5]. "Good grief[6]", she said.

CHAPTER 27

Later that evening I overheard my parents speaking[7].

"You said yes?" said Father.

"I believe he asked you too. You referred him to me[8]", replied Mother.

"Did I?"

"You did."

"I had a very busy day..."

1. si tu veux vraiment être croyant

2. Tu t'es épris de choses terriblement démodées.

3. Son visage a trahi une certaine incertitude.

4. front

5. Elle avait l'air vraiment fatiguée, Maman.

6. Bon sang

7. j'ai surpris une conversation de mes parents

8. Tu l'as envoyé me voir

1. Tu es
agréablement
désœuvré on
dirait.

2. faire
irruption dans
sa chambre d'un
pas décidé

3. vas-y

4. Je ne m'y
opposerai pas.

5. comme un
chien attire les
puces

6. en passe de

7. On ne peut
pas arrêter le
progrès.

8. C'est le
battement de
tambour au
rythme duquel
nous avançons
tous.

9. se répandent

10. à rester un
dinosaure

11. J'en suis
parfaitement
convaincu.

12. stupidité

13. a continué

14. commence à
parler en termes
affectueux de
Gandhi

"You're not busy now. You're quite comfortably unemployed by the looks of it.[1] If you want to march into his room[2] and pull the prayer rug from under his feet and discuss the question of Christian baptism with him, please go ahead[3]. I won't object.[4]"

"No, no." I could tell from his voice that Father was settling deeper into his chair. There was a pause.

"He seems to be attracting religions the way a dog attracts fleas[5]", he pursued. "I don't understand it. We're a modern Indian family; we live in a modern way, India is on the cusp of[6] becoming a truly modern and advanced nation—and here we've produced a son who thinks he's the reincarnation of Sri Ramakrishna."

"If Mrs. Gandhi is what being modern and advanced is about, I'm not sure I like it", Mother said.

"Mrs. Gandhi will pass! Progress is unstoppable.[7] It is a drumbeat to which we must all march.[8] Technology helps and good ideas spread[9]—these are two laws of nature. If you don't let technology help you, if you resist good ideas, you condemn yourself to dinosaurhood[10]! I am utterly convinced of this.[11] Mrs. Gandhi and her foolishness[12] will pass. The New India will come."

(Indeed she would pass. And the New India, or one family of it, would decide to move to Canada.)

Father went on[13]: "Did you hear when he said, 'Bapu Gandhi said, "All religions are true"'?"

"Yes."

"*Bapu* Gandhi? The boy is getting to be on affectionate terms with Gandhi[14]? After Daddy

102

Gandhi, what next? Uncle Jesus? And what's this nonsense—has he really become a *Muslim*?"

"It seems so."

"A Muslim! A devout[1] Hindu, all right, I can understand. A Christian in addition, it's getting to be a bit strange, but I can stretch my mind[2]. The Christians have been here for a long time—Saint Thomas, Saint Francis Xavier, the missionaries and so on. We owe them[3] good schools."

"Yes."

"So all that I can sort of accept. But *Muslim*? It's totally foreign to our tradition. They're outsiders[4]."

"They've been here a very long time too. They're a hundred times more numerous than the Christians."

"That makes no difference. They're outsiders."

"Perhaps Piscine is marching to a different drumbeat of progress."

"You're defending the boy? You don't mind it[5] that he's fancying himself a Muslim[6]?"

"What can we do, Santosh? He's taken it to heart[7], and it's not doing anyone any harm[8]. Maybe it's just a phase. It too may pass—like Mrs. Gandhi."

"Why can't he have the normal interests of a boy his age? Look at Ravi. All he can think about is cricket, movies and music."

"You think that's better?"

"No, no. Oh, I don't know what to think. It's been a long day." He sighed. "I wonder how far he'll go with[9] these interests."

Mother chuckled[10]. "Last week he finished a book called *The Imitation of Christ*."

"*The* Imitation *of Christ*! I say again, I wonder how far he'll go with these interests!" cried Father.

They laughed.

1. pieux

2. en faisant un effort, je peux l'accepter

3. On leur doit

4. des étrangers

5. Ça ne te dérange pas

6. il se prétende musulman

7. Ça lui tient à cœur

8. ça ne fait de mal à personne

9. jusqu'où il poursuivra

10. a gloussé

CHAPTER 28

1. Bien que de qualité ordinaire
2. il était d'une beauté étincelante
3. Où que je l'aie posé
4. le bout de terrain sur lequel il se trouvait
5. qu'elle est partout sacrée
6. motif
7. un fond rouge
8. simple
9. sommet
10. fioritures
11. des volutes
12. glands non noués
13. à quelques centimètres du haut de mon front
14. orteils
15. confortable
16. je déroulais
17. cour
18. isolé
19. à l'ombre d'un arbre corail
20. une rangée de poinsettias en pots
21. s'était glissé
22. bractées
23. une vraie volière pleine de corbeaux, de mainates, de passereaux
24. d'étourneaux roselins, de nectariniidés et de perruches
25. un peu plus loin
26. l'ombre laiteuse et marbrée
27. inondé de soleil

I loved my prayer rug. Ordinary in quality though it was[1], it glowed with beauty[2] in my eyes. I'm sorry I lost it. Wherever I laid it[3] I felt special affection for the patch of ground beneath it[4] and the immediate surroundings, which to me is a clear indication that it was a good prayer rug because it helped me remember that the earth is the creation of God and sacred the same all over[5]. The pattern[6], in gold lines upon a background of red[7], was plain[8]: a narrow rectangle with a triangular peak[9] at one extremity to indicate the qibla, the direction of prayer, and little curlicues[10] floating around it, like wisps[11] of smoke or accents from a strange language. The pile was soft. When I prayed, the short, unknotted tassels[12] were inches from the tip of my forehead[13] at one end of the carpet and inches from the tip of my toes[14] at the other, a cozy[15] size to make you feel at home anywhere upon this vast earth.

I prayed outside because I liked it. Most often I unrolled[16] my prayer rug in a corner of the yard[17] behind the house. It was a secluded[18] spot in the shade of a coral tree[19], next to a wall that was covered with bougainvillea. Along the length of the wall was a row of potted poinsettias[20]. The bougainvillea had also crept[21] through the tree. The contrast between its purple bracts[22] and the red flowers of the tree was very pretty. And when that tree was in bloom, it was a regular aviary of crows, mynahs, babblers[23], rosy pastors, sunbirds and parakeets[24]. The wall was to my right, at a wide angle[25]. Ahead of me and to my left, beyond the milky, mottled shade[26] of the tree, lay the sun-drenched[27] open space of the yard. The appearance of things changed, of course, depending on[1] the weather, the time of day, the time of year. But it's all very clear in my memory, as if it never changed. I faced[2] Mecca with the help of a line I scratched into[3] the pale yellow ground and carefully kept up[4].

Sometimes, upon finishing my prayers, I would turn and catch sight of[5] Father or Mother or Ravi observing me, until they got used to the sight[6].

My baptism was a slightly awkward affair[7]. Mother played along nicely[8], Father looked on stonily[9], and Ravi was mercifully[10] absent because of a cricket match, which did not prevent him from commenting at great length[11] on the event. The water trickled down[12] my face and down my neck; though just a beaker's worth[13], it had the refreshing effect of a monsoon rain[14].

CHAPTER 29

Why do people move? What makes them uproot[15] and leave everything they've known for a great unknown beyond the horizon? Why climb[16] this Mount Everest of formalities that makes you feel like a beggar[17]? Why enter this jungle of foreignness[18] where everything is new, strange and difficult?

The answer is the same the world over[19]: people move in the hope of a better life.

The mid-1970s were troubled times in India. I gathered that from[20] the deep furrows[21] that appeared on Father's forehead when he read the papers[22]. Or from snippets[23] of conversation that I caught between him and Mother and Mamaji and others. It's not that I didn't understand the drift of what they said[24]—it's that I wasn't interested. The

1. selon
2. Je me tournais vers
3. grattée dans
4. que je prenais soin de ne pas effacer
5. j'apercevais
6. jusqu'à ce qu'ils se soient habitués à me voir ainsi
7. s'est passé de manière un peu embarrassante
8. s'est bien prêtée au jeu
9. a observé froidement la scène
10. par chance
11. longuement
12. a dégouliné le long de
13. même s'il y en avait seulement de quoi remplir un gobelet
14. une pluie de mousson
15. se déraciner
16. escalader
17. mendiant
18. cette étrange jungle
19. partout
20. Je l'ai compris en voyant
21. les profondes rides
22. journaux
23. des bribes
24. où ils voulaient en venir

1. aimaient
toujours autant
les chapatis
2. gazouillaient
3. a eu raison de
4. suspendu
5. virulents
6. prise de
pouvoir
7. s'est faite
sans incident
8. les ministres
du Premier
ministre
Karunanidhi
9. ont disparu
discrètement,
ayant
« démissionné »
ou été assignés
à résidence
10. le
couronnement
11. est resté
imperturbable
12. pour mon
père, c'était la
goutte d'eau qui
a fait déborder
le vase
13. J'aurais
préféré qu'il
ne se fasse pas
autant de souci.
14. Mais il
s'inquiétait
vraiment.
15. ce sont
les petits
entrepreneurs
qui courent le
plus de risques
16. ceux qui
risquent leur
chemise
17. par
conséquent
18. ce n'est pas
une entreprise
très lucrative

orang-utans were as eager for chapattis as ever[1]; the monkeys never asked after the news from Delhi; the rhinos and goats continued to live in peace; the birds twittered[2]; the clouds carried rain; the sun was hot; the earth breathed; God was—there was no Emergency in my world.

Mrs. Gandhi finally got the best of[3] Father. In February 1976, the Tamil Nadu government was brought down[4] by Delhi. It had been one of Mrs. Gandhi's most vocal[5] critics. The takeover[6] was smoothly enforced[7]—Chief Minister Karunanidhi's ministry[8] vanished quietly into "resignation" or house arrest[9]—and what does the fall of one local government matter when the whole country's Constitution has been suspended these last eight months? But it was to Father the crowning touch[10] in Mrs. Gandhi's dictatorial takeover of the nation. The camel at the zoo was unfazed[11], but that straw broke Father's back[12].

He shouted, "Soon she'll come down to our zoo and tell us that her jails are full, she needs more space. Could we put Desai with the lions?"

Morarji Desai was an opposition politician. No friend of Mrs. Gandhi's. It makes me sad, my father's ceaseless worrying. Mrs. Gandhi could have personally bombed the zoo, it would have been fine with me if Father had been gay about it. I wish he hadn't fretted so much.[13] It's hard on a son to see his father sick with worry.

But worry he did.[14] Any business is risky business, and none more so than small *b* business[15], the one that risks the shirt on its back[16]. A zoo is a cultural institution. Like a public library, like a museum, it is at the service of popular education and science. And by this token[17], not much of a money-making venture[18], for the Greater Good and the

Greater Profit are not compatible aims[1], much to Father's chagrin[2]. The truth was, we were not a rich family, certainly not by Canadian standards[3]. We were a poor family that happened to own a lot of animals, though not the roof[4] above their heads (or above ours, for that matter). The life of a zoo, like the life of its inhabitants in the wild, is precarious. It is neither big enough a business to be above the law[5] nor small enough to survive on its margins[6]. To prosper, a zoo needs parliamentary government, democratic elections, freedom of speech[7], freedom of the press, freedom of association, rule of law[8] and everything else enshrined[9] in India's Constitution. Impossible to enjoy the animals otherwise. Long-term, bad politics[10] is bad for business.

People move because of the wear and tear of anxiety[11]. Because of the gnawing[12] feeling that no matter how hard they work[13] their efforts will yield nothing[14], that what they build up in one year will be torn down[15] in one day by others. Because of the impression that the future is blocked up[16], that *they* might do all right[17] but not their children. Because of the feeling that nothing will change, that happiness and prosperity are possible only somewhere else.

The New India split to pieces and collapsed[18] in Father's mind. Mother assented[19]. We would bolt.[20]

It was announced to us one evening during dinner. Ravi and I were thunderstruck[21]. *Canada!* If Andhra Pradesh, just north of us, was alien[22], if Sri Lanka, a monkey's hop across a strait[23], was the dark side of the moon, imagine what Canada was. Canada meant absolutely nothing to us. It was like Timbuktu, by definition a place permanently far away.

1. objectifs
2. au grand dam de mon père
3. selon des critères canadiens
4. toit
5. au-dessus des lois
6. en marge de la loi
7. la liberté d'expression
8. un État de droit
9. inscrit
10. Une politique durablement mauvaise
11. l'inquiétude les ronge
12. tenace
13. quelle que soit l'intensité avec laquelle ils travaillent
14. n'aboutiront à rien
15. détruit
16. l'avenir mène à une impasse
17. ils pourront peut-être s'en sortir
18. s'est morcelée et effondrée
19. a acquiescé
20. Nous allions déguerpir.
21. abasourdis
22. nous était étranger
23. à un saut de singe au-dessus du détroit

CHAPTER 30

He's married. I am bent down[1], taking my shoes off[2], when I hear him say, "I would like you to meet my wife." I look up and there beside him is... Mrs. Patel. "Hello", she says, extending her hand[3] and smiling. "Piscine has been telling me lots about you." I can't say the same of her. I had no idea. She's on her way out[4], so we talk only a few minutes. She's also Indian but has a more typically Canadian accent. She must be second generation. She's a little younger than him, skin slightly darker[5], long black hair woven in a tress. Bright dark eyes[6] and lovely[7] white teeth. She has in her arms a dry-cleaned white lab coat[8] in a protective plastic film. She's a pharmacist. When I say "Nice meeting you, Mrs. Patel", she replies, "Please, make it[9] Meena." After a quick kiss between husband and wife, she's off on a working Saturday[10].

This house is more than a box full of icons. I start noticing small signs of conjugal existence. They were there all along, but I hadn't seen them because I wasn't looking for them[11].

He's a shy[12] man. Life has taught him not to show off[13] what is most precious to him.

Is she the nemesis of my digestive tract?[14]

"I've made a special chutney[15] for you", he says. He's smiling.

No, he is[16].

1. Je suis accroupi
2. en train d'enlever mes chaussures
3. en me tendant la main
4. Elle est sur le point de sortir
5. un peu plus sombre
6. Elle a des yeux noirs brillants
7. jolies
8. une blouse blanche de laboratoire nettoyée à sec
9. appelez-moi
10. elle s'en va travailler
11. je ne les cherchais pas
12. timide
13. exhiber
14. Est-ce elle l'ennemi de mon appareil digestif ?
15. sauce aigre-douce de la cuisine indienne
16. c'est lui

CHAPTER 31

They met once, Mr. and Mr. Kumar, the baker and the teacher. The first Mr. Kumar had expressed the wish to see the zoo. "All these years and I've never seen it. It's so close by[1], too. Will you show it to me?" he asked.

"Yes, of course", I replied. "It would be an honour."

We agreed to meet at the main gate the next day after school.

I worried all that day. I scolded myself[2], "You fool![3] Why did you say the main gate? At any time there will be a crowd of people there. Have you forgotten how plain he looks[4]? You'll never recognize him!" If I walked by him without seeing him he would be hurt[5]. He would think I had changed my mind and didn't want to be seen with a poor Muslim baker. He would leave without saying a word. He wouldn't be angry—he would accept my claims[6] that it was the sun in my eyes—but he wouldn't want to come to the zoo any more. I could see it happening that way. I *had* to recognize him.[7] I would hide and wait until I was certain it was him, that's what I would do. But I had noticed before that it was when I tried my hardest[8] to recognize him that I was least able to pick him out[9]. The very effort seemed to blind me[10].

At the appointed hour[11] I stood squarely[12] before the main gate of the zoo and started rubbing my eyes[13] with both hands.

"What are you doing?"

It was Raj, a friend.

"I'm busy."

"You're busy rubbing your eyes?"

"Go away."

"Let's go to Beach Road."

"I'm waiting for someone."

"Well, you'll miss him[14] if you keep rubbing your eyes[15] like that."

"Thank you for the information. Have fun on Beach Road."

1. tout près

2. Je me suis fait des reproches

3. Espèce d'imbécile !

4. à quel point il a l'air ordinaire

5. vexé

6. il ne remettrait pas en cause mes dires quand j'affirmerai

7. Il fallait que je le reconnaisse.

8. je faisais de mon mieux

9. le repérer

10. m'aveugler

11. À l'heure convenue

12. directement

13. j'ai commencé à me frotter les yeux

14. tu vas le rater

15. tu continues à te frotter les yeux

"How about Government Park?"

"I can't, I tell you."

1. *Allez.*

"Come on.[1]"

2. *Va-t'en*

"Please, Raj, move on[2]!"

He left. I went back to rubbing my eyes.

3. *mes devoirs de maths*

"Will you help me with my math homework[3], Pi?"

It was Ajith, another friend.

"Later. Go away."

"Hello, Piscine."

4. *je l'ai tranquillement remise sur sa route*

It was Mrs. Radhakrishna, a friend of Mother's. In a few more words I eased her on her way[4].

"Excuse me. Where's Laporte Street?"

5. *Un inconnu.*

A stranger.[5]

"That way."

6. *Combien coûte l'entrée*

"How much is admission[6] to the zoo?"

Another stranger.

7. *roupies*

8. *guichet*

"Five rupees[7]. The ticket booth[8] is right there."

9. *Est-ce que le chlore est entré en contact avec tes yeux ?*

"Has the chlorine got to your eyes?[9]"

It was Mamaji.

"Hello, Mamaji. No, it hasn't."

10. *dans les parages*

"Is your father around[10]?"

"I think so."

"See you tomorrow morning."

"Yes, Mamaji."

"I am here, Piscine."

11. *me venir aux lèvres*

My hands froze over my eyes. That voice. Strange in a familiar way, familiar in a strange way. I felt a smile welling up in me[11].

"*Salaam alaykum*, Mr. Kumar! How good to see you."

"*Wa alaykum as-salaam.* Is something wrong with your eyes?"

12. *un peu de poussière*

"No, nothing. Just a bit of dust[12]."

"They look quite red."

"It's nothing."

He headed for[1] the ticket booth but I called him back[2].

"No, no. Not for you, master."

It was with pride that I waved the ticket collector's hand away[3] and showed Mr. Kumar into the zoo.

He marvelled at everything[4], at how to tall trees came tall giraffes, how carnivores were supplied with[5] herbivores and herbivores with grass[6], how some creatures crowded[7] the day and others the night, how some that needed sharp beaks[8] had sharp beaks and others that needed limber limbs[9] had limber limbs. It made me happy that he was so impressed.

He quoted from the Holy Qur'an: "In all this there are messages indeed for a people who use their reason."

We came to the zebras. Mr. Kumar had never heard of such creatures, let alone[10] seen one. He was dumbfounded[11].

"They're called zebras", I said.

"Have they been painted with a brush[12]?"

"No, no. They look like that naturally."

"What happens when it rains?"

"Nothing."

"The stripes don't melt?[13]"

"No."

I had brought some carrots. There was one left, a large and sturdy[14] specimen. I took it out of the bag. At that moment I heard a slight scraping of gravel[15] to my right. It was Mr. Kumar, coming up to the railing[16] in his usual limping and rolling gait[17].

"Hello, sir."

"Hello, Pi."

The baker, a shy but dignified man, nodded at the teacher, who nodded back[18].

1. Il s'est dirigé vers
2. je l'ai rappelé
3. j'ai fait signe au contrôleur de billets de nous laisser passer
4. Il s'est émerveillé de tout
5. étaient approvisionnés en
6. en herbe
7. s'attroupaient
8. des becs acérés
9. des membres agiles
10. encore moins
11. abasourdi
12. pinceau
13. Les rayures ne s'effacent pas ?
14. grand et robuste
15. un léger crissement de gravier
16. garde-fou
17. sa démarche chaloupée et boiteuse habituelle
18. qui lui a répondu par un signe de tête

An alert zebra had noticed my carrot and had come up to the low fence[1]. It twitched its ears[2] and stamped the ground softly[3]. I broke the carrot in two and gave one half to Mr. Kumar and one half to Mr. Kumar. "Thank you, Piscine", said one; "Thank you, Pi", said the other. Mr. Kumar went first, dipping his hand over the fence[4]. The zebra's thick, strong, black lips grasped the carrot eagerly[5]. Mr. Kumar wouldn't let go. The zebra sank its teeth into the carrot[6] and snapped it in two[7]. It crunched loudly on the treat[8] for a few seconds, then reached for the remaining piece[9], lips flowing over[10] Mr. Kumar's fingertips[11]. He released the carrot and touched the zebra's soft nose.

It was Mr. Kumar's turn. He wasn't so demanding of[12] the zebra. Once it had his half of the carrot between its lips, he let go[13]. The lips hurriedly[14] moved the carrot into the mouth.

Mr. And Mr. Kumar looked delighted.

"A *zebra*, you say?" said Mr. Kumar.

"That's right", I replied. "It belongs to the same family as the ass[15] and the horse."

"The Rolls-Royce of equids[16]", said Mr. Kumar.

"What a wondrous[17] creature", said Mr. Kumar.

"This one's a Grant's zebra[18]", I said.

Mr. Kumar said, *"Equus burchelli boehmi."*

Mr. Kumar said, *"Allahu akbar."*

I said, "It's very pretty."

We looked on.

CHAPTER 32

There are many examples of animals coming to surprising living arrangements[19]. All are instances of that animal equivalent of anthropomorphism: zoo-morphism, where an animal takes a human being, or another animal, to be one of its kind[1].

The most famous case is also the most common: the pet dog[2], which has so assimilated humans into the realm of doghood[3] as to want to mate with them, a fact that any dog owner[4] who has had to pull[5] an amorous dog from the leg of a mortified visitor will confirm.

Our golden agouti and spotted[6] paca got along very well[7], contentedly huddling together[8] and sleeping against each other until the first was stolen.

I have already mentioned our rhinoceros-and-goat herd, and the case of circus lions.

There are confirmed stories of drowning sailors[9] being pushed up to the surface of the water and held there by dolphins[10], a characteristic way in which these marine mammals[11] help each other.

A case is mentioned in the literature of a stoat[12] and a rat living in a companion relationship[13], while other rats presented to the stoat were devoured by it in the typical way of stoats.

We had our own case of the freak[14] suspension of the predator-prey relationship[15]. We had a mouse that lived for several *weeks* with the vipers. While other mice dropped[16] in the terrarium disappeared within two days, this little brown Methuselah[17] built itself a nest, stored the grains[18] we gave it in various hideaways[19] and scampered about in plain sight[20] of the snakes. We were amazed. We put up a sign[21] to bring the mouse to the public's attention. It finally met its end[22] in a curious way: a young viper bit it[23]. Was the viper unaware[24] of the mouse's special status? Unsocialized to it, perhaps? [25] Whatever the case, the mouse was bitten by a young viper but devoured—and immediately—by an adult.

1. pour l'un des siens
2. le chien de compagnie
3. le royaume canin
4. propriétaire de chien
5. détacher
6. tacheté
7. s'entendaient très bien
8. heureux de se blottir l'un contre l'autre
9. marins en train de se noyer
10. que des dauphins poussent et maintiennent vers la surface
11. mammifères
12. hermine
13. se côtoyant paisiblement
14. insolite
15. la relation entre le prédateur et la proie
16. d'autres souris lâchées
17. Mathusalem
18. a entreposé les graines
19. cachettes
20. trottinait sous les yeux
21. Nous avons mis un panneau
22. Elle a finalement trouvé la mort
23. l'a mordue
24. Est-ce que la vipère n'avait pas conscience
25. Elle n'en avait peut-être pas été informée ?

If there was a spell[1], it was broken by the young one. Things returned to normal after that. All mice disappeared down the vipers' gullets[2] at the usual rate.

In the trade, dogs are sometimes used as foster mothers for lion cubs[3]. Though the cubs grow to become larger than their caregiver[4], and far more dangerous, they never give their mother trouble[5] and she never loses her placid behaviour or her sense of authority over her litter[6]. Signs have to be put up to explain to the public that the dog is not live food[7] left for the lions (just as we had to put up a sign pointing out that rhinoceros are herbivores and do not eat goats).

What could be the explanation for zoomorphism? Can't a rhinoceros distinguish big from small, tough hide[8] from soft fur[9]? Isn't it plain[10] to a dolphin what a dolphin is like[11]? I believe the answer lies in something I mentioned earlier, that measure of madness that moves life in strange but saving ways. The golden agouti, like the rhinoceros, was in need of companionship[12]. The circus lions don't care to know that their leader is a weakling human[13]; the fiction guarantees their social well-being[14] and staves off[15] violent anarchy. As for the lion cubs, they would positively keel over with fright[16] if they knew their mother was a dog, for that would mean they were motherless[17], the absolute worst condition imaginable for any young, warm-blooded[18] life. I'm sure even the adult viper, as it swallowed[19] the mouse, must have felt somewhere in its undeveloped[20] mind a twinge of regret[21], a feeling that something greater was just missed, an imaginative leap away from[22] the lonely, crude[23] reality of a reptile.

CHAPTER 33

He shows me family memorabilia[1]. Wedding photos[2] first. A Hindu wedding with Canada prominently on the edges[3]. A younger him, a younger her. They went to Niagara Falls[4] for their honeymoon[5]. Had a lovely time.[6] Smiles to prove it. We move back in time. Photos from his student days at U of T[7]: with friends; in front of St. Mike's[8]; in his room; during Diwali[9] on Gerrard Street; reading at St. Basil's Church dressed in a white gown[10]; wearing another kind of white gown in a lab of the zoology department; on graduation day[11]. A smile every time, but his eyes tell another story.

Photos from Brazil, with plenty of three-toed sloths in situ.

With a turn of a page[12] we jump over the Pacific[13]—and there is next to nothing[14]. He tells me that the camera did click regularly[15]—on all the usual important occasions—but everything was lost. What little[16] there is consists of what was assembled by Mamaji and mailed over[17] after the events.

There is a photo taken at the zoo during the visit of a V.I.P. In black and white another world is revealed to me. The photo is crowded with people. A Union cabinet minister is the focus of attention[18]. There's a giraffe in the background. Near the edge of the group, I recognize a younger Mr. Adirubasamy.

"Mamaji?" I ask, pointing.

"Yes", he says.

There's a man next to the minister, with horn-rimmed glasses[19] and hair very cleanly combed[20]. He looks like a plausible Mr. Patel, face rounder than his son's.

"Is this your father?" I ask.

He shakes his head. "I don't know who that is."

---

1. souvenirs
2. Des photos de mariage
3. bien en évidence en marge
4. les chutes du Niagara
5. leur lune de miel
6. Ils y ont passé de très bons moments.
7. ses années d'étudiant à l'université de Toronto
8. Saint Michael's College [faculté de l'université de Toronto]
9. [grande fête indienne des lumières qui commémore le retour de Rama à Ayodhya]
10. robe
11. le jour de la remise des diplômes
12. Au détour d'une page
13. on se retrouve de l'autre côté du Pacifique
14. pratiquement rien
15. de nombreuses photos ont été prises
16. Le peu
17. envoyé
18. au centre de l'attention
19. des lunettes à monture en écaille
20. soigneusement peignés

There's a pause of a few seconds. He says, "It's my father who took the picture."

On the same page there's another group shot[1], mostly of schoolchildren. He taps the photo.[2]

"That's Richard Parker", he says.

I'm amazed. I look closely, trying to extract personality from appearance. Unfortunately, it's black and white again and a little out of focus[3]. A photo taken in better days[4], casually[5]. Richard Parker is looking away[6]. He doesn't even realize that his picture is being taken.

The opposing page is entirely taken up[7] by a colour photo of the swimming pool of the Aurobindo Ashram. It's a nice big outdoor pool with clear, sparkling[8] water, a clean blue bottom[9] and an attached diving pool[10].

The next page features a photo of the front gate of Petit Séminaire school. An arch has the school's motto[11] painted on it: Nil magnum nisi bonum. *No greatness without goodness.[12]*

And that's it. An entire childhood memorialized in four nearly irrelevant[13] photographs.

He grows sombre.[14]

"The worst of it[15]", he says, "is that I can hardly remember what my mother looks like any more[16]. I can see her in my mind, but it's fleeting[17]. As soon as I try to have a good look at her[18], she fades[19]. It's the same with her voice. If I saw her again in the street, it would all come back. But that's not likely to happen[20]. It's very sad not to remember what your mother looks like."

He closes the book.

1. photo de groupe
2. Il tape la photo du doigt.
3. floue
4. lors de jours meilleurs
5. par hasard
6. regarde ailleurs
7. entièrement couverte
8. scintillante
9. fond
10. bassin de plongée
11. devise
12. Pas de grandeur sans bonté.
13. pratiquement sans intérêt
14. Il s'assombrit.
15. Le pire dans tout cela
16. de ce à quoi ma mère ressemblait
17. éphémère
18. Dès que j'essaie de capter son image
19. elle disparaît
20. il est peu probable que ça arrive

CHAPTER 34

Father said, "We'll sail[1] like Columbus!"

"He was hoping to find India", I pointed out sullenly[2].

We sold the zoo, lock, stock and barrel[3]. To a new country, a new life. Besides assuring our collection of a happy future, the transaction would pay for our immigration and leave us with a good sum to make a fresh start[4] in Canada (though now, when I think of it, the sum is *laughable*[5]—how blinded we are by money). We could have sold our animals to zoos in India, but American zoos were willing to[6] pay higher prices. CITES, the Convention on International Trade in Endangered Species[7], had just come into effect[8], and the window on the trading of captured wild animals had slammed shut[9]. The future of zoos would now lie with other zoos[10]. The Pondicherry Zoo closed shop[11] at just the right time. There was a scramble[12] to buy our animals. The final buyers were a number of zoos, mainly the Lincoln Park Zoo in Chicago and the soon-to-open Minnesota Zoo, but odd animals[13] were going to Los Angeles, Louisville, Oklahoma City and Cincinnati.

And two animals were being shipped[14] to the Canada Zoo. That's how Ravi and I felt. We did not want to go. We did not want to live in a country of gale-force winds[15] and minus-two-hundred-degree winters[16]. Canada was not on the cricket map[17]. Departure was made easier—as far as getting us used to the idea[18]—by the time it took for all the pre-departure preparations. It took well over a year. I don't mean for us. I mean for the animals. Considering that animals dispense with[19] clothes,

1. Nous allons prendre la mer
2. d'un ton morose
3. l'ensemble du zoo, sans exception
4. prendre un nouveau départ
5. dérisoire
6. disposés à
7. la convention sur le commerce international d'espèces menacées d'extinction
8. venait d'entrer en application
9. le commerce d'animaux sauvages capturés s'en trouvait strictement réglementé
10. dépendrait à présent des autres zoos
11. a fermé ses portes
12. On s'est bousculé
13. quelques animaux
14. allaient être expédiés
15. où le vent soufflait très fort
16. où il faisait −130 °C en hiver
17. la carte des matchs de cricket
18. en ce qui concerne le fait de s'habituer à l'idée
19. n'ont pas besoin de

1. chaussures, linge, meubles, ustensiles de cuisine ou affaires de toilette
2. ils ne se soucient pas le moins du monde de
3. de leurs perspectives professionnelles
4. du coût du logement, des établissements de santé
5. le peu de choses qui leur sont nécessaires
6. paperasserie
7. pour humidifier les timbres
8. Cher Monsieur Untel
9. Des marchandages ont été effectués.
10. transmises aux autorités pour approbation
11. Des accords ont été conclus.
12. Des signatures ont été apposées.
13. Des permis d'exportation
14. Les réglementations en matière de quarantaine
15. éculée
16. musaraigne
17. pèse
18. baleine
19. une file indienne de bureaucrates tatillons
20. formulaire
21. abandonner
22. fourmiliers

footwear, linen, furniture, kitchenware, toiletries[1]; that nationality means nothing to them; that they care not a jot for[2] passports, money, employment prospects[3], schools, cost of housing, healthcare facilities[4]—considering, in short, their lightness of being[5], it's amazing how hard it is to move them. Moving a zoo is like moving a city.

The paperwork[6] was colossal. Litres of water used up in the wetting of stamps[7]. *Dear Mr. So-and-so*[8] written hundreds of times. Offers made. Sighs heard. Doubts expressed. Haggling gone through.[9] Decisions sent higher up for approval[10]. Prices agreed upon. Deals clinched.[11] Dotted lines signed.[12] Congratulations given. Certificates of origin sought. Certificates of health sought. Export permits[13] sought. Import permits sought. Quarantine regulations[14] clarified. Transportation organized. A fortune spent on telephone calls. It's a joke in the zoo business, a weary[15] joke, that the paperwork involved in trading a shrew[16] weighs[17] more than an elephant, that the paperwork involved in trading an elephant weighs more than a whale[18], and that you must never try to trade a whale, never. There seemed to be a single file of nit-picking bureaucrats[19] from Pondicherry to Minneapolis via Delhi and Washington, each with his form[20], his problem, his hesitation. Shipping the animals to the moon couldn't possibly have been more complicated. Father pulled nearly every hair off his head and came close to giving up[21] on a number of occasions.

There were surprises. Most of our birds and reptiles, and our lemurs, rhinos, orang-utans, mandrills, lion-tailed macaques, giraffes, anteaters[22], tigers, leopards, cheetahs, hyenas, zebras, Himalayan and sloth bears, Indian elephants and

Nilgiri tahrs[1], among others, were in demand, but others, Elfie for example, were met with silence. "A cataract operation!" Father shouted, waving[2] the letter. "They'll take her if we do a cataract operation on her right eye. On a hippopotamus! What next? Nose jobs on the rhinos?[3]" Some of our other animals were considered "too common", the lions and baboons, for example. Father judiciously traded these for[4] an extra orang-utan from the Mysore Zoo and a chimpanzee from the Manila Zoo. (As for Elfie, she lived out the rest of her days[5] at the Trivandrum Zoo.) One zoo asked for "an authentic Brahmin cow[6]" for their children's zoo. Father walked out into the urban jungle of Pondicherry and bought a cow with dark wet eyes, a nice fat hump[7] and horns so straight[8] and at such right angles to[9] its head that it looked as if it had licked an electrical outlet[10]. Father had its horns[11] painted bright orange and little plastic bells fitted to the tips[12], for added authenticity.

A deputation[13] of three Americans came. I was very curious. I had never seen real live Americans. They were pink, fat, friendly, very competent and sweated profusely[14]. They examined our animals. They put most of them to sleep and then applied stethoscopes to hearts, examined urine and feces[15] as if horoscopes, drew blood in syringes[16] and analyzed it, fondled humps and bumps[17], tapped teeth, blinded eyes with flashlights[18], pinched[19] skins, stroked and pulled[20] hairs. Poor animals. They must have thought they were being drafted into[21] the U.S. Army. We got big smiles from the Americans and bone-crushing handshakes[22].

The result was that the animals, like us, got their working papers. They were future Yankees[23], and we, future Canucks[24].

1. [chèvre du sud de l'Inde]
2. agitant
3. Faire refaire le nez des rhinos ?
4. les a judicieusement échangés contre
5. elle a passé le restant de ses jours
6. vache brahmane
7. bosse
8. des cornes si droites
9. si perpendiculaires à
10. prise
11. cornes
12. il a fait accrocher des clochettes à leur extrémité
13. groupe
14. ils transpiraient abondamment
15. excréments
16. ils ont prélevé du sang dans des seringues
17. ils ont caressé les grandes et petites bosses
18. des lampes torches
19. pincé
20. caressé et tiré
21. qu'on les enrôlait dans
22. des poignées de main qui broyaient les os
23. Ricains
24. Canadiens français

CHAPTER 35

We left Madras on June 21st, 1977, on the Panamanian-registered Japanese cargo ship[1] *Tsimtsum*. Her officers were Japanese, her crew was Taiwanese[2], and she was large and impressive. On our last day in Pondicherry I said goodbye to Mamaji, to Mr. and Mr. Kumar, to all my friends and even to many strangers. Mother was apparelled in her finest sari[3]. Her long tress, artfully folded back[4] and attached to the back of her head, was adorned with a garland of[5] fresh jasmine flowers. She looked beautiful. And sad. For she was leaving India, India of the heat and monsoons, of rice fields[6] and the Cauvery River, of coastlines[7] and stone temples, of bullock carts and colourful trucks[8], of friends and known shopkeepers[9], of Nehru Street and Goubert Salai, of this and that, India so familiar to her and loved by her. While her men—I fancied myself one already[10], though I was only sixteen—were in a hurry to get going[11], were Winnipeggers at heart already[12], she lingered[13].

The day before our departure she pointed at a cigarette wallah and earnestly asked, "Should we get a pack or two?"

Father replied, "They have tobacco in Canada. And why do you want to buy cigarettes? We don't smoke."

Yes, they have tobacco in Canada—but do they have Gold Flake cigarettes? Do they have Arun ice cream? Are the bicycles Heroes? Are the televisions Onidas? Are the cars Ambassadors? Are the bookshops Higginbothams'? Such, I suspect, were the questions that swirled in Mother's mind[14] as she contemplated[15] buying cigarettes.

Marginal notes (French):

1. sur le cargo japonais enregistré au Panama
2. son équipage était taïwanais
3. vêtue de son plus beau sari
4. soigneusement repliée
5. parée d'une guirlande de
6. des rizières
7. des littoraux
8. des chars à bœufs et des fourgons colorés
9. commerçants
10. je me prenais déjà pour un homme
11. étaient pressés de s'en aller
12. se sentaient déjà Winnipégois dans l'âme
13. elle prenait son temps
14. qui se bousculaient dans la tête de ma mère
15. elle envisageait

Animals were sedated[1], cages were loaded and secured[2], feed was stored[3], bunks were assigned[4], lines were tossed[5], and whistles were blown[6]. As the ship was worked out of the dock[7] and piloted out to sea, I wildly waved goodbye to India. The sun was shining, the breeze was steady, and seagulls shrieked[8] in the air above us. I was terribly excited.

Things didn't turn out the way they were supposed to[9], but what can you do? You must take life the way it comes at you and make the best of it.

CHAPTER 36

The cities are large and memorably crowded[10] in India, but when you leave them you travel through vast stretches of country[11] where hardly a soul is to be seen[12]. I remember wondering where 950 million Indians could be hiding.

I could say the same of his house.

I'm a little early. I've just set foot on the cement steps of the front porch[13] when a teenager bursts out[14] the front door. He's wearing a baseball uniform and carrying baseball equipment, and he's in a hurry. When he sees me he stops dead in his tracks[15], startled[16]. He turns around and hollers into the house[17], "Dad! The writer's here." To me he says, "Hi", and rushes off[18].

His father comes to the front door. "Hello", he says.

"That was your son?" I ask, incredulous.

"Yes." To acknowledge the fact brings a smile to his lips.[19] "I'm sorry you didn't meet properly[20]. He's late for practice.[21] His name is Nikhil. He goes by Nick.[22]"

1. ont reçu des sédatifs
2. ont été remplies et fermées à clé
3. la nourriture entreposée
4. les couchettes attribuées
5. larguées
6. les sirènes ont sonné
7. Tandis que l'on faisait sortir le bateau du dock
8. des mouettes criaient
9. Les choses ne se sont pas passées comme prévu
10. bondées
11. de vastes étendues
12. il n'y a quasiment pas âme qui vive
13. Je commence juste à monter les marches en ciment du perron
14. surgit de
15. il s'arrête brusquement
16. surpris
17. il crie vers l'intérieur de la maison
18. il part en courant
19. Il l'admet le sourire aux lèvres.
20. que vous n'ayez pas eu le temps de faire véritablement connaissance
21. Il est en retard pour son entraînement.
22. On le surnomme Nick.

I'm in the entrance hall. "I didn't know you had a son", I say. There's a barking[1]. A small mongrel mutt[2], black and brown, races up to me[3], panting and sniffing[4]. He jumps up against my legs.[5] "Or a dog", I add.

"He's friendly. Tata, down!"

Tata ignores him. I hear "Hello." Only this greeting is not short and forceful[6] like Nick's. It's a long, nasal and softly whining[7] Helloooooooooo, with the ooooooooo reaching for me like a tap on the shoulder or a gentle tug at my pants[8].

I turn. Leaning against the sofa in the living room, looking up at me bashfully[9], is a little brown girl, pretty in pink, very much at home[10]. She's holding an orange cat in her arms. Two front legs sticking straight up[11] and a deeply sunk head[12] are all that is visible of it above her crossed arms. The rest of the cat is hanging all the way down to the floor[13]. The animal seems quite relaxed about being stretched on the rack[14] in this manner.

"And this is your daughter", I say.

"Yes. Usha. Usha darling, are you sure Moccasin is comfortable[15] like that?"

Usha drops Moccasin. He flops to the floor unperturbed[16].

"Hello, Usha", I say.

She comes up to her father and peeks at me[17] from behind his leg.

"What are you doing, little one?" he says. "Why are you hiding?"

She doesn't reply, only looks at me with a smile and hides her face.

"How old are you, Usha?" I ask.

She doesn't reply.

Then Piscine Molitor Patel, known to all as Pi Patel, bends down and picks up his daughter[18].

"You know the answer to that question. Hmmm? You're four years old. One, two, three, four."

At each number he softly presses the tip of her nose with his index finger[1]. She finds this terribly funny. She giggles[2] and buries her face in the crook of his neck[3].

This story has a happy ending.

1. il appuie doucement sur le bout du nez de sa fille avec son index

2. Elle pouffe de rire

3. elle enfonce la tête dans le cou de son père

PART TWO

The Pacific Ocean

The ship sank.[1] It made a sound like a monstrous metallic burp[2]. Things bubbled at the surface and then vanished[3]. Everything was screaming: the sea, the wind, my heart. From the lifeboat[4] I saw something in the water.

I cried, "Richard Parker, is that you? It's so hard to see. Oh, that this rain would stop[5]! Richard Parker? Richard Parker? Yes, it is you!"

I could see his head. He was struggling[6] to stay at the surface of the water.

"Jesus, Mary, Muhammad and Vishnu, how good to see you, Richard Parker! Don't give up, please. Come to the lifeboat. Do you hear this whistle? TREEEEEE[7]! TREEEEEE! TREEEEEE! You heard right. Swim, swim! You're a strong swimmer. It's not a hundred feet.[8]"

He had seen me. He looked panic-stricken.[9] He started swimming my way[10]. The water about him was shifting wildly[11]. He looked small and helpless.

"Richard Parker, can you believe what has happened to us? Tell me it's a bad dream. Tell me it's not real. Tell me I'm still in my bunk[12] on the *Tsimtsum* and I'm tossing and turning[13] and soon I'll wake up from this nightmare[14]. Tell me I'm still happy. Mother, my tender guardian angel of wisdom[15], where are you? And you, Father, my loving worrywart[16]? And you, Ravi, dazzling[17] hero of my childhood? Vishnu preserve me, Allah protect me, Christ save me, I can't bear it![18] TREEEEEE! TREEEEEE! TREEEEEE!"

I was not wounded[19] in any part of my body, but I had never experienced such intense pain[20], such a ripping of the nerves[21], such an ache of the heart[22].

1. Le bateau a coulé.
2. rot
3. faisaient des bulles à la surface, puis disparaissaient
4. canot de sauvetage
5. si seulement cette pluie pouvait s'arrêter
6. Il luttait
7. [bruit d'un sifflet]
8. Il te reste moins de trente mètres.
9. Il avait l'air affolé.
10. dans ma direction
11. était très agitée
12. couchette
13. je me tourne et me retourne dans mon lit
14. cauchemar
15. ange gardien plein de sagesse
16. mon tendre angoisé
17. éblouissant
18. je ne peux pas le supporter !
19. blessé
20. douleur
21. je n'avais jamais eu les nerfs aussi à vif
22. je n'avais jamais eu le cœur aussi brisé

He would not make it.[1] He would drown[2]. He was hardly moving forward[3] and his movements were weak. His nose and mouth kept dipping underwater[4]. Only his eyes were steadily[5] on me.

"What are you doing, Richard Parker? Don't you love life? Keep swimming then! TREEEEEE! TREEEEEE! TREEEEEE! Kick with your legs.[6] Kick! Kick! Kick!"

He stirred[7] in the water and made to swim[8].

"And what of my extended[9] family—birds, beasts and reptiles? They too have drowned. Every single thing I value in life[10] has been destroyed. And I am allowed [11] no explanation? I am to suffer hell[12] without any account from heaven[13]? In that case, what is the purpose[14] of reason, Richard Parker? Is it no more than to shine at practicalities[15]—the getting of food, clothing and shelter[16]? Why can't reason give greater answers? Why can we throw a question further than we can pull in an answer?[17] Why such a vast net[18] if there's so little fish to catch?"

His head was barely[19] above water. He was looking up, taking in[20] the sky one last time. There was a lifebuoy[21] in the boat with a rope tied to it[22]. I took hold of it and waved it in the air.

"Do you see this lifebuoy, Richard Parker? Do you see it? Catch hold of it![23] *HUMPF!* I'll try again. *Humpf!*"

He was too far. But the sight of the lifebuoy flying his way gave him hope. He revived[24] and started beating the water with vigorous, desperate strokes.

"That's right! One, two. One, two. One, two. Breathe when you can. Watch for[25] the waves. TREEEEEE! TREEEEEE! TREEEEEE!"

My heart was chilled to ice[26]. I felt ill with grief[27]. But there was no time for frozen shock[28]. It was shock in activity. Something in me did not want to give up on life[1], was unwilling to let go[2], wanted to fight to the very end[3]. Where that part of me got the heart[4], I don't know.

"Isn't it ironic[5], Richard Parker? We're in hell yet still we're afraid of immortality. Look how close you are! TREEEEEE! TREEEEEE! TREEEEEE! Hurrah, hurrah! You've made it[6], Richard Parker, you've made it. Catch! *Humpf!*"

I threw the lifebuoy mightily[7]. It fell in the water right in front of him. With his last energies he stretched forward and took hold of it[8].

"Hold on tight[9], I'll pull you in[10]. Don't let go. Pull with your eyes while I pull with my hands. In a few seconds you'll be aboard[11] and we'll be together. Wait a second. Together? We'll be *together*? Have I gone mad?"

I woke up to what I was doing. I yanked[12] on the rope.

"Let go of that lifebuoy, Richard Parker! Let go, I said. I don't want you here, do you understand? Go somewhere else. Leave me alone. Get lost.[13] Drown! Drown!"

He was kicking vigorously with his legs. I grabbed an oar[14]. I thrust it at him[15], meaning to push him away[16]. I missed and lost hold of the oar.

I grabbed another oar. I dropped it in an oar-lock[17] and pulled as hard as I could, meaning to move the lifeboat away. All I accomplished was to turn the lifeboat a little, bringing one end closer to Richard Parker.

I would hit him on the head! I lifted the oar in the air.

He was too fast. He reached up and pulled himself aboard.

"Oh my God!"

1. renoncer à la vie
2. ne voulait pas laisser tomber
3. jusqu'au bout
4. courage
5. C'est drôle, n'est-ce pas ?
6. Tu as réussi
7. avec force
8. il s'est étiré vers l'avant et l'a attrapée
9. Tiens-toi bien
10. je vais te tirer dans le canot
11. à bord
12. J'ai tiré d'un coup sec
13. Va-t'en
14. rame
15. Je l'ai jetée dans sa direction
16. dans le but de le repousser
17. Je l'ai placée dans son encoche

Ravi was right. Truly I was to be the next goat. I had a wet, trembling, half-drowned, heaving and coughing[1] three-year-old adult Bengal tiger in my lifeboat. Richard Parker rose unsteadily to his feet[2] on the tarpaulin[3], eyes blazing as they met mine[4], ears laid tight to his head[5], all weapons drawn[6]. His head was the size and colour of the lifebuoy, with teeth.

I turned around, stepped over[7] the zebra and threw myself overboard[8].

CHAPTER 38

I don't understand. For days the ship had pushed on[9], bullishly[10] indifferent to its surroundings. The sun shone, rain fell, winds blew, currents flowed[11], the sea built up hills[12], the sea dug up valleys[13]— the *Tsimtsum* did not care. It moved with the slow, massive confidence[14] of a continent.

I had bought a map of the world for the trip; I had set it up in our cabin against a cork billboard[15]. Every morning I got our position from the control bridge and marked it on the map with an orange tipped pin[16]. We sailed from Madras across the Bay of Bengal, down through the Strait of Malacca[17], around Singapore and up to Manila. I loved every minute of it. It was a thrill[18] to be on a ship. Taking care of the animals kept us very busy. Every night we fell into bed weary to our bones[19]. We were in Manila for two days, a question of fresh feed[20], new cargo[21] and, we were told, the performing of routine maintenance work on the engines[22]. I paid attention only to the first two. The fresh feed included a ton of bananas, and the new cargo, a female Congo chimpanzee, part of Father's wheeling and dealing[1]. A ton of bananas bristles with a good three, four pounds of big black spiders.[2] A chimpanzee is like a smaller, leaner[3] gorilla, but meaner-looking[4], with less of the melancholy gentleness of its larger cousin. A chimpanzee shudders and grimaces[5] when it touches a big black spider, like you and I would do, before squashing it angrily with its knuckles[6], not something you and I would do. I thought bananas and a chimpanzee were more interesting than a loud, filthy mechanical contraption[7] in the dark bowels[8] of a ship. Ravi spent his days there, watching the men work. Something was wrong with the engines, he said. Did something go wrong with the fixing of them[9]? I don't know. I don't think anyone will ever know. The answer is a mystery lying at the bottom of thousands of feet of water[10].

We left Manila and entered the Pacific. On our fourth day out[11], midway to Midway[12], we sank. The ship vanished into a pinprick hole[13] on my map. A mountain collapsed before my eyes and disappeared beneath my feet. All around me was the vomit of a dyspeptic ship[14]. I felt sick to my stomach.[15] I felt shock. I felt a great emptiness within me, which then filled with silence. My chest[16] hurt with pain and fear for days afterwards.

I think there was an explosion. But I can't be sure. It happened while I was sleeping. It woke me up. The ship was no luxury liner[17]. It was a grimy, hardworking cargo ship[18] not designed for paying passengers[19] or for their comfort. There were all kinds of noises all the time. It was precisely because the level of noise was so uniform that we slept like babies. It was a form of silence that nothing disturbed, not Ravi's snoring[20] nor my talking

1. magouilles
2. Il y a dans une tonne de bananes deux bons kilos de grosses araignées noires qui grouillent.
3. plus mince
4. à l'air plus méchant
5. frémit et fait une grimace
6. avant de l'écraser furieusement avec les articulations de ses doigts
7. un engin mécanique crasseux et bruyant
8. entrailles
9. leur réparation
10. à plusieurs milliers de mètres de profondeur, sous l'eau
11. Le quatrième jour de notre voyage
12. à mi-chemin des îles Midway
13. un trou d'épingle
14. bateau dyspeptique [atteint de troubles digestifs]
15. J'avais la nausée.
16. poitrine
17. n'était pas un paquebot de luxe
18. un cargo crasseux, conçu pour travailler dur
19. le transport de passagers payants
20. ronflements

in my sleep. So the explosion, if there was one, was not a new noise. It was an irregular noise. I woke up with a start[1], as if Ravi had burst a balloon in my ears[2]. I looked at my watch. It was just after four-thirty in the morning. I leaned over[3] and looked down at the bunk below. Ravi was still sleeping.

I dressed and climbed down.[4] Normally I'm a sound sleeper[5]. Normally I would have gone back to sleep. I don't know why I got up that night. It was more the sort of thing Ravi would do. He liked the word *beckon*[6]; he would have said, "Adventure beckons[7]", and would have gone off to prowl around the ship[8]. The level of noise was back to normal again, but with a different quality perhaps, muffled[9] maybe.

I shook[10] Ravi. I said, "Ravi! There was a funny[11] noise. Let's go exploring."

He looked at me sleepily. He shook his head and turned over[12], pulling the sheet up to his cheek[13]. Oh, Ravi!

I opened the cabin door.

I remember walking down the corridor. Day or night it looked the same. But I felt the night in me. I stopped at Father and Mother's door and considered knocking on it[14]. I remember looking at my watch and deciding against it. Father liked his sleep. I decided I would climb to the main deck[15] and catch the dawn[16]. Maybe I would see a shooting star[17]. I was thinking about that, about shooting stars, as I climbed the stairs. We were two levels below the main deck. I had already forgotten about the funny noise.

It was only when I had pushed open the heavy door leading onto the main deck that I realized what the weather was like. Did it qualify as a storm?[18] It's true there was rain, but it wasn't so very hard. It certainly wasn't a driving rain[1], like you see during the monsoons. And there was wind. I suppose some of the gusts[2] would have upset umbrellas[3]. But I walked through it without much difficulty. As for the sea, it looked rough[4], but to a landlubber[5] the sea is always impressive and forbidding[6], beautiful and dangerous. Waves were reaching up[7], and their white foam[8], caught by the wind, was being whipped[9] against the side of the ship. But I'd seen that on other days and the ship hadn't sunk[10]. A cargo ship is a huge and stable structure, a feat of engineering[11]. It's designed to stay afloat[12] under the most adverse[13] conditions. Weather like this surely wouldn't sink a ship? Why[14], I only had to close a door and the storm was gone. I advanced onto the deck. I gripped the railing[15] and faced[16] the elements. This was adventure.

"Canada, here I come[17]!" I shouted as I was soaked and chilled[18]. I felt very brave. It was dark still, but there was enough light to see by. Light on pandemonium[19] it was. Nature can put on a thrilling show[20]. The stage[21] is vast, the lighting is dramatic[22], the extras are innumerable[23], and the budget for special effects is absolutely unlimited. What I had before me was a spectacle of wind and water, an earthquake[24] of the senses, that even Hollywood couldn't orchestrate. But the earthquake stopped at the ground beneath my feet. The ground beneath my feet was solid. I was a spectator safely ensconced[25] in his seat.

It was when I looked up at a lifeboat on the bridge castle that I started to worry. The lifeboat wasn't hanging straight down[26]. It was leaning in from its davits.[27] I turned and looked at my hands. My knuckles[28] were white. The thing was, I wasn't holding on so tightly[29] because of the weather, but

1. une pluie battante
2. bourrasques
3. auraient retourné des parapluies
4. agitée
5. marin d'eau douce
6. menaçante
7. Les vagues prenaient de la hauteur
8. écume
9. venait s'écraser
10. n'avait pas fait naufrage
11. une prouesse d'ingénierie
12. se maintenir à flot
13. défavorables
14. Ma foi
15. Je me suis agrippé au garde-fou
16. j'ai affronté
17. me voilà
18. trempé et gelé
19. tumulte
20. peut assurer un spectacle palpitant
21. scène
22. les lumières sont spectaculaires
23. les figurants sont innombrables
24. séisme
25. installé
26. était suspendu de travers
27. Il penchait vers l'arrière.
28. jointures
29. je ne me tenais pas si fermement

because otherwise I would fall in towards the ship[1]. The ship was listing to port[2], to the other side. It wasn't a severe list[3], but enough to surprise me. When I looked overboard[4] the drop wasn't sheer any more[5]. I could see the ship's great black side.

A shiver of cold went through me.[6] I decided it was a storm after all. Time to return to safety. I let go[7], hotfooted it to the wall[8], moved over and pulled open the door.

Inside the ship, there were noises. Deep structural groans. I stumbled[9] and fell. No harm done.[10] I got up. With the help of the handrails[11] I went down the stairwell[12] four steps at a time. I had gone down just one level when I saw water. Lots of water. It was blocking my way. It was surging from below like a riotous crowd[13], raging, frothing[14] and boiling. Stairs vanished into watery darkness. I couldn't believe my eyes. What was this water doing here? Where had it come from? I stood nailed to the spot[15], frightened and incredulous and ignorant of what I should do next. Down there was where my family was.

I ran up the stairs. I got to the main deck. The weather wasn't entertaining[16] any more. I was very afraid. Now it was plain and obvious[17]: the ship was listing badly[18]. And it wasn't level the other way either[19]. There was a noticeable incline going from bow to stern.[20] I looked overboard. The water didn't look to be eighty feet away[21]. The ship was sinking. My mind could hardly conceive it. It was as unbelievable as the moon catching fire[22].

Where were the officers and the crew? What were they doing? Towards the bow[23] I saw some men running in the gloom[24]. I thought I saw some animals too, but I dismissed the sight as illusion[25] crafted by rain and shadow[26]. We had the hatch covers over their bay pulled open[1] when the weather was good, but at all times the animals were kept confined to their cages. These were dangerous wild animals we were transporting, not farm livestock[2]. Above me, on the bridge, I thought I heard some men shouting.

The ship shook and there was that sound, the monstrous metallic burp. What was it? Was it the collective scream of humans and animals protesting their oncoming death[3]? Was it the ship itself giving up the ghost[4]? I fell over.[5] I got to my feet.[6] I looked overboard again. The sea was rising. The waves were getting closer. We were sinking fast[7].

I clearly heard monkeys shrieking. Something was shaking the deck. A gaur—an Indian wild ox[8]—exploded out of the rain and thundered by me[9], terrified, out of control, berserk[10]. I looked at it, dumbstruck[11] and amazed. Who in God's name had let it out?

I ran for the stairs to the bridge.[12] Up there was where the officers were, the only people on the ship who spoke English, the masters of our destiny here, the ones who would right this wrong[13]. They would explain everything. They would take care of my family and me. I climbed to the middle bridge. There was no one on the starboard side[14]. I ran to the port side. I saw three men, crew members. I fell. I got up. They were looking overboard. I shouted. They turned. They looked at me and at each other. They spoke a few words. They came towards me quickly. I felt gratitude and relief[15] welling up in me[16]. I said, "Thank God I've found you. What is happening? I am very scared.[17] There is water at the bottom of the ship. I am worried about my family. I can't get to the level where our cabins are. Is this normal? Do you think—"

1. Nous faisions sortir les panneaux d'écoutille de leur compartiment

2. du bétail

3. leur mort prochaine

4. qui rendait l'âme

5. Je suis tombé.

6. Je me suis relevé.

7. rapidement

8. bœuf

9. a poussé un énorme grognement à côté de moi

10. fou furieux

11. stupéfait

12. J'ai couru vers les escaliers qui menaient à la passerelle de commandement.

13. qui nous sortiraient de ce mauvais pas

14. à tribord

15. soulagement

16. monter en moi

17. J'ai très peur.

One of the men interrupted me by thrusting a life jacket into my arms[1] and shouting something in Chinese. I noticed an orange whistle dangling[2] from the life jacket. The men were nodding vigorously at me[3]. When they took hold of me and lifted me[4] in their strong arms, I thought nothing of it. I thought they were helping me. I was so full of trust in them that I felt grateful[5] as they carried me in the air. Only when they threw me overboard[6] did I begin to have doubts.

CHAPTER 39

I landed with a trampoline-like bounce[7] on the half-unrolled tarpaulin[8] covering a lifeboat forty feet below[9]. It was a miracle I didn't hurt myself. I lost the life jacket, except for the whistle, which stayed in my hand. The lifeboat had been lowered partway[10] and left to hang. It was leaning out from its davits[11], swinging[12] in the storm, some twenty feet above the water[13]. I looked up. Two of the men were looking down at me, pointing wildly at the lifeboat and shouting. I didn't understand what they wanted me to do. I thought they were going to jump in after me. Instead they turned their heads, looked horrified, and this creature appeared in the air, leaping with the grace of a racehorse[14]. The zebra missed the tarpaulin. It was a male Grant, weighing over five hundred pounds[15]. It landed with a loud crash[16] on the last bench[17], smashing it[18] and shaking the whole lifeboat. The animal called out[19]. I might have expected[20] the braying of an ass or the neighing of a horse[21]. It was nothing of the sort. It could only be called a burst of barking, a *kwa-*

ha-ha, *kwa-ha-ha*, *kwa-ha-ha* put out at the highest pitch of distress[1]. The creature's lips were widely parted, standing upright and quivering[2], revealing yellow teeth and dark pink gums[3]. The lifeboat fell through the air and we hit the seething water[4].

CHAPTER 40

Richard Parker did not jump into the water after me[5]. The oar I intended to use as a club[6] floated. I held on to it[7] as I reached for the lifebuoy, now vacant of its previous occupant[8]. It was terrifying to be in the water. It was black and cold and in a rage. I felt as if I were at the bottom of a crumbling well[9]. Water kept crashing down on me.[10] It stung[11] my eyes. It pulled me down.[12] I could hardly breathe.[13] If there hadn't been the lifebuoy I wouldn't have lasted[14] a minute.

I saw a triangle slicing the water fifteen feet away[15]. It was a shark's fin[16]. An awful tingle[17], cold and liquid, went up and down my spine[18]. I swam as fast as I could to one end of the lifeboat, the end still covered by the tarpaulin. I pushed myself up on the lifebuoy with my arms. I couldn't see Richard Parker. He wasn't on the tarpaulin or on a bench. He was at the bottom of the lifeboat. I pushed myself up again. All I could see, briefly, at the other end, was the zebra's head thrashing about[19]. As I fell back into the water another shark's fin glided right before me[20].

The bright orange tarpaulin was held down by[21] a strong nylon rope that wove its way between metal grommets in the tarpaulin and blunt hooks[22] on the side of the boat. I happened to be tread-

1. *empreint de la plus grande détresse*
2. *grandes ouvertes, relevées et tremblantes*
3. *gencives*
4. *nous sommes tombés sur l'eau bouillonnante*
5. *n'a pas sauté à l'eau pour m'attraper*
6. *massue*
7. *Je m'y suis accroché*
8. *que son occupant précédent avait libérée*
9. *au fond d'un puits en train de s'effondrer*
10. *L'eau venait sans cesse s'écraser contre moi.*
11. *Elle me piquait*
12. *Elle me tirait vers le bas.*
13. *Je pouvais à peine respirer.*
14. *je n'aurais pas survécu*
15. *fendre l'eau à 4 m de moi*
16. *un aileron de requin*
17. *frisson*
18. *ma colonne vertébrale*
19. *qui s'agitait dans tous les sens*
20. *est passé juste devant moi*
21. *maintenu par*
22. *qui serpentait entre des anneaux en métal dans la bâche et des crochets émoussés*

1. Je nageais sur place
2. étrave [partie saillante à l'avant d'un bateau]
3. proue
4. un nez retroussé
5. La bâche était un peu relâchée
6. j'ai poussé son manche dans ce trou
7. qui faisait saillie au-dessus des vagues
8. bien qu'un peu de travers
9. j'ai serré les jambes
10. même si je n'en étais éloigné que d'une distance fluctuant entre 60 et 90 centimètres
11. La crête des vagues les plus hautes
12. orphelin
13. Si j'avais considéré mes chances de survie à la lumière de la raison
14. je ne me souviens pas
15. le lever du jour
16. Au bout d'un moment
17. jusqu'à ce que je me retrouve à l'intérieur de la bouée
18. plus difficile de me détacher de la rame

ing water[1] at the bow. The tarpaulin was not as securely fixed going over the stem[2]—which had a very short prow[3], what in a face would be called a snub nose[4]—as it was elsewhere around the boat. There was a little looseness in the tarpaulin[5] as the rope went from one hook on one side of the stem to the next hook on the other side. I lifted the oar in the air and I shoved its handle into this looseness[6], into this lifesaving detail. I pushed the oar in as far as it would go. The lifeboat now had a prow projecting over the waves[7], if crookedly[8]. I pulled myself up and wrapped my legs[9] around the oar. The oar handle pushed up against the tarpaulin, but tarpaulin, rope and oar held. I was out of the water, if only by a fluctuating two, three feet[10]. The crest of the larger waves[11] kept striking me.

I was alone and orphaned[12], in the middle of the Pacific, hanging on to an oar, an adult tiger in front of me, sharks beneath me, a storm raging about me. Had I considered my prospects in the light of reason[13], I surely would have given up and let go of the oar, hoping that I might drown before being eaten. But I don't recall[14] that I had a single thought during those first minutes of relative safety. I didn't even notice daybreak[15]. I held on to the oar, I just held on, God only knows why.

After a while[16] I made good use of the lifebuoy. I lifted it out of the water and put the oar through its hole. I worked it down until the ring was hugging me[17]. Now it was only with my legs that I had to hold on. If Richard Parker appeared, it would be more awkward to drop from the oar[18], but one terror at a time, Pacific before tiger.

CHAPTER 41

The elements allowed me to go on living. The lifeboat did not sink. Richard Parker kept out of sight[1]. The sharks prowled but did not lunge.[2] The waves splashed me[3] but did not pull me off[4].

I watched the ship as it disappeared with much burbling and belching[5]. Lights flickered and went out[6]. I looked about for my family, for survivors, for another lifeboat, for anything that might bring me hope. There was nothing. Only rain, marauding[7] waves of black ocean and the flotsam[8] of tragedy.

The darkness melted away[9] from the sky. The rain stopped.

I could not stay in the position I was in forever. I was cold. My neck was sore[10] from holding up my head and from all the craning I had been doing[11]. My back hurt from leaning against the lifebuoy.[12] And I needed to be higher up[13] if I were to see other lifeboats.

I inched my way[14] along the oar till my feet were against the bow of the boat. I had to proceed with extreme caution[15]. My guess was that Richard Parker was on the floor of the lifeboat beneath the tarpaulin, his back to me, facing the zebra, which he had no doubt killed by now. Of the five senses, tigers rely the most on their sight[16]. Their eyesight is very keen[17], especially in detecting motion[18]. Their hearing[19] is good. Their smell is average. I mean compared to other animals, of course. Next to Richard Parker, I was deaf, blind and nose-dead[20]. But at the moment he could not see me, and in my wet condition could probably not smell me, and what with the whistling[21] of the wind and the hissing[22] of the sea as waves broke, if I were careful,

1. n'est plus apparu
2. Les requins rodaient, mais ils n'ont pas attaqué.
3. m'éclaboussaient
4. elles ne m'ont pas fait tomber
5. beaucoup de glouglous et de bruits de renvoi
6. ont vacillé et se sont éteintes
7. à l'affût
8. les débris flottants
9. s'est dissipée
10. J'avais mal à la nuque
11. à force de dresser la tête et de tendre le cou
12. J'avais mal au dos à cause de la bouée.
13. plus en hauteur
14. J'ai avancé lentement
15. procéder avec une extrême prudence
16. se fient le plus à la vue
17. Leur vue est perçante
18. les mouvements
19. ouïe
20. sourd, aveugle et dépourvu d'odorat
21. avec le sifflement
22. bruit strident

he would not hear me. I had a chance so long as he did not sense me[1]. If he did, he would kill me right away. Could he burst through[2] the tarpaulin, I wondered.

Fear and reason fought over the answer. Fear said Yes. He was a fierce, 450-pound carnivore[3]. Each of his claws was as sharp[4] as a knife. Reason said No. The tarpaulin was sturdy canvas[5], not a Japanese paper wall[6]. I had landed upon it from a height.[7] Richard Parker could shred it[8] with his claws with a little time and effort, but he couldn't pop through it like a jack-in-the-box[9]. And he had not seen me. Since he had not seen me, he had no reason to claw his way through it[10].

I slid[11] along the oar. I brought both my legs to one side of the oar and placed my feet on the gunnel[12]. The gunnel is the top edge[13] of a boat, the rim[14] if you want. I moved a little more till my legs were on the boat. I kept my eyes fixed on the horizon[15] of the tarpaulin. Any second I expected to see Richard Parker rising up[16] and coming for me. Several times I had fits of fearful trembling[17]. Precisely where I wanted to be most still[18]—my legs—was where I trembled most. My legs drummed upon[19] the tarpaulin. A more obvious rapping on Richard Parker's door couldn't be imagined.[20] The trembling spread[21] to my arms and it was all I could do to hold on[22]. Each fit passed[23].

When enough of my body was on the boat I pulled myself up. I looked beyond the end of the tarpaulin. I was surprised to see that the zebra was still alive. It lay near the stern[24], where it had fallen, listless[25], but its stomach was still panting and its eyes were still moving, expressing terror. It was on its side[26], facing me, its head and neck awkwardly propped against[27] the boat's side bench. It had badly broken a rear leg[1]. The angle of it was completely unnatural. Bone protruded through[2] skin and there was bleeding[3]. Only its slim front legs[4] had a semblance of normal position. They were bent and neatly tucked[5] against its twisted[6] torso. From time to time the zebra shook its head and barked and snorted[7]. Otherwise it lay quietly.

It was a lovely animal. Its wet markings glowed[8] brightly white and intensely black. I was so eaten up by[9] anxiety that I couldn't dwell on it[10]; still, in passing, as a faint afterthought[11], the queer, clean, artistic boldness of its design[12] and the fineness of its head struck me. Of greater significance to me was the strange fact that Richard Parker had not killed it. In the normal course of things[13] he should have killed the zebra. That's what predators do: they kill prey. In the present circumstances, where Richard Parker would be under tremendous mental strain[14], fear should have brought out an exceptional level of aggression. The zebra should have been properly butchered[15].

The reason behind its spared[16] life was revealed shortly. It froze my blood[17]—and then brought a slight measure of relief. A head appeared beyond the end of the tarpaulin. It looked at me in a direct, frightened way, ducked under[18], appeared again, ducked under again, appeared once more, disappeared a last time. It was the bear-like, balding-looking[19] head of a spotted hyena. Our zoo had a clan of six, two dominant females and four subordinate males. They were supposed to be going to Minnesota. The one here was a male. I recognized it by its right ear, which was badly torn[20], its healed jagged edge[21] testimony to old violence[22]. Now I understood why Richard Parker had not killed the zebra: he was no longer aboard. There couldn't be

1. une jambe arrière

2. traversait

3. des saignements

4. minces jambes antérieures

5. repliées

6. tordu

7. s'ébrouait

8. Ses rayures mouillées brillaient

9. dévoré par

10. m'y attarder

11. en y repensant vaguement après coup

12. l'étrange audace artistique épurée de son apparence

13. Normalement,

14. devait subir un énorme stress mental

15. massacré

16. épargnée

17. Cela m'a glacé le sang

18. s'est cachée

19. ayant l'air d'avoir des problèmes de calvitie

20. lacérée

21. son bord déchiqueté, qui avait cicatrisé

22. témoignait qu'elle avait participé à des combats

both a hyena and a tiger in such a small space. He must have fallen off the tarpaulin and drowned.

I had to explain to myself how a hyena had come to be on the lifeboat. I doubted hyenas were capable of swimming in open seas[1]. I concluded that it must have been on board all along, hiding under the tarpaulin, and that I hadn't noticed it when I landed with a bounce[2]. I realized something else: the hyena was the reason those sailors[3] had thrown me into the lifeboat. They weren't trying to save my life. That was the last of their concerns[4]. They were using me as fodder[5]. They were hoping that the hyena would attack me and that somehow I would get rid of it[6] and make the boat safe for them, no matter if[7] it cost me my life. Now I knew what they were pointing at so furiously just before the zebra appeared.

I never thought that finding myself confined in a small space with a spotted hyena would be good news[8], but there you go[9]. In fact, the good news was double: if it weren't for[10] this hyena, the sailor wouldn't have thrown me into the lifeboat and I would have stayed on the ship and I surely would have drowned; and if I had to share quarters[11] with a wild animal, better the upfront[12] ferocity of a dog than the power and stealth[13] of a cat. I breathed the smallest sigh of relief.[14] As a precautionary measure I moved onto the oar. I sat astride it[15], on the rounded edge of the speared[16] lifebuoy, my left foot against the tip of the prow, my right foot on the gunnel. It was comfortable enough and I was facing the boat.

I looked about. Nothing but sea and sky. The same when we were at the top of a swell[17]. The sea briefly imitated every land feature[18]—every hill, every valley, every plain. Accelerated geotectonics.

1. au large

2. j'ai atterri dans le canot

3. marins

4. le dernier de leurs soucis

5. nourriture

6. je m'en débarrasserais

7. peu importe si

8. une bonne nouvelle

9. ce fut le cas

10. s'il n'y avait pas eu

11. cohabiter

12. franche

13. furtivité

14. J'ai poussé un très léger soupir de soulagement.

15. Je l'ai chevauchée

16. pointue

17. portés par la houle

18. les caractéristiques des différents types de terrains

Around the world in eighty swells.[1] But nowhere on it could I find my family. Things floated in the water but none that brought me hope. I could see no other lifeboats.

The weather was changing rapidly. The sea, so immense, so breathtakingly immense[2], was settling into a smooth and steady motion[3], with the waves at heel[4]; the wind was softening to a tuneful breeze[5]; fluffy, radiantly white clouds[6] were beginning to light up in a vast fathomless[7] dome of delicate pale blue. It was the dawn of a beautiful day in the Pacific Ocean. My shirt was already beginning to dry. The night had vanished as quickly as the ship.

I began to wait. My thoughts swung wildly[8]. I was either fixed on practical details of immediate survival or transfixed[9] by pain, weeping[10] silently, my mouth open and my hands at my head.

CHAPTER 42

She came floating on an island of bananas in a halo of light, as lovely the Virgin Mary. The rising sun[11] was behind her. Her flaming hair[12] looked stunning[13].

I cried, "Oh blessed Great Mother, Pondicherry fertility goddess[14], provider of[15] milk and love, wondrous arm spread of comfort[16], terror of ticks[17], picker-up of crying ones[18], are you to witness[19] this tragedy too? It's not right that gentleness meet horror. Better that you had died right away. How bitterly glad I am to see you.[20] You bring joy and pain in equal measure[21]. Joy because you are with me, but pain because it won't be for long. What

1. Le tour du monde en quatre-vingts houles.

2. immense à couper le souffle

3. se calmait pour prendre un mouvement fluide et régulier

4. sous contrôle

5. mollissait pour devenir une brise mélodieuse

6. des nuages cotonneux, d'un blanc éclatant

7. infini

8. passaient d'un extrême à l'autre

9. paralysé

10. pleurant

11. Le soleil levant

12. Sa chevelure flamboyante

13. magnifique

14. déesse

15. qui procure

16. dont l'enver-gure des bras est merveilleu-sement grande et confortable

17. tiques

18. qui s'occupe des éplorés

19. faut-il que tu assistes à

20. Te voir me procure une joie amère.

21. autant de joie que de peine

do you know about the sea? Nothing. What do I know about the sea? Nothing. Without a driver[1] this bus is lost. Our lives are over[2]. Come aboard if your destination is oblivion[3]—it should be our next stop[4]. We can sit together. You can have the window seat[5], if you want. But it's a sad view. Oh, enough of this dissembling[6]. Let me say it plainly[7]: I love you, I love you, I love you. I love you, I love you, I love you. Not the spiders, please."

It was Orange Juice—so called because she tended to drool[8]—our prize[9] Borneo orang-utan matriarch, zoo star and mother of two fine boys, surrounded by a mass of black spiders that crawled[10] around her like malevolent worshippers[11]. The bananas on which she floated were held together by the nylon net[12] with which they had been lowered[13] into the ship. When she stepped off the bananas into the boat, they bobbed up and rolled over[14]. The net became loose[15]. Without thinking about it, only because it was at hand's reach and about to sink, I took hold of the net and pulled it aboard, a casual gesture[16] that would turn out to be a lifesaver in many ways[17]; this net would become one of my most precious possessions.

The bananas came apart[18]. The black spiders crawled as fast as they could, but their situation was hopeless. The island crumbled[19] beneath them. They all drowned. The lifeboat briefly floated in a sea of fruit.

I had picked up what I thought was a useless net, but did I think of reaping from this banana manna[20]? No. Not a single one. It was banana split[21] in the wrong sense of the term: the sea dispersed them. This colossal waste[22] would later weigh on me heavily[23]. I would nearly go into convulsions of dismay[24] at my stupidity.

Orange Juice was in a fog[1]. Her gestures were slow and tentative[2] and her eyes reflected deep mental confusion. She was in a state of profound shock. She lay flat[3] on the tarpaulin for several minutes, quiet and still, before reaching over and falling into the lifeboat proper. I heard a hyena's scream.

CHAPTER 43

The last trace I saw of the ship was a patch of oil[4] glimmering[5] on the surface of the water.

I was certain I wasn't alone. It was inconceivable that the *Tsimtsum* should sink without eliciting a peep of concern[6]. Right now in Tokyo, in Panama City, in Madras, in Honolulu, why, even in Winnipeg, red lights were blinking[7] on consoles, alarm bells were ringing, eyes were opening wide in horror, mouths were gasping[8], "My God! The *Tsimtsum* has sunk!" and hands were reaching for phones. More red lights were starting to blink and more alarm bells were starting to ring. Pilots were running to their planes with their shoelaces still untied[9], such was their hurry[10]. Ship officers were spinning their wheels[11] till they were feeling dizzy[12]. Even submarines were swerving[13] underwater to join in the rescue effort. We would be rescued soon. A ship would appear on the horizon. A gun would be found to kill the hyena and put the zebra out of its misery[14]. Perhaps Orange Juice could be saved. I would climb aboard[15] and be greeted[16] by my family. They would have been picked up in another lifeboat. I only had to ensure my survival for the next few hours until this rescue ship[17] came.

1. dans le brouillard
2. hésitants
3. Elle est restée étendue
4. une flaque de pétrole
5. étincelant
6. sans susciter la moindre inquiétude
7. clignotaient
8. les gens étaient bouche bée
9. sans même avoir fait leurs lacets
10. tellement ils étaient pressés
11. faisaient tourner leur gouvernail
12. jusqu'à en avoir le tournis
13. déviaient de leur course
14. mettre fin aux souffrances du zèbre
15. Je monterai à bord
16. je serai accueilli
17. bateau de sauvetage

I reached from my perch[1] for the net. I rolled it up and tossed it midway on the tarpaulin[2] to act as a barrier, however small[3]. Orange Juice had seemed practically cataleptic. My guess was she was dying of shock. It was the hyena that worried me. I could hear it whining[4]. I clung to the hope that a zebra, a familiar prey, and an orang-utan, an unfamiliar one, would distract it from thoughts of me.

I kept one eye on the horizon, one eye on the other end of the lifeboat. Other than the hyena's whining, I heard very little from the animals[5], no more than claws scuffing against[6] a hard surface and occasional groans and arrested cries[7]. No major fight seemed to be taking place.

Mid-morning the hyena appeared again. In the preceding minutes its whining had been rising in volume to a scream[8]. It jumped over the zebra onto the stern, where the lifeboat's side benches came together to form a triangular bench. It was a fairly exposed position, the distance between bench and gunnel being about twelve inches[9]. The animal nervously peered[10] beyond the boat. Beholding[11] a vast expanse of shifting water[12] seemed to be the last thing it wanted to see, for it instantly brought its head down and dropped to the bottom of the boat behind the zebra. That was a cramped[13] space; between the broad back of the zebra and the sides of the buoyancy tanks[14] that went all round the boat beneath the benches, there wasn't much room[15] left for a hyena. It thrashed about[16] for a moment before climbing to the stern again and jumping back over the zebra to the middle of the boat, disappearing beneath the tarpaulin. This burst of activity[17] lasted less than ten seconds. The hyena came to within fifteen feet of me[1]. My only reaction was to freeze with fear[2]. The zebra, by comparison, swiftly reared its head[3] and barked.

I was hoping the hyena would stay under the tarpaulin. I was disappointed. Nearly immediately it leapt over the zebra and onto the stern bench again. There it turned on itself a few times, whimpering[4] and hesitating. I wondered what it was going to do next. The answer came quickly: it brought its head low and ran around the zebra in a circle, transforming the stern bench, the side benches and the cross bench[5] just beyond the tarpaulin into a twenty-five-foot indoor track[6]. It did one lap[7]—two—three—four—five—and onwards, non-stop, till I lost count[8]. And the whole time, lap after lap, it went yip yip yip yip yip in a high-pitched way[9]. My reaction, once again, was very slow. I was seized by fear and could only watch. The beast was going at a good clip[10], and it was no small animal; it was an adult male that looked to be about 140 pounds[11]. The beating of its legs against the benches made the whole boat shake, and its claws were loudly clicking on their surface. Each time it came from the stern I tensed[12]. It was hair-raising enough[13] to see the thing racing my way[14]; worse still was the fear[15] that it would keep going straight[16]. Clearly, Orange Juice, wherever she was[17], would not be an obstacle. And the rolled-up tarpaulin and the bulge[18] of the net were even more pitiful[19] defences. With the slightest of efforts the hyena could be[20] at the bow right at my feet. It didn't seem intent on that course of action[21]; every time it came to the cross bench, it took it, and I saw the upper half of its body moving rapidly along the edge of the tarpaulin. But in this state, the hyena's behaviour was highly

1. à moins de 4,5 mètres de moi
2. rester pétrifié de peur
3. a levé la tête
4. en gémissant
5. le banc à l'arrière, les bancs sur les côtés et le banc transversal
6. une piste intérieure de 7 mètres
7. tour
8. j'arrête de compter
9. elle poussait un petit aboiement aigu
10. à un bon rythme
11. environ 65 kilos
12. je me crispais
13. C'était suffisamment effrayant
14. de la voir courir dans ma direction
15. plus grande encore était ma peur
16. tout droit
17. où qu'elle soit
18. renflement
19. pitoyables
20. L'hyène n'avait qu'un tout petit effort à faire pour se retrouver
21. Elle ne semblait pas en avoir l'intention

unpredictable[1] and it could decide to attack me without warning.

After a number of laps it stopped short[2] at the stern bench and crouched[3], directing its gaze downwards, to the space below the tarpaulin. It lifted its eyes and rested them[4] upon me. The look was nearly the typical look of a hyena—blank[5] and frank, the curiosity apparent with nothing of the mental set revealed[6], jaw hanging open[7], big ears sticking up[8] rigidly, eyes bright and black—were it not for the strain that exuded from every cell of its body[9], an anxiety that made the animal glow[10], as if with a fever. I prepared for my end. For nothing. It started running in circles again.

When an animal decides to do something, it can do it for a very long time. All morning the hyena ran in circles going *yip yip yip yip yip*. Once in a while it briefly stopped at the stern bench, but otherwise every lap was identical to the previous one, with no variations in movement, in speed, in the pitch[11] or the volume of the yipping, in the counter-clockwise direction of travel[12]. Its yipping was shrill and annoying in the extreme[13]. It became so tedious and draining[14] to watch that I eventually turned my head to the side, trying to keep guard[15] with the corner of my eyes. Even the zebra, which at first snorted[16] each time the hyena raced by its head, fell into a stupor.

Yet every time the hyena paused at the stern bench, my heart jumped. And as much as I wanted to[17] direct my attention to the horizon, to where my salvation lay[18], it kept straying back to[19] this maniacal[20] beast.

I am not one to hold a prejudice against[21] any animal, but it is a plain fact[22] that the spotted hyena is not well served by its appearance. It is ugly beyond redemption[1]. Its thick neck and high shoulders that slope to the hindquarters[2] look as if they've come from a discarded[3] prototype for the giraffe, and its shaggy, coarse coat[4] seems to have been patched together from the leftovers of creation[5]. The colour is a bungled mix of tan[6], black, yellow, grey, with the spots having none of the classy ostentation of a leopard's rosettes[7]; they look rather like the symptoms of a skin disease, a virulent form of mange[8]. The head is broad and too massive, with a high forehead, like that of a bear, but suffering from a receding hairline[9], and with ears that look ridiculously mouse-like, large and round, when they haven't been torn off[10] in battle. The mouth is forever open and panting[11]. The nostrils[12] are too big. The tail is scraggly and unwagging[13]. The gait is shambling.[14] All the parts put together look doglike, but like no dog anyone would want as a pet.

But I had not forgotten Father's words. These were not cowardly carrion-eaters[15]. If *National Geographic* portrayed them as such, it was because *National Geographic* filmed during the day. It is when the moon rises that the hyena's day starts, and it proves to be a devastating hunter[16]. Hyenas attack in packs whatever animal can be run down[17], its flanks opened while still in full motion[18]. They go for[19] zebras, gnus and water buffaloes, and not only the old or the infirm in a herd—full-grown members[20] too. They are hardy[21] attackers, rising up from buttings and kickings immediately[22], never giving up for simple lack of will[23]. And they are clever[24]; anything that can be distracted[25] from its mother is good. The ten-minute-old gnu is a favourite dish, but hyenas also eat young lions and young rhinoceros. They

1. horriblement laide
2. ses hautes épaules et son arrière-train bas
3. rejeté
4. son pelage rugueux et ébouriffé
5. assemblé à partir des restes de la création
6. un mélange raté de fauve
7. le chic ostentatoire des taches d'un léopard
8. gale
9. dégarni
10. arrachées
11. haletante
12. narines
13. est hirsute et ne bouge pas
14. Sa démarche est traînante.
15. charognards
16. un chasseur vorace
17. tout animal qui peut être renversé
18. alors qu'il est encore en train de courir
19. Elles s'attaquent aux
20. des adultes
21. robustes
22. qui se relèvent immédiatement après avoir reçu un coup de corne ou de patte
23. manque de volonté
24. futées
25. soustrait

1. efficaces
2. récompensés
3. pile
4. grignoté librement
5. tanière
6. Rien n'est gaspillé
7. se soulèvent
8. morceaux de leur proie
9. elles recrachent de denses boules de poils
10. qu'elles nettoient de tout ce qui peut être comestible
11. arrive fréquemment
12. un repas
13. en voulant arracher un morceau de zèbre
14. sans mauvaise intention
15. Elle a trop de plaisirs
16. les goûts d'une hyène sont tellement éclectiques
17. au moment même où
18. vessie
19. en formant un rafraîchissant bain de boue avec ses pattes
20. grignotent
21. gloussements
22. d'autres hyènes
23. dont elles ont englouti les oreilles et le nez comme amuse-gueules
24. les phares, le pot d'échappement, les rétroviseurs

are diligent[1] when their efforts are rewarded[2]. In fifteen minutes flat[3], all that will be left of a zebra is the skull, which may yet be dragged away and gnawed down at leisure[4] by young ones in the lair[5]. Nothing goes to waste[6]; even grass upon which blood has been spilt will be eaten. Hyenas' stomachs swell[7] visibly as they swallow huge chunks of kill[8]. If they are lucky, they become so full they have difficulty moving. Once they've digested their kill, they cough up dense hairballs[9], which they pick clean of edibles[10] before rolling in them. Accidental cannibalism is a common occurrence[11] during the excitement of a feeding[12]; in reaching for a bite of zebra[13], a hyena will take in the ear or nostril of a clan member, no hard feelings intended[14]. The hyena feels no disgust at this mistake. Its delights are too many[15] to admit to disgust at anything.

In fact, a hyena's catholicity of taste is so indiscriminate[16] it nearly forces admiration. A hyena will drink from water even as[17] it is urinating in it. The animal has another original use for its urine: in hot, dry weather it will cool itself by relieving its bladder[18] on the ground and stirring up a refreshing mud bath with its paws[19]. Hyenas snack on[20] the excrement of herbivores with clucks[21] of pleasure. It's an open question as to what hyenas *won't* eat. They eat their own kind[22] (the rest of those whose ears and noses they gobbled down as appetizers[23]) once they're dead, after a period of aversion that lasts about one day. They will even attack motor vehicles—the headlights, the exhaust pipe, the side mirrors[24]. It is not their gastric juices that limit hyenas, but the power of their jaws, which is formidable.

That was the animal I had[1] racing around in circles before me. An animal to pain the eye and chill the heart[2].

Things ended in typical hyena fashion. It stopped at the stern and started producing deep groans interrupted by fits of heavy panting[3]. I pushed myself away on the oar till only the tips of my feet were holding on to the boat. The animal hacked and coughed[4]. Abruptly it vomited. A gush[5] landed behind the zebra. The hyena dropped into what it had just produced. It stayed there, shaking and whining and turning around on itself, exploring the furthest confines of animal anguish[6]. It did not move from the restricted[7] space for the rest of the day. At times the zebra made noises about the predator just behind it, but mostly it lay in hopeless and sullen[8] silence.

CHAPTER 44

The sun climbed through the sky, reached its zenith, began to come down. I spent the entire day perched on the oar, moving only as much as was necessary to stay balanced[9]. My whole being tended towards the spot[10] on the horizon that would appear and save me. It was a state of tense, breathless boredom[11]. Those first hours are associated in my memory with one sound, not one you'd guess[12], not the yipping of the hyena or the hissing[13] of the sea: it was the buzzing of flies[14]. There were flies aboard the lifeboat. They emerged and flew about in the way of flies, in great, lazy orbits except when they came close to each other, when they spiralled together with dizzying speed[15] and

1. que je voyais
2. qui heurte la vue et vous glace le sang
3. de profonds halètements
4. crachait et toussait
5. jet
6. les limites ultimes de l'angoisse animale
7. restreint
8. lugubre
9. pour garder mon équilibre
10. point
11. ennui tendu, haletant
12. que vous pourriez deviner
13. chuintement
14. le bourdonnement des mouches
15. elles formaient ensemble des spirales à une vitesse étourdissante

1. elles bourdonnaient d'autant plus

2. Elles formaient des cercles autour de moi

3. des avions monomoteurs pétaradants

4. dans le canot avant nous

5. elles n'ont pas survécu longtemps

6. essayait de les mordre

7. balayées vers la mer

8. sont mortes de vieillesse

9. cachaient

10. il n'y avait presque pas de vent

11. me repérer à l'aide des bruits

12. a commencé à grogner

13. à aboyer et couiner

14. des coups répétés

15. je me suis fais pipi dessus

16. infernale

a burst of buzzing[1]. Some were brave enough to venture out to where I was. They looped around me[2], sounding like sputtering, single-prop airplanes[3], before hurrying home. Whether they were native to the boat[4] or had come with one of the animals, the hyena most likely, I can't say. But whatever their origin, they didn't last long[5]; they all disappeared within two days. The hyena, from behind the zebra, snapped at them[6] and ate a number. Others were probably swept out to sea[7] by the wind. Perhaps a few lucky ones came to their life's term and died of old age[8].

As evening approached, my anxiety grew. Everything about the end of the day scared me. At night a ship would have difficulty seeing me. At night the hyena might become active again and maybe Orange Juice too.

Darkness came. There was no moon. Clouds hid[9] the stars. The contours of things became hard to distinguish. Everything disappeared, the sea, the lifeboat, my own body. The sea was quiet and there was hardly any wind[10], so I couldn't even ground myself in sound[11]. I seemed to be floating in pure, abstract blackness. I kept my eyes fixed on where I thought the horizon was, while my ears were on guard for any sign of the animals. I couldn't imagine lasting the night.

Sometime during the night the hyena began snarling[12] and the zebra barking and squealing[13], and I heard a repeated knocking sound[14]. I shook with fright and—I will hide nothing here—relieved myself in my pants[15]. But these sounds came from the other end of the lifeboat. I couldn't feel any shaking that indicated movement. The hellish[16] beast was apparently staying away from me. From nearer in the blackness I began hearing loud expirations and groans and grunts[1] and various wet mouth sounds. The idea of Orange Juice stirring[2] was too much for my nerves to bear, so I did not consider it. I simply ignored the thought. There were also noises coming from beneath me, from the water, sudden flapping sounds and swishing sounds[3] that were over and done with in an instant[4]. The battle for life was taking place there too.

The night passed, minute by slow minute.

CHAPTER 45

I was cold. It was a distracted[5] observation, as if it didn't concern me. Daybreak came. It happened quickly, yet by imperceptible degrees. A corner of the sky changed colours. The air began filling with light. The calm sea opened up around me like a great book. Still it felt like night. Suddenly it was day.

Warmth came only when the sun, looking like an electrically lit orange, broke across the horizon[6], but I didn't need to wait that long to feel it. With the very first rays[7] of light it came alive in me: hope. As things emerged in outline[8] and filled with colour, hope increased until it was like a song in my heart. Oh, what it was to bask in it[9]! Things would work out yet.[10] The worst was over. I had survived the night. Today I would be rescued. To think that, to string those words together[11] in my mind, was itself a source of hope. Hope fed on hope.[12] As the horizon became a

1. des gémissements, des grognements

2. en train de bouger

3. des battements et des sifflements soudains

4. qui ne duraient qu'un instant

5. distraite

6. s'est montré à l'horizon

7. rayons

8. Tandis que le contour des choses émergeait

9. quel plaisir de s'y prélasser

10. Les choses allaient s'arranger à présent.

11. associer ces mots

12. L'espoir nourrissait l'espoir.

neat, sharp line[1], I scanned it eagerly[2]. The day was clear again and visibility was perfect. I imagined Ravi would greet me first and with a tease[3]. "What's this?" he would say. "You find yourself a great big lifeboat and you fill it with animals? You think you're Noah[4] or something[5]?" Father would be unshaven and dishevelled[6]. Mother would look to the sky and take me in her arms. I went through a dozen versions of what it was going to be like on the rescue ship, variations on the theme of sweet reunion. That morning the horizon might curve[7] one way, my lips resolutely curved the other, in a smile.

Strange as it might sound[8], it was only after a long time that I looked to see what was happening in the lifeboat. The hyena had attacked the zebra. Its mouth was bright red and it was chewing on a piece of hide[9]. My eyes automatically searched for the wound[10], for the area under attack. I gasped with horror.[11]

The zebra's broken leg was missing[12]. The hyena had bitten it off[13] and dragged it to the stern, behind the zebra. A flap[14] of skin hung limply over the raw stump[15]. Blood was still dripping[16]. The victim bore its suffering[17] patiently, without showy remonstrations[18]. A slow and constant grinding[19] of its teeth was the only visible sign of distress. Shock, revulsion and anger surged through me[20]. I felt intense hatred[21] for the hyena. I thought of doing something to kill it. But I did nothing. And my outrage was short-lived[22]. I must be honest about that. I didn't have pity to spare for long[23] for the zebra. When your own life is threatened[24], your sense of empathy is blunted[25] by a terrible, selfish hunger for survival. It was sad that it was suffering so much—and being such a big, strapping[1] creature it wasn't at the end of its ordeal[2]—but there was nothing I could do about it. I felt pity and then I moved on. This is not something I am proud of[3]. I am sorry I was so callous[4] about the matter. I have not forgotten that poor zebra and what it went through[5]. Not a prayer goes by that I don't think of it.

There was still no sign of Orange Juice. I turned my eyes to the horizon again.

That afternoon the wind picked up[6] a little and I noticed something about the lifeboat: despite its weight, it floated lightly on the water, no doubt because it was carrying less than its capacity. We had plenty of freeboard[7], the distance between the water and the gunnel; it would take a mean sea[8] to swamp us[9]. But it also meant that whatever end of the boat was facing the wind tended to fall away, bringing us broadside to the waves[10]. With small waves the result was a ceaseless, fist-like beating against the hull[11], while larger waves made for a tiresome rolling of the boat[12] as it leaned from side to side[13]. This jerky and incessant motion[14] was making me feel queasy[15].

Perhaps I would feel better in a new position. I slid down the oar and shifted back onto the bow. I sat facing the waves, with the rest of the boat to my left. I was closer to the hyena, but it wasn't stirring[16].

It was as I was breathing deeply and concentrating on making my nausea go away that I saw Orange Juice. I had imagined her completely out of sight[17], near the bow beneath the tarpaulin, as far

1. bien bâtie
2. calvaire
3. dont je suis fier
4. insensible
5. ce qu'il a enduré

6. s'est levé
7. franc-bord
8. une mer mauvaise
9. nous inonder
10. ce qui faisait que le canot était perpendiculaire aux vagues
11. comme des coups de poing incessants sur la coque
12. provoquaient un pénible mouvement de roulis
13. car le canot oscillait sur son axe
14. Ces mouvements saccadés et incessants
15. me donnaient mal au cœur
16. elle ne bougeait pas
17. hors de vue

from the hyena as she could get. Not so. She was on the side bench, just beyond the edge of the hyena's indoor track and barely hidden from me by the bulge of rolled-up tarpaulin. She lifted her head only an inch or so[1] and right away I saw her.

Curiosity got the best of me[2]. I had to see her better. Despite the rolling of the boat I brought myself to a kneeling position[3]. The hyena looked at me, but did not move. Orange Juice came into sight[4]. She was deeply slouched[5] and holding on to the gunnel with both her hands, her head sunk[6] very low between her arms. Her mouth was open and her tongue was lolling about[7]. She was visibly panting. Despite the tragedy afflicting me, despite not feeling well, I let out a laugh. Everything about Orange Juice at that moment spelled one word[8]: *seasickness*[9]. The image of a new species popped[10] into my head: the rare seafaring[11] *green* orang-utan. I returned to my sitting position. The poor dear looked so *humanly* sick! It is a particularly funny thing to read human traits in animals, especially in apes[12] and monkeys, where it is so easy. Simians[13] are the clearest mirrors we have in the animal world. That is why they are so popular in zoos. I laughed again. I brought my hands to my chest, surprised at how I felt. Oh my.[14] This laughter was like a volcano of happiness erupting in me. And Orange Juice had not only cheered me up[15]; she had also taken on both our feelings of seasickness. I was feeling fine now.

I returned to scrutinizing the horizon, my hopes high.

Besides being deathly seasick[16], there was something else about Orange Juice that was remark-

---

1. de quelques centimètres seulement

2. a pris le dessus

3. je me suis mis à genoux

4. est apparue

5. complètement avachie

6. baissée

7. pendait

8. évoquait un seul mot

9. mal de mer

10. a surgi

11. marin

12. chez les grands singes

13. Les simiens

14. Mon Dieu.

15. ne m'avait pas seulement remonté le moral

16. Hormis son terrible mal de mer

able: she was uninjured[1]. And she had her back turned to the hyena, as if she felt she could safely ignore it. The ecosystem on this lifeboat was decidedly baffling[2]. Since there are no natural conditions in which a spotted hyena and an orangutan can meet, there being none of the first in Borneo and none of the second in Africa, there is no way of knowing how they would relate[3]. But it seemed to me highly improbable, if not totally incredible, that when brought together these frugivorous tree-dwellers[4] and carnivorous savannah-dwellers[5] would so radically carve out their niches[6] as to pay no attention to each other. Surely an orang-utan would smell of prey to a hyena, albeit a strange one[7], one to be remembered afterwards for producing stupendous[8] hairballs, nonetheless better-tasting[9] than an exhaust pipe and well worth looking out for when near trees. And surely a hyena would smell of a predator to an orang-utan, a reason for being vigilant when a piece of durian[10] has been dropped to the ground accidentally. But nature forever holds surprises[11]. Perhaps it was not so. If goats could be brought to live amicably with rhinoceros, why not orangutans with hyenas? That would be a big winner at a zoo. A sign would have to be put up. I could see it already: "Dear Public, Do not be afraid for the orang-utans! They are in the trees because that is where they live, not because they are afraid of the spotted hyenas. Come back at mealtime[12], or at sunset when they get thirsty, and you will see them climbing down from[13] their trees and moving about the grounds, absolutely unmolested by the hyenas[14]." Father would be fascinated.

1. elle n'était pas blessée

2. déconcertant

3. quelle serait leur relation

4. ces mangeurs de fruits arboricoles

5. ces habitants de la savane carnivores

6. délimiteraient leur territoire de façon si marquée

7. fût-elle étrange

8. extraordinaires

9. ayant un meilleur goût

10. un morceau de durian [fruit asiatique]

11. nous réserve toujours des surprises

12. au moment des repas

13. descendre de

14. sans que les hyènes ne les attaquent

Sometime that afternoon I saw the first specimen of what would become a dear, reliable[1] friend of mine. There was a bumping and scraping sound[2] against the hull[3] of the lifeboat. A few seconds later, so close to the boat I could have leaned down and grabbed it[4], a large sea turtle appeared, a hawksbill[5], flippers[6] lazily turning, head sticking out of the water[7]. It was striking-looking[8] in an ugly sort of way, with a rugged, yellowish brown shell[9] about three feet[10] long and spotted with patches of algae[11], and a dark green face with a sharp beak[12], no lips, two solid holes for nostrils, and black eyes that stared at me intently. The expression was haughty[13] and severe, like that of an ill-tempered[14] old man who has complaining on his mind[15]. The queerest thing[16] about the reptile was simply that it was. It looked incongruous, floating there in the water, so odd in its shape compared to the sleek, slippery design of fish[17]. Yet it was plainly in its element and it was I who was the odd one out[18]. It hovered by the boat[19] for several minutes.

I said to it, "Go tell a ship I'm here. Go, go." It turned and sank out of sight, back flippers pushing water in alternate strokes.

CHAPTER 46

Clouds that gathered[20] where ships were supposed to appear, and the passing of the day, slowly did the job of unbending my smile[21]. It is pointless[22] to say that this or that night was the worst of my life.

I have so many bad nights to choose from that I've made none the champion. Still, that second night at sea stands in my memory as one of exceptional suffering, different from the frozen anxiety of the first night in being a more conventional sort of suffering, the broken-down kind[1] consisting of weeping and sadness and spiritual pain, and different from later ones in that I still had the strength to appreciate fully what I felt. And that dreadful[2] night was preceded by a dreadful evening.

I noticed the presence of sharks[3] around the lifeboat. The sun was beginning to pull the curtains[4] on the day. It was a placid explosion of orange and red, a great chromatic symphony, a colour canvas of supernatural proportions[5], truly a splendid Pacific sunset, quite wasted on me[6]. The sharks were makos—swift, pointy-snouted predators[7] with long, murderous teeth that protruded[8] noticeably from their mouths. They were about six or seven feet long[9], one was larger still. I watched them anxiously. The largest one came at the boat quickly, as if to attack, its dorsal fin[10] rising out of the water by several inches[11], but it dipped below[12] just before reaching us and glided underfoot[13] with fearsome[14] grace. It returned, not coming so close this time, then disappeared. The other sharks paid a longer visit[15], coming and going at different depths[16], some in plain sight at hand's reach[17] below the surface of the water, others deeper down. There were other fish too, big and small, colourful, differently shaped. I might have considered them more closely had my attention not been drawn elsewhere: Orange Juice's head came into sight.

She turned and brought her arm onto the tarpaulin in a motion that imitated exactly the way

1. une forme de dépression

2. épouvantable

3. requins

4. fermer les rideaux

5. une toile colorée aux dimensions surnaturelles

6. que je n'étais pas en mesure d'apprécier

7. des prédateurs rapides, au museau pointu

8. dépassaient

9. Ils faisaient environ deux mètres de long

10. sa nageoire dorsale

11. s'élevait au-dessus de l'eau d'une dizaine de centimètres

12. il a plongé

13. a glissé sous nos pieds

14. effrayante

15. sont restés plus longtemps

16. profondeurs

17. bien visibles et à portée de main

you or I would bring out an arm and place it on the back of the chair next to our own in a gesture of expansive[1] relaxation. But such was clearly not her disposition[2]. Bearing an expression profoundly sad and mournful[3], she began to look about[4], slowly turning her head from side to side. Instantly the likeness of apes lost its amusing character. She had given birth[5] at the zoo to two young ones, strapping males five and eight years old that were her—and our—pride. It was unmistakably[6] these she had on her mind as she searched over the water, unintentionally mimicking[7] what I had been doing these last thirty-six hours. She noticed me and expressed nothing about it. I was just another animal that had lost everything and was vowed to death[8]. My mood plummeted[9].

Then, with only a snarl for notice[10], the hyena went amok[11]. It hadn't moved from its cramped quarters[12] all day. It put its front legs on the zebra's side, reached over and gathered a fold[13] of skin in its jaws. It pulled roughly[14]. A strip of hide came off[15] the zebra's belly[16] like gift-wrap paper comes off a gift[17], in a smooth-edged swath[18], only silently, in the way of tearing skin[19], and with greater resistance. Immediately blood poured forth[20] like a river. Barking, snorting and squealing, the zebra came to life to defend itself. It pushed on its front legs and reared its head in an attempt to bite[21] the hyena, but the beast was out of reach[22]. It shook its good hind[23] leg, which did no more than explain the origin of the previous night's knocking: it was the hoof[24] beating against the side of the boat. The zebra's attempts at self-preservation only whipped the hyena into a frenzy of snarling and biting[25]. It made a gaping wound[26] in the zebra's side. When it was no longer satisfied with the reach it had[1] from behind the zebra, the hyena climbed onto its haunches[2]. It started pulling out coils[3] of intestines and other viscera. There was no order to what it was doing. It bit here, swallowed there, seemingly overwhelmed by the riches before it[4]. After devouring half the liver[5], it started tugging on[6] the whitish, balloon-like stomach bag. But it was heavy, and with the zebra's haunches being higher than its belly—and blood being slippery[7]—the hyena started to slide[8] into its victim. It plunged head and shoulders into the zebra's guts[9], up to the knees[10] of its front legs. It pushed itself out[11], only to slide back down. It finally settled in this position, half in, half out. The zebra was being eaten alive from the inside.

It protested with diminishing vigour. Blood started coming out its nostrils[12]. Once or twice it reared its head straight up[13], as if appealing to heaven[14]—the abomination of the moment was perfectly expressed.

Orange Juice did not view these doings indifferently. She raised herself to her full height[15] on her bench. With her incongruously small legs and massive torso, she looked like a refrigerator on crooked wheels[16]. But with her giant arms lifted in the air, she looked impressive. Their span[17] was greater than her height—one hand hung over the water, the other reached across the width[18] of the lifeboat nearly to the opposite side. She pulled back her lips[19], showing off enormous canines, and began to *roar*. It was a deep, powerful, huffing[20] roar, amazing for an animal normally as silent as a giraffe. The hyena was as startled as I was by the outburst[21]. It cringed and retreated.[22] But not for long. After an intense stare at Orange Juice, the hairs on its neck and shoulders stood up[23] and its tail rose straight

1. ce qu'elle pouvait atteindre
2. hanches
3. des morceaux entortillés
4. apparemment dépassée par l'abondance qui s'offrait à elle
5. foie
6. elle s'est mise à tirailler sur
7. glissant
8. s'introduire
9. boyaux
10. jusqu'aux genoux
11. Elle s'est dégagée
12. narines
13. il a levé la tête à la verticale
14. il en appelait au ciel
15. Elle s'est dressée de toute sa hauteur
16. monté sur des roues tordues
17. Leur envergure
18. largeur
19. Elle a retroussé les babines
20. plein de hargne
21. cette explosion de colère
22. Elle a eu un mouvement de recul, puis a battu en retraite.
23. se sont hérissés

in the air. It climbed back onto the dying zebra. There, blood dripping from its mouth, it responded to Orange Juice in kind, with a higher-pitched roar. The two animals were three feet apart[1], wide-open jaws[2] directly facing. They put all their energies into their cries, their bodies shaking with the effort. I could see deep down the hyena's throat. The Pacific air, which until a minute before had been carrying the whistling and whispering of the sea, a natural melody I would have called soothing[3] had the circumstances been happier, was all at once filled with this appalling[4] noise, like the fury of an all-out battle[5], with the ear-splitting firing[6] of guns and cannons and the thunderous blasts[7] of bombs. The hyena's roar filled the higher range[8] of what my ears could hear, Orange Juice's bass roar filled the lower range[9], and somewhere in between I could hear the cries of the helpless zebra. My ears were full. Nothing more, not one more sound, could push into them and be registered.

I began to tremble uncontrollably. I was convinced the hyena was going to lunge at[10] Orange Juice.

I could not imagine that matters[11] could get worse, but they did. The zebra snorted some of its blood overboard[12]. Seconds later there was a hard knock against the boat, followed by another. The water began to churn[13] around us with sharks. They were searching for the source of the blood, for the food so close at hand[14]. Their tail fins flashed out of the water[15], their heads swung out[16]. The boat was hit repeatedly. I was not afraid we would capsize[17]—I thought the sharks would actually punch through[18] the metal hull[19] and sink us.

With every bang[20] the animals jumped and looked alarmed, but they were not to be distracted

Margin notes:
1. à un mètre l'un de l'autre
2. les mâchoires grandes ouvertes
3. apaisante
4. terrifiant
5. une guerre totale
6. les détonations stridentes
7. les explosions tonitruantes
8. la limite aiguë
9. la limite grave
10. bondir sur
11. situation
12. a rejeté par les narines du sang, qui est allé par-dessus bord
13. bouillonner
14. si proche
15. Leurs queues apparaissaient subitement hors de l'eau
16. surgissaient
17. chavirer
18. transperceraient
19. coque
20. coup

from their main business of roaring in each other's faces[1]. I was certain the shouting match[2] would turn physical[3]. Instead it broke off[4] abruptly after a few minutes. Orange Juice, with huffs and lip-smacking noises[5], turned away[6], and the hyena lowered its head and retreated behind the zebra's butchered[7] body. The sharks, finding nothing, stopped knocking on the boat and eventually left. Silence fell at last.

A foul and pungent smell[8], an earthy[9] mix of rust[10] and excrement, hung in the air. There was blood everywhere, coagulating to a deep red crust[11]. A single fly buzzed about, sounding to me like an alarm bell of insanity[12]. No ship, nothing at all, had appeared on the horizon that day, and now the day was ending. When the sun slipped below[13] the horizon, it was not only the day that died and the poor zebra, but my family as well. With that second sunset, disbelief gave way to[14] pain and grief[15]. They were dead; I could no longer deny it[16]. What a thing to acknowledge in your heart! To lose a brother is to lose someone with whom you can share the experience of growing old, who is supposed to bring you a sister-in-law and nieces and nephews[17], creatures to people the tree of your life and give it new branches. To lose your father is to lose the one whose guidance and help you seek[18], who supports you like a tree trunk supports its branches. To lose your mother, well, that is like losing the sun above you. It is like losing—I'm sorry, I would rather not go on. I lay down on the tarpaulin and spent the whole night weeping and grieving, my face buried[19] in my arms. The hyena spent a good part of the night eating.

1. se hurler dessus

2. les cris belliqueux

3. allait se transformer en lutte corporelle

4. s'est arrêté

5. des claquements de lèvres

6. s'est retournée

7. massacré

8. Une odeur âcre et nauséabonde

9. terreux

10. rouille

11. croûte

12. un signal m'avertissant de l'imminence de la folie

13. a disparu derrière

14. l'incrédulité a fait place à

15. deuil

16. le nier

17. une belle-sœur, des nièces et des neveux

18. auprès duquel vous cherchez à obtenir des conseils et de l'aide

19. enfouie

CHAPTER 47

1. couvert

2. couche

3. des draps de coton sales entassés

4. un trou de 60 centimètres

5. des organes à moitié mangés brillaient

6. prenaient un éclat terne et sec

7. le sang battait encore dans ses veines

8. tremblement

9. clignement

10. être à ce point blessé

11. tendue

12. repos

13. Elle ne tenait pas en place

14. recroquevillé

15. à midi

16. Il avait les yeux vitreux

17. a éclaté

18. glapissait

The day broke, humid and overcast[1], with the wind warm and the sky a dense blanket[2] of grey clouds that looked like bunched-up, dirty cotton sheets[3]. The sea had not changed. It heaved the lifeboat up and down in a regular motion.

The zebra was still alive. I couldn't believe it. It had a two-foot-wide hole[4] in its body, a fistula like a freshly erupted volcano, spewed half-eaten organs glistening[5] in the light or giving off a dull, dry shine[6], yet, in its strictly essential parts, it continued to pump with life[7], if weakly. Movement was confined to a tremor[8] in the rear leg and an occasional blinking[9] of the eyes. I was horrified. I had no idea a living being could sustain so much injury[10] and go on living.

The hyena was tense[11]. It was not settling down to its night of rest[12] despite the daylight. Perhaps it was a result of taking in so much food; its stomach was grossly dilated. Orange Juice was in a dangerous mood too. She was fidgeting[13] and showing her teeth.

I stayed where I was, curled up[14] near the prow. I was weak in body and in soul. I was afraid I would fall into the water if I tried to balance on the oar.

The zebra was dead by noon[15]. It was glassy-eyed[16] and had become perfectly indifferent to the hyena's occasional assaults.

Violence broke out[17] in the afternoon. Tension had risen to an unbearable level. The hyena was yipping[18]. Orange Juice was grunting and making loud lip-smacking noises. All of a sudden their complaining fused and shot up to top volume. The hyena jumped over the remains[1] of the zebra and made for[2] Orange Juice.

I believe I have made clear the menace of a hyena. It was certainly so clear in my mind that I gave up on Orange Juice's life before she even had a chance to defend it. I underestimated her.[3] I underestimated her grit[4].

She thumped[5] the beast on the head. It was something shocking. It made my heart melt[6] with love and admiration and fear. Did I mention she was a former pet[7], callously discarded[8] by her Indonesian owners? Her story was like that of every inappropriate pet. It goes something like this: The pet is bought when it is small and cute. It gives much amusement to its owners. Then it grows in size and in appetite. It reveals itself incapable of being house-trained.[9] Its increasing strength makes it harder to handle[10]. One day the maid[11] pulls the sheet from its nest[12] because she has decided to wash it, or the son jokingly pinches a morsel of food from its hands[13]—over some such seemingly small matter[14], the pet flashes[15] its teeth in anger and the family is frightened. The very next day the pet finds itself bouncing at the back of[16] the family Jeep in the company of its human brothers and sisters. A jungle is entered. Everyone in the vehicle finds it a strange and formidable[17] place. A clearing is come to.[18] It is briefly explored. All of a sudden the Jeep roars to life[19] and its wheels kick up dirt[20] and the pet sees all the ones it has known and loved looking at it from the back window as the Jeep speeds away[21]. It has been left behind[22]. The pet does not understand. It is as unprepared for this jungle as its human siblings[23] are. It waits around for their return, trying to quell[24] the panic rising in it. They do not return. The sun sets.

1. a sauté par-dessus les restes
2. s'est dirigée vers
3. Je l'ai sous-estimée.
4. courage
5. Elle a frappé violemment
6. fondre
7. c'était un animal familier
8. brutalement abandonné
9. Il s'avère impossible de lui apprendre la propreté.
10. de s'en occuper
11. la femme de ménage
12. enlève le drap de sa couche
13. lui pique un morceau de nourriture des mains, pour plaisanter
14. à propos de ce qui ne semble être qu'une bagatelle
15. montre
16. ballotté à l'arrière de
17. impression-nant
18. On arrive à une clairière.
19. démarre en grondant
20. ses roues soulèvent la poussière
21. disparaît à toute allure
22. abandonné
23. frères et sœurs
24. calmer

Quickly it becomes depressed and gives up on life[1]. It dies of hunger and exposure[2] in the next few days. Or is attacked by dogs.

Orange Juice could have been one of these forlorn[3] pets. Instead she ended up at the Pondicherry Zoo. She remained gentle and unaggressive her whole life. I have memories from when I was a child of her never-ending[4] arms surrounding me, her fingers, each as long as my whole hand, picking at my hair[5]. She was a young female practising her maternal skills[6]. As she matured into her full wild self[7], I observed her at a distance. I thought I knew her so well that I could predict her every move[8]. I thought I knew not only her habits but also her limits. This display[9] of ferocity, of savage courage, made me realize that I was wrong. All my life I had known only a part of her.

She thumped the beast on the head. And what a thump it was[10]. The beast's head hit the bench it had just reached, making such a sharp[11] noise, besides splaying its front legs flat out[12], that I thought surely either the bench or its jaw or both must break. The hyena was up again in an instant, every hair on its body as erect as the hairs on my head, but its hostility wasn't quite so kinetic now[13]. It withdrew.[14] I exulted. Orange Juice's stirring[15] defence brought a glow to my heart[16].

It didn't last long.

An adult female orang-utan cannot defeat an adult male spotted hyena. That is the plain empirical truth. Let it become known among zoologists. Had Orange Juice been a male, had she loomed as large on the scales as she did in my heart[17], it might have been another matter[18]. But portly and overfed though she was[19] from living in the comfort of a zoo, even so she tipped the scales at barely

110 pounds[1]. Female orang-utans are half the size[2] of males. But it is not simply a question of weight and brute strength. Orange Juice was far from defenceless. What it comes down to[3] is attitude and knowledge. What does a fruit eater know about killing? Where would it learn where to bite, how hard, for how long? An orang-utan may be taller, may have very strong and agile arms and long canines, but if it does not know how to use these as weapons, they are of little use[4]. The hyena, with only its jaws, will overcome[5] the ape because it knows what it wants and how to get it.

The hyena came back. It jumped on the bench and caught Orange Juice at the wrist[6] before she could strike[7]. Orange Juice hit the hyena on the head with her other arm, but the blow[8] only made the beast snarl viciously. She made to bite[9], but the hyena moved faster. Alas, Orange Juice's defence lacked[10] precision and coherence. Her fear was something useless that only hampered her[11]. The hyena let go of her wrist and expertly got to her throat.

Dumb[12] with pain and horror, I watched as Orange Juice thumped the hyena ineffectually[13] and pulled at its hair while her throat was being squeezed by its jaws[14]. To the end[15] she reminded me of us[16]: her eyes expressed fear in such a humanlike way, as did her strained whimpers[17]. She made an attempt to climb onto the tarpaulin. The hyena violently shook her. She fell off the bench to the bottom of the lifeboat, the hyena with her. I heard noises but no longer saw anything.

I was next. That much was clear to me. With some difficulty I stood up. I could hardly see through the tears in my eyes. I was no longer crying because of my family or because of my impending death[18]. I was far too numb to consider either.[19] I was crying

1. elle atteignait à peine 50 kilos sur la balance
2. font la moitié de la taille
3. Ce qui compte
4. elles ne lui sont pas très utiles
5. vaincra
6. au poignet
7. frapper
8. coup
9. Elle a essayé de la mordre
10. manquait de
11. la gênait
12. Muet
13. en vain
14. tandis que les mâchoires de l'hyène lui serraient la gorge
15. Jusqu'au bout
16. elle me faisait penser à un être humain
17. ses gémissements anxieux
18. ma mort prochaine
19. J'étais trop sonné pour penser à l'une ou l'autre.

because I was exceedingly tired and it was time to get rest[1].

I advanced over the tarpaulin. Though tautly stretched[2] at the end of the boat, it sagged a little[3] in the middle; it made for three or four toilsome, bouncy steps[4]. And I had to reach over the net and the rolled-up tarpaulin. And these efforts in a lifeboat that was constantly rolling. In the condition I was in, it felt like a great trek[5]. When I laid my foot on the middle cross bench, its hardness had an invigorating effect on me[6], as if I had just stepped on solid ground[7]. I planted both my feet on the bench and enjoyed my firm stand[8]. I was feeling dizzy[9], but since the capital moment of my life was coming up[10] this dizziness only added to my sense of frightened sublimity. I raised my hands to the level of my chest—the weapons I had against the hyena. It looked up at me. Its mouth was red. Orange Juice lay next to it, against the dead zebra. Her arms were spread wide open[11] and her short legs were folded[12] together and slightly turned to one side[13]. She looked like a simian Christ on the Cross. Except for her head. She was beheaded[14]. The neck wound was still bleeding. It was a sight horrible to the eyes and killing to the spirit. Just before throwing myself upon the hyena, to collect myself[15] before the final struggle, I looked down.

Between my feet, under the bench, I beheld[16] Richard Parker's head. It was gigantic. It looked the size of the planet Jupiter to my dazed[17] senses. His paws were like volumes of *Encyclopaedia Britannica*.

I made my way back to the bow[18] and collapsed[19].

I spent the night in a state of delirium. I kept thinking I had slept and was awaking[20] after dreaming of a tiger.

CHAPTER 48

Richard Parker was so named because of a cleric-al error[1]. A panther was terrorizing the Khulna district of Bangladesh, just outside the Sundarbans. It had recently carried off[2] a little girl. All that was found of her was a tiny[3] hand with a henna pattern on the palm[4] and a few plastic bangles[5]. She was the seventh person killed in two months by the marauder. And it was growing bolder[6]. The previous victim was a man who had been attacked in broad daylight[7] in his field[8]. The beast dragged him off into the forest, where it ate a good part of his head, the flesh off his right leg and all his innards[9]. His corpse[10] was found hanging in the fork of a tree[11]. The villagers kept a watch[12] nearby that night, hoping to surprise the panther and kill it, but it never appeared. The Forest Department hired[13] a professional hunter[14]. He set up a small, hidden platform in a tree near a river where two of the attacks had taken place. A goat was tied[15] to a stake[16] on the river's bank[17]. The hunter waited several nights. He assumed the panther would be an old, wasted[18] male with worn[19] teeth, incapable of catching anything more difficult than a human. But it was a sleek[20] tiger that stepped into the open[21] one night. A female with a single cub[22]. The goat bleated[23]. Oddly[24], the cub, who looked to be about three months old, paid little attention to the goat. It raced to the water's edge[25], where it drank eagerly[26]. Its mother followed suit[27]. Of hunger and thirst, thirst is the greater imperative. Only once the tiger had quenched her thirst[28] did she turn to the goat to satisfy her hunger. The hunter had two rifles[29] with him: one with real bullets[30], the other with immo-

---

1. l'erreur d'un employé de bureau
2. enlevé
3. petite
4. un motif dessiné au henné sur la paume
5. bracelets
6. elle s'enhardissait
7. en plein jour
8. champ
9. entrailles
10. cadavre
11. suspendu à la fourche d'un arbre
12. faisaient le guet
13. a engagé
14. chasseur
15. attachée
16. piquet
17. bord
18. décharné
19. usées
20. au pelage soyeux
21. s'est montré
22. lionceau
23. a bêlé
24. Étrangement
25. Il a couru jusqu'au bord de l'eau
26. avec avidité
27. a fait de même
28. a eu étanché sa soif
29. fusils
30. balles

bilizing darts[1]. This animal was not the man-eater, but so close to human habitation she might pose a threat to[2] the villagers, especially as she was with cub. He picked up the gun with the darts. He fired as the tiger was about to fell[3] the goat. The tiger reared up[4] and snarled[5] and raced away. But immobilizing darts don't bring on sleep gently, like a good cup of tea; they knock out like a bottle of hard liquor straight up[6]. A burst[7] of activity on the animal's part makes it act all the faster[8]. The hunter called his assistants on the radio. They found the tiger about two hundred yards[9] from the river. She was still conscious. Her back legs had given way[10] and her balance on her front legs was woozy[11]. When the men got close, she tried to get away but could not manage it. She turned on them, lifting a paw that was meant to kill. It only made her lose her balance. She collapsed and the Pondicherry Zoo had two new tigers. The cub was found in a bush[12] close by[13], meowing with fear[14]. The hunter, whose name was Richard Parker, picked it up with his bare hands[15] and, remembering how it had rushed to drink in the river, baptized it Thirsty. But the shipping clerk[16] at the Howrah train station was evidently a man both befuddled and diligent[17]. All the papers we received with the cub clearly stated that its name was Richard Parker, that the hunter's first name was Thirsty and that his family name was None Given[18]. Father had had a good chuckle over the mix-up[19] and Richard Parker's name had stuck[20].

I don't know if Thirsty None Given ever got the man-eating panther.

CHAPTER 49

In the morning I could not move. I was pinned by weakness to the tarpaulin.[1] Even thinking was exhausting. I applied myself to thinking straight.[2] At length[3], as slowly as a caravan of camels crossing a desert, some thoughts came together.

The day was like the previous one, warm and overcast, the clouds low, the breeze light. That was one thought. The boat was rocking gently[4], that was another.

I thought of sustenance[5] for the first time. I had not had a drop to drink or a bite to eat[6] or a minute of sleep in three days. Finding this obvious explanation for my weakness brought me a little strength.

Richard Parker was still on board. In fact, he was directly beneath me. Incredible that such a thing should need consent to be true[7], but it was only after much deliberation, upon assessing various mental items[8] and points of view, that I concluded that it was not a dream or a delusion[9] or a misplaced memory[10] or a fancy[11] or any other such falsity[12], but a solid, true thing witnessed while in a weakened, highly agitated state. The truth of it would be confirmed as soon as I felt well enough to investigate[13].

How I had failed to notice for two and a half days a 450-pound Bengal tiger[14] in a lifeboat twenty-six feet long[15] was a conundrum I would have to try to crack[16] later, when I had more energy. The feat[17] surely made Richard Parker the largest stowaway[18], proportionally speaking, in the history of navigation. From tip[19] of nose to tip of tail he took up over a third of the length of the ship he was on.

1. L'épuisement me clouait à la bâche.

2. Je me suis efforcé d'avoir les idées claires.

3. Finalement

4. oscillait doucement

5. ma subsistance

6. Je n'avais pas bu une goutte ou mangé un morceau

7. Il est incroyable qu'il faille s'assurer d'une telle chose pour être sûr qu'elle est vraie

8. après avoir évalué mon état mental

9. une hallucination

10. un souvenir déplacé

11. mon imagination

12. illusion

13. me pencher sur la question

14. un tigre du Bengale de 200 kilos

15. de 8 mètres de long

16. une énigme qu'il me faudrait résoudre

17. Cet exploit

18. passager clandestin

19. Depuis le bout

You might think I lost all hope at that point. I did. And as a result I perked up[1] and felt much better. We see that in sports all the time, don't we? The tennis challenger starts strong but soon loses confidence in his playing[2]. The champion racks up the games[3]. But in the final set, when the challenger has nothing left to lose, he becomes relaxed again, insouciant, daring[4]. Suddenly he's playing like the devil[5] and the champion must work hard to get those last points. So it was with me. To cope with[6] a hyena seemed remotely[7] possible, but I was so obviously outmatched by[8] Richard Parker that it wasn't even worth worrying about. With a tiger aboard, my life was over. That being settled[9], why not do something about my parched[10] throat?

I believe it was this that saved my life that morning, that I was quite literally dying of thirst. Now that the word had popped into my head I couldn't think of anything else, as if the word itself were salty and the more I thought of it, the worse the effect. I have heard that the hunger for air exceeds as a compelling sensation the thirst for water[11]. Only for a few minutes, I say. After a few minutes you die and the discomfort of asphyxiation goes away. Whereas thirst is a drawn-out affair[12]. Look: Christ on the Cross died of suffocation, but His only complaint was of thirst[13]. If thirst can be so taxing[14] that even God Incarnate complains about it, imagine the effect on a regular[15] human. It was enough to make me go raving mad[16]. I have never known a worse physical hell than this putrid taste and pasty feeling in the mouth[17], this unbearable pressure[18] at the back of the throat, this sensation that my blood was turning to a thick syrup[19] that barely flowed[20]. Truly, by comparison, a tiger was nothing.

And so I pushed aside all thoughts of Richard Parker and fearlessly went exploring for fresh water[1].

The divining rod[2] in my mind dipped sharply[3] and a spring gushed water[4] when I remembered that I was on a genuine, regulation lifeboat[5] and that such a lifeboat was surely outfitted with supplies[6]. That seemed like a perfectly reasonable proposition. What captain would fail in so elementary a way to ensure[7] the safety of his crew? What ship chandler[8] would not think of making a little extra money[9] under the noble guise of[10] saving lives? It was settled.[11] There was water aboard. All I had to do was find it.

Which meant I had to move.

I made it to the middle of the boat, to the edge of the tarpaulin. It was a hard crawl. I felt I was climbing the side of a volcano and I was about to look over the rim[12] into a boiling cauldron[13] of orange lava. I lay flat.[14] I carefully brought my head over. I did not look over any more than I had to. I did not see Richard Parker. The hyena was plainly visible, though. It was back behind what was left of the zebra. It was looking at me.

I was no longer afraid of it. It wasn't ten feet away[15], yet my heart didn't skip a beat[16]. Richard Parker's presence had at least that useful aspect. To be afraid of this ridiculous dog when there was a tiger about was like being afraid of splinters[17] when trees are falling down. I became very angry at the animal. "You ugly, foul creature[18]", I muttered. The only reason I didn't stand up and beat it off the lifeboat with a stick[19] was lack of strength and stick, not lack of heart[20].

Did the hyena sense something of my mastery? Did it say to itself, "Super alpha is watching me[21]— I better not move[22]?" I don't know. At any rate, it

1. à la recherche d'eau douce
2. La baguette de sourcier
3. a creusé vivement
4. une source a jailli
5. un véritable canot de sauvetage, conforme à la réglementation
6. approvisionné en vivres
7. assurer
8. fournisseur maritime
9. gagner un peu plus d'argent
10. sous le noble prétexte de
11. C'était sûr.
12. à l'intérieur du cratère
13. chaudron
14. Je me suis mis à plat ventre.
15. Elle était à moins de trois mètres de moi
16. a continué de battre normalement
17. des échardes
18. Tu n'es qu'une créature laide et repoussante
19. je ne l'ai pas chassée du canot à coups de bâton
20. courage
21. Un vrai mâle dominant m'observe
22. je ferais mieux de ne pas bouger

didn't move. In fact, in the way it ducked its head it seemed to want to hide from me. But it was no use hiding[1]. It would get its just deserts[2] soon enough.

Richard Parker also explained the animals' strange behaviour. Now it was clear why the hyena had confined itself to such an absurdly small space behind the zebra and why it had waited so long before killing it. It was fear of the greater beast and fear of touching the greater beast's food. The strained[3], temporary peace between Orange Juice and the hyena, and my reprieve[4], were no doubt due to the same reason: in the face of such a superior predator, all of us were prey, and normal ways of preying[5] were affected. It seemed the presence of a tiger had saved me from a hyena—surely a textbook example[6] of jumping from the frying pan into the fire[7].

But the great beast was not behaving like a great beast, to such an extent that the hyena had taken liberties. Richard Parker's passivity, and for three long days, needed explaining[8]. Only in two ways could I account for it: sedation[9] and seasickness. Father regularly sedated a number of the animals to lessen[10] their stress. Might he have sedated Richard Parker shortly before the ship sank? Had the shock of the shipwreck[11]—the noises, the falling into the sea, the terrible struggle to swim to the lifeboat—increased the effect of the sedative? Had seasickness taken over[12] after that? These were the only plausible explanations I could come up with[13].

I lost interest in the question. Only water interested me.

I took stock of the lifeboat.[14]

174

CHAPTER 50

It was three and a half feet deep[1], eight feet wide[2] and twenty-six feet long[3], exactly. I know because it was printed on one of the side benches in black letters. It also said that the lifeboat was designed to accommodate[4] a maximum of thirty-two people. Wouldn't that have been merry[5], sharing it with so many? Instead we were three and it was awfully crowded[6]. The boat was symmetrically shaped, with rounded ends that were hard to tell apart[7]. The stern was hinted at by a small fixed rudder[8], no more than a rearward extension of the keel[9], while the bow[10], except for my addition, featured a stem with the saddest, bluntest prow[11] in boat-building history. The aluminum hull was studded with rivets[12] and painted white.

That was the outside of the lifeboat. Inside, it was not as spacious as might be expected because of the side benches and the buoyancy tanks. The side benches ran the whole length of the boat, merging at[13] the bow and stern to form end benches that were roughly[14] triangular in shape. The benches were the top surfaces of the sealed[15] buoyancy tanks. The side benches were one and a half feet[16] wide and the end benches were three feet deep[17]; the open space of the lifeboat was thus twenty feet[18] long and five feet[19] wide. That made a territory of one hundred square feet[20] for Richard Parker. Spanning this space widthwise were three cross benches[21], including the one smashed[22] by the zebra. These benches were two feet[23] wide and were evenly spaced[24]. They were two feet above the floor of the boat—the play Richard Parker had before he would knock his head against

1. 1 mètre de profondeur
2. 2,43 mètres de large
3. 7,90 mètres de large
4. transporter
5. drôle
6. terriblement bondé
7. qu'il était difficile de distinguer l'une de l'autre
8. L'arrière se reconnaissait à son petit gouvernail fixe
9. une extension vers l'arrière de la quille
10. l'avant
11. avait une étrave dotée de la proue la plus triste et la plus plate
12. garnie de rivets
13. se rencontraient au niveau de
14. à peu près
15. scellées
16. 45 cm
17. avaient une hauteur de 90 cm
18. 6 m
19. 1,5 m
20. 9 m²
21. Trois bancs latéraux traversaient cet espace dans le sens de la largeur
22. détruit
23. 60 cm
24. régulièrement espacés

1. l'espace restant à Richard Parker avant qu'il ne se cogne la tête au plafond

2. pour ainsi dire

3. un espace supplémentaire de 30 centimètres

4. 90 cm

5. planches étroites

6. lui étaient perpendiculaires

7. sifflets sans roulette

8. simples

9. solide toile traitée

10. rugueuse

11. tanière

12. des encoches en forme de « u »

13. un moyen de

14. un bateau de course

15. bien flotter

the ceiling[1], so to speak[2], if he were beneath a bench. Under the tarpaulin, he had another twelve inches of space[3], the distance between the gunnel, which supported the tarpaulin, and the benches, so three feet[4] in all, barely enough for him to stand. The floor, consisting of narrow planks[5] of treated wood, was flat and the vertical sides of the buoyancy tanks were at right angles to it[6]. So, curiously, the boat had rounded ends and rounded sides, but the interior volume was rectangular.

It seems orange—such a nice Hindu colour—is the colour of survival because the whole inside of the boat and the tarpaulin and the life jackets and the lifebuoy and the oars and most every other significant object aboard was orange. Even the plastic, beadless whistles[7] were orange.

The words *Tsimtsum* and *Panama* were printed on each side of the bow in stark[8], black, roman capitals.

The tarpaulin was made of tough, treated canvas[9], rough[10] on the skin after a while. It had been unrolled to just past the middle cross bench. So one cross bench was hidden beneath the tarpaulin, in Richard Parker's den[11]; the middle cross bench was just beyond the edge of the tarpaulin, in the open; and the third cross bench lay broken beneath the dead zebra.

There were six oarlocks, U-shaped notches[12] in the gunnel for holding an oar in place, and five oars, since I had lost one trying to push Richard Parker away. Three oars rested on one side bench, one rested on the other and one made up my life-saving prow. I doubted the usefulness of these oars as a means of[13] propulsion. This lifeboat was no racing shell[14]. It was a heavy, solid construction designed for stolid floating[15], not for navigating, though I suppose that if we had been thirty-two to row we could have made some headway[1].

I did not grasp[2] all these details—and many more—right away. They came to my notice with time and as a result of necessity. I would be in the direst of dire straits[3], facing a bleak future[4], when some small thing, some detail, would transform itself and appear in my mind in a new light. It would no longer be the small thing it was before, but the most important thing in the world, the thing that would save my life. This happened time and again[5]. How true it is that necessity is the mother of invention, how very true.

CHAPTER 51

But that first time I had a good look at the lifeboat I did not see the detail I wanted. The surface of the stern and side benches was continuous and unbroken[6], as were the sides of the buoyancy tanks. The floor lay flat against the hull[7]; there could be no cache[8] beneath it. It was certain: there was no locker[9] or box or any other sort of container[10] anywhere. Only smooth[11], uninterrupted orange surfaces.

My estimation of captains and ship chandlers wavered[12]. My hopes for survival flickered[13]. My thirst remained.

And what if the supplies were at the bow, beneath the tarpaulin? I turned and crawled back. I felt like a dried-out lizard[14]. I pushed down on the tarpaulin. It was tautly stretched[15]. If I unrolled it, I would give myself access to what supplies might be

1. nous aurions pu avancer
2. compris

3. dans la plus désespérée des situations

4. promis à un avenir sombre

5. à maintes reprises

6. régulière
7. reposait à plat sur la coque
8. cachette
9. caisson
10. récipient
11. lisses
12. a faibli
13. ont vacillé

14. un lézard desséché
15. bien tendue

1. aux
provisions,
quelles qu'elles
soient, qui
pourraient être
entreposées en
dessous
2. ouverture
3. J'ai dégagé
4. taille
5. pouces
6. crochets
7. s'est affaissée
sous mes coudes
8. J'étais couché
à plat ventre
9. un loquet
scintillait
10. On pouvait
distinguer un
couvercle.
11. battre la
chamade
12. J'ai jeté un
coup d'œil
13. arrondi
14. de 90 cm de
large
15. 60 cm de
haut
16. J'ai
brusquement
redressé la tête.
17. frisson
18. j'ai pu, pour
la première
fois, apercevoir
Richard
Parker sans
ambiguïté, avec
l'esprit clair
19. Fauve et
rayé
20. immobile
21. J'ai cligné
des yeux,
incrédule, en le
voyant si près.
22. En tendant
la main

stored below[1]. But that meant creating an opening[2] onto Richard Parker's den.

There was no question. Thirst pushed me on. I eased[3] the oar from under the tarpaulin. I placed the lifebuoy around my waist[4]. I laid the oar across the bow. I leaned over the gunnel and with my thumbs[5] pushed from under one of the hooks[6] the rope that held down the tarpaulin. I had a difficult time of it. But after the first hook, it was easier with the second and the third. I did the same on the other side of the stem. The tarpaulin became slack beneath my elbows[7]. I was lying flat[8] on it, my legs pointed towards the stern.

I unrolled it a little. Immediately I was rewarded. The bow was like the stern; it had an end bench. And upon it, just a few inches from the stem, a hasp glittered[9] like a diamond. There was the outline of a lid.[10] My heart began to pound[11]. I unrolled the tarpaulin further. I peeked[12] under. The lid was shaped like a rounded-out[13] triangle, three feet wide[14] and two feet deep[15]. At that moment I perceived an orange mass. I jerked my head back.[16] But the orange wasn't moving and didn't look right. I looked again. It wasn't a tiger. It was a life jacket. There were a number of life jackets at the back of Richard Parker's den.

A shiver[17] went through my body. Between the life jackets, partially, as if through some leaves, I had my first, unambiguous, clear-headed glimpse of Richard Parker[18]. It was his haunches I could see, and part of his back. Tawny and striped[19] and simply enormous. He was facing the stern, lying flat on his stomach. He was still[20] except for the breathing motion of his sides. I blinked in disbelief at how close he was.[21] He was right there, two feet beneath me. Stretching[22], I could have pinched his

178

bottom[1]. And between us there was nothing but a thin tarpaulin, easily got round[2].

"God preserve me!" No supplication was ever more passionate yet more gently carried by the breath. I lay absolutely motionless.

I had to have water. I brought my hand down and quietly undid the hasp[3]. I pulled on the lid. It opened onto a locker.

I have just mentioned the notion of details that become lifesavers. Here was one: the lid was hinged an inch or so[4] from the edge of the bow bench—which meant that as the lid opened, it became a barrier that closed off the twelve inches[5] of open space between tarpaulin and bench through which Richard Parker could get to me after pushing aside the life jackets. I opened the lid till it fell against the crosswise[6] oar and the edge of the tarpaulin. I moved onto the stem, facing the boat, one foot on the edge of the open locker, the other against the lid. If Richard Parker decided to attack me from below, he would have to push on the lid. Such a push would both warn me and help me fall backwards into the water with the lifebuoy. If he came the other way, climbing atop the tarpaulin from astern[7], I was in the best position to see him early and, again, take to the water[8]. I looked about the lifeboat. I couldn't see any sharks.

I looked down between my legs. I thought I would faint for joy.[9] The open locker glistened with shiny new things. Oh, the delight of the manufactured good[10], the man-made device[11], the created thing! That moment of material revelation brought an intensity of pleasure—a heady mix[12] of hope, surprise, disbelief, thrill[13], gratitude, all crushed into one—unequalled[14] in my life by any Christ-

1. j'aurais pu lui pincer les fesses
2. contournable
3. loquet
4. les charnières du couvercle étaient à 2 ou 3 cm
5. les 30 cm
6. posée en travers
7. de la poupe
8. plonger dans l'eau
9. J'ai cru que j'allais m'évanouir de bonheur.
10. la joie de voir des produits manufacturés
11. dispositifs
12. un enivrant mélange
13. excitation
14. inégalé

mas, birthday, wedding, Diwali or other gift-giving occasion[1]. I was positively giddy with happiness[2].

My eyes immediately fell upon what I was looking for. Whether in a bottle, a tin can[3] or a carton[4], water is unmistakably packaged[5]. On this lifeboat, the wine of life was served in pale golden cans that fit nicely in the hand. *Drinking Water* said the vintage label[6] in black letters. *HP Foods Ltd.*[7] were the vintners[8]. *500 ml* were the contents. There were stacks[9] of these cans, too many to count at a glance[10].

With a shaking hand I reached down and picked one up. It was cool to the touch and heavy. I shook it. The bubble of air inside made a dull glub glub glub sound[11]. I was about to be delivered from my hellish[12] thirst. My pulse raced[13] at the thought. I only had to open the can.

I paused. How would I do that?

I had a can—surely I had a can opener[14]? I looked in the locker. There was a great quantity of things. I rummaged about.[15] I was losing patience. Aching expectation had run its fruitful course.[16] I had to drink *now*—or I would die. I could not find the desired instrument. But there was no time for useless distress. Action was needed. Could I prise it open with my fingernails?[17] I tried. I couldn't. My teeth? It wasn't worth trying.[18] I looked over the gunnel. The tarpaulin hooks. Short, blunt[19], solid. I kneeled on the bench and leaned over. Holding the can with both my hands, I sharply brought it up against a hook. A good dint[20]. I did it again. Another dint next to the first. By dint of dinting[21], I managed the trick[22]. A pearl of water appeared. I licked it off.[23] I turned the can and banged the opposite side of the top against the hook to make another hole. I worked like a fiend[24]. I made a larger hole. I sat back on the gunnel. I held the can up to my face. I opened my mouth. I tilted the can.[1]

My feelings can perhaps be imagined, but they can hardly be described. To the gurgling beat[2] of my greedy[3] throat, pure, delicious, beautiful, crystalline water flowed into my system. Liquid life, it was. I drained that golden cup to the very last drop[4], sucking[5] at the hole to catch any remaining moisture[6]. I went, "Ahhhhhh!", tossed[7] the can overboard and got another one. I opened it the way I had the first and its contents vanished just as quickly. That can sailed overboard too, and I opened the next one. Which, shortly, also ended up in the ocean. Another can was dispatched. I drank four cans, two litres of that most exquisite of nectars, before I stopped. You might think such a rapid intake[8] of water after prolonged thirst might upset[9] my system. Nonsense! I never felt better in my life. Why, feel my brow[10]! My forehead was wet with fresh, clean, refreshing perspiration[11]. Everything in me, right down to the pores of my skin, was expressing joy.

A sense of well-being quickly overcame me[12]. My mouth became moist[13] and soft. I forgot about the back of my throat. My skin relaxed. My joints[14] moved with greater ease. My heart began to beat like a merry drum[15] and blood started flowing through my veins like cars from a wedding party honking their way through town[16]. Strength and suppleness[17] came back to my muscles. My head became clearer. Truly, I was coming back to life from the dead. It was glorious, it was glorious. I tell you, to be drunk on alcohol is disgraceful[18], but to be drunk on water is noble and ecstatic. I basked in bliss[19] and plenitude for several minutes.

1. J'ai incliné la canette.
2. Au rythme des lampées
3. avide
4. J'ai vidé cette coupe dorée jusqu'à la dernière goutte
5. suçant
6. toute trace d'humidité restante
7. j'ai jeté
8. absorption
9. perturber
10. front
11. transpiration
12. m'a rapidement envahi
13. humide
14. articulations
15. s'est mis à tambouriner joyeusement
16. qui klaxonnent à travers la ville
17. souplesse
18. déshonorant
19. J'ai nagé dans le bonheur

1. creuse
2. [crêpe à base de farine de lentilles farcie de pommes de terre aux épices]
3. [pizza de l'Inde]
4. [gâteaux salés à base de riz et de lentilles]
5. s'est agitée de manière incontrôlée
6. les délicieuses boules aplaties de riz blanchi
7. chaude matière fumante
8. gorgée de
9. J'ai mâché
10. venant de la lointaine et exotique ville de Bergen, en Norvège
11. compenser
12. sans parler des quelques snacks
13. emballés sous vide
14. blé cuit
15. Tant pis pour la graisse
16. étant donné
17. se boucherait simplement le nez et ferait avec
18. Déchirer ici
19. flèche
20. s'est déchiré
21. emballées dans du papier sulfurisé
22. en sont tombées
23. J'en ai ouvert une.

A certain emptiness made itself felt. I touched my belly. It was a hard and hollow[1] cavity. Food would be nice now. A masala dosai[2] with a coconut chutney—hmmmmm! Even better: oothappam[3]! HMMMMM! Oh! I brought my hands to my mouth—IDLI[4]! The mere thought of the word provoked a shot of pain behind my jaws and a deluge of saliva in my mouth. My right hand started twitching[5]. It reached and nearly touched the delicious flattened balls of parboiled rice[6] in my imagination. It sank its fingers into their steaming hot flesh[7]... It formed a ball soaked with[8] sauce ... It brought it to my mouth ... I chewed[9] ... Oh, it was exquisitely painful!

I looked into the locker for food. I found cartons of Seven Oceans Standard Emergency Ration, from faraway, exotic Bergen, Norway[10]. The breakfast that was to make up for[11] nine missed meals, not to mention odd tiffins[12] that Mother had brought along, came in a half-kilo block, dense, solid and vacuum-packed[13] in silver-coloured plastic that was covered with instructions in twelve languages. In English it said the ration consisted of eighteen fortified biscuits of baked wheat[14], *animal fat* and glucose, and that no more than six should be eaten in a twenty-four-hour period. Pity about the fat[15], but given[16] the exceptional circumstances the vegetarian part of me would simply pinch its nose and bear it[17].

At the top of the block were the words *Tear here*[18] *to open* and a black arrow[19] pointing to the edge of the plastic. The edge gave way[20] under my fingers. Nine wax-paper-wrapped[21] rectangular bars tumbled out[22]. I unwrapped one.[23] It naturally broke into two. Two nearly square biscuits, pale in colour and fragrant in smell. I bit into one. Lord, who would have thought? I never suspected. It was a secret held from me: Norwegian cuisine was the best in the world! These biscuits were amazingly good. They were savoury and delicate to the palate[1], neither too sweet nor too salty. They broke up under the teeth with a delightful crunching sound[2]. Mixed with saliva, they made a granular paste that was enchantment to[3] the tongue and mouth. And when I swallowed, my stomach had only one thing to say: Hallelujah!

The whole package disappeared in a few minutes, wrapping paper flying away in the wind. I considered opening another carton, but I thought better. No harm in exercising a little restraint.[4] Actually, with half a kilo of emergency ration in my stomach, I felt quite heavy.

I decided I should find out what exactly was in the treasure chest[5] before me. It was a large locker, larger than its opening. The space extended right down to the hull and ran some little ways into the side benches. I lowered my feet into the locker and sat on its edge, my back against the stem. I counted the cartons of Seven Ocean. I had eaten one; there were thirty-one left. According to the instructions, each 500-gram carton was supposed to last one survivor three days[6]. That meant I had food rations to last me—31 × 3—93 days! The instructions also suggested survivors restrict themselves to half a litre of water every twenty-four hours. I counted the cans of water. There were 124. Each contained half a litre. So I had water rations to last me 124 days. Never had simple arithmetic brought such a smile to my face.

What else did I have? I plunged my arm eagerly into the locker and brought up one marvellous object after another. Each one, no matter what it was[7],

1. *délicieux et fins au palais*

2. *craquement*

3. *une pâte granuleuse qui ravissait*

4. *Un peu de restriction ne fait pas de mal.*

5. *coffre au trésor*

6. *permettre à un survivant de tenir pendant trois jours*

7. *quel qu'il fût*

1. m'a réconforté

2. Mon besoin de compagnie et de réconfort était tel

3. J'ai marmonné plusieurs fois

4. Après un examen approfondi

5. comprimés

6. couvertures en laine

7. distillateurs solaires d'eau salée

8. seringues contenant de la morphine

9. feux à main

10. rames pouvant flotter

11. fusées à parachute

12. résistants

13. gobelets en verre gradués

14. allumettes étanches

15. seaux

16. écopes

soothed me[1]. I was so sorely in need of company and comfort[2] that the attention brought to making each one of these mass-produced goods felt like a special attention paid to me. I repeatedly mumbled[3], "Thank you! Thank you! Thank you!"

CHAPTER 52

After a thorough investigation[4], I made a complete list:

- 192 tablets[5] of anti-seasickness medicine
- 124 tin cans of fresh water, each containing 500 millilitres, so 62 litres in all
- 32 plastic vomit bags
- 31 cartons of emergency rations, 500 grams each, so 15.5 kilos in all
- 16 wool blankets[6]
- 12 solar stills[7]
- 10 or so orange life jackets, each with an orange, beadless whistle attached by a string
- 6 morphine ampoule syringes[8]
- 6 hand flares[9]
- 5 buoyant oars[10]
- 4 rocket parachute flares[11]
- 3 tough[12], transparent plastic bags, each with a capacity of about 50 litres
- 3 can openers
- 3 graduated glass beakers[13] for drinking
- 2 boxes of waterproof matches[14]
- 2 buoyant orange smoke signals
- 2 mid-size orange plastic buckets[15]
- 2 buoyant orange plastic bailing cups[16]

- 2 multi-purpose plastic containers with air-tight lids[1]
- 2 yellow rectangular sponges
- 2 buoyant synthetic ropes, each 50 metres long
- 2 non-buoyant synthetic ropes of unspecified length, but each at least 30 metres long
- 2 fishing kits[2] with hooks, lines and sinkers[3]
- 2 gaffs with very sharp barbed hooks[4]
- 2 sea anchors[5]
- 2 hatchets[6]
- 2 rain catchers[7]
- 2 black ink ballpoint pens[8]
- 1 nylon cargo net[9]
- 1 solid lifebuoy with an inner diameter of 40 centimetres and an outer diameter of 80 centimetres, and an attached rope
- 1 large hunting knife with a solid handle[10], a pointed end and one edge a sharp blade and the other a sawtoothed blade[11]; attached by a long string to a ring[12] in the locker
- 1 sewing kit[13] with straight and curving needles[14] and strong white thread[15]
- 1 first-aid kit[16] in a waterproof plastic case[17]
- 1 signalling mirror[18]
- 1 pack of filter-tipped[19] Chinese cigarettes
- 1 large bar of dark chocolate
- 1 survival manual
- 1 compass[20]
- 1 notebook[21] with 98 lined[22] pages
- 1 boy with a complete set of light clothing[23] but for one lost shoe[24]

1. aux couvercles hermétiques
2. kits de pêche
3. avec des hameçons, des lignes et des plombs
4. perches munies de crochets métalliques très acérés
5. ancres
6. hachettes
7. récupérateurs d'eau de pluie
8. stylos à bille noirs
9. filet à fret en Nylon
10. couteau de chasse avec un manche solide
11. une lame en dents de scie
12. anneau
13. nécessaire à couture
14. des aiguilles droites et courbées
15. fil
16. trousse de premiers secours
17. dans une pochette en plastique étanche
18. miroir de signalisation
19. avec filtre
20. boussole
21. carnet de notes
22. lignées
23. ensemble complet de vêtements légers pour garçon
24. auquel ne manquait qu'une chaussure

185

- 1 spotted hyena
- 1 Bengal tiger
- 1 lifeboat
- 1 ocean
- 1 God

I ate a quarter of the large chocolate bar. I examined one of the rain catchers. It was a device that looked like an inverted umbrella[1] with a good-sized catchment pouch[2] and a connecting rubber tube[3].

I crossed my arms on the lifebuoy around my waist, brought my head down and fell soundly asleep.

CHAPTER 53

I slept all morning. I was roused[4] by anxiety. That tide[5] of food, water and rest that flowed through my weakened system, bringing me a new lease on life[6], also brought me the strength to see how desperate my situation was. I awoke to the reality of Richard Parker. There was a tiger in the lifeboat. I could hardly believe it, yet I knew I had to. And I had to save myself.

I considered jumping overboard and swimming away, but my body refused to move. I was hundreds of miles from landfall[7], if not over a thousand miles[8]. I couldn't swim such a distance, even with a lifebuoy. What would I eat? What would I drink? How would I keep the sharks away? How would I keep warm? How would I know which way to go? There was not a shadow of doubt about the matter: to leave the lifeboat meant certain death. But what was staying aboard? He would come at me like a

1. un parapluie retourné
2. une poche de récupération de bonne taille
3. tube en caoutchouc
4. réveillé
5. marée
6. qui me faisait renaître
7. la terre ferme
8. voire à plus de mille kilomètres

typical cat, without a sound. Before I knew it he would seize the back of my neck or my throat and I would be pierced by fang-holes[1]. I wouldn't be able to speak. The lifeblood would flow out of me unmarked by a final utterance[2]. Or he would kill me by clubbing me[3] with one of his great paws, breaking my neck.

"I'm going to die", I blubbered through quivering lips[4].

Oncoming death[5] is terrible enough, but worse still[6] is oncoming death with time to spare[7], time in which all the happiness that was yours and all the happiness that might have been yours becomes clear to you. You see with utter[8] lucidity all that you are losing. The sight brings on an oppressive sadness that no car about to hit you[9] or water about to drown you can match[10]. The feeling is truly unbearable. The words *Father, Mother, Ravi, India, Winnipeg* struck me with searing poignancy[11].

I was giving up. I would have given up—if a voice hadn't made itself heard in my heart. The voice said, "I will not die. I refuse it. I will make it through[12] this nightmare. I will beat the odds[13], as great as they are[14]. I have survived so far, miraculously. Now I will turn miracle into routine. The amazing will be seen every day. I will put in all the hard work necessary. Yes, so long as God is with me, I will not die. Amen."

My face set to a grim and determined expression[15]. I speak in all modesty as I say this, but I discovered at that moment that I have a fierce will[16] to live. It's not something evident, in my experience. Some of us give up on life with only a resigned sigh. Others fight a little, then lose hope. Still others—and I am one of those—never give up. We fight and fight and fight. We fight no matter[17]

1. transpercé à coups de crocs

2. sans même un dernier mot

3. en m'assommant

4. ai-je dit en pleurant, les lèvres tremblantes

5. Savoir que l'on va mourir prochainement

6. plus terrible encore

7. en ayant un peu de temps libre devant soi

8. parfaite

9. sur le point de vous renverser

10. ne peuvent égaler

11. une douloureuse intensité

12. Je vais survivre à

13. déjouer les pronostics

14. si mauvais soient-ils

15. a pris une expression sévère et déterminée

16. une volonté farouche

17. quels que soient

the cost of battle, the losses we take[1], the improbability of success. We fight to the very end[2]. It's not a question of courage. It's something constitutional, an inability to let go[3]. It may be nothing more than life-hungry[4] stupidity.

Richard Parker started growling that very instant, as if he had been waiting for me to become a worthy opponent[5]. My chest became tight[6] with fear.

"Quick, man, quick", I wheezed[7]. I had to organize my survival. Not a second to waste. I needed shelter and right away. I thought of the prow[8] I had made with an oar. But now the tarpaulin was unrolled at the bow; there was nothing to hold the oar in place. And I had no proof that hanging at the end of an oar provided real safety from Richard Parker. He might easily reach and nab me[9]. I had to find something else. My mind worked fast.

I built a raft[10]. The oars, if you remember, floated. And I had life jackets and a sturdy[11] lifebuoy.

With bated breath[12] I closed the locker and reached beneath the tarpaulin for the extra oars on the side benches. Richard Parker noticed[13]. I could see him through the life jackets. As I dragged each oar out[14]—you can imagine how carefully—he stirred in reaction. But he did not turn. I pulled out three oars. A fourth was already resting crosswise on the tarpaulin. I raised the locker lid to close the opening onto Richard Parker's den.

I had four buoyant oars. I set them on the tarpaulin around the lifebuoy. The lifebuoy was now squared by the oars[15]. My raft looked like a game of tic-tac-toe[16] with an O in the centre as the first move.

Now came the dangerous part. I needed the life jackets. Richard Parker's growling was now a deep rumble[17] that shook the air. The hyena responded with a whine[1], a wavering, high-pitched whine, a sure sign that trouble was on the way[2].

I had no choice. I had to act. I lowered the lid again. The life jackets were at hand's reach. Some were right against[3] Richard Parker. The hyena broke into a scream[4].

I reached for the closest life jacket. I had difficulty grasping it, my hand was trembling so much. I pulled the jacket out. Richard Parker did not seem to notice. I pulled another one out. And another. I was feeling faint with fear.[5] I was having great difficulty breathing. If need be[6], I told myself, I could throw myself overboard with these life jackets. I pulled a last one out. I had four life jackets.

Pulling the oars in one after the next, I worked them through the armholes[7] of the life jackets—in one armhole, out the other[8]—so that the life jackets became secured[9] to the four corners of the raft. I tied each one shut.[10]

I found one of the buoyant ropes in the locker. With the knife, I cut four segments. I tightly lashed[11] the four oars where they met[12]. Ah, to have had a practical education in knots[13]! At each corner I made ten knots and still I worried that the oars would come apart[14]. I worked feverishly, all the while cursing[15] my stupidity. A tiger aboard and I had waited three days and three nights to save my life!

I cut four more segments of the buoyant rope and tied the lifebuoy to each side of the square. I wove the lifebuoy's rope through[16] the life jackets, around the oars, in and out of the lifebuoy—all round the raft—as yet another precaution against[17] the raft breaking into pieces.

The hyena was now screaming at top pitch.

1. gémissement
2. il allait y avoir du grabuge
3. tout contre
4. s'est mise à hurler
5. Je défaillais d'angoisse.
6. Si nécessaire
7. je les ai fait passer dans les emmanchures
8. les glissant dans une emmanchure et les faisant ressortir par l'autre
9. attachées
10. Je les ai refermées.
11. J'ai fermement arrimé
12. aux endroits où elles se rejoignaient
13. si seulement j'avais appris à faire des nœuds
14. ne se détachent
15. pestant contre
16. J'ai enfilé la corde de la bouée à travers
17. un moyen supplémentaire d'éviter que

One last thing to do. "God, give me the time", I implored. I took the rest of the buoyant line. There was a hole that went through the stem of the boat, near the top. I brought the buoyant rope through it and hitched it[1]. I only had to hitch the other end of the rope to the raft and I might be saved.

The hyena fell silent. My heart stopped and then beat triple speed[2]. I turned.

"Jesus, Mary, Muhammad and Vishnu!"

I saw a sight[3] that will stay with me for the rest of my days. Richard Parker had risen and emerged. He was not fifteen feet[4] from me. Oh, the size of him[5]! The hyena's end had come, and mine. I stood rooted to the spot[6], paralyzed, in thrall to[7] the action before my eyes. My brief experience with the relations of unconfined[8] wild animals in lifeboats had made me expect great noise and protest when the time came for bloodshed[9]. But it happened practically in silence. The hyena died neither whining nor whimpering, and Richard Parker killed without a sound. The flame-coloured carnivore emerged from beneath the tarpaulin and made for the hyena. The hyena was leaning against the stern bench, behind the zebra's carcass, transfixed[10]. It did not put up a fight.[11] Instead it shrank[12] to the floor, lifting a forepaw in a futile gesture of defence. The look on its face was of terror. A massive paw landed on its shoulders. Richard Parker's jaws closed on the side of the hyena's neck. Its glazed eyes[13] widened[14]. There was a noise of organic crunching[15] as windpipe[16] and spinal cord[17] were crushed[18]. The hyena shook. Its eyes went dull[19]. It was over.

Richard Parker let go and growled. But a quiet growl, private and half-hearted[20], it seemed. He was panting, his tongue hanging from his mouth. He licked his chops[21]. He shook his head. He

1. je l'ai accrochée

2. a battu à tout rompre

3. une scène

4. à moins de 5 mètres

5. la taille qu'il faisait

6. cloué sur place

7. subjugué par

8. non enfermés

9. l'effusion de sang

10. pétrifiée

11. Elle ne s'est pas défendue.

12. elle s'est tapie

13. Ses yeux vitreux

14. se sont écarquillés

15. craquement

16. la trachée

17. la moelle épinière

18. broyées

19. se sont éteints

20. dépourvu d'enthousiasme

21. côtes

sniffed[1] the dead hyena. He raised his head high and smelled the air. He placed his forepaws on the stern bench and lifted himself. His feet were wide apart. The rolling of the boat, though gentle, was visibly not to his liking. He looked beyond the gunnel at the open seas. He put out a low, mean[2] snarl. He smelled the air again. He slowly turned his head. It turned—turned—turned full round—till he was looking straight at me.

I wish I could describe what happened next, not as I saw it, which I might manage[3], but as I felt it. I beheld Richard Parker from the angle that showed him off to greatest effect[4]: from the back, half-raised, with his head turned. The stance[5] had something of a pose to it[6], as if it were an intentional, even affected, display of mighty art[7]. And what art, what might. His presence was overwhelming[8], yet equally evident was the lithesome[9] grace of it. He was incredibly muscular, yet his haunches were thin and his glossy coat hung loosely on his frame[10]. His body, bright brownish orange streaked with black vertical stripes[11], was incomparably beautiful, matched[12] with a tailor[13]'s eye for harmony by his pure white chest and underside[14] and the black rings[15] of his long tail. His head was large and round, displaying formidable sideburns[16], a stylish goatee[17] and some of the finest whiskers[18] of the cat world, thick, long and white. Atop the head were small, expressive ears shaped like perfect arches. His carrot orange face had a broad bridge[19] and a pink nose, and it was made up with brazen flair[20]. Wavy dabs of black[21] circled[22] the face in a pattern that was striking yet subtle, for it brought less attention to itself than it did to the one part of the face left untouched by it, the bridge, whose rufous lustre[23] shone near-

1. Il a reniflé

2. méchant

3. ce dont j'étais capable

4. qui le montrait sous son côté le plus impressionnant

5. Cette position

6. ressemblait à une pose

7. démonstration de puissance et d'art

8. imposante

9. élégante

10. son pelage brillant pendait sur son squelette

11. rayé de bandes verticales noires

12. assorti

13. tailleur

14. ventre

15. anneaux

16. roufla-quettes

17. un élégant bouc

18. moustaches

19. arête

20. un talent insolent

21. Des rayures noires ondulées

22. entouraient

23. dont l'éclat rouge orangé

1. brillait presque
2. taches
3. joues
4. ajoutaient les touches finales
5. [théâtre dansé du sud de l'Inde, aux maquillages et costumes multicolores]
6. les ailes d'un papillon
7. déterminé
8. fuyant
9. sang-froid
10. elles ont pivoté sur elles-mêmes
11. subreptice-ment
12. hérissé
13. Venu de nulle part
14. maigrichon
15. rongeur
16. a sauté par-dessus
17. cuir chevelu
18. comme si sa vie en dépendait
19. pesante
20. recourbée
21. étaient plaquées contre

ly with a radiance[1]. The patches[2] of white above the eyes, on the cheeks[3] and around the mouth came off as finishing touches[4] worthy of a Kathakali[5] dancer. The result was a face that looked like the wings of a butterfly[6] and bore an expression vaguely old and Chinese. But when Richard Parker's amber eyes met mine, the stare was intense, cold and unflinching[7], not flighty[8] or friendly, and spoke of self-possession[9] on the point of exploding with rage. His ears twitched and then swivelled right around[10]. One of his lips began to rise and fall. The yellow canine thus coyly[11] revealed was as long as my longest finger.

Every hair on me was standing up[12], shrieking with fear.

That's when the rat appeared. Out of nowhere[13], a scrawny[14] brown rat materialized on the side bench, nervous and breathless. Richard Parker looked as astonished as I was. The rat leapt onto the tarpaulin and raced my way. At the sight, in shock and surprise, my legs gave way beneath me and I practically fell into the locker. Before my incredulous eyes the rodent[15] hopped over[16] the various parts of the raft, jumped onto me and climbed to the top of my head, where I felt its little claws clamping down on my scalp[17], holding on for dear life[18].

Richard Parker's eyes had followed the rat. They were now fixed on my head.

He completed the turn of his head with a slow turn of his body, moving his forepaws sideways along the side bench. He dropped to the floor of the boat with ponderous[19] ease. I could see the top of his head, his back and his long, curled[20] tail. His ears lay flat against[21] his skull. In three paces he was at the middle of the boat. Without effort the front half of his body rose in the air and his forepaws came to rest on the rolled-up edge of the tarpaulin.

He was less than ten feet away[1]. His head, his chest, his paws—so big! so big! His teeth—an entire army battalion in a mouth. He was making to jump onto the tarpaulin. I was about to die.

But the tarpaulin's strange softness bothered him[2]. He pressed at it tentatively[3]. He looked up anxiously—the exposure to[4] so much light and open space did not please him either. And the rolling motion of the boat continued to unsettle him[5]. For a brief moment, Richard Parker was hesitating.

I grabbed the rat and threw it his way[6]. I can still see it in my mind as it sailed[7] through the air—its outstretched[8] claws and erect[9] tail, its tiny elongated scrotum[10] and pinpoint[11] anus. Richard Parker opened his maw[12] and the squealing rat disappeared into it like a baseball into a catcher's mitt[13]. Its hairless tail vanished like a spaghetti noodle sucked into a mouth.

He seemed satisfied with the offering[14]. He backed down[15] and returned beneath the tarpaulin. My legs instantly became functional[16] again. I leapt up and raised the locker lid again to block the open space between bow bench and tarpaulin.

I heard loud sniffing and the noise of a body being dragged. His shifting weight made the boat rock a little. I began hearing the sound of a mouth eating. I peeked beneath the tarpaulin. He was in the middle of the boat. He was eating the hyena by great chunks, voraciously. This chance would not come again. I reached and retrieved the remaining life jackets[17]—six in all—and the last oar. They would go to improving[18] the raft. I noticed in passing a smell. It was not the sharp smell of cat piss. It was vomit. There was a patch of it on the floor of

1. à moins de 3 mètres

2. le dérangeait

3. d'une manière hésitante

4. être exposé à

5. le déstabiliser

6. dans sa direction

7. en train de voler

8. sorties

9. dressée

10. son minuscule scrotum allongé

11. tout petit

12. la gueule

13. le gant d'un receveur

14. cette offrande

15. Il s'est éloigné

16. ont retrouvé leur usage

17. J'ai attrapé les gilets de sauvetage restants

18. Ils serviraient à améliorer

the boat. It must have come from Richard Parker. So he was indeed seasick.

I hitched the long rope to the raft. Lifeboat and raft were now tethered[1]. Next I attached a life jacket to each side of the raft, on its underside. Another life jacket I strapped across the hole of the lifebuoy to act as a seat. I turned the last oar into a foot-rest[2], lashing it[3] on one side of the raft, about two feet[4] from the lifebuoy, and tying[5] the remaining life jacket to it. My fingers trembled as I worked, and my breath was short and strained[6]. I checked and rechecked all my knots.

I looked about the sea. Only great, gentle swells[7]. No whitecaps.[8] The wind was low and constant. I looked down. There were fish—big fish with protruding[9] foreheads and very long dorsal fins[10], *dorados* they are called, and smaller fish, lean[11] and long, unknown to me, and smaller ones still—and there were sharks.

I eased the raft off the lifeboat.[12] If for some reason it did not float, I was as good as dead[13]. It took to the water beautifully. In fact, the buoyancy of the life jackets was such that they pushed the oars and the lifebuoy right out of the water. But my heart sank[14]. As soon as the raft touched the water, the fish scattered[15]—except for the sharks. They remained. Three or four of them. One swam directly beneath the raft. Richard Parker growled.

I felt like a prisoner being pushed off a plank by pirates.

I brought the raft as close to the lifeboat as the protruding tips[16] of the oars would allow[17]. I leaned out and lay my hands on the lifebuoy. Through the "cracks[18]" in the floor of the raft—yawning crevasses[19] would be more accurate[20]—I looked directly into the bottomless depths[21] of the sea. I heard

---

Marginal glossary:

1. attachés
2. un repose-pied
3. en la ficelant
4. à environ 60 centimètres
5. attachant
6. je respirais rapidement et difficilement
7. vagues
8. Pas de crêtes.
9. protubérants
10. nageoires
11. fins
12. J'ai mis le radeau à l'eau.
13. condamné
14. s'est serré
15. se sont dispersés
16. les bouts saillants
17. le permettaient
18. fissures
19. les gouffres
20. approprié
21. les profondeurs insondables

Richard Parker again. I flopped[1] onto the raft on my stomach. I lay flat and spread-eagled[2] and did not move a finger. I expected the raft to overturn[3] at any moment. Or a shark to lunge and bite right through the life jackets and oars. Neither happened. The raft sank lower[4] and pitched and rolled[5], the tips of the oars dipping underwater, but it floated robustly. Sharks came close, but did not touch.

I felt a gentle tug[6]. The raft swung round[7]. I raised my head. The lifeboat and the raft had already separated as far as the rope would go, about forty feet[8]. The rope tensed and lifted out of the water and wavered[9] in the air. It was a highly distressing sight.[10] I had fled the lifeboat to save my life. Now I wanted to get back. This raft business was far too precarious. It only needed a shark to bite the rope, or a knot to become undone[11], or a large wave to crash upon me[12], and I would be lost. Compared to the raft, the lifeboat now seemed a haven[13] of comfort and security.

I gingerly turned over.[14] I sat up. Stability was good, so far. My footrest worked well enough. But it was all too small. There was just enough space to sit on and no more. This toy raft[15], mini-raft, micro-raft, might do for a pond[16], but not for the Pacific Ocean. I took hold of the rope and pulled. The closer I got to the lifeboat, the slower I pulled. When I was next to the lifeboat, I heard Richard Parker. He was still eating.

I hesitated for long minutes.

I stayed on the raft. I didn't see what else I could do. My options were limited to perching above a tiger or hovering[17] over sharks. I knew perfectly well how dangerous Richard Parker was. Sharks, on the other hand, had not yet proved to be dangerous. I checked the knots that held the rope to the lifeboat

1. Je me suis laissé tomber

2. bras et jambes écartés

3. se retourner

4. s'est enfoncé dans l'eau

5. a tangué

6. un petit coup sec

7. a pivoté sur lui-même

8. 12 mètres

9. s'est alternativement tendue et relâchée

10. J'observais ce spectacle avec angoisse.

11. qu'un nœud se défasse

12. qu'une grosse vague vienne s'écraser sur moi

13. havre

14. Je me suis retourné précautionneusement.

15. Ce radeau miniature

16. étang

17. flotter

1. à environ
9 mètres

2. contrebalan-
çait à peu près
correctement

3. Le bout de
corde qui restait

4. je l'ai enroulé

5. lâcher du mou

6. si nécessaire

7. déluge

8. criblant

9. J'ai claqué
le couvercle du
caisson.

10. a glissé

11. lui bouchait
la vue

12. jaillir

13. fendant l'air

and to the raft. I let the rope out until I was thirty or so feet[1] from the lifeboat, the distance that about rightly balanced[2] my two fears: being too close to Richard Parker and being too far from the lifeboat. The extra rope[3], ten feet or so, I looped[4] around the footrest oar. I could easily let out slack[5] if the need arose[6].

The day was ending. It started to rain. It had been overcast and warm all day. Now the temperature dropped, and the downpour[7] was steady and cold. All around me heavy drops of fresh water plopped loudly and wastefully into the sea, dimpling[8] its surface. I pulled on the rope again. When I was at the bow I turned onto my knees and took hold of the stem. I pulled myself up and carefully peeped over the gunnel. He wasn't in sight.

I hurriedly reached down into the locker. I grabbed a rain catcher, a fifty-litre plastic bag, a blanket and the survival manual. I slammed the locker lid shut.[9] I didn't mean to slam it—only to protect my precious goods from the rain—but the lid slipped[10] from my wet hand. It was a bad mistake. In the very act of revealing myself to Richard Parker by bringing down what blocked his view[11], I made a great loud noise to attract his attention. He was crouched over the hyena. His head turned instantly. Many animals intensely dislike being disturbed while they are eating. Richard Parker snarled. His claws tensed. The tip of his tail twitched electrically. I fell back onto the raft, and I believe it was terror as much as wind and current that widened the distance between raft and lifeboat so swiftly. I let out all the rope. I expected Richard Parker to burst forth[12] from the boat, sailing through the air[13], teeth and claws reaching for me.

I kept my eyes on the boat. The longer I looked, the more unbearable was the expectation[1].

He did not appear.

By the time[2] I had opened the rain catcher above my head and tucked[3] my feet into the plastic bag, I was already soaked to the bones[4]. And the blanket had got wet when I fell back onto the raft. I wrapped myself with it nonetheless.

Night crept up[5]. My surroundings disappeared into pitch-black darkness[6]. Only the regular tugging[7] of the rope at the raft told me that I was still attached to the lifeboat. The sea, inches beneath me yet too far for my eyes, buffeted[8] the raft. Fingers of water reached up[9] furtively through the cracks and wet my bottom.

CHAPTER 54

It rained all night. I had a horrible, sleepless time of it. It was noisy. On the rain catcher the rain made a drumming sound[10], and around me, coming from the darkness beyond, it made a hissing sound[11], as if I were at the centre of a great nest[12] of angry snakes. Shifts in the wind changed the direction of the rain so that parts of me that were beginning to feel warm were soaked anew[13]. I shifted the rain catcher, only to be unpleasantly surprised a few minutes later when the wind changed once more. I tried to keep a small part of me dry and warm, around my chest, where I had placed the survival manual, but the wetness spread with perverse determination. I spent the whole night shivering with cold. I worried constantly that the raft would come apart[14], that the knots holding me to the lifeboat

1. plus l'attente était insupportable
2. Lorsque
3. j'ai eu glissé
4. trempé jusqu'aux os
5. est tombée lentement
6. une obscurité totale
7. tiraillements
8. ballottait
9. s'introduisaient
10. un bruit de tambour
11. un sifflement
12. nid
13. trempées de nouveau
14. J'avais constamment peur que le radeau se défasse

would become loose[1], that a shark would attack. With my hands I checked the knots and lashings incessantly, trying to read them the way a blind man[2] would read Braille.

The rain grew stronger and the sea rougher[3] as the night progressed. The rope to the lifeboat tautened with a jerk[4] rather than with a tug[5], and the rocking[6] of the raft became more pronounced and erratic[7]. It continued to float, rising above every wave, but there was no freeboard[8] and the surf of every breaking wave rode clear across it[9], washing around me like a river washing around a boulder[10]. The sea was warmer than the rain, but it meant that not the smallest part of me stayed dry that night.

At least I drank. I wasn't really thirsty, but I forced myself to drink. The rain catcher looked like an inverted umbrella, an umbrella blown open by the wind. The rain flowed to its centre, where there was a hole. The hole was connected by a rubber tube to a catchment pouch[11] made of thick, transparent plastic. At first the water had a rubbery[12] taste, but quickly the rain rinsed[13] the catcher and the water tasted fine.

During those long, cold, dark hours, as the pattering[14] of the invisible rain got to be deafening[15], and the sea hissed[16] and coiled[17] and tossed me about[18], I held on to one thought: Richard Parker. I hatched[19] several plans to get rid of him[20] so that the lifeboat might be mine.

Plan Number One: Push Him off the Lifeboat[21]. What good would that do?[22] Even if I did manage to shove[23] 450 pounds[24] of living, fierce animal off the lifeboat, tigers are accomplished swimmers[25]. In the Sundarbans they have been known to swim five miles[26] in open, choppy waters[27]. If he found himself unexpectedly overboard, Richard Parker would simply tread water[1], climb back aboard and make me pay the price for my treachery[2].

Plan Number Two: Kill Him with the Six Morphine Syringes. But I had no idea what effect they would have on him. Would they be enough to kill him? And how exactly was I supposed to get the morphine into his system? I could remotely[3] conceive surprising him once, for an instant, the way his mother had been when she was captured—but to surprise him long enough to give him *six consecutive injections*? Impossible. All I would do by pricking him with a needle[4] would be to get a cuff[5] in return that would take my head off[6].

Plan Number Three: Attack Him with All Available Weaponry[7]. Ludicrous.[8] I wasn't Tarzan. I was a puny[9], feeble, vegetarian life form. In India it took riding atop[10] great big elephants and shooting with powerful rifles to kill tigers. What was I supposed to do here? Fire off a rocket flare in his face?[11] Go at him with a hatchet in each hand and a knife between my teeth? Finish him off with straight and curving sewing needles? If I managed to *nick* him[12], it would be a feat[13]. In return he would tear me apart limb by limb, organ by organ. For if there's one thing more dangerous than a healthy animal, it's an injured animal.

Plan Number Four: Choke Him[14]. I had rope. If I stayed at the bow and got the rope to go around the stern and a noose[15] to go around his neck, I could pull on the rope while he pulled to get at me. And so, in the very act of reaching for me, he would choke himself. A clever, suicidal plan.

Plan Number Five: Poison Him, Set Him on Fire[16], Electrocute Him. How? With what?

Plan Number Six: Wage a War of Attrition[17]. All I had to do was let the unforgiving[18] laws of na-

---

1. nagerait sur place
2. trahison
3. vaguement
4. en le piquant avec une aiguille
5. une claque
6. m'arracherait la tête
7. toutes les armes disponibles
8. Ridicule.
9. chétive
10. il fallait chevaucher
11. Lui envoyer une fusée en pleine tête ?
12. lui faire une petite entaille
13. exploit
14. l'étrangler
15. nœud coulant
16. le brûler
17. livrer une guerre d'usure
18. impitoyables

1. suivre leur cours
2. Attendre qu'il dépérisse
3. ne nécessitait
4. des provisions pour plusieurs mois
5. quelle que soit sa force
6. une période prolongée
7. Une petite lueur d'espoir s'est allumée
8. le mettre en œuvre

ture run their course[1] and I would be saved. Waiting for him to waste away[2] and die would require[3] no effort on my part. I had supplies for months to come[4]. What did he have? Just a few dead animals that would soon go bad. What would he eat after that? Better still: where would he get water? He might last for weeks without food, but no animal, however mighty[5], can do without water for any extended period of time[6].

A modest glow of hope flickered to life[7] within me, like a candle in the night. I had a plan and it was a good one. I only needed to survive to put it into effect[8].

CHAPTER 55

9. L'aube
10. depuis des hauteurs vertigineuses
11. se jetaient sur moi
12. m'écrasaient
13. Les yeux ternes
14. engourdi
15. soudaineté
16. accentuée
17. s'enfuir
18. lisse

Dawn[9] came and matters were worse for it. Because now, emerging from the darkness, I could see what before I had only felt, the great curtains of rain crashing down on me from towering heights[10] and the waves that threw a path over me[11] and trod me underfoot[12] one after another.

Dull-eyed[13], shaking and numb[14], one hand gripping the rain catcher, the other clinging to the raft, I continued to wait.

Sometime later, with a suddenness[15] emphasized[16] by the silence that followed, the rain stopped. The sky cleared and the waves seemed to flee[17] with the clouds. The change was as quick and radical as changing countries on land. I was now in a different ocean. Soon the sun was alone in the sky, and the ocean was a smooth[18] skin reflecting the light with a million mirrors.

I was stiff, sore[1] and exhausted, barely grateful to be still alive. The words "Plan Number Six, Plan Number Six, Plan Number Six" repeated themselves in my mind like a mantra and brought me a small measure of comfort, though I couldn't recall for the life of me[2] what Plan Number Six was. Warmth started coming to my bones. I closed the rain catcher. I wrapped myself with the blanket and curled up[3] on my side in such a way that no part of me touched the water. I fell asleep. I don't know how long I slept. It was mid-morning when I awoke, and hot. The blanket was nearly dry. It had been a brief bout of deep sleep[4]. I lifted myself onto an elbow[5].

All about me was flatness and infinity, an endless panorama of blue. There was nothing to block my view. The vastness hit me like a punch[6] in the stomach. I fell back, winded[7]. This raft was a joke. It was nothing but a few sticks[8] and a little cork[9] held together by string. Water came through every crack. The depth beneath would make a bird dizzy. I caught sight of the lifeboat. It was no better than half a walnut shell[10]. It held on to the surface of the water like fingers gripping the edge of a cliff[11]. It was only a matter of time before gravity pulled it down.

My fellow castaway[12] came into view. He raised himself onto the gunnel and looked my way. The sudden appearance of a tiger is arresting[13] in any environment, but it was all the more so here. The weird contrast between the bright, striped, living orange of his coat and the inert white of the boat's hull was incredibly compelling[14]. My overwrought[15] senses screeched to a halt[16]. Vast as the Pacific was[17] around us, suddenly, between us, it seemed a very narrow moat[18], with no bars[19] or walls.

1. courbaturé, plein de douleurs

2. il m'était impossible de me souvenir

3. je me suis pelotonné

4. une courte période de sommeil profond

5. coude

6. coup de poing

7. essoufflé

8. bouts de bois

9. un peu de liège

10. une demi-coquille de noix

11. falaise

12. Mon compagnon de naufrage

13. saisissante

14. fascinant

15. émoussés

16. se sont brusquement figés

17. Malgré l'immensité du Pacifique

18. il ne semblait y avoir que d'étroites douves

19. barreaux

"Plan Number Six, Plan Number Six, Plan Number Six", my mind whispered urgently. But what *was* Plan Number Six? Ah yes. The war of attrition. The waiting game. Passivity. Letting things happen. The unforgiving laws of nature. The relentless march[1] of time and the hoarding[2] of resources. That was Plan Number Six.

A thought rang in my mind like an angry shout: "You fool and idiot! You dimwit![3] You brainless[4] baboon! *Plan Number Six is the worst plan of all!* Richard Parker is afraid of the sea right now. It was nearly his grave[5]. But crazed with[6] thirst and hunger he will surmount his fear, and he will do whatever is necessary to appease his need. He will turn this moat into a bridge.[7] He will swim as far as he has to, to catch the drifting raft and the food upon it. As for water, have you forgotten that tigers from the Sundarbans are known to drink saline water? Do you really think you can outlast his kidneys[8]? I tell you, if you wage a war of attrition, you will lose it! You will *die*! IS THAT CLEAR?"

CHAPTER 56

I must say a word about fear. It is life's only true opponent[9]. Only fear can defeat life. It is a clever, treacherous[10] adversary, how well I know. It has no decency, respects no law or convention, shows no mercy[11]. It goes for your weakest spot[12], which it finds with unerring ease[13]. It begins in your mind, always. One moment you are feeling calm, self-possessed, happy. Then fear, disguised in the garb of mild-mannered doubt[14], slips[15] into your mind like a spy[16]. Doubt meets disbelief and disbelief tries to

1. La marche inexorable
2. stockage

3. Espèce d'imbécile !
4. sans cervelle
5. tombe
6. une fois rendu fou par
7. Il transformera ces douves en pont.

8. survivre plus longtemps que ses reins

9. adversaire
10. traître
11. pitié
12. Elle cible votre point faible
13. avec une grande facilité
14. déguisée sous les traits du placide doute
15. s'introduit
16. espion

push it out. But disbelief is a poorly armed foot sol-dier[1]. Doubt does away with it with little trouble. You become anxious. Reason comes to do battle for you. You are reassured. Reason is fully equipped with the latest weapons technology[2]. But, to your amazement[3], despite superior tactics and a number of undeniable victories, reason is laid low[4]. You feel yourself weakening, wavering[5]. Your anxiety becomes dread[6].

Fear next turns fully to your body, which is already aware that something terribly wrong is going on. Already your lungs[7] have flown away[8] like a bird and your guts have slithered away[9] like a snake. Now your tongue drops dead like an opossum[10], while your jaw begins to gallop on the spot[11]. Your ears go deaf[12]. Your muscles begin to shiver as if they had malaria and your knees to shake as though they were dancing. Your heart strains too hard[13], while your sphincter relaxes too much. And so with the rest of your body. Every part of you, in the manner most suited to it[14], falls apart[15]. Only your eyes work well. They always pay proper attention to fear.

Quickly you make rash[16] decisions. You dismiss[17] your last allies: hope and trust. There[18], you've defeated yourself. Fear, which is but an impression, has triumphed over you.

The matter is difficult to put into words. For fear, real fear, such as shakes you to your foundation[19], such as you feel when you are brought face to face with your mortal end, nestles[20] in your memory like a gangrene: it seeks to rot[21] everything, even the words with which to speak of it. So you must fight hard to express it. You must fight hard to shine the light of words upon it[22]. Because if you don't, if your fear becomes a wordless darkness that you

1. un fantassin mal armé

2. la technologie militaire la plus récente

3. à votre surprise

4. dépose les armes

5. hésitant

6. de l'effroi

7. poumons

8. se sont envolés

9. vos intestins se sont enfuis

10. fait la morte

11. sur place

12. n'entendent plus rien

13. fait trop d'efforts

14. qui lui est la plus appropriée

15. tombe en morceaux

16. inconsidérées

17. Vous congédiez

18. Voilà

19. celle qui vous ébranle jusque dans vos fondations

20. est nichée

21. pourrir

22. pour que la lumière des mots l'éclaire

avoid[1], perhaps even manage to forget, you open yourself to further attacks of fear because you never truly fought the opponent who defeated you[2].

CHAPTER 57

It was Richard Parker who calmed me down. It is the irony of this story that the one who scared me witless[3] to start with was the very same who brought me peace, purpose[4], I dare say even wholeness[5].

He was looking at me intently. After a time I recognized the gaze[6]. I had grown up with it. It was the gaze of a contented animal looking out from its cage or pit the way you or I would look out from a restaurant table after a good meal, when the time has come for conversation and people-watching. Clearly, Richard Parker had eaten his fill of hyena[7] and drunk all the rainwater he wanted. No lips were rising and falling, no teeth were showing, no growling or snarling was coming from him. He was simply taking me in, observing me, in a manner that was sober but not menacing. He kept twitching[8] his ears and varying the sideways turn[9] of his head. It was all so, well, *catlike*[10]. He looked like a nice, big, fat domestic cat, a 450-pound tabby[11].

He made a sound, a snort[12] from his nostrils. I pricked up my ears.[13] He did it a second time. I was astonished. *Prusten*?

Tigers make a variety of sounds. They include a number of roars and growls, the loudest of these being most likely the full-throated[14] *aaonh*, usually made during the mating season[15] by males and oestrous[16] females. It's a cry that travels far and wide[17], and is absolutely petrifying when heard close up[18].

1. vous évitez
2. qui vous a vaincu
3. me faisait une peur bleue
4. la détermination
5. un sentiment de plénitude
6. ce regard
7. avait eu tout son content d'hyène
8. remuer
9. rotation
10. félin
11. chat tigré
12. reniflement
13. J'ai tendu l'oreille.
14. retentissant
15. la saison des amours
16. en chaleur
17. a une très longue portée
18. de près

Tigers go *woof*[1] when they are caught unawares[2], a short, sharp detonation[3] of fury that would instantly make your legs jump up and run away if they weren't frozen to the spot[4]. When they charge, tigers put out throaty, coughing roars[5]. The growl they use for purposes of threatening has yet another guttural quality. And tigers hiss and snarl, which, depending on the emotion behind it, sounds either like autumn leaves rustling[6] on the ground, but a little more resonant, or, when it's an infuriated[7] snarl, like a giant door with rusty hinges[8] slowly opening—in both cases, utterly spine—chilling[9]. Tigers make other sounds too. They grunt and they moan. They purr[10], though not as melodiously or as frequently as small cats, and only as they breathe out[11]. (Only small cats purr breathing both ways. It is one of the characteristics that distinguishes big cats from small cats. Another is that only big cats can roar. A good thing that is. I'm afraid the popularity of the domestic cat would drop very quickly if little kitty[12] could roar its displeasure.) Tigers even go *meow*[13], with an inflection similar to that of domestic cats, but louder and in a deeper range[14], not as encouraging to one to bend down[15] and pick them up[16]. And tigers can be utterly[17], majestically silent, that too.

I had heard all these sounds growing up. Except for prusten. If I knew of it, it was because Father had told me about it. He had read descriptions of it in the literature. But he had heard it only once, while on a working visit[18] to the Mysore Zoo, in their animal hospital, from a young male being treated for pneumonia. Prusten is the quietest of tiger calls, a puff through the nose[19] to express friendliness[20] and harmless intentions[21].

1. ouah
2. pris par surprise
3. explosion
4. clouées sur place
5. poussent des rugissements gutturaux, comme s'ils toussaient
6. bruissant
7. furieux
8. des charnières rouillées
9. à vous glacer le sang
10. Ils ronronnent
11. ils expirent
12. le petit matou
13. miaou
14. plus grave
15. se baisser
16. les prendre dans ses bras
17. parfaitement
18. en visite de travail
19. un reniflement
20. une attitude amicale
21. de bonnes intentions

Richard Parker did it again, this time with a rolling of the head[1]. He looked exactly as if he were asking me a question.

I looked at him, full of fearful wonder[2]. There being no immediate threat, my breath slowed down, my heart stopped knocking about in my chest, and I began to regain my senses.

I had to tame him.[3] It was at that moment that I realized this necessity. It was not a question of him or me, but of him *and* me. We were, literally and figuratively, in the same boat. We would live—or we would die—together. He might be killed in an accident, or he could die shortly of natural causes, but it would be foolish[4] to count on such an eventuality. More likely the worst would happen: the simple passage of time, in which his animal toughness[5] would easily outlast my human frailty[6]. Only if I tamed him could I possibly trick him into[7] dying first, if we had to come to that sorry business[8].

But there's more to it. I will come clean.[9] I will tell you a secret: a part of me was glad[10] about Richard Parker. A part of me did not want Richard Parker to die at all, because if he died I would be left alone with despair, a foe[11] even more formidable[12] than a tiger. If I still had the will to live[13], it was thanks to Richard Parker. He kept me from[14] thinking too much about my family and my tragic circumstances. He pushed me to go on living. I hated him for it, yet at the same time I was grateful. I *am* grateful. It's the plain truth: without Richard Parker, I wouldn't be alive today to tell you my story.

I looked around at the horizon. Didn't I have here a perfect circus ring, inescapably[15] round, without a single corner for him to hide in? I looked down at the sea. Wasn't this an ideal source of treats[16] with which to condition him to obey? I noticed a whistle hanging from one of the life jackets. Wouldn't this make a good whip[1] with which to keep him in line[2]? What was missing here to tame[3] Richard Parker? Time? It might be weeks before a ship sighted me[4]. I had all the time in the world. Resolve?[5] There's nothing like extreme need to give you resolve. Knowledge? Was I not a zookeeper's son? Reward? Was there any reward greater than life? Any punishment worse than death? I looked at Richard Parker. My panic was gone. My fear was dominated. Survival was at hand[6].

Let the trumpets blare.[7] Let the drums roll.[8] Let the show begin. I rose to my feet.[9] Richard Parker noticed. The balance was not easy.[10] I took a deep breath[11] and shouted, "Ladies and gentlemen, boys and girls, hurry to your seats! Hurry, hurry. You don't want to be late. Sit down, open your eyes, open your hearts and prepare to be amazed. Here it is, for your enjoyment and instruction, for your gratification[12] and edification, the show you've been waiting for all your life, THE GREATEST SHOW ON EARTH! Are you ready for the miracle of it? Yes? Well then: they are amazingly adaptable. You've seen them in freezing, snow-covered temperate forests. You've seen them in dense, tropical monsoon jungles. You've seen them in sparse, semi-arid scrublands[13]. You've seen them in brackish mangrove swamps[14]. Truly, they would fit anywhere. But you've never seen them where you are about to see them now! Ladies and gentlemen, boys and girls, without further ado[15], it is my pleasure and honour to present to you: THE PI PATEL, INDO-CANADIAN, TRANS-PACIFIC, FLOATING CIRCUUUUUSSSSSSSSSSSS!!! *TREEEEEE! TREEEEEE! TREEEEEE! TREEEEEE! TREEEEEE! TREEEEEE!*"

---

1. fouet
2. le faire obéir
3. apprivoiser
4. ne me voie
5. De la détermination ?

6. à portée de main
7. Sonnez trompettes.
8. Battez tambours.
9. Je me suis mis debout.
10. J'avais du mal à tenir en équilibre.
11. J'ai inspiré profondément
12. satisfaction

13. des garrigues semi-arides, à la végétation clairsemée
14. des mangroves saumâtres
15. sans plus attendre

1. il s'est recroquevillé

I had an effect on Richard Parker. At the very first blow of the whistle he cringed[1] and he snarled. Ha! Let him jump into the water if he wanted to! Let him try!

"*TREEEEEE! TREEEEEE! TREEEEEE! TREEEEEE! TREEEEEE! TREEEEEE!*"

2. a griffé

3. sur laquelle je pouvais compter

He roared and he clawed[2] the air. But he did not jump. He might not be afraid of the sea when he was driven mad by hunger and thirst, but for the time being it was a fear I could rely on[3].

"*TREEEEEE! TREEEEEE! TREEEEEE! TREEEEEE! TREEEEEE! TREEEEEE!*"

4. Il a reculé

5. séance d'entraînement

6. un franc succès

7. hors d'haleine

8. le garder en vie

He backed off[4] and dropped to the bottom of the boat. The first training session[5] was over. It was a resounding success[6]. I stopped whistling and sat down heavily on the raft, out of breath[7] and exhausted.

And so it came to be:

Plan Number Seven: Keep Him Alive[8].

CHAPTER 58

9. J'ai sorti

10. un commandant de la marine britannique

11. beaucoup de

12. des conseils de

I pulled out[9] the survival manual. Its pages were still wet. I turned them carefully. The manual was written by a British Royal Navy commander[10]. It contained a wealth of[11] practical information on surviving at sea after a shipwreck. It included survival tips[12] such as:

- Always read instructions carefully.

- Do not drink urine. Or sea water. Or bird blood.

13. de méduses

14. piquants

15. des becs de perroquet

16. se gonflent

- Do not eat jellyfish[13]. Or fish that are armed with spikes[14]. Or that have parrot-like beaks[15]. Or that puff up[16] like balloons.

- Pressing the eyes of fish will paralyze them.

- The body can be a hero in battle. If a cast-away[1] is injured, beware of[2] well-meaning but ill-founded[3] medical treatment. Ignorance is the worst doctor, while rest and sleep are the best nurses[4].

- Put up your feet[5] at least five minutes every hour.

- Unnecessary exertion[6] should be avoided. But an idle mind[7] tends to sink[8], so the mind should be kept occupied with whatever light[9] distraction may suggest itself. Playing card games, Twenty Questions[10] and I Spy With My Little Eye[11] are excellent forms of simple recreation. Community singing[12] is another sure-fire way to lift the spirits[13]. Yarn spinning[14] is also highly recommended.

- Green water is shallower[15] than blue water.

- Beware of far-off[16] clouds that look like mountains. Look for green. Ultimately, a foot is the only good judge of land.

- Do not go swimming. It wastes energy. Besides, a survival craft[17] may drift[18] faster than you can swim. Not to mention the danger of sea life. If you are hot, wet your clothes instead.

- Do not urinate in your clothes. The momentary warmth is not worth the nappy rash[19].

- Shelter yourself.[20] Exposure can kill faster than thirst or hunger.

- So long as no excessive water is lost through perspiration[21], the body can survive up to fourteen days without water. If you feel thirsty, suck[22] a button.

- Turtles are an easy catch[23] and make for ex-

1. naufragé
2. méfiez-vous des
3. bien intentionnés mais injustifiés
4. infirmières
5. Surélevez vos pieds
6. efforts
7. un esprit inactif
8. sombrer dans la déprime
9. légère
10. des jeux de devinette
11. « Je vois quelque chose qui commence par. . . »
12. Chanter à plusieurs
13. moyen infaillible de se remonter le moral
14. Les travaux de filature
15. moins profonde
16. éloignés
17. embarcation
18. dériver
19. ne vaut pas des fesses irritées
20. Abritez-vous.
21. transpiration
22. sucez
23. sont faciles à attraper

1. nourrissante

2. un vrai régal

3. Attention aux

4. Ne vous laissez pas abattre.

5. Vous pouvez vous sentir découragé

6. énigmatiques

7. vu d'une hauteur de 1,50 m

8. à 4 km

9. ne sera jamais, au grand jamais, vu avec

10. pipi

11. brochure

12. mariné dans l'eau salée

13. sujet

14. abordé

15. relations de domination

16. parasites

17. concevoir un programme d'entraînement

18. formellement interdit

cellent meals. Their blood is a good, nutritious, salt-free drink; their flesh is tasty and filling[1]; their fat has many uses; and the castaway will find turtle eggs a real treat[2]. Mind the[3] beak and the claws.

• Don't let your morale flag.[4] Be daunted[5], but not defeated. Remember: the spirit, above all else, counts. If you have the will to live, you will. Good luck!

There were also a few highly cryptic[6] lines distilling the art and science of navigation. I learned that the horizon, as seen from a height of five feet[7] on a calm day, was two and a half miles away[8].

The injunction not to drink urine was quite unnecessary. No one called "Pissing" in his childhood would be caught dead with[9] a cup of pee[10] at his lips, even alone in a lifeboat in the middle of the Pacific. And the gastronomic suggestions only confirmed to my mind that the English didn't know the meaning of the word *food*. Otherwise, the manual was a fascinating pamphlet[11] on how to avoid being pickled in brine[12]. Only one important topic[13] was not addressed[14]: the establishing of alpha-omega relationships[15] with major lifeboat pests[16].

I had to devise a training program[17] for Richard Parker. I had to make him understand that I was the top tiger and that his territory was limited to the floor of the boat, the stern bench and the side benches as far as the middle cross bench. I had to fix in his mind that the top of the tarpaulin and the bow of the boat, bordered by the neutral territory of the middle bench, was *my* territory and utterly forbidden[18] to him.

I had to start fishing very soon. It would not take long for Richard Parker to finish the animal carcasses. At the zoo the adult lions and tigers ate on average ten pounds[1] of meat a day.

1. 4,5 kilos

There were many other things I had to do. I had to find a means of sheltering myself. If Richard Parker stayed under the tarpaulin all the time, it was for a good reason. To be continuously outside, exposed to sun, wind, rain and sea, was exhausting, and not only to the body but also to the mind. Hadn't I just read that exposure could inflict[2] a quick death? I had to devise some sort of canopy[3].

2. provoquer
3. toit

I had to tie the raft to the lifeboat with a second rope, in case the first should break or become loose.

I had to improve the raft. At present it was seaworthy[4], but hardly[5] habitable. I would have to make it fit for living in until I could move to my permanent quarters[6] on the lifeboat. For example, I had to find a way to stay dry on it. My skin was wrinkled and swollen all over[7] from being constantly wet. That had to change. And I had to find a way to store[8] things on the raft.

4. en état de naviguer
5. à peine
6. quartiers
7. ridée et gonflée de partout
8. entreposer

I had to stop hoping so much that a ship would rescue me. I should not count on outside help. Survival had to start with me. In my experience, a castaway's worst mistake is to hope too much and do too little. Survival starts by paying attention to what is close at hand[9] and immediate. To look out[10] with idle hope[11] is tantamount to[12] dreaming one's life away[13].

9. à portée de main
10. Regarder autour de soi
11. sans rien faire d'autre qu'espérer
12. revient à
13. gâcher sa vie à rêvasser

There was much I had to do.

I looked out at the empty horizon. There was so much water. And I was all alone. All alone.

I burst into hot tears. I buried my face in my crossed arms and sobbed[14]. My situation was patently[15] hopeless.

14. j'ai sangloté
15. manifestement

CHAPTER 59

Alone or not, lost or not, I was thirsty and hungry. I pulled on the rope. There was a slight tension. As soon as I lessened my grip on it[1], it slid out[2], and the distance between the lifeboat and the raft increased. So the lifeboat drifted faster than the raft, pulling it along[3]. I noted the fact without thinking anything of it. My mind was more focused on the doings of Richard Parker.

By the looks of it, he was under the tarpaulin.

I pulled the rope till I was right next to the bow. I reached up to the gunnel.[4] As I was crouched[5], preparing myself for a quick raid[6] on the locker[7], a series of waves got me thinking[8]. I noticed that with the raft next to it, the lifeboat had changed directions. It was no longer perpendicular to the waves but broadside to them[9] and was beginning to roll from side to side, that rolling that was so unsettling[10] for the stomach. The reason for this change became clear to me: the raft, when let out[11], was acting as a sea anchor[12], as a drag[13] that pulled on the lifeboat and turned its bow to face the waves. You see, waves and steady winds are usually perpendicular to each other. So, if a boat is pushed by a wind but held back[14] by a sea anchor, it will turn until it offers the least resistance to the wind—that is, until it is in line with it[15] and at right angles[16] to the waves, which makes for a front-to-back pitching[17] that is much more comfortable than a side-to-side rolling[18]. With the raft next to the boat, the dragging effect was gone[19], and there was nothing to steer[20] the boat head into the wind[21]. Therefore it turned broadside and rolled.

---

1. j'ai desserré la main
2. elle s'est déroulée
3. le tirant derrière lui
4. J'ai posé la main sur le plat-bord.
5. accroupi
6. à foncer vers
7. caisson
8. m'ont fait réfléchir
9. en travers de la lame
10. perturbant
11. quand la corde était relâchée
12. ancre
13. frein
14. retenu
15. jusqu'à ce qu'il aille dans le sens du vent
16. soit perpendiculaire
17. une oscillation d'avant en arrière
18. un balancement latéral
19. la résistance disparaissait
20. diriger
21. dans le sens du vent

What may seem like a detail to you was something which would save my life and which Richard Parker would come to regret.

As if to confirm my fresh insight[1], I heard him growl. It was a disconsolate[2] growl, with something indefinably green and queasy[3] in its tone. He was maybe a good swimmer, but he was not much of a sailor[4].

I had a chance yet.[5]

Lest[6] I got cocky[7] about my abilities to manipulate him, I received at that moment a quiet[8] but sinister warning[9] about what I was up against[10]. It seemed Richard Parker was such a magnetic pole of life, so charismatic in his vitality, that other expressions of life found it intolerable. I was on the point of raising myself over the bow when I heard a gentle thrashing buzz[11]. I saw something small land[12] in the water next to me.

It was a cockroach[13]. It floated for a second or two before being swallowed by an underwater mouth. Another cockroach landed in the water. In the next minute, ten or so cockroaches plopped into the water[14] on either side of the bow. Each was claimed[15] by a fish.

The last of the foreign life forms was abandoning ship.

I carefully brought my eyes over the gunnel. The first thing I saw, lying in a fold[16] of the tarpaulin above the bow bench, was a large cockroach, perhaps the patriarch of the clan. I watched it, strangely interested. When it decided it was time, it deployed its wings, rose in the air with a minute clattering[17], hovered[18] above the lifeboat momentarily, as if making sure no one had been left behind, and then veered overboard[19] to its death.

1. ma nouvelle découverte

2. plaintif

3. nauséeux

4. il n'avait pas le pied marin

5. Il me restait encore une chance.

6. De peur que

7. trop sûr de moi

8. silencieux

9. avertissement

10. ce à quoi je me confrontais

11. un léger vrombissement

12. tomber

13. cafard

14. sont tombés dans l'eau

15. a été attrapé

16. pli

17. un léger cliquetis

18. a voltigé

19. a viré par-dessus bord

Now we were two. In five days the populations of orang-utans, zebras, hyenas, rats, flies and cockroaches had been wiped out[1]. Except for the bacteria and worms[2] that might still be alive in the remains of the animals, there was no other life left on the lifeboat but Richard Parker and me.

It was not a comforting thought[3].

I lifted myself and breathlessly opened the locker lid. I deliberately did not look under the tarpaulin for fear that looking would be like shouting and would attract Richard Parker's attention. Only once the lid was leaning against the tarpaulin did I dare let my senses consider what was beyond it.

A smell came to my nose, a musky[4] smell of urine, quite sharp[5], what every cat cage in a zoo smells of. Tigers are highly territorial, and it is with their urine that they mark the boundaries[6] of their territory. Here was good news wearing a foul dress[7]: the odour was coming exclusively from below the tarpaulin. Richard Parker's territorial claims seemed to be limited to the floor of the boat. This held promise. If I could make the tarpaulin mine, we might get along.

I held my breath, lowered my head and cocked it to the side[8] to see beyond the edge of the lid. There was rainwater, about four inches[9] of it, sloshing about the floor of the lifeboat[10]—Richard Parker's own freshwater pond[11]. He was doing exactly what I would be doing in his place: cooling off in the shade[12]. The day was getting beastly[13] hot. He was flat[14] on the floor of the boat, facing away from me, his hind legs sticking straight back and splayed out[15], back paws facing up[16], and stomach and inner thighs[17] lying directly against the floor. The position looked silly but was no doubt very pleasant.

1. éliminées
2. vers
3. une pensée réconfortante
4. musquée
5. assez forte
6. frontières
7. qui ne présageait rien de bon
8. l'ai penchée sur le côté
9. 10 centimètres
10. qui clapotait au fond du canot
11. bassin d'eau douce
12. se rafraîchir à l'ombre
13. horriblement
14. collé
15. étendues vers l'arrière et écartées
16. tournées vers le ciel
17. cuisses

I returned to the business of survival. I opened a carton of emergency ration and ate my fill[1], about one-third of the package. It was remarkable how little it took[2] to make my stomach feel full. I was about to drink from the rain-catcher pouch slung across my shoulder when my eyes fell upon the graduated drinking beakers. If I couldn't go for a dip[3], could I at least have a sip[4]? My own supplies of water would not last forever. I took hold of one of the beakers, leaned over[5], lowered the lid just as much as I needed to and tremulously dipped[6] the beaker into Parker's Pond, four feet[7] from his back paws. His upturned pads with their wet fur looked like little desert islands surrounded by seaweed[8].

I brought back a good 500 millilitres. It was a little discoloured.[9] Specks[10] were floating in it. Did I worry about ingesting some horrid bacteria? I didn't even think about it. All I had on my mind was my thirst. I drained that beaker to the dregs[11] with great satisfaction.

Nature is preoccupied with balance, so it did not surprise me that nearly right away I felt the urge to urinate. I relieved myself[12] in the beaker. I produced so exactly the amount I had just downed[13] that it was as if a minute hadn't passed and I were still considering Richard Parker's rainwater. I hesitated. I felt the urge[14] to tilt the beaker[15] into my mouth once more. I resisted the temptation. But it was hard. Mockery be damned[16], my urine looked delicious! I was not suffering yet from dehydration, so the liquid was pale in colour. It glowed in the sunlight, looking like a glass of apple juice. And it was guaranteed fresh, which certainly couldn't be said of the canned water[17] that was my staple[18]. But I heeded my better judgment[19]. I splashed[20] my

1. de quoi me rassasier

2. le peu de nourriture dont j'avais besoin

3. je ne pouvais pas m'y baigner

4. en prendre une gorgée

5. je me suis penché

6. j'ai plongé en tremblant

7. à à peine plus d'un mètre

8. des algues

9. L'eau était un peu trouble.

10. Des petites particules

11. J'ai vidé ce gobelet jusqu'à la dernière goutte

12. Je me suis soulagé

13. la quantité que je venais de boire

14. l'envie pressante

15. verser le contenu du gobelet

16. Au diable les railleries

17. des cannettes d'eau

18. ma boisson de base

19. j'ai écouté mon bon sens

20. J'ai versé

urine on the tarpaulin and over the locker lid to stake my claim[1].

I stole another two beakers of water from Richard Parker, without urinating this time. I felt as freshly watered[2] as a potted plant[3].

Now it was time to improve my situation. I turned to the contents of the locker and the many promises they held.

I brought out a second rope and tethered[4] the raft to the lifeboat with it.

I discovered what a solar still is. A solar still is a device to produce fresh water from salt water. It consists of an inflatable[5] transparent cone set upon[6] a round lifebuoy-like buoyancy chamber that has a surface of black rubberized canvas[7] stretched[8] across its centre. The still operates on the principle of distillation: sea water lying beneath the sealed[9] cone on the black canvas is heated[10] by the sun and evaporates, gathering[11] on the inside surface of the cone. This salt-free water trickles down[12] and collects[13] in a gully[14] on the perimeter of the cone, from which it drains[15] into a pouch. The lifeboat came equipped with twelve solar stills. I read the instructions carefully, as the survival manual told me to. I inflated[16] all twelve cones with air and I filled each buoyancy chamber with the requisite ten litres of sea water. I strung[17] the stills together, tying one end of the flotilla to the lifeboat and the other to the raft, which meant that not only would I not lose any stills should one of my knots become loose[18], but also that I had, in effect, a second emergency rope to keep me tethered to the lifeboat. The stills looked pretty and very technological as they floated on the water, but they also looked flimsy[19], and I was doubtful of their capacity to produce fresh water.

I directed my attention to improving the raft. I examined every knot that held it together, making sure each was tight and secure. After some thought[1], I decided to transform the fifth oar, the footrest oar, into a mast of sorts[2]. I undid the oar. With the sawtoothed edge[3] of the hunting knife I painstakingly cut a notch[4] into it, about halfway down[5], and with the knife's point I drilled[6] three holes through its flat[7] part. Work was slow but satisfying. It kept my mind busy. When I had finished I lashed[8] the oar in a vertical position to the inside of one of the corners of the raft, flat part, the masthead[9], rising in the air, handle[10] disappearing underwater. I ran the rope tightly into the notch, to prevent the oar from slipping down[11]. Next, to ensure[12] that the mast would stand straight[13], and to give myself lines[14] from which to hang a canopy and supplies, I threaded[15] ropes through the holes I had drilled in the masthead and tied them to the tips of the horizontal oars. I strapped[16] the life jacket that had been attached to the footrest oar to the base of the mast. It would play a double role: it would provide extra flotation[17] to compensate for the vertical weight of the mast, and it would make for a slightly raised seat for me[18].

I threw a blanket over the lines. It slid down.[19] The angle of the lines was too steep.[20] I folded the lengthwise edge of the blanket over once[21], cut two holes midway down[22], about a foot apart[23], and linked the holes with a piece of string, which I made by unweaving a length of rope[24]. I threw the blanket over the lines again, with the new girdle string going around the masthead. I now had a canopy.

It took me a good part of the day to fix up the raft. There were so many details to look after. The

1. Après réflexion
2. une sorte de mât
3. le côté en dents de scie
4. j'ai minutieusement creusé une encoche
5. au milieu
6. j'ai percé
7. plate
8. j'ai arrimé
9. la tête de mât
10. le manche
11. pour empêcher la rame de glisser vers le bas
12. pour m'assurer
13. serait droit
14. des cordes
15. j'ai enfilé
16. J'ai attaché
17. une meilleure flottaison
18. elle me permettrait d'avoir un siège légèrement surélevé
19. Elle a glissé.
20. Les cordes étaient trop inclinées.
21. J'ai plié la couverture une fois dans le sens de la longueur
22. au milieu
23. à environ 30 cm l'un de l'autre
24. en détachant les fils d'une corde

constant motion of the sea, though gentle, didn't make my work any easier. And I had to keep an eye on Richard Parker. The result was no galleon[1]. The mast, so called, ended hardly a few inches above my head. As for the deck, it was just big enough to sit on cross-legged[2] or to lie on in a tight, near-ly-to-term fetal position[3]. But I wasn't complaining. It was seaworthy and it would save me from Richard Parker.

By the time I had finished my work, the afternoon was nearing its end[4]. I gathered a can of water, a can opener, four biscuits of survival ration and four blankets. I closed the locker (very softly this time), sat down on the raft and let out[5] the rope. The life-boat drifted away. The main rope tensed, while the security rope, which I had deliberately measured out longer, hung limply[6]. I laid two blankets beneath me, carefully folding them so that they didn't touch the water. I wrapped the other two around my shoulders and rested[7] my back against the mast. I enjoyed the slight[8] elevation I gained from sitting on the extra life jacket. I was hardly higher up from the water than one would be from a floor sitting on a thick cushion; still, I hoped not to get wet so much.

I enjoyed my meal as I watched the sun's descent in a cloudless sky. It was a relaxing moment. The vault[9] of the world was magnificently tinted[10]. The stars were eager[11] to participate; hardly[12] had the blanket of colour been pulled a little than they started to shine through[13] the deep blue. The wind blew with a faint[14], warm breeze and the sea moved about kindly, the water peaking and troughing[15] like people dancing in a circle who come together and raise[16] their hands and move apart[17] and come together[18] again, over and over[19].

Side glossary (left margin):

1. galion
2. en tailleur
3. dans la position inconfortable d'un fœtus proche du terme
4. approchait de sa fin
5. j'ai lâché
6. pendait mollement
7. j'ai appuyé
8. légère
9. voûte
10. avait des teintes magnifiques
11. pressées
12. à peine
13. briller à travers
14. légère
15. montant et descendant
16. lèvent
17. s'éloignent
18. se rapprochent
19. encore et encore

Richard Parker sat up. Only his head and a little of his shoulders showed above the gunnel. He looked out.[1] I shouted, "Hello, Richard Parker!" and I waved. He looked at me. He snorted or sneezed[2], neither word quite captures it[3]. Prusten again. What a stunning[4] creature. Such a noble mien[5]. How apt[6] that in full it is[7] a *Royal* Bengal tiger. I counted myself lucky[8] in a way. What if I had ended up with a creature that looked silly or ugly, a tapir or an ostrich or a flock of turkeys[9]? That would have been a more trying[10] companionship in some ways.

I heard a splash. I looked down at the water. I gasped. I thought I was alone. The stillness[11] in the air, the glory of the light, the feeling of comparative safety[12]—all had made me think so. There is commonly an element of silence and solitude to peace, isn't there? It's hard to imagine being at peace in a busy subway station[13], isn't it? So what was all this commotion[14]?

With just one glance I discovered that the sea is a city. Just below me, all around, unsuspected by me[15], were highways[16], boulevards, streets and roundabouts[17] bustling with[18] submarine traffic. In water that was dense, glassy and flecked by millions of lit-up specks of plankton[19], fish like trucks[20] and buses and cars and bicycles and pedestrians[21] were madly racing about[22], no doubt honking and hollering[23] at each other. The predominant colour was green. At multiple depths, as far as I could see, there were evanescent trails[24] of phosphorescent green bubbles, the wake[25] of speeding fish. As soon as one trail faded[26], another appeared. These trails came from all directions and disappeared in all directions. They were like those time-exposure[27] photographs you see of cities at night, with the long red streaks[28] made by the tail lights of cars. Ex-

1. Il a regardé autour de lui.
2. il a éternué
3. ne correspond parfaitement
4. sensationnelle
5. air
6. Comme il est approprié
7. son nom complet soit
8. Je me considérais chanceux
9. un troupeau de dindes
10. pénible
11. tranquillité
12. relative sécurité
13. une station de métro très fréquentée
14. agitation
15. sans que je ne me doute de rien
16. des autoroutes
17. des ronds-points
18. animés de
19. mouchetée de millions d'organismes planctoniques lumineux
20. des camions
21. des piétons haxonnant et braillant
24. traînées
25. sillage
26. s'estompait
27. prises avec un long temps de pose
28. traits

cept that here the cars were driving above and under each other as if they were on interchanges that were stacked ten storeys high[1]. And here the cars were of the craziest colours. The dorados—there must have been over fifty patrolling beneath the raft—showed off their bright gold, blue and green as they whisked by[2]. Other fish that I could not identify were yellow, brown, silver, blue, red, pink, green, white, in all kinds of combinations, solid, streaked and speckled[3]. Only the sharks stubbornly[4] refused to be colourful. But whatever the size or colour of a vehicle, one thing was constant: the furious driving[5]. There were many collisions—all involving fatalities[6], I'm afraid—and a number of cars spun wildly out of control[7] and collided against[8] barriers, bursting[9] above the surface of the water and splashing down in showers of luminescence. I gazed upon this urban hurly-burly[10] like someone observing a city from a hot-air balloon[11]. It was a spectacle wondrous and awe-inspiring[12]. This is surely what Tokyo must look like at rush hour[13].

I looked on until the lights went out in the city.

From the *Tsimtsum* all I had seen were dolphins. I had assumed that the Pacific, but for passing schools of fish[14], was a sparsely inhabited waste of water[15]. I have learned since that cargo ships travel too quickly for fish. You are as likely to see sea life from a ship as you are to see wildlife[16] in a forest from a car on a highway. Dolphins, very fast swimmers, play about boats and ships much like dogs chase[17] cars: they race along[18] until they can no longer keep up[19]. If you want to see wildlife, it is on foot, and quietly, that you must explore a forest. It is the same with the sea. You must stroll[20] through the Pacific at a walking pace[21], so to speak, to see the wealth[22] and abundance that it holds.

I settled on my side. For the first time in five days I felt a measure of calm[1]. A little bit of hope—hard earned[2], well deserved[3], reasonable—glowed in me. I fell asleep.

CHAPTER 60

I awoke once during the night. I pushed the canopy aside and looked out. The moon was a sharply defined crescent[4] and the sky was perfectly clear. The stars shone with such fierce, contained brilliance[5] that it seemed absurd to call the night dark. The sea lay quietly, bathed in a shy, light-footed light[6], a dancing play of black and silver that extended without limits all about me. The volume of things was confounding[7]—the volume of air above me, the volume of water around and beneath me. I was half-moved, half-terrified. I felt like the sage Markandeya, who fell out of Vishnu's mouth while Vishnu was sleeping and so beheld the entire universe, everything that there is. Before the sage could die of fright[8], Vishnu awoke and took him back into his mouth. For the first time I noticed—as I would notice repeatedly during my ordeal[9], between one throe of agony and the next[10]—that my suffering was taking place in a grand setting[11]. I saw my suffering for what it was, finite[12] and insignificant, and I was still[13]. My suffering did not fit anywhere[14], I realized. And I could accept this. It was all right. (It was daylight that brought my protest: "No! No! No! My suffering *does* matter. I want to live! I can't help but mix my life with that of the universe. Life is a peephole[15], a single tiny entry onto a vastness[16]—how can I not dwell[17] on this

1. un certain calme
2. durement gagné
3. bien mérité
4. un croissant très nettement dessiné
5. un éclat si vif et si clairement délimité
6. baignée d'une lumière discrète et douce
7. déconcertant
8. peur
9. mon calvaire
10. entre deux moments d'angoisse
11. dans un cadre exceptionnel
12. limitée
13. calme
14. n'avait sa place nulle part
15. un judas
16. un vaste univers
17. m'attarder

1. perspective brève et limitée

brief, cramped view[1] I have of things? This peep-hole is all I've got!") I mumbled words of Muslim prayer and went back to sleep.

CHAPTER 61

The next morning I was not too wet and I was feeling strong. I thought this was remarkable considering[2] the strain I was under[3] and how little I had eaten in the last several days.

2. étant donné
3. la fatigue que j'éprouvais

It was a fine day. I decided to try my hand at fishing, for the first time in my life. After a breakfast of three biscuits and one can of water, I read what the survival manual had to say on the subject. The first problem arose: bait[4]. I thought about it. There were the dead animals, but stealing food from under a tiger's nose was a proposition I was not up to[5]. He would not realize that it was an investment that would bring him an excellent return[6]. I decided to use my leather[7] shoe. I had only one left. The other I had lost when the ship sank.

4. les appâts
5. une possibilité dont je ne me sentais pas capable
6. rendement
7. en cuir

I crept up to the lifeboat and I gathered from the locker one of the fishing kits, the knife and a bucket for my catch[8]. Richard Parker was lying on his side. His tail jumped to life[9] when I was at the bow but his head did not lift. I let the raft out.

8. les poissons que je prendrais
9. a bougé
10. hameçon
11. un bas de ligne en acier
12. plombs
13. de torpille
14. épais
15. J'ai prudemment enfoncé

I attached a hook[10] to a wire leader[11], which I tied to a line. I added some lead weights[12]. I picked three that had an intriguing torpedo[13] shape. I removed my shoe and cut it into pieces. It was hard work; the leather was tough[14]. I carefully worked[15] the hook into a flat piece of hide, not through it but into it, so that the point of the hook was hidden. I let the line down deep. There had been so many fish the previous evening that I expected easy success.

I had none. The whole shoe disappeared bit by bit[1], slight tug on the line by slight tug on the line[2], happy freeloading[3] fish by happy freeloading fish, bare hook by bare hook, until I was left with only the rubber sole[4] and the shoelace[5]. When the shoelace proved an unconvincing earthworm[6], out of sheer[7] exasperation I tried the sole, all of it. It was not a good idea. I felt a slight, promising tug and then the line was unexpectedly[8] light. All I pulled in was line. I had lost the whole tackle[9].

This loss did not strike me as a terrible blow.[10] There were other hooks, leader wires and weights in the kit, besides a whole other kit. And I wasn't even fishing for myself. I had plenty of food in store[11].

Still, a part of my mind—the one that says what we don't want to hear—rebuked me[12]. "Stupidity has a price. You should show more care and wisdom next time."

Later that morning a second turtle appeared. It came right up to the raft. It could have reached up[13] and bit my bottom[14] if it had wanted to. When it turned I reached for its hind flipper[15], but as soon as I touched it I recoiled in horror[16]. The turtle swam away.

The same part of my mind that had rebuked me over my fishing fiasco scolded me again. "What exactly do you intend to feed that tiger of yours? How much longer do you think he'll last on three dead animals? Do I need to remind you that tigers are not carrion[17] eaters? Granted[18], when he's on his last legs[19] he probably won't lift his nose at much. But don't you think that before he submits to eating puffy[20], putrefied zebra he'll try the fresh, juicy

1. peu à peu
2. après chaque tiraillement sur la ligne
3. resquilleur
4. la semelle en caoutchouc
5. lacet
6. ver de terre
7. pure
8. étonnamment
9. tout le matériel
10. Cette perte ne m'a pas semblé terrible.
11. en stock
12. m'a fait des reproches
13. Elle aurait pu lever la tête
14. me mordre les fesses
15. nageoire postérieure
16. j'ai reculé d'horreur
17. de charognes
18. Certes
19. au bout du rouleau
20. bouffi

Indian boy just a short dip away[1]? And how are we doing with the water situation? You know how tigers get impatient with thirst. Have you smelled his breath[2] recently? It's pretty awful. That's a bad sign. Perhaps you're hoping that he'll lap up the Pacific[3] and in quenching[4] his thirst allow you to walk to America[5]? Quite amazing, this limited capacity to excrete salt that Sundarbans tigers have developed. Comes from living in a tidal mangrove forest, I suppose. But it *is* a limited capacity. Don't they say that drinking too much saline water makes a man-eater of a tiger? Oh, look. Speak of the devil.[6] There he is. He's yawning.[7] My, my[8], what an enormous pink cave[9]. Look at those long yellow stalactites and stalagmites. Maybe today you'll get a chance to visit."

Richard Parker's tongue, the size and colour of a rubber hot-water bottle[10], retreated and his mouth closed. He swallowed.

I spent the rest of the day worrying myself sick[11]. I stayed away from the lifeboat. Despite my own dire[12] predictions, Richard Parker passed the time calmly enough. He still had water from the rainfall and he didn't seem too concerned with hunger. But he did make various tiger noises—growls and moans and the like[13]—that did nothing to put me at ease[14]. The riddle seemed irresolvable[15]: to fish I needed bait, but I would have bait only once I had fish. What was I supposed to do? Use one of my toes[16]? Cut off one of my ears?[17]

A solution appeared in the late afternoon in a most unexpected way. I had pulled myself up to the lifeboat.[18] More than that: I had climbed aboard and was rummaging through[19] the locker, feverishly looking for an idea that would save my life. I had tied the raft so that it was about six feet[20] from the boat. I fancied[21] that with a jump[22] and a pull at a loose knot[1] I could save myself from Richard Parker. Desperation had pushed me to take such a risk.

Finding nothing, no bait and no new idea, I sat up—only to discover that I was dead centre in the focus of his stare[2]. He was at the other end of the lifeboat, where the zebra used to be, turned my way and sitting up, looking as if he'd been patiently waiting for me to notice him. How was it that I hadn't heard him stir? What delusion was I under[3] that I thought I could outwit him[4]? Suddenly I was hit hard across the face[5]. I cried out[6] and closed my eyes. With feline speed he had leapt across the lifeboat and struck me. I was to have my face clawed off[7]—this was the gruesome[8] way I was to die. The pain was so severe I felt nothing. Blessed be shock.[9] Blessed be that part of us that protects us from too much pain and sorrow[10]. At the heart of life is a fuse box[11]. I whimpered, "Go ahead, Richard Parker, finish me off[12]. But please, what you must do, do it quickly. A blown fuse[13] should not be overtested[14]."

He was taking his time. He was at my feet, making noises. No doubt he had discovered the locker and its riches. I fearfully opened an eye.

It was a fish. There was a fish in the locker. It was flopping about like a fish out of water. It was about fifteen inches long[15] and it had wings. A flying fish. Slim and dark grey-blue, with dry, featherless[16] wings and round, unblinking[17], yellowish eyes. It was this flying fish that had struck me across the face, not Richard Parker. He was still fifteen feet away[18], no doubt wondering what I was going on about. But he had seen the fish. I could read a keen[19] curiosity on his face. He seemed about ready to investigate[20].

1. en tirant sur un nœud à peine serré

2. il avait les yeux rivés sur moi

3. Quelle illusion m'avait fait croire

4. me montrer plus malin que lui

5. j'ai reçu un grand coup au visage

6. J'ai poussé un cri

7. déchirée à coups de griffes

8. horrible

9. Béni soit le choc.

10. chagrin

11. une boîte à fusibles

12. achève-moi

13. Un fusible grillé

14. trop testé

15. Il faisait environ 40 cm de long

16. sans plumes

17. qui ne clignaient pas

18. à 4,50 mètres de moi

19. vive

20. l'examiner

I bent down, picked up the fish and threw it towards him. This was the way to tame him![1] Where a rat had gone, a flying fish would follow. Unfortunately, the flying fish flew. In mid-air, just ahead of Richard Parker's open mouth, the fish swerved[2] and dropped into the water. It happened with lightning speed[3]. Richard Parker turned his head and snapped[4] his mouth, jowls flapping[5], but the fish was too quick for him. He looked astonished and displeased[6]. He turned to me again. "Where's my treat?" his face seemed to inquire. Fear and sadness gripped me[7]. I turned with the half-hearted[8], half-abandoned hope that I could jump onto the raft before he could jump onto me.

At that precise instant there was a vibration in the air and we were struck by a school[9] of flying fish. They came like a swarm of locusts[10]. It was not only their numbers; there was also something insect-like about the clicking, whirring sound[11] of their wings. They burst out of the water, dozens of them at a time, some of them flick-flacking over a hundred yards[12] through the air. Many dived[13] into the water just before the boat. A number sailed clear over it[14]. Some crashed into[15] its side, sounding like firecrackers going off[16]. Several lucky ones returned to the water after a bounce[17] on the tarpaulin. Others, less fortunate[18], fell directly into the boat, where they started a racket[19] of flapping and flailing and splashing[20]. And still others flew right into us. Standing unprotected as I was, I felt I was living the martyrdom[21] of Saint Sebastian. Every fish that hit me was like an arrow[22] entering my flesh. I clutched at[23] a blanket to protect myself while also trying to catch some of the fish. I received cuts and bruises[24] all over my body.

The reason for this onslaught[1] became evident immediately: dorados were leaping out of the water in hot pursuit of them. The much larger dorados couldn't match their flying[2], but they were faster swimmers and their short lunges[3] were very powerful. They could overtake[4] flying fish if they were just behind them and lunging from the water at the same time and in the same direction. There were sharks too; they also leapt out of the water, not so cleanly but with devastating consequence for some dorados. This aquatic mayhem[5] didn't last long, but while it did, the sea bubbled and boiled, fish jumped and jaws worked hard.

Richard Parker was tougher than I was in the face of these fish, and far more efficient. He raised himself and went about[6] blocking, swiping[7] and biting all the fish he could. Many were eaten live and whole, struggling wings beating in his mouth. It was a dazzling display[8] of might and speed. Actually, it was not so much the speed that was impressive as the pure animal confidence, the total absorption in the moment. Such a mix of ease and concentration, such a being-in-the-present, would be the envy of the highest yogis.

When it was over, the result, besides a very sore body[9] for me, was six flying fish in the locker and a much greater number in the lifeboat. I hurriedly wrapped a fish in a blanket, gathered a hatchet and made for the raft.

I proceeded with great deliberation. The loss of my tackle[10] that morning had had a sobering effect on me[11]. I couldn't allow myself another mistake. I unwrapped the fish carefully, keeping a hand pressed down[12] on it, fully aware that it would try to jump away to save itself. The closer the fish was to appearing, the more afraid and disgusted I be-

1. attaque

2. ne pouvaient pas voler comme eux

3. bonds

4. dépasser

5. pagaille

6. s'est mis à

7. frapper à toute volée

8. une impressionnante démonstration

9. un corps tout endolori

10. matériel de pêche

11. m'avait donné à réfléchir

12. appuyée

came. Its head came into sight[1]. The way I was holding it, it looked like a scoop of loathsome fish ice cream[2] sticking out[3] of a wool blanket cone[4]. The thing was gasping for water[5], its mouth and gills[6] opening and closing slowly. I could feel it pushing with its wings against my hand. I turned the bucket over[7] and brought its head against the bottom. I took hold of the hatchet. I raised it in the air.

Several times I started bringing the hatchet down, but I couldn't complete the action. Such sentimentalism may seem ridiculous considering what I had witnessed[8] in the last days, but those were the deeds[9] of others, of predatory animals. I suppose I was partly responsible for the rat's death, but I'd only thrown it; it was Richard Parker who had killed it. A lifetime of peaceful vegetarianism stood between me and the willful beheading[10] of a fish.

I covered the fish's head with the blanket and turned the hatchet around[11]. Again my hand wavered[12] in the air. The idea of beating a soft, living head with a hammer[13] was simply too much.

I put the hatchet down. I would break its neck, sight unseen[14], I decided. I wrapped the fish tightly[15] in the blanket. With both hands I started bending it[16]. The more I pressed, the more the fish struggled. I imagined what it would feel like if I were wrapped in a blanket and someone were trying to break my neck. I was appalled[17]. I gave up a number of times. Yet I knew it had to be done, and the longer I waited, the longer the fish's suffering would go on.

Tears flowing down my cheeks, I egged myself on[18] until I heard a cracking sound and I no longer felt any life fighting in my hands. I pulled back the folds of the blanket. The flying fish was dead. It was split open[1] and bloody on one side of its head, at the level of the gills.

I wept heartily over[2] this poor little deceased[3] soul. It was the first sentient being[4] I had ever killed. I was now a killer. I was now as guilty[5] as Cain. I was sixteen years old, a harmless[6] boy, bookish[7] and religious, and now I had blood on my hands. It's a terrible burden[8] to carry. All sentient life is sacred. I never forget to include this fish in my prayers.

After that it was easier. Now that it was dead, the flying fish looked like fish I had seen in the markets of Pondicherry. It was something else, something outside the essential scheme of creation. I chopped it up into pieces[9] with the hatchet and put it in the bucket.

In the dying hours of the day[10] I tried fishing again. At first I had no better luck[11] than I'd had in the morning. But success seemed less elusive[12]. The fish nibbled at[13] the hook with fervour. Their interest was evident. I realized that these were small fish, too small for the hook. So I cast my line further out[14] and let it sink deeper[15], beyond the reach of the small fish that concentrated around the raft and lifeboat.

It was when I used the flying fish's head as bait, and with only one sinker[16], casting my line out and pulling it in quickly, making the head skim over[17] the surface of the water, that I finally had my first strike[18]. A dorado surged forth and lunged for the fish head. I let out a little slack[19], to make sure it had properly swallowed the bait, before giving the line a good yank[20]. The dorado exploded out of the water, tugging on the line so hard I thought it was going to pull me off the raft[21]. I braced myself.[22] The line became very taut[23]. It was good line; it

1.	ouvert
2.	J'ai pleuré à chaudes larmes sur
3.	décédée
4.	être sensible
5.	coupable
6.	inoffensif
7.	aimant les livres
8.	fardeau
9.	Je l'ai découpé en morceaux
10.	En fin de journée
11.	pas plus de succès
12.	hors d'atteinte
13.	mordillaient
14.	j'ai envoyé ma ligne plus loin
15.	plus profondément
16.	plomb
17.	raser
18.	prise
19.	J'ai donné un peu de mou
20.	avant de tirer sur la ligne d'un coup sec
21.	me faire tomber du radeau
22.	Je me suis accroché.
23.	tendue

would not break. I started bringing the dorado in. It struggled with all its might, jumping and diving and splashing. The line cut into my hands[1]. I wrapped my hands in the blanket. My heart was pounding. The fish was as strong as an ox[2]. I was not sure I would be able to pull it in[3].

I noticed all the other fish had vanished from around the raft and boat. No doubt they had sensed the dorado's distress. I hurried. Its struggling would attract sharks. But it fought like a devil. My arms were aching[4]. Every time I got it close to the raft, it beat about with such frenzy that I was cowed into[5] letting out some line.

At last I managed to haul it[6] aboard. It was over three feet long.[7] The bucket was useless. It would fit the dorado like a hat. I held the fish down by kneeling on it and using my hands. It was a writhing[8] mass of pure muscle, so big its tail stuck out[9] from beneath me, pounding hard[10] against the raft. It was giving me a ride[11] like I imagine a bucking bronco[12] would give a cowboy. I was in a wild and triumphant mood. A dorado is a magnificent-looking fish, large, fleshy and sleek[13], with a bulging[14] forehead that speaks of a forceful personality, a very long dorsal fin as proud as a cock's comb[15], and a coat of scales[16] that is smooth and bright. I felt I was dealing fate a serious blow[17] by engaging[18] such a handsome adversary. With this fish I was retaliating against[19] the sea, against the wind, against the sinking of ships, against all circumstances that were working against me. "Thank you, Lord Vishnu, thank you!" I shouted. "Once you saved the world by taking the form of a fish. Now you have saved *me* by taking the form of a fish. Thank you, thank you!"

Killing it was no problem. I would have spared myself the trouble[1]—after all, it was for Richard Parker and he would have dispatched it[2] with expert ease—but for[3] the hook that was embedded[4] in its mouth. I exulted at having a dorado at the end of my line—I would be less keen[5] if it were a tiger. I went about the job in a direct way. I took the hatchet in both my hands and vigorously beat the fish on the head with the hammerhead (I still didn't have the stomach[6] to use the sharp edge[7]). The dorado did a most extraordinary thing as it died: it began to flash all kinds of colours in rapid succession. Blue, green, red, gold and violet flickered and shimmered neon-like on its surface as it struggled. I felt I was beating a rainbow to death[8]. (I found out later that the dorado is famed for its death-knell iridescence[9].) At last it lay still and dull-coloured[10], and I could remove the hook. I even managed to retrieve[11] a part of my bait.

You may be astonished that in such a short period of time I could go from weeping over the muffled[12] killing of a flying fish to gleefully bludgeoning to death a dorado[13]. I could explain it by arguing[14] that profiting from a pitiful[15] flying fish's navigational mistake made me shy and sorrowful[16], while the excitement of actively capturing a great dorado made me sanguinary and self-assured[17]. But in point of fact the explanation lies elsewhere. It is simple and brutal: a person can get used to anything, even to killing.

It was with a hunter's pride that I pulled the raft up to the lifeboat. I brought it along the side, keeping very low[18]. I swung my arm[19] and dropped the dorado into the boat. It landed with a heavy thud and provoked a gruff[20] expression of surprise from Richard Parker. After a sniff or two, I heard the wet

1. Je me serais épargné cette peine
2. il s'en serait chargé
3. s'il n'y avait pas eu
4. enfoncé
5. enthousiaste
6. courage
7. le côté tranchant

8. je battais à mort un arc-en-ciel
9. connue pour émettre toutes les couleurs de l'arc-en-ciel au moment où elle meurt
10. terne
11. récupérer
12. étouffé
13. matraquer joyeusement une dorade jusqu'à ce qu'elle en meure
14. en alléguant
15. misérable
16. triste
17. sûr de moi
18. sans me faire voir
19. J'ai balancé le bras
20. bourrue

1. bruit de mastication
2. Je me suis éloigné

mashing sound[1] of a mouth at work. I pushed myself off[2], not forgetting to blow the whistle hard several times, to remind Richard Parker of who had so graciously provided him with fresh food. I stopped to pick up some biscuits and a can of water. The five remaining flying fish in the locker were dead. I pulled their wings off, throwing them away, and wrapped the fish in the now-consecrated[3] fish blanket.

3. à présent consacrée
4. mon matériel de pêche

By the time I had rinsed myself of blood, cleaned up my fishing gear[4], put things away and had my supper, night had come on. A thin layer of clouds masked the stars and the moon, and it was very dark. I was tired, but still excited by the events of the last hours. The feeling of busyness[5] was profoundly satisfying; I hadn't thought at all about my plight[6] or myself. Fishing was surely a better way of passing the time than yarn-spinning or playing I Spy. I determined to start again the next day as soon as there was light.

5. Se sentir occupé
6. situation dramatique

I fell asleep, my mind lit up by the chameleon-like flickering[7] of the dying dorado.

7. scintillement

CHAPTER 62

8. en pointillé
9. je me suis appuyé sur un coude
10. [première phrase du jeu « I Spy », « Je vois quelque chose... »]
11. agité
12. il marchait de long en large dans
13. J'ai analysé
14. pantelant

I slept in fits[8] that night. Shortly before sunrise I gave up trying to fall asleep again and lifted myself on an elbow[9]. I spied with my little eye[10] a tiger. Richard Parker was restless[11]. He was moaning and growling and pacing about[12] the lifeboat. It was impressive. I assessed[13] the situation. He couldn't be hungry. Or at least not dangerously hungry. Was he thirsty? His tongue hung from his mouth, but only on occasion, and he was not panting[14]. And his stomach and paws were still wet. But they were not dripping wet[1]. There probably wasn't much water left in the boat. Soon he would be thirsty.

I looked up at the sky. The cloud cover had vanished. But for a few wisps[2] on the horizon, the sky was clear. It would be another hot, rainless day. The sea moved in a lethargic way, as if already exhausted by the oncoming heat[3].

I sat against the mast and thought over our problem. The biscuits and the fishing gear assured us of the solid part of our diet. It was the liquid part that was the rub[4]. It all came down to what was so abundant around us but marred[5] by salt. I could perhaps mix some sea water with his fresh water, but I had to procure more fresh water to start with. The cans would not last long between the two of us—in fact, I was loath to[6] share even one with Richard Parker—and it would be foolish to rely on[7] rainwater.

The solar stills were the only other possible source of drinkable[8] water. I looked at them doubtfully[9]. They had been out two days now. I noticed that one of them had lost a little air. I pulled on the rope to tend to it[10]. I topped off[11] its cone with air. Without any real expectation[12] I reached underwater for the distillate pouch that was clipped to[13] the round buoyancy chamber. My fingers took hold of a bag that was unexpectedly fat. A shiver of thrill[14] went through me. I controlled myself. As likely as not[15], salt water had leaked in[16]. I unhooked[17] the pouch and, following the instructions, lowered it and tilted[18] the still so that any more water from beneath the cone might flow into it. I closed the two small taps[19] that led to the pouch, detached it and pulled it out of the water. It was rectangular in shape and made of thick, soft, yellow plastic, with calibration

1. trempés
2. volutes
3. la chaleur qui s'annonçait
4. posait problème
5. gâté
6. je n'étais pas disposé à
7. compter sur
8. potable
9. d'un air sceptique
10. m'en occuper
11. J'ai rempli
12. Sans grand espoir
13. attachée à
14. Un frisson d'excitation
15. Probablement
16. avait coulé à l'intérieur
17. J'ai décroché
18. j'ai penché
19. robinets

233

marks[1] on one side. I tasted the water. I tasted it again. It was salt-free.

"My sweet sea cow!" I exclaimed to the solar still. "You've produced, and how! What a delicious milk. Mind you[2], a little rubbery[3], but I'm not complaining. Why[4], look at me drink!"

I finished the bag. It had a capacity of one litre and was nearly full. After a moment of sigh-producing, shut-eyed satisfaction, I reattached the pouch. I checked the other stills. Each one had an udder[5] similarly heavy. I collected the fresh milk, over eight litres of it, in the fish bucket. Instantly these technological contraptions[6] became as precious to me as cattle[7] are to a farmer. Indeed, as they floated placidly in an arc, they looked almost like cows grazing in a field[8]. I ministered to their needs[9], making sure that there was enough sea water inside each and that the cones and chambers were inflated to just the right pressure[10].

After adding a little sea water to the bucket's contents, I placed it on the side bench just beyond the tarpaulin. With the end of the morning coolness[11], Richard Parker seemed safely settled below. I tied the bucket in place using rope and the tarpaulin hooks on the side of the boat. I carefully peeked over the gunnel. He was lying on his side. His den was a foul sight[12]. The dead mammals were heaped together[13], a grotesque pile of decayed[14] animal parts. I recognized a leg or two, various patches of hide[15], parts of a head, a great number of bones. Flying-fish wings were scattered about[16].

I cut up a flying fish and tossed a piece onto the side bench. After I had gathered what I needed for the day from the locker and was ready to go, I tossed another piece over the tarpaulin in front of Richard Parker. It had the intended effect[17]. As I

Marginal footnotes:

1. des repères
2. Cela dit
3. il a un petit goût de caoutchouc
4. Tiens
5. pis
6. engins
7. du bétail
8. en train de brouter dans un pré
9. Je pourvoyais à leur besoins
10. gonflés comme il le fallait
11. fraîcheur
12. n'était pas beau à voir
13. empilés les uns sur les autres
14. en décomposition
15. morceaux de peau
16. éparpillées partout
17. l'effet voulu

drifted away[1] I saw him come out into the open to fetch the morsel[2] of fish. His head turned and he noticed the other morsel and the new object next to it. He lifted himself. He hung his huge head over the bucket. I was afraid he would tip it over.[3] He didn't. His face disappeared into it, barely fitting, and he started to lap up the water[4]. In very little time the bucket started shaking and rattling[5] emptily with each strike of his tongue. When he looked up, I stared him aggressively in the eyes and I blew on the whistle a few times. He disappeared under the tarpaulin.

It occurred to me that with every passing day the lifeboat was resembling a zoo enclosure more and more: Richard Parker had his sheltered area for sleeping and resting, his food stash[6], his lookout[7] and now his water hole.

The temperature climbed. The heat became stifling[8]. I spent the rest of the day in the shade[9] of the canopy, fishing. It seems I had had beginner's luck with that first dorado. I caught nothing the whole day, not even in the late afternoon, when marine life appeared in abundance. A turtle turned up, a different kind this time, a green sea turtle, bulkier[10] and smoother-shelled[11], but curious in the same fixed way as a hawksbill[12]. I did nothing about it, but I started thinking that I should.

The only good thing about the day being so hot was the sight the solar stills presented. Every cone was covered on the inside with drops and rivulets[13] of condensation.

The day ended. I calculated that the next morning would make it a week since the *Tsimtsum* had sunk.

1. Alors que mon radeau s'éloignait

2. morceau

3. J'avais peur qu'il le renverse.

4. boire l'eau à grands coups de langue

5. à faire un bruit de ferraille

6. son stock de nourriture

7. poste de guet

8. étouffante

9. à l'ombre

10. plus grosse

11. à la carapace plus lisse

12. caret

13. ruisseaux

CHAPTER 63

The Robertson family survived thirty-eight days at sea. Captain Bligh of the celebrated mutinous *Bounty*[1] and his fellow castaways survived forty-seven days. Steven Callahan survived seventy-six. Owen Chase, whose account[2] of the sinking of the whaling ship[3] *Essex* by a whale inspired Herman Melville, survived eighty-three days at sea with two mates[4], interrupted by a one-week stay on an inhospitable[5] island. The Bailey family survived 118 days. I have heard of a Korean merchant sailor[6] named Poon, I believe, who survived the Pacific for 173 days in the 1950s.

I survived 227 days. That's how long my trial[7] lasted, over seven months.

I kept myself busy. That was one key to my survival. On a lifeboat, even on a raft, there's always something that needs doing[8]. An average day[9] for me, if such a notion can be applied to a castaway, went like this:

Sunrise to mid-morning:
> wake up
> prayers
> breakfast for Richard Parker
> general inspection of raft and lifeboat, with
>> particular attention paid to all knots and
>> ropes
> tending of solar stills[10] (wiping[11], inflating[12],
>> topping off with water[13])
> breakfast and inspection of food stores
> fishing and preparing of fish if any caught (gut-
>> ting[14], cleaning, hanging of strips of flesh[15]
>> on lines to cure in the sun[16])

Mid-morning to late afternoon:
> prayers

1. du navire « Le Bounty », célèbre pour sa mutinerie
2. dont le récit
3. baleinier
4. compagnons
5. inhospitalière
6. un marin marchand coréen
7. épreuve
8. qu'il faut faire
9. Une journée type
10. s'occuper des distillateurs d'eau salée
11. les essuyer
12. les gonfler
13. les remplir d'eau
14. les vider
15. étendre les lanières de chair
16. pour les laisser sécher au soleil

light[1] lunch

rest and restful[2] activities (writing in diary, examining of scabs and sores[3], upkeeping[4] of equipment, puttering about locker[5], observation and study of Richard Parker, picking at of[6] turtle bones, etc.)

Late afternoon to early evening:

prayers

fishing and preparing of fish

tending of curing strips of flesh[7] (turning over[8], cutting away of[9] putrid parts)

dinner preparations

dinner for self and Richard Parker

Sunset:

general inspection of raft and lifeboat (knots and ropes again)

collecting and safekeeping of distillate[10] from solar stills

storing of[11] all foods and equipment

arrangements for night (making of bed, safe storage on raft of flare, in case of ship, and rain catcher, in case of rain)

prayers

Night:

fitful sleeping[12]

prayers

Mornings were usually better than late afternoons, when the emptiness of time tended to make itself felt. Any number of events affected this routine. Rainfall, at any time of the day or night, stopped all other business; for as long as it fell, I held up the rain catchers and was feverishly occupied storing their catch[13]. A turtle's visit was another major disruption[14]. And Richard Parker, of course, was a regular disturbance[15]. Accommodating him[16] was a priority I could not neglect for an instant. He didn't have much of a

1. léger
2. reposantes
3. croûtes et endroits douloureux
4. entretenir
5. tourner autour du caisson sans but précis
6. rogner
7. s'occuper des lanières de chair en train de sécher
8. les retourner
9. enlever
10. recueillir et mettre à l'abri l'eau distillée
11. ranger
12. sommeil agité
13. à récupérer ce qu'ils captaient
14. pouvait également interrompre mes activités
15. régulièrement une source de perturbation
16. Répondre à ses besoins

routine beyond eating, drinking and sleeping, but there were times when he stirred from his lethargy and rambled about[1] his territory, making noises and being cranky[2]. Thankfully, every time, the sun and the sea quickly tired him and he returned to beneath the tarpaulin, to lying on his side again, or flat on his stomach, his head on top of his crossed front legs.

But there was more to my dealings with him[3] than strict necessity. I also spent hours observing him because it was a distraction. A tiger is a fascinating animal at any time, and all the more so when it is your sole[4] companion.

At first, looking out for a ship[5] was something I did all the time, compulsively[6]. But after a few weeks, five or six, I stopped doing it nearly entirely.

And I survived because I made a point of forgetting[7]. My story started on a calendar day—July 2nd, 1977—and ended on a calendar day—February 14th, 1978—but in between there was no calendar. I did not count the days or the weeks or the months. Time is an illusion that only makes us pant[8]. I survived because I forgot even the very notion of time.

What I remember are events and encounters[9] and routines, markers[10] that emerged here and there from the ocean of time and imprinted themselves on[11] my memory. The smell of spent hand-flare shells[12], and prayers at dawn, and the killing of turtles, and the biology of algae, for example. And many more. But I don't know if I can put them in order for you. My memories come in a jumble.[13]

CHAPTER 64

My clothes disintegrated[14], victims of the sun and the salt. First they became gauze-thin[15]. Then they

1. errait sur
2. grincheux

3. mes rapports avec lui

4. unique
5. chercher un bateau à l'horizon
6. de manière obsessionnelle
7. je me suis efforcé d'oublier

8. nous tient en haleine
9. des rencontres
10. des repères
11. se sont gravés dans
12. des feux à main utilisés

13. Mes souvenirs arrivent pêle-mêle.

14. se sont désagrégés
15. fins comme de la gaze

tore[1] until only the seams[2] were left. Lastly, the seams broke. For months I lived stark naked[3] except for the whistle that dangled from my neck[4] by a string.

Salt-water boils[5]—red, angry, disfiguring—were a leprosy[6] of the high seas, transmitted by the water that soaked me[7]. Where they burst, my skin was exceptionally sensitive[8]; accidentally rubbing an open sore[9] was so painful I would gasp and cry out. Naturally, these boils developed on the parts of my body that got the most wet and the most wear on[10] the raft; that is, my backside[11]. There were days when I could hardly find a position in which I could rest. Time and sunshine healed a sore[12], but the process was slow, and new boils appeared if I didn't stay dry.

CHAPTER 65

I spent hours trying to decipher[13] the lines in the survival manual on navigation. Plain and simple explanations on living off the sea[14] were given in abundance, but a basic knowledge of seafaring[15] was assumed by the author of the manual. The castaway was to his mind[16] an experienced sailor[17] who, compass, chart and sextant[18] in hand, knew how he found his way into trouble, if not how he would get out of it. The result was advice such as "Remember, time is distance. Don't forget to wind your watch[19]", or "Latitude can be measured with the fingers, if need be[20]. " I had a watch, but it was now at the bottom of the Pacific. I lost it when the *Tsimtsum* sank. As for latitude and longitude, my marine knowledge was strictly limited to what lived *in* the sea and did not extend to what cruised on top of it[21]. Winds and

1. ils se sont déchirés
2. coutures
3. complètement nu
4. pendait à mon cou
5. furoncles
6. lèpre
7. me trempait
8. sensible
9. frotter une plaie ouverte
10. étaient le plus en contact avec
11. dos
12. guérissaient les plaies
13. déchiffrer
14. la vie en mer
15. navigation
16. selon lui
17. un marin expérimenté
18. une boussole, une carte et un sextant
19. remonter votre montre
20. si nécessaire
21. ce qui naviguait à sa surface

currents were a mystery to me. The stars meant nothing to me. I couldn't name a single constellation. My family lived by one star alone: the sun. We were early to bed and early to rise[1]. I had in my life looked at a number of beautiful starry[2] nights, where with just two colours and the simplest of styles nature draws the grandest of pictures, and I felt the feelings of wonder and smallness that we all feel, and I got a clear sense of direction from the spectacle, most definitely[3], but I mean that in a spiritual sense, not in a geographic one. I hadn't the faintest idea[4] how the night sky might serve as a road map[5]. How could the stars, sparkle as they might[6], help me find my way if they kept moving?

I gave up trying to find out[7]. Any knowledge I might gain was useless. I had no means of controlling where I was going—no rudder[8], no sails[9], no motor, some oars but insufficient brawn[10]. What was the point of plotting a course[11] if I could not act on it? And even if I could, how should I know where to go? West, back to where we came from? East, to America? North, to Asia? South, to where the shipping lanes[12] were? Each seemed a good and bad course in equal measure[13].

So I drifted[14]. Winds and currents decided where I went. Time became distance for me in the way it is for all mortals—I travelled down the road of life—and I did other things with my fingers than try to measure latitude. I found out later that I travelled a narrow[15] road, the Pacific equatorial counter-current[16].

CHAPTER 66

I fished with a variety of hooks at a variety of depths for a variety of fish, from deep-sea fishing[17]

1. nous nous levions tôt
2. étoilées
3. assurément
4. la moindre idée
5. servir de feuille de route
6. aussi étincelantes qu'elles pouvaient être
7. le découvrir
8. pas de gouvernail
9. pas de voiles
10. force
11. définir la route à suivre
12. les voies maritimes
13. avait autant d'avantages que d'inconvénients
14. je dérivais
15. étroite
16. le contre-courant nord-équatorial du Pacifique
17. la pêche en eaux profondes

240

with large hooks and many sinkers to surface fishing with smaller hooks and only one or two sinkers. Success was slow to come[1], and when it did, it was much appreciated, but the effort seemed out of proportion to the reward[2]. The hours were long, the fish were small, and Richard Parker was forever hungry[3].

It was the gaffs[4] that finally proved to be my most valuable fishing equipment. They came in three screw-in pieces[5]: two tubular sections that formed the shaft[6]—one with a moulded plastic handle[7] at its end and a ring for securing[8] the gaff with a rope—and a head that consisted of a hook measuring about two inches across its curve[9] and ending in a needle-sharp, barbed point[10]. Assembled, each gaff was about five feet long[11] and felt as light and sturdy[12] as a sword[13].

At first I fished in open water[14]. I would sink the gaff to a depth of four feet[15] or so, sometimes with a fish speared[16] on the hook as bait, and I would wait. I would wait for hours, my body tense till it ached[17]. When a fish was in just the right spot, I jerked the gaff up[18] with all the might and speed I could muster[19]. It was a split-second[20] decision. Experience taught me that it was better to strike when I felt I had a good chance of success than to strike wildly[21], for a fish learns from experience too, and rarely falls for the same trap[22] twice.

When I was lucky, a fish was properly snagged[23] on the hook, impaled[24], and I could confidently bring it aboard. But if I gaffed a large fish in the stomach or tail, it would often get away with a twist[25] and a forward spurt of speed[26]. Injured, it would be easy prey for another predator, a gift I had not meant to make. So with large fish I aimed for the ventral area beneath their gills and their

1. tardait à venir
2. disproportionné par rapport à la récompense
3. toujours affamé
4. perches
5. trois pièces à visser ensemble
6. manche
7. une poignée en plastique moulé
8. un anneau pour attacher
9. un crochet de 5 cm de large
10. une pointe acérée comme une aiguille
11. faisait environ 1,50 m de long
12. robuste
13. épée
14. en eaux profondes
15. 1,20 m
16. accroché
17. jusqu'à la souffrance
18. je redressais la gaffe
19. rassembler
20. qu'il fallait prendre en une fraction de seconde
21. frénétiquement
22. dans le même piège
23. accroché
24. empalé
25. il se libérait souvent en se tortillant
26. de plus en plus vite

1. nager vers le haut
2. piqué
3. pouvait surgir
4. bégueule
5. qui se jetait sur lui à mains nues et sans aucune retenue
6. que le poisson n'était pas bien accroché à la gaffe
7. j'attrapais
8. bien que non acérés
9. agiles
10. glissants
11. manier
12. je devais faire avec deux
13. j'enfonçais
14. j'écrasais
15. le décapiter
16. Je suis devenu plus audacieux
17. une intuition
18. raide
19. tissage
20. serré
21. leurre
22. Quand je le laissais traîner
23. qui vivaient dans un espace restreint

lateral fins, for a fish's instinctive reaction when struck there was to swim *up*[1], away from the hook, in the very direction I was pulling. Thus it would happen: sometimes more pricked[2] than actually gaffed, a fish would burst out[3] of the water in my face. I quickly lost my revulsion at touching sea life. None of this prissy[4] fish blanket business any more. A fish jumping out of water was confronted by a famished boy with a hands-on no-holds-barred approach to capturing it[5]. If I felt the gaff's hold was uncertain[6], I would let go of it—I had not forgotten to secure it with a rope to the raft—and I would clutch at[7] the fish with my hands. Fingers, though blunt[8], were far more nimble[9] than a hook. The struggle would be fast and furious. Those fish were slippery[10] and desperate, and I was just plain desperate. If only I had had as many arms as the goddess Durga—two to hold the gaffs, four to grasp the fish and two to wield[11] the hatchets. But I had to make do with two[12]. I stuck fingers into eyes, jammed[13] hands into gills, crushed[14] soft stomachs with knees, bit tails with my teeth—I did whatever was necessary to hold a fish down until I could reach for the hatchet and chop its head off[15].

With time and experience I became a better hunter. I grew bolder[16] and more agile. I developed an instinct, a feel[17], for what to do.

My success improved greatly when I started using part of the cargo net. As a fishing net it was useless—too stiff[18] and heavy and with a weave[19] that wasn't tight[20] enough. But it was perfect as a lure[21]. Trailing freely[22] in the water, it proved irresistibly attractive to fish, and even more so when seaweed started growing on it. Fish that were local in their ambit[23] made the net their neighbourhood, and the quick ones, the ones that tended to streak by[1], the dorados, slowed down to visit the new development. Neither the residents nor the travellers ever suspected that a hook was hidden in the weave. There were some days—too few unfortunately[2]—when I could have all the fish I cared to gaff. At such times I hunted far beyond the needs of my hunger or my capacity to cure[3]; there simply wasn't enough space on the lifeboat, or lines on the raft, to dry so many strips of dorado, flying fish, jacks, groupers and mackerels[4], let alone space in my stomach to eat them. I kept what I could and gave the rest to Richard Parker. During those days of plenty, I laid hands on so many fish that my body began to glitter[5] from all the fish scales[6] that became stuck to it. I wore these spots of shine and silver[7] like tilaks, the marks of colour that we Hindus wear on our foreheads as symbols of the divine. If sailors had come upon me then, I'm sure they would have thought I was a fish god standing atop his kingdom[8] and they wouldn't have stopped. Those were the good days. They were rare.

Turtles were an easy catch indeed, as the survival manual said they were. Under the "hunting and gathering" heading, they would go under "gathering." Solid in build though they were[9], like tanks[10], they were neither fast nor powerful swimmers; with just one hand gripped around a back flipper, it was possible to hold on to[11] a turtle. But the survival manual failed to mention[12] that a turtle caught[13] was not a turtle had. It still needed to be brought aboard. And hauling a struggling 130-pound turtle[14] aboard a lifeboat was anything but easy[15]. It was a labour that demanded feats of strength[16] worthy of Hanuman[17]. I did it by bringing the victim alongside the bow of the boat, carapace against hull, and tying a rope to its neck, a

1. passer en trombe

2. trop peu malheureusement

3. apprêter la chair

4. de carangues, de mérous et de maquereaux

5. briller

6. écailles

7. ces marques brillantes et argentées

8. au sommet de son royaume

9. Malgré leur robustesse

10. des chars d'assaut

11. attraper

12. oubliait de mentionner

13. capturée

14. porter une tortue de 60 kilos

15. tout sauf simple

16. des tours de force

17. [dieu du Ramayana à la force prodigieuse]

5. *sans le vouloir*
6. *En essayant*
7. *ses pattes douloureusement tordues*

front flipper and a back flipper. Then I pulled until I thought my arms would come apart[1] and my head would explode. I ran the ropes around the tarpaulin hooks on the opposite side of the bow; every time a rope yielded a little[2], I secured my gain before the rope slipped back[3]. Inch by inch, a turtle was heaved[4] out of the water. It took time. I remember one green sea turtle that hung from the side of the lifeboat for two days, the whole while thrashing about madly, free flippers beating in the air. Luckily, at the last stage, on the lip of the gunnel, it would often happen that a turtle would help me without meaning to[5]. In an attempt[6] to free its painfully twisted flippers[7], it would pull on them; if I pulled at the same moment, our conflicting efforts sometimes came together and suddenly it would happen, easily: in the most dramatic fashion imaginable, a turtle would surge over the gunnel and slide onto the tarpaulin. I would fall back[8], exhausted but jubilant.

Green sea turtles gave more meat than hawksbills, and their belly shells were thinner. But they tended to be bigger than hawksbills, often too big to lift out of the water for the weakened castaway that I became.

Lord, to think[9] that I'm a strict vegetarian. To think that when I was a child I always shuddered[10] when I snapped open[11] a banana because it sounded to me like the breaking of an animal's neck. I descended to a level of savagery I never imagined possible.

CHAPTER 67

The underside of the raft became host to a multitude of sea life, like the net but smaller in form. It started with a soft green algae that clung[1] to the life jackets. Stiffer algae[2] of a darker kind joined it. They did well[3] and became thick. Animal life appeared. The first that I saw were tiny, translucent shrimp[4], hardly half an inch long[5]. They were followed by fish no bigger that looked like they were permanently under X-ray[6]; their internal organs showed through[7] their transparent skins. After that I noticed the black worms[8] with the white spines, the green gelatinous slugs[9] with the primitive limbs[10], the inch-long, motley-coloured fish[11] with the potbellies[12], and lastly the crabs, half to three-quarters of an inch across[13] and brown in colour. I tried everything but the worms, including the algae. Only the crabs didn't have an unpalatably bitter or salty taste[14]. Every time they appeared, I popped them[15] one after another into my mouth like candy[16] until there were none left. I couldn't control myself. It was always a long wait between fresh crops[17] of crabs.

The hull of the lifeboat invited life too, in the form of small gooseneck barnacles[18]. I sucked their fluid. Their flesh made for good fishing bait.

I became attached to these oceanic hitchhikers[19], though they weighed the raft down a little[20]. They provided distraction, like Richard Parker. I spent many hours doing nothing but lying on my side, a life jacket pushed out of place a few inches[21], like a curtain from a window, so that I might have a clear view. What I saw was an upside-down[22] town, small, quiet and peaceable, whose citizens went about with the sweet civility[23] of angels. The sight was a welcome relief for my frayed[24] nerves.

1. s'est accrochée
2. Des algues plus rigides
3. Elles ont prospéré
4. de minuscules crevettes translucides
5. d'à peine plus d'un centimètre
6. sous rayons X
7. se voyaient à travers
8. vers
9. limaces
10. membres
11. les poissons bigarrés de 2 ou 3 centimètres
12. bedaines
13. de 1 ou 2 cm de large
14. un goût affreusement amer ou salé
15. je les fourrais
16. des bonbons
17. récoltes
18. pouces-pieds
19. auto-stoppeurs
20. leur poids faisait s'enfoncer un peu le radeau
21. déplacée de quelques centimètres
22. à l'envers
23. courtoisie
24. à vif

CHAPTER 68

My sleep pattern[1] changed. Though I rested all the time, I rarely slept longer than an hour or so at a stretch[2], even at night. It was not the ceaseless motion of the sea that disturbed me, nor the wind; you get used to those the way you get used to lumps in a mattress[3]. It was apprehension and anxiety that roused me[4]. It was remarkable how little sleep I got by on[5].

Unlike Richard Parker. He became a champion napper[6]. Most of the time he rested beneath the tarpaulin. But on calm days when the sun was not too harsh and on calm nights, he came out. One of his favourite positions in the open was lying on the stern bench on his side, stomach overhanging the edge of it[7], front and back legs extending down[8] the side benches. It was a lot of tiger to squeeze onto a fairly narrow ledge[9], but he managed it by making his back very round[10]. When he was truly sleeping, he laid his head on his front legs, but when his mood was slightly more active, when he might choose to open his eyes and look about, he turned his head and lay his chin[11] on the gunnel.

Another favourite position of his was sitting with his back to me, his rear half resting on the floor[12] of the boat and his front half on the bench, his face buried into the stern, paws right next to his head, looking as if we were playing hide-and-seek[13] and he were the one counting[14]. In this position he tended to lie very still, with only the occasional twitching of his ears to indicate that he was not necessarily sleeping.

CHAPTER 69

On many nights I was convinced I saw a light in the distance[1]. Each time I set off a flare[2]. When I had used up the rocket flares, I expended the hand flares[3]. Were they ships that failed to see me[4]? The light of rising or setting stars bouncing off[5] the ocean? Breaking waves that moonlight[6] and forlorn hope[7] fashioned into illusion[8]? Whatever the case, every time it was for nothing. Never a result. Always the bitter emotion of hope raised and dashed[9]. In time[10] I gave up entirely[11] on being saved by a ship. If the horizon was two and a half miles away at an altitude of five feet[12], how far away was it when I was sitting against the mast of my raft, my eyes not even three feet[13] above the water? What chance was there that a ship crossing the whole great big Pacific would cut into such a tiny circle[14]? Not only that: that it would cut into such a tiny circle *and see me*— what chance was there of that? No, humanity and its unreliable[15] ways could not be counted upon. It was land I had to reach, hard, firm, certain land.

I remember the smell of the spent[16] hand-flare shells. By some freak of chemistry[17] they smelled exactly like cumin. It was intoxicating[18]. I sniffed the plastic shells[19] and immediately Pondicherry came to life in my mind, a marvellous relief[20] from the disappointment of calling for help and not being heard. The experience was very strong, nearly a hallucination. From a single smell a whole town arose. (Now, when I smell cumin, I see the Pacific Ocean.)

Richard Parker always froze when a hand flare hissed to life. His eyes, round pupils the size of pinpricks[21], fixed on the light steadily[22]. It was

1. au loin

2. j'ai envoyé une fusée de détresse

3. les feux à main

4. ne m'ont pas vu

5. qui se reflétait

6. le clair de lune

7. un vain espoir

8. transformaient en un mirage

9. ranimé puis réduit à néant

10. Avec le temps

11. j'ai complètement abandonné l'idée

12. à 4 km, à une hauteur de 1,50 m

13. à 90 cm

14. entre dans le périmètre de ce petit cercle

15. imprévisibles

16. utilisés

17. Par une aberration chimique,

18. enivrant

19. Je reniflais les enveloppes en plastique

20. consolation

21. piqûres d'épingle

22. sans ciller

too bright for me, a blinding[1] white centre with a pinkish red aureole. I had to turn away.[2] I held the flare in the air at arm's length[3] and waved it[4] slowly. For about a minute heat showered down upon[5] my forearm and everything was weirdly lit[6]. Water around the raft, until a moment before opaquely black, showed itself to be crowded with fish.

CHAPTER 70

Butchering[7] a turtle was hard work. My first one was a small hawksbill. It was its blood that tempted me, the "good, nutritious, salt-free drink" promised by the survival manual. My thirst was that bad.[8] I took hold of the turtle's shell and grappled with[9] one of its back flippers. When I had a good grip[10], I turned it over in the water and attempted to pull it onto the raft. The thing was thrashing violently. I would never be able to deal with it on the raft. Either I let it go—or I tried my luck on the lifeboat. I looked up. It was a hot and cloudless day. Richard Parker seemed to tolerate my presence at the bow on such days, when the air was like the inside of

an oven[11] and he did not move from under the tarpaulin until sunset.

I held on to one of the turtle's back flippers with one hand and I pulled on the rope to the lifeboat with the other. It was not easy climbing aboard. When I had managed it, I jerked the turtle in the air and brought it onto its back on the tarpaulin. As I had hoped, Richard Parker did no more than growl once or twice. He was not up to exerting himself[12]

in such heat.

My determination was grim and blind[1]. I felt I had no time to waste. I turned to the survival manual as to a cookbook[2]. It said to lay the turtle on its back. Done. It advised that a knife should be "inserted into the neck" to sever[3] the arteries and veins running through it. I looked at the turtle. There was no neck. The turtle had retracted[4] into its shell; all that showed[5] of its head was its eyes and its beak, surrounded by circles of skin. It was looking at me upside down[6] with a stern[7] expression. I took hold of the knife and, hoping to goad it[8], poked[9] a front flipper. It only shrank further[10] into its shell. I decided on a more direct approach. As confidently as if I had done it a thousand times, I jammed the knife just to the right of the turtle's head, at an angle[11]. I pushed the blade[12] deep into the folds of skin and twisted it[13]. The turtle retreated even further, favouring[14] the side where the blade was, and suddenly shot its head forward, beak snapping at me viciously[15]. I jumped back. All four flippers came out and the creature tried to make its getaway[16]. It rocked[17] on its back, flippers beating wildly and head shaking from side to side. I took hold of a hatchet and brought it down on the turtle's neck, gashing it[18]. Bright red blood shot out[19]. I grabbed the beaker and collected about three hundred millilitres, a pop can's worth[20]. I might have got much more, a litre I would guess, but the turtle's beak was sharp and its front flippers were long and powerful, with two claws on each. The blood I managed to collect gave off no particular smell. I took a sip.[21] It tasted warm and animal, if my memory is right. It's hard to remember first impressions. I drank the blood to the last drop[22].

I thought I would use the hatchet to remove the tough belly shell, but it proved easier with the saw-

1. terrible et aveugle
2. livre de cuisine
3. couper
4. s'était retirée
5. tout ce que je pouvais voir
6. à l'envers
7. sévère
8. l'aiguillonner
9. j'ai piqué
10. Elle n'a fait que s'enfoncer davantage

11. en biais
12. lame
13. je l'ai vrillée
14. privilégiant
15. essayait de me mordre violemment
16. prendre la fuite
17. Elle s'est balancée

18. le tailladant
19. a jailli
20. de quoi remplir une canette

21. J'en ai bu une gorgée.
22. jusqu'à la dernière goutte

249

toothed edge of the knife. I set one foot at the centre of the shell, the other clear of the[1] flailing flippers. The leathery skin[2] at the head end of the shell was easy cutting[3], except around the flippers. Sawing away at the rim[4], however, where shell met shell, was very hard work, especially as the turtle wouldn't stop moving. By the time I had gone all the way around I was bathed in sweat[5] and exhausted. I pulled on the belly shell. It lifted reluctantly[6], with a wet sucking sound[7]. Inner life was revealed, twitching and jerking—muscles, fat, blood, guts and bones. And still the turtle thrashed about. I slashed its neck[8] to the vertebrae. It made no difference. Flippers continued to beat. With two blows of the hatchet I cut its head right off[9]. The flippers did not stop. Worse, the separated head went on gulping for air and blinking its eyes. I pushed it into the sea. The living rest of the turtle I lifted and dropped into Richard Parkers territory. He was making noises and sounded as if he were about to stir. He had probably smelled the turtle's blood. I fled to the raft.

I watched sullenly[10] as he loudly appreciated my gift and made a joyous mess of himself[11]. I was utterly spent[12]. The effort of butchering the turtle had hardly seemed worth the cup of blood.

I started thinking seriously about how I was going to deal with Richard Parker. This forbearance[13] on his part on hot, cloudless days, if that is what it was and not simple laziness[14], was not good enough. I couldn't always be running away from him[15]. I needed safe access to the locker and the top of the tarpaulin, no matter the time of day or the weather, no matter his mood[16]. It was rights I needed, the sort of rights that come with might[17].

It was time to impose myself and carve out[1] my territory.

CHAPTER 71

To those who should ever find themselves in a predicament such as I was in[2], I would recommend the following program:

1. Choose a day when the waves are small but regular. You want a sea that will put on a good show[3] when your lifeboat is broadside[4] to it, though without capsizing[5] your boat.

2. Stream your sea anchor full out to make your lifeboat as stable and comfortable as possible. Prepare your safe haven[6] from the lifeboat in case you should need it (you most likely will[7]). If you can, devise[8] some means of bodily protection. Almost anything can make a shield[9]. Wrapping clothes or blankets around your limbs will make for a minimal form of armour[10].

3. Now comes the difficult part: you must provoke the animal that is afflicting you[11]. Tiger, rhinoceros, ostrich, wild boar, brown bear—no matter the beast, you must get its goat[12]. The best way to do this will most likely be to go to the edge of your territory and noisily intrude into[13] the neutral zone. I did just that: I went to the edge of the tarpaulin and stamped[14] upon the middle bench as I mildly blew into the whistle. It is important that you make a consistent, recognizable noise[15] to signal your aggression. But you must be careful. You want to provoke your animal, but only so much[16]. You

1. délimiter

2. dans une situation aussi difficile que celle où je me trouvais

3. fera un beau spectacle

4. perpendiculaire

5. mais sans faire chavirer

6. refuge

7. ce qui sera très probablement le cas

8. trouvez

9. bouclier

10. armure

11. vous tourmente

12. le ou la rendre chèvre

13. faire bruyamment intrusion dans

14. j'ai tapé du pied

15. un bruit reconnaissable, toujours le même

16. pas trop

don't want it to attack you outright[1]. If it does, God be with you. You will be torn to pieces[2], trampled flat[3], disembowelled[4], very likely eaten. You don't want that. You want an animal that is piqued, peeved, vexed, bothered, irked, annoyed[5]—but not homicidal. Under no circumstances should you step into your animal's territory. Contain your aggression to staring into its eyes and hurling toots and taunts[6].

4. When your animal has been roused[7], work in all bad faith[8] to provoke a border intrusion[9]. A good way of bringing this about in my experience is to back off slowly as you are making your noises. BE SURE NOT TO BREAK EYE CONTACT! As soon as the animal has laid a paw in your territory, or even made a determined advance into the neutral territory, you have achieved your goal[10]. Don't be picky[11] or legalistic as to where its paw actually landed. Be quick to be affronted[12]. Don't wait to construe[13]—misconstrue as fast as you can. The point here is to make your animal understand that its upstairs neighbour[14] is exceptionally persnickety[15] about territory.

5. Once your animal has trespassed upon[16] your territory, be unflagging in[17] your outrage. Whether you have fled to your safe haven off the lifeboat or retreated to the back of your territory on the lifeboat, START BLOWING YOUR WHISTLE AT FULL BLAST[18] and IMMEDIATELY TRIP[19] THE SEA ANCHOR. These two actions are of pivotal[20] importance. You must not delay putting them into effect.[21] If you can help your lifeboat get broadside to the waves by other means, with an oar for example, apply yourself

right away. The faster[1] your lifeboat broaches to the waves[2], the better[3].

6. Blowing a whistle continuously is exhausting for the weakened castaway, but you must not falter[4]. Your alarmed animal must associate its increasing nausea with the shrill[5] cries of the whistle. You can help things move along by standing at the end of your boat, feet on opposing gunnels, and swaying in rhythm to the motion imparted by the sea[6]. However slight you are[7], however large your lifeboat, you will be amazed at the difference this will make. I assure you, in no time you'll have your lifeboat rocking and rolling[8] like Elvis Presley. Just don't forget to be blowing your whistle all the while, and mind you don't make your lifeboat capsize.

7. You want to keep going until the animal that is your burden—your tiger, your rhinoceros, whatever[9]—is properly green about the gills[10] with seasickness. You want to hear it heaving and dry retching[11]. You want to see it lying at the bottom of the lifeboat, limbs trembling, eyes rolled back[12], a deathly rattle[13] coming from its gaping[14] mouth. And all the while you must be shattering[15] the animal's ears with the piercing blows of your whistle. If you become sick yourself, don't waste your vomit by sending it overboard. Vomit makes an excellent border guard[16]. Puke[17] on the edges of your territory.

8. When your animal appears good and sick[18], you can stop. Seasickness comes on quickly, but it takes a long while to go away. You don't want to overstate your case[19]. No one dies of nausea, but it can seriously sap[20] the will to live. When enough is enough, stream the sea anchor, try

1. *Plus vite*

2. *viendra en travers des vagues*

3. *mieux ce sera*

4. *faiblir*

5. *stridents*

6. *vous balancer au rythme du mouvement de la mer*

7. *Peu importe votre poids*

8. *dansant le rock and roll*

9. *peu importe*

10. *sur le point de vomir*

11. *en train d'avoir des haut-le-cœur*

12. *révulsés*

13. *un râle d'agonie*

14. *béante*

15. *vous devez écorcher*

16. *garde-frontière*

17. *Gerbez*

18. *semble bien malade*

19. *dépasser les bornes*

20. *miner*

to give shade to your animal if it has collapsed in direct sunlight, and make sure it has water available[1] when it recovers[2], with anti-seasickness tablets dissolved in it, if you have any. Dehydration is a serious danger at this point. Otherwise retreat to your territory and leave your animal in peace. Water, rest and relaxation, besides a stable lifeboat, will bring it back to life. The animal should be allowed to recover fully before going through steps 1 to 8 again.

9. Treatment should be repeated until the association in the animal's mind between the sound of the whistle and the feeling of intense, incapacitating[3] nausea is fixed and totally unambiguous. Thereafter[4], the whistle alone will deal with[5] trespassing or any other untoward[6] behaviour. Just one shrill blow and you will see your animal shudder with malaise and repair at top speed[7] to the safest, furthest[8] part of its territory. Once this level of training is reached, use of the whistle should be sparing[9].

CHAPTER 72

In my case, to protect myself from Richard Parker while I trained him, I made a shield with a turtle shell. I cut a notch[10] on each side of the shell and connected them with a length of rope[11]. The shield was heavier than I would have liked, but do soldiers ever get to choose their ordnance[12]?

The first time I tried, Richard Parker bared his teeth[13], rotated his ears full round[14], vomited a short guttural roar and charged. A great, full-clawed[15]

1. à disposition
2. il se remettra
3. handicapante
4. Par la suite
5. sera la réponse à
6. inapproprié
7. se retirer à toute vitesse
8. la plus éloignée
9. il faut utiliser le sifflet le plus rarement possible
10. J'ai fait une encoche
11. un morceau de corde
12. équipement militaire
13. a montré les crocs
14. a fait complètement pivoter ses oreilles
15. toutes griffes dehors

paw rose in the air and cuffed[1] my shield. The blow sent me flying off the boat. I hit the water and instantly let go of the shield. It sank without a trace after hitting me in the shin[2]. I was beside myself with[3] terror—of Richard Parker, but also of being in the water. In my mind a shark was at that very second shooting up for me[4]. I swam for the raft in frantic strokes, precisely the sort of wild thrashing[5] that sharks find so deliciously inviting. Luckily there were no sharks. I reached the raft, let out all the rope and sat with my arms wrapped around my knees and my head down, trying to put out[6] the fire of fear that was blazing[7] within me. It was a long time before the trembling of my body stopped completely. I stayed on the raft for the rest of that day and the whole night. I did not eat or drink.

I was at it again next time I caught a turtle. Its shell was smaller, lighter, and made for a better shield. Once more I advanced and started stamping on the middle bench with my foot.

I wonder if those who hear this story will understand that my behaviour was not an act of insanity[8] or a covert suicide attempt[9] but a simple necessity. Either I tamed him, made him see who was Number One and who was Number Two—or I died the day I wanted to climb aboard the lifeboat during rough weather[10] and he objected[11].

If I survived my apprenticeship[12] as a high seas animal trainer it was because Richard Parker did not really want to attack me. Tigers, indeed all animals, do not favour[13] violence as a means of settling scores[14]. When animals fight, it is with the intent to kill and with the understanding that[15] they may be killed. A clash[16] is costly[17]. And so animals have a full system of cautionary signals[18] designed to avoid a showdown[19], and they are quick to

1. a frappé

2. tibia

3. fou de

4. était en train de foncer vers moi

5. gesticulations

6. éteindre

7. brûlait

8. un accès de folie

9. une tentative de suicide déguisée

10. un jour de mauvais temps

11. il s'y opposait

12. apprentissage

13. ne privilégient pas

14. moyen de régler leurs comptes

15. en sachant que

16. affrontement

17. coûte cher

18. avertissements

19. confrontation

1. ils font
rapidement
machine arrière
2. une attaque
frontale de
3. un profond
grondement
menaçant
4. Il évaluera
5. il s'est bien
fait comprendre

back down[1] when they feel they can. Rarely will a tiger attack a fellow predator without warning. Typically a head-on rush for[2] the adversary will be made, with much snarling and growling. But just before it is too late, the tiger will freeze, the menace rumbling deep[3] in its throat. It will appraise[4] the situation. If it decides that there is no threat, it will turn away, feeling that its point has been made[5].

Richard Parker made his point with me four times. Four times he struck at me with his right paw and sent me overboard, and four times I lost my shield. I was terrified before, during and after each attack, and I spent a long time shivering with fear on the raft. Eventually I learned to read the signals he was sending me. I found that with his ears, his eyes, his whiskers, his teeth, his tail and his throat, he spoke a simple, forcefully punctuated[6] language that told me what his next move might be[7]. I learned to back down before he lifted his paw in the air.

6. clairement
accentué
7. ce qu'il allait
faire ensuite
8. mon langage
basé sur une
seule note

Then I made *my* point, feet on the gunnel, boat rolling, my single-note language[8] blasting from the whistle, and Richard Parker moaning and gasping at the bottom of the boat.

My fifth shield lasted me the rest of his training.

CHAPTER 73

9. interminable
10. pas de livre
sacré
11. inconsolable
12. un char
cabossé

My greatest wish—other than salvation—was to have a book. A long book with a never-ending[9] story. One I could read again and again, with new eyes and a fresh understanding each time. Alas, there was no scripture[10] in the lifeboat. I was a disconsolate[11] Arjuna in a battered chariot[12] without the benefit of Krishna's words. The first time I came upon a Bible in the bedside table[1] of a hotel room in Canada, I burst into tears[2]. I sent a contribution to the Gideons[3] the very next day, with a note urging them to spread the range of their activity[4] to all places where worn and weary[5] travellers might lay down their heads, not just to hotel rooms, and that they should leave not only Bibles, but other sacred writings as well. I cannot think of a better way to spread the faith[6]. No thundering from a pulpit[7], no condemnation from bad churches, no peer pressure[8], just a book of scripture[9] quietly waiting to say hello, as gentle and powerful as a little girl's kiss on your cheek.

At the very least[10], if I had had a good novel! But there was only the survival manual, which I must have read ten thousand times over the course of my ordeal.

I kept a diary[11]. It's hard to read. I wrote as small as I could. I was afraid I would run out of paper.[12] There's not much to it.[13] Words scratched[14] on a page trying to capture a reality that overwhelmed me[15]. I started it a week or so after the sinking of the *Tsimtsum*. Before that I was too busy and scattered[16]. The entries are not dated or numbered. What strikes me now is how time is captured. Several days, several weeks, all on one page. I talked about what you might expect: about things that happened and how I felt, about what I caught and what I didn't, about seas and weather, about problems and solutions, about Richard Parker. All very practical stuff.[17]

CHAPTER 74

I practised religious rituals that I adapted to the

1. la table de chevet

2. j'ai fondu en larmes

3. les Gédéons [organisation chrétienne qui distribue gratuitement la Bible]

4. les pressant d'élargir le champ de leur activité

5. épuisés

6. diffuser la foi

7. Pas besoin de prêches tonitruants

8. de pression sociale

9. un texte sacré

10. Au moins

11. journal intime

12. J'avais peur de manquer de papier.

13. Ce n'est pas grand-chose.

14. gribouillés

15. me dépassait

16. je me dispersais trop

17. Que des choses pratiques.

circumstances—solitary Masses[1] without priests or consecrated Communion hosts[2], darshans without murtis, and pujas[3] with turtle meat for prasad[4], acts of devotion to Allah not knowing where Mecca was and getting my Arabic wrong[5]. They brought me comfort[6], that is certain. But it was hard, oh, it was hard. Faith in God is an opening up[7], a letting go[8], a deep trust, a free act of love—but sometimes it was so hard to love. Sometimes my heart was sinking so fast with anger, desolation[9] and weariness[10], I was afraid it would sink to the very bottom of the Pacific and I would not be able to lift it back up[11].

At such moments I tried to elevate myself. I would touch the turban I had made with the remnants[12] of my shirt and I would say aloud[13], "THIS IS GOD'S HAT!"

I would pat my pants[14] and say aloud, "THIS IS GOD'S ATTIRE[15]!"

I would point to[16] Richard Parker and say aloud, "THIS IS GOD'S CAT!"

I would point to the lifeboat and say aloud, "THIS IS GOD'S ARK[17]!"

I would spread my hands wide[18] and say aloud, "THESE ARE GOD'S WIDE ACRES[19]!"

I would point at the sky and say aloud, "THIS IS GOD'S EAR!"

And in this way I would remind myself of creation and of my place in it.

But God's hat was always unravelling[20]. God's pants were falling apart[21]. God's cat was a constant danger. God's ark was a jail[22]. God's wide acres were slowly killing me. God's ear didn't seem to be listening.

Despair was a heavy blackness that let no light in or out[23]. It was a hell beyond expression[24]. I thank God it always passed. A school of fish appeared around the net or a knot cried out to be reknotted[1]. Or I thought of my family, of how they were spared[2] this terrible agony[3]. The blackness would stir[4] and eventually go away, and God would remain, a shining point of light in my heart. I would go on loving.

1. il fallait refaire un nœud

2. ils avaient échappé à

3. souffrance

4. se levait

CHAPTER 75

On the day when I estimated it was Mother's birthday, I sang "Happy Birthday" to her out loud[5].

5. à voix haute

CHAPTER 76

I got into the habit of cleaning up after[6] Richard Parker. As soon as I became aware that he had had a bowel movement[7], I went about getting to it, a risky operation involving[8] nudging his feces my way[9] with the gaff and reaching for them from the tarpaulin. Feces can be infected with parasites. This does not matter with animals in the wild since they rarely spend any time next to their feces and mostly have a neutral relationship to them; tree dwellers hardly see them at all and land animals normally excrete[10] and move on[11]. In the compact territory of a zoo, however, the case is quite different, and to leave feces in an animal's enclosure is to invite reinfection by encouraging the animal to eat them, animals being gluttons for anything that remotely[12] resembles food. That is why enclosures are cleaned, out of concern for the intestinal health of animals, not to spare[13] the eyes and noses of visitors. But upholding[14] the Patel family's reputation

6. ramasser les excréments de

7. un mouvement intestinal

8. qui impliquait que

9. je ramène ses déjections vers moi

10. font leurs besoins

11. s'en vont

12. vaguement

13. épargner

14. maintenir

1. pour la haute qualité
2. ce qui me préoccupait
3. dans ce cas précis
4. travaux de nettoyage

5. J'ai bien compris pourquoi.
6. Montrer
7. imprégner l'atmosphère de leur odeur
8. domination
9. Inversement
10. respect
11. penchée en arrière
12. continu
13. vigilance
14. après mûre réflexion
15. j'ai dirigé mon regard vers lui
16. de manière bien visible
17. le fixant avec les yeux écarquillés
18. lui ficher la trouille
19. en le harcelant
20. sinistres

21. seigneurial
22. caresser
23. intimidation

for high standards[1] in zookeeping was not my concern[2] in the case at hand[3]. In a matter of weeks Richard Parker became constipated and his bowel movements came no more than once a month, so my dangerous janitoring[4] was hardly worth it from a sanitary point of view. It was for another reason that I did it: it was because the first time Richard Parker relieved himself in the lifeboat, I noticed that he tried to hide the result. The significance of this was not lost on me.[5] To display[6] his feces openly, to flaunt the smell of them[7], would have been a sign of social dominance[8]. Conversely[9], to hide them, or try to, was a sign of deference[10]—of deference to *me*.

I could tell that it made him nervous. He stayed low, his head cocked back[11] and his ears flat to the sides, a quiet, sustained[12] growl coming from him. I proceeded with exceptional alertness[13] and deliberation[14], not only to preserve my life but also to give him the right signal. The right signal was that when I had his feces in my hand, I rolled them about for some seconds, brought them close to my nose and sniffed them loudly, and swung my gaze his way[15] a few times in a showy manner[16], glaring at him wide-eyed[17] (with fear, if only he knew) long enough to give him the willies[18], but not so long as to provoke him. And with each swing of my gaze, I blew in a low, menacing way in the whistle. By doing this, by badgering him[19] with my eyes (for, of course, with all animals, including us, to stare is an aggressive act) and by sounding that whistle cry that had such ominous[20] associations in his mind, I made clear to Richard Parker that it was my right, my lordly[21] right, to fondle[22] and sniff his feces if I wanted to. So you see, it was not good zookeeping I was up to, but psychological bullying[23].

And it worked. Richard Parker never stared back[1]; his gaze always floated in mid-air, neither on me nor off me. It was something I could feel as much as I felt his balls of excrement in my hand: mastery in the making[2]. The exercise always left me utterly drained[3] from the tension, yet exhilarated.

Since we are on the subject, I became as constipated as Richard Parker. It was the result of our diet[4], too little water and too much protein. For me, relieving myself[5], also a monthly act, was hardly that[6]. It was a long-drawn[7], arduous and painful event that left me bathing in sweat and helpless with exhaustion, a trial worse than a high fever[8].

CHAPTER 77

As the cartons of survival rations diminished, I reduced my intake[9] till I was following instructions exactly, holding myself to[10] only two biscuits every eight hours. I was continuously hungry. I thought about food obsessively. The less I had to eat, the larger became the portions I dreamed of. My fantasy meals[11] grew to be the size of India. A Ganges of dhal soup[12]. Hot chapattis the size of Rajasthan. Bowls of rice as big as Uttar Pradesh. Sambars to flood[13] all of Tamil Nadu. Ice cream heaped[14] as high as the Himalayas. My dreaming became quite expert: all ingredients for my dishes[15] were always in fresh and plentiful supply[16]; the oven[17] or frying pan[18] was always at just the right temperature; the proportion of things was always bang on[19]; nothing was ever burnt or undercooked[20], nothing too hot or too cold. Every meal was simply perfect—only just beyond the reach of my hands.

1. ne m'a jamais fixé en retour
2. une relation de domination en train de s'établir
3. complètement épuisé
4. régime alimentaire
5. l'acte de me soulager
6. portait mal son nom
7. interminable
8. forte fièvre
9. j'ai réduit ma consommation
10. en m'en tenant à
11. Mes repas imaginaires
12. [soupe de lentilles]
13. inonder
14. amoncelée
15. plats
16. disponibles en abondance
17. four
18. poêle à frire
19. parfaite
20. pas assez cuit

By degrees[1] the range of my appetite increased[2]. Whereas at first I gutted[3] fish and peeled their skin fastidiously, soon I no more than rinsed off their slimy slipperiness[4] before biting into them, delighted to have such a treat between my teeth. I recall flying fish as being quite tasty[5], their flesh rosy white and tender. Dorado had a firmer texture and a stronger taste. I began to pick at[6] fish heads rather than toss them to Richard Parker or use them as bait. It was a great discovery when I found that a fresh-tasting fluid could be sucked out not only from the eyes of larger fish but also from their vertebrae. Turtles—which previously I had roughly[7] opened up with the knife and tossed onto the floor of the boat for Richard Parker, like a bowl of hot soup—became my favourite dish.

It seems impossible to imagine that there was a time when I looked upon a live sea turtle as a ten-course meal[8] of great delicacy[9], a blessed respite[10] from fish. Yet so it was. In the veins of turtles coursed[11] a sweet lassi that had to be drunk as soon as it spurted[12] from their necks, because it coagulated in less than a minute. The best poriyals and kootus[13] in the land could not rival turtle flesh, either cured brown[14] or fresh deep red. No cardamom payasam[15] I ever tasted was as sweet or as rich as creamy turtle eggs or cured turtle fat[16]. A chopped-up mixture[17] of heart, lungs, liver, flesh and cleaned-out[18] intestines sprinkled with[19] fish parts, the whole soaked[20] in a yolk-and-serum gravy[21], made an unsurpassable, finger-licking[22] thali[23]. By the end of my journey[24] I was eating everything a turtle had to offer. In the algae that covered the shells of some hawksbills I sometimes found small crabs and barnacles[25]. Whatever I found in a turtle's stomach became my turn to eat[1]. I whiled away many a pleasant hour gnawing at[2] a flipper joint or splitting open[3] bones and licking out their marrow[4]. And my fingers were forever picking away at bits of dry fat and dry flesh that clung to the inner sides of shells, rummaging for food[5] in the automatic way of monkeys.

Turtle shells were very handy[6]. I couldn't have done without them. They served not only as shields, but as cutting boards[7] for fish and as bowls for mixing food. And when the elements had destroyed the blankets beyond repair[8], I used the shells to protect myself from the sun by propping them against each other[9] and lying beneath them.

It was frightening, the extent to which[10] a full belly made for a good mood[11]. The one would follow the other measure for measure[12]: so much food and water, so much good mood. It was such a terribly fickle[13] existence. I was at the mercy of turtle meat for smiles.

By the time the last of the biscuits had disappeared, anything was good to eat, no matter the taste. I could put anything in my mouth, chew it and swallow it—delicious, foul or plain[14]—so long as it wasn't salty. My body developed a revulsion for salt that I still experience to this day.

I tried once to eat Richard Parker's feces. It happened early on[15], when my system hadn't learned yet to live with hunger and my imagination was still wildly searching for solutions. I had delivered fresh solar-still water to his bucket not long before. After draining it in one go[16], he had disappeared below the tarpaulin and I had returned to attending to[17] some small matter in the locker. As I always did in those early days, I glanced below the tarpaulin every so often[18] to make sure he wasn't up

1. je le mangeais à mon tour

2. J'ai passé bien des heures agréables à rogner

3. à casser

4. à lécher leur moelle

5. farfouillant à la recherche de nourriture

6. pratiques

7. planches à découper

8. irrémédiable-ment

9. en les appuyant les unes contre les autres

10. de voir à quel point

11. me mettait de bonne humeur

12. L'un n'allait pas sans l'autre

13. instable

14. répugnant ou ordinaire

15. assez tôt

16. Après l'avoir vidé d'un trait

17. m'occuper de

18. régulière-ment

263

1. qu'il n'était pas en train de manigancer quelque chose

2. voilà

3. accroupi

4. ses pattes arrière étaient écartées

5. révélatrice

6. J'ai pris une écope

7. pile au bon moment

8. une boule de chewing-gum

9. tintement

10. humanité

11. la tasse d'un mendiant

12. m'a fendu les lèvres

13. crotte

14. [boulette de pâte frite]

15. En chargeant un mousquet avec cette balle

16. J'en ai eu l'eau à la bouche

17. je n'ai plus pu supporter d'attendre

18. âcre

19. des déchets

20. éléments nutritifs

21. Je l'ai recrachée

22. amer d'avoir gâché

to something[1]. Well, this one time, lo[2], he was. He was crouched[3], his back was rounded and his rear legs were spread[4]. His tail was raised, pushing up against the tarpaulin. The position was tell-tale[5]. Right away I had food in mind, not animal hygiene. I decided there was little danger. He was turned the other way and his head was out of sight. If I respected his peace and quiet, he might not even notice me. I grabbed a bailing cup[6] and stretched my arm forward. My cup arrived in the nick of time[7]. At the second it was in position at the base of his tail, Richard Parker's anus distended, and out of it, like a bubble-gum balloon[8], came a black sphere of excrement. It fell into my cup with a clink[9], and no doubt I will be considered to have abandoned the last vestiges of humanness[10] by those who do not understand the degree of my suffering when I say that it sounded to my ears like the music of a five-rupee coin dropped into a beggar's cup[11]. A smile cracked my lips[12] and made them bleed. I felt deep gratitude towards Richard Parker. I pulled back the cup. I took the turd[13] in my fingers. It was very warm, but the smell was not strong. In size it was like a big ball of gulab jamun[14], but with none of the softness. In fact, it was as hard as a rock. Load a musket with it[15] and you could have shot a rhino.

I returned the ball to the cup and added a little water. I covered it and set it aside. My mouth watered[16] as I waited. When I couldn't stand the wait any longer[17], I popped the ball into my mouth. I couldn't eat it. The taste was acrid[18], but it wasn't that. It was rather my mouth's conclusion, immediate and obvious: there's nothing to be had here. It was truly waste matter[19], with no nutrients[20] in it. I spat it out[21] and was bitter at the loss of[22] precious water. I took the gaff and went about collecting the rest of Richard Parker's feces. They went straight to the fish.

After just a few weeks my body began to deteriorate. My feet and ankles[1] started to swell[2] and I was finding it very tiring to stand.

1. chevilles
2. enfler

CHAPTER 78

There were many skies. The sky was invaded by great white clouds, flat on the bottom but round and billowy[3] on top. The sky was completely cloudless, of a blue quite shattering[4] to the senses. The sky was a heavy, suffocating blanket of grey cloud, but without promise of rain. The sky was thinly overcast[5]. The sky was dappled[6] with small, white, fleecy[7] clouds. The sky was streaked with[8] high, thin clouds that looked like a cotton ball stretched apart[9]. The sky was a featureless milky haze[10]. The sky was a density of dark and blustery[11] rain clouds that passed by without delivering rain. The sky was painted with a small number of flat clouds that looked like sandbars[12]. The sky was a mere block to allow a visual effect on the horizon: sunlight flooding[13] the ocean, the vertical edges[14] between light and shadow perfectly distinct. The sky was a distant black curtain of falling rain. The sky was many clouds at many levels, some thick and opaque, others looking like smoke. The sky was black and spitting rain[15] on my smiling face. The sky was nothing but falling water, a ceaseless deluge that wrinkled and bloated[16] my skin and froze me stiff[17].

There were many seas. The sea roared like a tiger. The sea whispered in your ear like a friend telling

3. pleins de volutes
4. étourdissant
5. légèrement couvert
6. tacheté
7. cotonneux
8. tacheté de
9. étirée
10. une brume laiteuse aux contours indéfinis
11. de tempête
12. des bancs de sable
13. inondant
14. frontières
15. du crachin
16. ridait et gonflait
17. me frigorifiait

1. tintait comme des pièces

2. du papier de verre

3. complètement silencieuse

4. Quand bien même les choses semblent changer

5. se déplace toujours dans un certain rayon

6. atroce

7. tournoient

8. vous tourmente

9. envahissante

10. vous boucher les oreilles

11. en vous rappelant silencieusement

12. pris au piège de

13. le désespoir

14. sinistres

15. verser

you secrets. The sea clinked like small change[1] in a pocket. The sea thundered like avalanches. The sea hissed like sandpaper[2] working on wood. The sea sounded like someone vomiting. The sea was dead silent[3].

And in between the two, in between the sky and the sea, were all the winds.

And there were all the nights and all the moons.

To be a castaway is to be a point perpetually at the centre of a circle. However much things may appear to change[4]—the sea may shift from whisper to rage, the sky might go from fresh blue to blinding white to darkest black—the geometry never changes. Your gaze is always a radius[5]. The circumference is ever great. In fact, the circles multiply. To be a castaway is to be caught in a harrowing[6] ballet of circles. You are at the centre of one circle, while above you two opposing circles spin about[7]. The sun distresses you[8] like a crowd, a noisy, invasive[9] crowd that makes you cup your ears[10], that makes you close your eyes, that makes you want to hide. The moon distresses you by silently reminding you of[11] your solitude; you open your eyes wide to escape your loneliness. When you look up, you sometimes wonder if at the centre of a solar storm, if in the middle of the Sea of Tranquillity, there isn't another one like you also looking up, also trapped by[12] geometry, also struggling with fear, rage, madness, hopelessness[13], apathy.

Otherwise, to be a castaway is to be caught up in grim[14] and exhausting opposites. When it is light, the openness of the sea is blinding and frightening. When it is dark, the darkness is claustrophobic. When it is day, you are hot and wish to be cool and dream of ice cream and pour[15] sea water on yourself. When it is night you are cold and wish to be warm and dream of hot curries and wrap your-self in blankets. When it is hot, you are parched[1] and wish to be wet. When it rains, you are nearly drowned and wish to be dry. When there is food, there is too much of it and you must feast[2]. When there is none, there is truly none and you starve[3]. When the sea is flat and motionless, you wish it would stir. When it rises up and the circle that im-prisons you is broken by hills of water, you suf-fer that peculiarity of the high seas, suffocation in open spaces, and you wish the sea would be flat again. The opposites often take place at the same moment, so that when the sun is scorching you[4] till you are stricken down[5], you are also aware that it is drying the strips of fish and meat that are hanging from your lines and that it is a blessing[6] for your so-lar stills. Conversely[7], when a rain squall[8] is replen-ishing[9] your fresh-water supplies, you also know that the humidity will affect your cured provisions and that some will probably go bad, turning pasty[10] and green. When rough weather abates[11], and it be-comes clear that you have survived the sky's attack and the sea's treachery, your jubilation is tempered by the rage that so much fresh water should fall dir-ectly into the sea and by the worry that it is the last rain you will ever see, that you will die of thirst be-fore the next drops fall.

The worst pair of opposites is boredom[12] and terror. Sometimes your life is a pendulum swing[13] from one to the other. The sea is without a wrin-kle[14]. There is not a whisper of wind. The hours last forever. You are so bored you sink into a state of apathy close to a coma. Then the sea becomes rough and your emotions are whipped into a fren-zy[15]. Yet even these two opposites do not remain distinct. In your boredom there are elements of ter-

1. assoiffé

2. faire un festin
3. êtes affamé

4. cogne sur vous
5. jusqu'à vous terrasser
6. bénédiction
7. Inversement
8. averse
9. remplit
10. pâteuses
11. le mauvais temps se calme

12. l'ennui
13. un va-et-vient permanent
14. ride

15. vous submergent

1. vous vous
effondrez en
pleurs
2. effroi
3. lassitude
4. systémati-
quement
5. fade

6. la fin d'une
partie d'échecs
7. enjeux

8. superflu

9. des requins
pointes blanches
du large
10. L'aube et le
crépuscule
11. a frappé

12. claque
13. le nez du
contrevenant
14. en toute hâte

ror: you break down into tears[1]; you are filled with dread[2]; you scream; you deliberately hurt yourself. And in the grip of terror—the worst storm—you yet feel boredom, a deep weariness[3] with it all.

Only death consistently[4] excites your emotions, whether contemplating it when life is safe and stale[5], or fleeing it when life is threatened and precious.

Life on a lifeboat isn't much of a life. It is like an end game in chess[6], a game with few pieces. The elements couldn't be more simple, nor the stakes[7] higher. Physically it is extraordinarily arduous, and morally it is killing. You must make adjustments if you want to survive. Much becomes expendable[8]. You get your happiness where you can. You reach a point where you're at the bottom of hell, yet you have your arms crossed and a smile on your face, and you feel you're the luckiest person on earth. Why? Because at your feet you have a tiny dead fish.

CHAPTER 79

There were sharks every day, mainly makos and blue sharks, but also oceanic whitetips[9], and once a tiger shark straight from the blackest of nightmares. Dawn and dusk[10] were their favourite times. They never seriously troubled us. On occasion one knocked[11] the hull of the lifeboat with its tail. I don't think it was accidental (other marine life did it too, turtles and even dorados). I believe it was part of a shark's way of determining the nature of the lifeboat. A good whack[12] on the offender's nose[13] with a hatchet sent it vanishing post-haste[14] into the deep. The main nuisance of sharks was that they made being in the water risky, like trespassing on[1] a property where there's a sign saying Beware of Dog[2]. Otherwise, I grew quite fond of sharks[3]. They were like curmudgeonly[4] old friends who would never admit that they liked me yet came round to see me all the time. The blue sharks were smaller, usually no more than four or five feet long[5], and the most attractive, sleek[6] and slender[7], with small mouths and discreet gill slits[8]. Their backs were a rich ultramarine[9] and their stomachs snow white, colours that vanished to grey or black when they were at any depth[10], but which close to the surface sparkled[11] with surprising brilliance. The makos were larger and had mouths bursting with[12] frightening teeth, but they too were nicely coloured, an indigo blue that shimmered[13] beautifully in the sun. The oceanic whitetips were often shorter than the makos—some of which stretched to twelve feet[14]—but they were much stockier[15] and had enormous dorsal fins that they sailed high above the surface of the water, like a war banner[16], a rapidly moving sight that was always nerve-racking[17] to behold[18]. Besides, they were a dull[19] colour, a sort of greyish brown, and the mottled[20] white tips of their fins held no special attraction[21].

I caught a number of small sharks, blue sharks for the most part, but some makos too. Each time it was just after sunset, in the dying light of the day, and I caught them with my bare hands as they came close to the lifeboat.

The first one was my largest, a mako over four feet long[22]. It had come and gone near the bow several times. As it was passing by yet again[23], I impulsively dropped my hand into the water and grabbed it just ahead of the tail, where its body was thin-

1. quand on pénètre illégalement dans

2. Attention au chien

3. je me suis attaché aux requins

4. grincheux

5. 1 ou 1,50 m

6. luisants

7. élancés

8. fentes branchiales

9. bleu outremer

10. ils plongeaient

11. scintillaient

12. remplies de

13. miroitait

14. faisaient plus de 3,50 m

15. beaucoup plus trapus

16. bannière

17. angoissant

18. voir

19. terne

20. tachetés

21. n'avaient rien de remarquable

22. de plus d'un mètre

23. une fois encore

1. *dure*
2. *était si facile à tenir*
3. *grande joie*
4. *a sauté*
5. *embruns*
6. *téméraire*
7. *a commencé à s'agiter vigoureusement*
8. *énergie*
9. *a commencé à frapper*
10. *je tremblais*
11. *coup*
12. *ferait voler en éclats n'importe quel meuble*
13. *un tas de gravats*
14. *il se tortillait*
15. *affûtés*
16. *être empoté*
17. *a été brusquement soulevé*

nest. Its harsh[1] skin afforded such a marvellously good grip[2] that without thinking about what I was doing, I pulled. As I pulled, it jumped, giving my arm a terrific shake. To my horror and delight[3] the thing vaulted[4] in the air in an explosion of water and spray[5]. For the merest fraction of a second I didn't know what to do next. The thing was smaller than I—but wasn't I being a foolhardy[6] Goliath here? Shouldn't I let go? I turned and swung, and falling on the tarpaulin, I threw the mako towards the stern. The fish fell from the sky into Richard Parker's territory. It landed with a crash and started thwacking about[7] with such thunder[8] that I was afraid it would demolish the boat. Richard Parker was startled. He attacked immediately.

An epic battle began. Of interest to zoologists I can report the following: a tiger will not at first attack a shark out of water with its jaws but will rather strike at it with its forepaws. Richard Parker started clubbing[9] the shark. I shuddered[10] at every blow[11]. They were simply terrible. Just one delivered to a human would break every bone, would turn any piece of furniture into splinters[12], would reduce an entire house into a pile of rubble[13]. That the mako was not enjoying the treatment was evident from the way it was twisting and turning[14] and beating its tail and reaching with its mouth.

Perhaps it was because Richard Parker was not familiar with sharks, had never encountered a predatory fish—whatever the case, it happened: an accident, one of those few times when I was reminded that Richard Parker was not perfect, that despite his honed[15] instincts he too could bumble[16]. He put his left paw into the mako's mouth. The mako closed its jaws. Immediately Richard Parker reared onto his back legs. The shark was jerked up[17], but it wouldn't let go[1]. Richard Parker fell back down, opened his mouth wide and full-out roared[2]. I felt a blast[3] of hot air against my body. The air visibly shook, like the heat coming off a road[4] on a hot day. I can well imagine that somewhere far off[5], 150 miles away[6], a ship's watch[7] looked up, startled, and later reported the oddest thing, that he thought he heard a cat's meow coming from three o'clock[8]. Days later that roar was still ringing[9] in my guts. But a shark is deaf, conventionally speaking. So while I, who wouldn't think of pinching[10] a tiger's paw, let alone of trying to swallow one, received a volcanic roar full in the face and quaked[11] and trembled and turned liquid with fear and collapsed, the shark perceived only a dull[12] vibration.

Richard Parker turned and started clawing[13] the shark's head with his free front paw and biting it with his jaws, while his rear legs began tearing at[14] its stomach and back. The shark held on to his paw, its only line of defence and attack, and thrashed its tail. Tiger and shark twisted and tumbled about[15]. With great effort I managed to gain enough control of my body to get onto the raft and release it. The lifeboat drifted away. I saw flashes of orange and deep blue, of fur and skin, as the lifeboat rocked from side to side. Richard Parker's snarling was simply terrifying.

At last the boat stopped moving. After several minutes Richard Parker sat up, licking his left paw. In the following days he spent much time tending[16] his four paws. A shark's skin is covered with minute tubercles[17] that make it as rough[18] as sandpaper[19]. He had no doubt cut himself while repeatedly raking[20] the shark. His left paw was injured, but the damage did not seem permanent; no toes or claws were missing. As for the mako, except for the

1. lâcher prise
2. a émis un énorme rugissement
3. souffle
4. qui s'élève d'une route
5. au loin
6. à plus de 200 kilomètres
7. un homme de quart sur un bateau
8. à l'est
9. résonnait encore
10. pincer
11. je frémissais
12. sourde
13. à donner des coups de griffes
14. se sont mises à déchirer
15. roulaient sur le sol
16. à s'occuper de
17. tubercules
18. rugueux
19. du papier de verre
20. à force de frapper

tips of the tail and the mouth area, incongruously untouched, it was a half-eaten, butchered mess. Chunks[1] of reddish grey flesh and clumps[2] of internal organs were strewn about[3].

I managed to gaff some of the shark's remains, but to my disappointment[4] the vertebrae of sharks do not hold fluid. At least the flesh was tasty and unfishy[5], and the crunchiness[6] of cartilage was a welcome respite[7] from so much soft food.

Subsequently[8] I went for smaller sharks, pups[9] really, and I killed them myself. I found that stabbing them through the eyes with the knife was a faster, less tiresome[10] way of killing them than hacking at the tops of their heads with the hatchet.

CHAPTER 80

Of all the dorados, I remember one in particular, a special dorado. It was early morning on a cloudy day, and we were in the midst of a storm of flying fish. Richard Parker was actively swatting at them[11]. I was huddled[12] behind a turtle shell, shielding myself[13] from the flying fish. I had a gaff with a piece of net hanging from it extended into the open[14]. I was hoping to catch fish in this way. I wasn't having much luck. A flying fish whizzed by[15]. The dorado that was chasing it burst out of the water. It was a bad calculation. The anxious flying fish got away, just missing my net, but the dorado hit the gunnel like a cannonball[16]. The thud it made shook the whole boat. A spurt[17] of blood sprayed the tarpaulin. I reacted quickly. I dropped beneath the hail[18] of flying fish and reached for the dorado just ahead of a shark. I pulled it aboard. It was dead, or nearly there, and turning all kinds of colours. What a

1. De gros morceaux
2. des paquets
3. éparpillés partout
4. à mon grand regret
5. n'avait pas le goût de poisson
6. croquant
7. répit
8. Par la suite
9. des bébés
10. pénible
11. leur tapait dessus énergiquement
12. blotti
13. me protégeant
14. déployé dans l'air
15. est passé tout près
16. un boulet de canon
17. jet
18. grêle

catch![1] What a catch! I thought excitedly. Thanks be to you, Jesus-Matsya. The fish was fat and fleshy[2]. It must have weighed a good forty pounds[3]. It would feed[4] a horde. Its eyes and spine would irrigate a desert.

Alas[5], Richard Parker's great head had turned my way. I sensed it from the corner of my eyes[6]. The flying fish were still coming, but he was no longer interested in them; it was the fish in my hands that was now the focus of his attention. He was eight feet away[7]. His mouth was half open, a fish wing dangling from it[8]. His back became rounder. His rump wriggled.[9] His tail twitched. It was clear: he was in a crouch[10] and he was making to[11] attack me. It was too late to get away, too late even to blow my whistle. My time had come.

But enough was enough. I had suffered so much. I was so hungry. There are only so many days you can go without eating.

And so, in a moment of insanity brought on by hunger—because I was more set on[12] eating than I was on staying alive—without any means of defence, naked in every sense of the term, I looked Richard Parker dead in the eyes[13]. Suddenly his brute strength meant only moral weakness. It was nothing compared to the strength in my mind. I stared into his eyes, wide-eyed and defiant[14], and we faced off[15]. Any zookeeper will tell you that a tiger, indeed any cat, will not attack in the face of a direct stare but will wait until the deer or antelope or wild ox has turned its eyes[16]. But to know that and to apply it are two very different things (and it's a useless bit of knowledge if you're hoping to stare down[17] a gregarious cat. While you hold one lion in the thrall of your gaze[18], another will come up to you from behind). For two, perhaps three seconds,

1. Quelle prise !

2. charnu

3. un peu moins de 20 kilos

4. nourrir

5. Hélas

6. du coin de l'œil

7. à 2,50 mètres de moi

8. en sortait

9. Il a remué l'arrière-train.

10. il s'était ramassé sur lui-même

11. il se préparait à

12. déterminé à

13. j'ai fusillé Richard Parker du regard

14. d'un air de défi

15. nous nous sommes fait face

16. ait détourné les yeux

17. défier du regard

18. vous tenez en respect un lion du regard

a terrific battle of minds for status and authority was waged[1] between a boy and a tiger. He needed to make only the shortest of lunges[2] to be on top of me. But I held my stare[3].

Richard Parker licked his nose, groaned and turned away. He angrily batted[4] a flying fish. I had won. I gasped with disbelief, heaved the dorado into my hands and hurried away to the raft. Shortly thereafter[5], I delivered to Richard Parker a fair chunk of the fish.

From that day onwards I felt my mastery was no longer in question, and I began to spend progressively more time on the lifeboat, first at the bow, then, as I gained confidence, on the more comfortable tarpaulin. I was still scared of Richard Parker, but only when it was necessary. His simple presence no longer strained me[6]. You can get used to[7] anything—haven't I already said that? Isn't that what all survivors say?

Initially I lay on the tarpaulin with my head against its rolled-up bow edge[8]. It was raised a little[9]—since the ends of the lifeboat were higher than its middle—and so I could keep an eye on Richard Parker.

Later on I turned the other way, with my head resting just above the middle bench, my back to Richard Parker and his territory. In this position I was further away from the edges of the boat and less exposed to wind and spray.

CHAPTER 81

I know my survival is hard to believe. When I think back[10], I can hardly believe it myself.

My crude exploitation of Richard Parker's weak sea legs[1] is not the only explanation. There is another: I was the source of food and water. Richard Parker had been a zoo animal as long as he could remember[2], and he was used to sustenance coming to him[3] without his lifting[4] a paw. True, when it rained and the whole boat became a rain catcher, he understood where the water came from. And when we were hit by a school of flying fish, there too my role was not apparent. But these events did not change the reality of things, which was that when he looked beyond the gunnel, he saw no jungle that he could hunt in and no river from which he could drink freely. Yet I brought him food and I brought him fresh water. My agency[5] was pure and miraculous. It conferred power upon me. Proof[6]: I remained alive day after day, week after week. Proof: he did not attack me, even when I was asleep on the tarpaulin. Proof: I am here to tell you this story.

CHAPTER 82

I kept rainwater and the water I collected from the solar stills in the locker, out of Richard Parker's sight, in the three 50-litre plastic bags. I sealed them with string.[7] Those plastic bags wouldn't have been more precious to me had they contained gold, sapphires, rubies and diamonds. I worried incessantly about them. My worst nightmare was that I would open the locker one morning and find that all three had spilled[8] or, worse still, had split[9]. To forestall[10] such a tragedy, I wrapped them in blankets to keep them from rubbing[11] against the met-

1. du fait que Richard Parker n'avait pas le pied marin

2. aussi loin que sa mémoire remontait

3. il avait l'habitude d'être nourri

4. lever

5. intervention

6. La preuve

7. Je les fermais avec une ficelle.

8. s'étaient renversés

9. s'étaient déchirés

10. empêcher

11. frotter

1. pour qu'ils
s'usent moins
vite
2. je me
tracassais à
propos de
3. goulot
4. La ficelle
n'allait-elle pas
les user ?
5. déchirés
6. tout allait bien
7. écopes
8. seaux
9. gobelets
10. en
entortillant
l'ouverture
11. nœud
12. sécheresse
13. Parfois
14. il plongeait
la tête
15. gorgées
16. nous avions
à peine de quoi
survivre
17. manque
18. tout au
long de
19. la part du
lion
20. Il remarquait
immédiatement
21. j'attrapais
22. j'ai battu le
record du monde
d'ouverture de
23. coupés en
morceaux
24. quasiment
25. ils frétillaient
encore
26. si peu
difficile
27. parce
que j'avais
terriblement
faim

al hull of the lifeboat, and I moved them as little as possible to reduce wear and tear[1]. But I fretted over[2] the necks[3] of the bags. Would the string not wear them thin?[4] How would I seal the bags if their necks were torn[5]?

When the going was good[6], when the rain was torrential, when the bags had as much water as I thought they could take, I filled the bailing cups[7], the two plastic buckets[8], the two multi-purpose plastic containers, the three beakers[9] and the empty cans of water (which I now preciously kept). Next I filled all the plastic vomit bags, sealing them by twisting them shut[10] and making a knot[11]. After that, if the rain was still coming down, I used myself as a container. I stuck the end of the rain-catcher tube in my mouth and I drank and I drank and I drank.

I always added a little sea water to Richard Parker's fresh water, in a greater proportion in the days following a rainfall, in a lesser during periods of drought[12]. On occasion[13], in the early days, he dipped his head[14] overboard, sniffed the sea and took a few sips[15], but quickly he stopped doing it.

Still, we barely got by[16]. The scarcity[17] of fresh water was the single most constant source of anxiety and suffering throughout[18] our journey.

Of whatever food I caught, Richard Parker took the lion's share[19], so to speak. I had little choice in the matter. He was immediately aware[20] when I landed[21] a turtle or a dorado or a shark, and I had to give quickly and generously. I think I set world records for sawing open[22] the belly shells of turtles. As for fish, they were hewn to pieces[23] practically[24] while they were still flopping about[25]. If I got to be so indiscriminate[26] about what I ate, it was not simply because of appalling hunger[27]; it was also plain rush[1]. Sometimes I just didn't have the time to consider what was before me. It either went into my mouth that instant or was lost to Richard Parker, who was pawing and stamping the ground[2] and huffing[3] impatiently on the edge of his territory. It came as an unmistakable indication to me of how low I had sunk the day I noticed, with a pinching of the heart, that I ate like an animal, that this noisy, frantic, unchewing wolfing-down of mine[4] was exactly the way Richard Parker ate.

CHAPTER 83

The storm came on slowly one afternoon. The clouds looked as if they were stumbling along[5] before the wind, frightened. The sea took its cue[6]. It started rising and falling in a manner that made my heart sink. I took in[7] the solar stills and the net. Oh, you should have seen that landscape! What I had seen up till now were mere hillocks[8] of water. These swells[9] were truly mountains. The valleys we found ourselves in were so deep they were gloomy[10]. Their sides were so steep[11] the lifeboat started sliding down them, nearly surfing. The raft was getting exceptionally rough treatment[12], being pulled out of the water and dragged along bouncing every which way[13]. I deployed both sea anchors fully, at different lengths so that they would not interfere with each other.

Climbing the giant swells, the boat clung to the sea anchors like a mountain climber[14] to a rope. We would rush up[15] until we reached a snow-white crest[16] in a burst[17] of light and foam[18] and a tipping forward of the lifeboat. The view would be

1. une simple question de vitesse

2. qui trépignait

3. soufflait

4. cette façon que j'avais d'engloutir la nourriture bruyamment, frénétiquement, sans la mâcher

5. ils s'enfuyaient en trébuchant

6. a suivi

7. J'ai mis à l'abri

8. que des petits monticules

9. vagues

10. sombres

11. abrupts

12. était terriblement malmené

13. ballotté dans toutes les directions

14. alpiniste

15. Nous montions à toute allure

16. crête

17. explosion

18. écume

1. *dégagée*
2. *bougeait*
3. *commençait à s'effondrer d'une manière qui retournait l'estomac*
4. *fragile*
5. *se tendaient brusquement*
6. *les montagnes russes*

7. *nous culbuter*
8. *j'étais trempé jusqu'aux os*
9. *décidée à nous emmener avec elle*
10. *gelé*
11. *complètement terrorisé*
12. *inondé*

13. *une machine à coudre cousant un bout de tissu*
14. *j'ai agrafé*
15. *montait en tanguant*
16. *garder l'équilibre*
17. *complètement dépliée*
18. *je me suis glissé*

clear[1] for miles around. But the mountain would shift[2], and the ground beneath us would start sinking in a most stomach-sickening way[3]. In no time we would be sitting once again at the bottom of a dark valley, different from the last but the same, with thousands of tons of water hovering above us and with only our flimsy[4] lightness to save us. The land would move once more, the sea-anchor ropes would snap to tautness[5], and the roller coaster[6] would start again.

The sea anchors did their job well—in fact, nearly too well. Every swell at its crest wanted to take us for a tumble[7], but the anchors, beyond the crest, heaved mightily and pulled us through, but at the expense of pulling the front of the boat down. The result was an explosion of foam and spray at the bow. I was soaked through and through[8] each time.

Then a swell came up that was particularly intent on taking us along[9]. This time the bow vanished underwater. I was shocked and chilled[10] and scared witless[11]. I barely managed to hold on. The boat was swamped[12]. I heard Richard Parker roar. I felt death was upon us. The only choice left to me was death by water or death by animal. I chose death by animal.

While we sank down the back of the swell, I jumped onto the tarpaulin and unrolled it towards the stern, closing in Richard Parker. If he protested, I did not hear him. Faster than a sewing machine working a piece of cloth[13], I hooked down[14] the tarpaulin on both sides of the boat. We were climbing again. The boat was lurching upwards steadily[15]. It was hard to keep my balance[16]. The lifeboat was now covered and the tarpaulin battened down[17], except at my end. I squeezed in[18] between the side bench and the tarpaulin and pulled the remaining tarpaulin over my head. I did not have much space. Between bench and gunnel there was twelve inches[1], and the side benches were only one and a half feet wide[2]. But I was not so foolhardy[3], even in the face of death, as to move onto the floor of the boat. There were four hooks[4] left to catch. I slipped a hand through the opening and worked the rope. With each hook done, it was getting harder to get the next. I managed two. Two hooks left. The boat was rushing upwards in a smooth and unceasing motion[5]. The incline[6] was over thirty degrees. I could feel myself being pulled down towards the stern. Twisting[7] my hand frantically[8] I succeeded in catching one more hook with the rope. It was the best I could do. This was not a job meant to be done from the inside of the lifeboat but from the outside. I pulled hard on the rope, something made easier by the fact that holding on to it was preventing me from sliding down the length of the boat. The boat swiftly passed[9] a forty-five-degree incline.

We must have been at a sixty-degree incline when we reached the summit of the swell and broke through its crest onto the other side. The smallest portion of the swell's supply of water crashed down on us. I felt as if I were being pummelled[10] by a great fist[11]. The lifeboat abruptly tilted forward[12] and everything was reversed[13]: I was now at the lower end[14] of the lifeboat, and the water that had swamped it, with a tiger soaking in it, came my way. I did not feel the tiger—I had no precise idea of where Richard Parker was; it was pitch-black[15] beneath the tarpaulin—but before we reached the next valley I was half-drowned.

For the rest of that day and into the night, we went up and down, up and down, up and down, until terror became monotonous and was replaced

1. 30 cm
2. larges de 45 cm
3. imprudent
4. crochets
5. un mouvement fluide et continu
6. inclinaison
7. En tordant
8. frénétiquement
9. a rapidement dépassé
10. roué de coups
11. poing
12. s'est penché vers l'avant
13. s'est inversé
14. la partie la plus basse
15. il faisait noir comme dans un four

1. la torpeur
2. abandon

3. tandis que
l'eau entrait
et sortait en
trombes
4. me réduisait
en bouillie

5. Nous
voguions
6. déchirure

7. poutre
8. détruite par
un incendie
9. son proprié-
taire
10. quart
11. fidèlement

12. dans un état
déplorable

13. J'avais mal
partout
14. entaille
15. cuisse
16. enflée

by numbness[1] and a complete giving-up[2]. I held on to the tarpaulin rope with one hand and the edge of the bow bench with the other, while my body lay flat against the side bench. In this position—water pouring in, water pouring out[3]—the tarpaulin beat me to a pulp[4], I was soaked and chilled, and I was bruised and cut by bones and turtle shells. The noise of the storm was constant, as was Richard Parker's snarling.

Sometime during the night my mind noted that the storm was over. We were bobbing[5] on the sea in a normal way. Through a tear[6] in the tarpaulin I glimpsed the night sky. Starry and cloudless. I undid the tarpaulin and lay on top of it.

I noticed the loss of the raft at dawn. All that was left of it were two tied oars and the life jacket between them. They had the same effect on me as the last standing beam[7] of a burnt-down[8] house would have on a householder[9]. I turned and scrutinized every quarter[10] of the horizon. Nothing. My little marine town had vanished. That the sea anchors, miraculously, were not lost—they continued to tug at the lifeboat faithfully[11]—was a consolation that had no effect. The loss of the raft was perhaps not fatal to my body, but it felt fatal to my spirits.

The boat was in a sorry state[12]. The tarpaulin was torn in several places, some tears evidently the work of Richard Parker's claws. Much of our food was gone, either lost overboard or destroyed by the water that had come in. I was sore all over[13] and had a bad cut[14] on my thigh[15]; the wound was swollen[16] and white. I was nearly too afraid to check the contents of the locker. Thank God none of the water bags had split. The net and the solar stills, which I had not entirely deflated, had filled the empty space and prevented the bags from moving too much.

I felt exhausted and depressed[1]. I unhooked[2] the tarpaulin at the stern. Richard Parker was so silent I wondered whether he had drowned. He hadn't. As I rolled back[3] the tarpaulin to the middle bench and daylight came to him, he stirred and growled. He climbed out of the water and set himself on the stern bench. I took out needle and thread[4] and went about mending[5] the tears in the tarpaulin.

Later I tied one of the buckets to a rope and bailed[6] the boat. Richard Parker watched me distractedly[7]. He seemed to find nearly everything I did boring. The day was hot and I proceeded slowly. One haul brought me[8] something I had lost. I considered it.[9] Cradled[10] in the palm of my hand was all that remained between me and death: the last of the orange whistles.

CHAPTER 84

I was on the tarpaulin, wrapped in a blanket, sleeping and dreaming and awakening and daydreaming and generally passing the time. There was a steady breeze. From time to time spray was blown off[11] the crest of a wave and wet the boat. Richard Parker had disappeared under the tarpaulin. He liked neither getting wet nor the ups and downs of the boat. But the sky was blue, the air was warm, and the sea was regular in its motion. I awoke because there was a blast[12]. I opened my eyes and saw water in the sky. It crashed down[13] on me. I looked up again. Cloudless blue sky. There was another blast, to my left, not as powerful as the first. Richard Par-

1. abattu
2. J'ai détaché
3. j'ai enroulé
4. une aiguille et du fil
5. je me suis mis à raccommoder
6. j'ai écopé
7. distraitement
8. En écopant, j'ai retrouvé
9. Je l'ai regardé.
10. Niché
11. des embruns se détachaient de
12. une rafale
13. Elle s'est abattue

ker growled fiercely. More water crashed against me. It had an unpleasant smell.

I looked over the edge of the boat. The first thing I saw was a large black object floating in the water. It took me a few seconds to understand what it was. An arching wrinkle[1] around its edge[2] was my clue[3]. It was an eye. It was a whale. Its eye, the size of my head, was looking directly at me.

Richard Parker came up from beneath the tarpaulin. He hissed. I sensed from a slight change in the glint[4] of the whale's eye that it was now looking at Richard Parker. It gazed for thirty seconds or so before gently sinking under[5]. I worried that it might strike us with its tail, but it went straight down and vanished in the dark blue. Its tail was a huge, fading, round bracket[6].

I believe it was a whale looking for a mate[7]. It must have decided that my size wouldn't do[8], and besides, I already seemed to have a mate.

We saw a number of whales but none so close up as that first one. I would be alerted to their presence by their spouting[9]. They would emerge a short distance away, sometimes three or four of them, a short-lived archipelago[10] of volcanic islands. These gentle behemoths[11] always lifted my spirits. I was convinced that they understood my condition, that at the sight of me one of them exclaimed, "Oh! It's that castaway with the pussy cat[12] Bamphoo was telling me about. Poor boy. Hope he has enough plankton. I must tell Mumphoo and Tomphoo and Stimphoo about him. I wonder if there isn't a ship around I could alert. His mother would be very happy to see him again. Goodbye, my boy. I'll try to help. My name's Pimphoo." And so, through the grapevine[13], every whale of the Pacific knew of me, and I would have been saved long ago if Pimphoo

1. *Un pli en arc de cercle*
2. *à son pourtour*
3. *indice*
4. *reflet*
5. *avant de replonger doucement*
6. *une énorme parenthèse qui s'estompait*
7. *un compagnon*
8. *ma taille ne lui convenait pas*
9. *leurs jets d'eau*
10. *un archipel éphémère*
11. *géants*
12. *petit chat*
13. *grâce au bouche-à-oreille*

hadn't sought help from a Japanese ship whose dastardly crew[1] harpooned her[2], the same fate[3] as befell[4] Lamphoo at the hands of a Norwegian ship. The hunting of whales is a heinous[5] crime.

Dolphins were fairly regular visitors. One group stayed with us a whole day and night. They were very gay. Their plunging and turning and racing just beneath the hull seemed to have no purpose other than sporting fun[6]. I tried to catch one. But none came close to the gaff. And even if one had, they were too fast and too big. I gave up and just watched them.

I saw six birds in all. I took each one to be an angel announcing nearby land[7]. But these were seafaring[8] birds that could span[9] the Pacific with hardly a flutter[10] of the wings. I watched them with awe[11] and envy and self-pity[12].

Twice I saw an albatross. Each flew by high in the air without taking any notice of us[13]. I stared with my mouth open. They were something supernatural[14] and incomprehensible.

Another time, a short distance from the boat, two Wilson's petrels[15] skimmed by[16], feet skipping[17] on the water. They, too, took no notice of us, and left me similarly amazed[18].

We at last attracted the attention of a short-tailed shearwater[19]. It circled above us, eventually dropping down. It kicked out its legs[20], turned its wings and alighted in the water[21], floating as lightly as a cork[22]. It eyed me[23] with curiosity. I quickly baited a hook with a bit of flying fish and threw the line its way. I put no weights on the line and had difficulty getting it close to the bird. On my third try the bird paddled up to the sinking bait[24] and plunged its head underwater to get at it. My heart pounded with excitement. I did not pull on the line for some

1. dont l'infâme équipage

2. l'avait harponnée

3. destin

4. qu'avait connu

5. abominable

6. pas d'autre but que de s'amuser

7. que nous approchions de la terre ferme

8. marins

9. traverser

10. battement

11. émerveillement

12. en m'apitoyant sur mon sort

13. sans nous remarquer

14. surnaturel

15. océanites de Wilson

16. sont passés au ras de l'eau

17. sautillant

18. surpris

19. puffin à bec grêle

20. Il a tendu les pattes

21. a amerri

22. bouchon de liège

23. Il m'a regardé

24. s'est approché de l'appât qui s'enfonçait en agitant les pattes

seconds. When I did, the bird merely squawked[1] and regurgitated what it had just swallowed. Before I could try again, it unfolded[2] its wings and pulled itself up into the air[3]. Within two, three beatings of its wings it was on its way.

I had better luck with a masked booby[4]. It appeared out of nowhere, gliding[5] towards us, wings spanning over three feet[6]. It landed on the gunnel within hand's reach of me[7]. Its round eyes took me in, the expression puzzled and serious. It was a large bird with a pure snowy white body and wings that were jet-black[8] at their tips and rear edges[9]. Its big, bulbous[10] head had a very pointed orange-yellow beak and the red eyes behind the black mask made it look like a thief who had had a very long night. Only the oversized, brown webbed feet[11] left something to be desired in their design. The bird was fearless. It spent several minutes tweaking[12] its feathers with its beak, exposing soft down[13]. When it was finished, it looked up and everything fell into place, and it showed itself for what it was: a smooth, beautiful, aerodynamic airship[14]. When I offered it a bit of dorado, it pecked it[15] out of my hand, jabbing the palm[16].

I broke its neck by leveraging[17] its head backwards, one hand pushing up the beak, the other holding the neck. The feathers were so well attached that when I started pulling them out, skin came off[18]—I was not plucking[19] the bird; I was tearing it apart[20]. It was light enough as it was, a volume with no weight. I took the knife and skinned it[21] instead. For its size there was a disappointing amount of flesh, only a little on its chest. It had a more chewy[22] texture than dorado flesh, but I didn't find there was much of a difference in taste. In its stomach, besides the morsel of dorado I had just given it, I found three small fish. After rinsing them of digestive juices[1], I ate them. I ate the bird's heart, liver and lungs. I swallowed its eyes and tongue with a gulp[2] of water. I crashed its head and picked out its small brain. I ate the webbings[3] of its feet. The rest of the bird was skin, bone and feathers. I dropped it beyond the edge of the tarpaulin for Richard Parker, who hadn't seen the bird arrive. An orange paw reached out[4].

Days later feathers and down were still floating up from his den and being blown out to sea. Those that landed in the water were swallowed by fish.

None of the birds ever announced land.

CHAPTER 85

Once there was lightning[5]. The sky was so black, day looked like night. The downpour was heavy.[6] I heard thunder[7] far away. I thought it would stay at that. But a wind came up, throwing the rain this way and that. Right after, a white splinter[8] came crashing down from the sky, puncturing[9] the water. It was some distance from the lifeboat, but the effect was perfectly visible. The water was shot through with what looked like white roots[10]; briefly, a great celestial tree stood in the ocean. I had never imagined such a thing possible, lightning striking the sea. The clap of thunder[11] was tremendous[12]. The flash of light was incredibly vivid[13].

I turned to Richard Parker and said, "Look, Richard Parker, a bolt of lightning[14]." I saw how he felt about it. He was flat on the floor of the boat, limbs splayed[15] and visibly trembling.

1. sucs digestifs

2. gorgée
3. palmures

4. est apparue

5. de la foudre
6. Il pleuvait à verse.
7. le tonnerre

8. éclair
9. perçant

10. racines

11. coup de tonnerre
12. épouvantable
13. éclatant

14. éclair

15. écartés

285

1. Cela me permettait d'échapper à ma condition de mortel

2. m'émerveillait et m'exaltait
3. éclat de verre
4. immatériel
5. extrêmement
6. tambours
7. complètement assourdissant

8. sidéré
9. foudroyé

10. Jugement dernier
11. manifestation divine
12. à bout de souffle
13. muet
14. me gelait jusqu'aux os
15. des brûlures au troisième degré
16. je me suis senti véritablement heureux

The effect on me was completely the opposite. It was something to pull me out of my limited mortal ways[1] and thrust me into a state of exalted wonder[2].

Suddenly a bolt struck much closer. Perhaps it was meant for us: we had just fallen off the crest of a swell and were sinking down its back when its top was hit. There was an explosion of hot air and hot water. For two, perhaps three seconds, a gigantic, blinding white shard of glass[3] from a broken cosmic window danced in the sky, insubstantial[4] yet overwhelmingly[5] powerful. Ten thousand trumpets and twenty thousand drums[6] could not have made as much noise as that bolt of lightning; it was positively deafening[7]. The sea turned white and all colour disappeared. Everything was either pure white light or pure black shadow. The light did not seem to illuminate so much as to penetrate. As quickly as it had appeared, the bolt vanished—the spray of hot water had not finished landing upon us and already it was gone. The punished swell returned to black and rolled on indifferently.

I was dazed[8], thunderstruck[9]—nearly in the true sense of the word. But not afraid.

"Praise be to Allah, Lord of All Worlds, the Compassionate, the Merciful, Ruler of Judgment Day[10]!" I muttered. To Richard Parker I shouted, "Stop your trembling! This is miracle. This is an outbreak of divinity[11]. This is... This is..." I could not find what it was, this thing so vast and fantastic. I was breathless[12] and wordless[13]. I lay back on the tarpaulin, arms and legs spread wide. The rain chilled me to the bone[14]. But I was smiling. I remember that close encounter with electrocution and third-degree burns[15] as one of the few times during my ordeal when I felt genuine happiness[16].

At moments of wonder, it is easy to avoid small thinking[1], to entertain thoughts[2] that span[3] the universe, that capture both thunder and tinkle[4], thick and thin, the near and the far.

CHAPTER 86

"Richard Parker, a ship!"

I had the pleasure of shouting that once. I was overwhelmed with happiness[5]. All hurt and frustration fell away[6] and I positively blazed[7] with joy.

"We've made it![8] We're saved! Do you understand, Richard Parker? WE'RE SAVED! Ha, ha, ha, ha!"

I tried to control my excitement. What if the ship passed too far away to see us? Should I launch[9] a rocket flare? Nonsense!

"It's coming right towards us, Richard Parker! Oh, I thank you, Lord Ganesha! Blessed be you[10] in all your manifestations, Allah-Brahman!"

It couldn't miss us. Can there be any happiness greater than the happiness of salvation? The answer—believe me—is No. I got to my feet[11], the first time in a long time I had made such an effort.

"Can you believe it, Richard Parker? People, food, a bed. Life is ours once again. Oh, what bliss[12]!"

The ship came closer still. It looked like an oil tanker[13]. The shape of its bow was becoming distinct. Salvation wore a robe of black metal with white trim[14].

"And what if... ?"

I did not dare[15] say the words. But might there not be a chance that Father and Mother and Ravi were still alive? The *Tsimtsum* had had a number of lifeboats. Perhaps they had reached Canada weeks

1. de penser au quotidien

2. d'avoir des pensées

3. aussi grandes que

4. les tintements

5. fou de joie

6. ont disparu

7. rayonnais

8. Nous avons réussi !

9. lancer

10. Soyez béni

11. Je me suis levé

12. c'est merveilleux

13. pétrolier

14. ornée de blanc

15. Je n'ai pas osé

ago and were anxiously waiting for news from me. Perhaps I was the only person from the wreck[1] unaccounted for[2].

"My God, oil tankers are big!"

It was a mountain creeping up[3] on us.

"Perhaps they're already in Winnipeg. I wonder what our house looks like. Do you suppose, Richard Parker, that Canadian houses have inner courtyards[4] in the traditional Tamil style? Probably not. I suppose they would fill up[5] with snow in winter. Pity.[6] There's no peace like the peace of an inner courtyard on a sunny day. I wonder what spices[7] grow in Manitoba?"

The ship was very close. The crew better be stopping short[8] or turning sharply[9] soon.

"Yes, what spices… ? Oh my God!"

I realized with horror that the tanker was not simply coming our way—it was in fact bearing down on us[10]. The bow was a vast wall of metal that was getting wider every second. A huge wave girdling it[11] was advancing towards us relentlessly[12]. Richard Parker finally sensed the looming juggernaut[13]. He turned and went "Woof! Woof!" but not doglike—it was tigerlike: powerful, scary and utterly suited to[14] the situation.

"Richard Parker, it's going to run us over[15]! What are we going to do? Quick, quick, a flare! No! Must row.[16] Oar in oarlock… there! *HUMPF! HUMPF! HUMPF! HUMPF! HUMPF! HUM—*"

The bow wave[17] pushed us up. Richard Parker crouched, and the hairs on him stood up. The lifeboat slid off[18] the bow wave and missed the tanker by less than two feet[19].

The ship slid by for what seemed like a mile[20], a mile of high, black canyon wall[21], a mile of castle fortification[22] with not a single sentinel to notice us languishing in the moat[1]. I fired off a rocket flare, but I aimed it poorly[2]. Instead of surging over the bulwarks[3] and exploding in the captain's face, it ricocheted off the ship's side and went straight into the Pacific, where it died with a hiss. I blew on my whistle with all my might[4]. I shouted at the top of my lungs[5]. All to no avail[6].

Its engines rumbling loudly and its propellers[7] chopping explosively underwater, the ship churned past us[8] and left us bouncing and bobbing in its frothy wake[9]. After so many weeks of natural sounds, these mechanical noises were strange and awesome[10] and stunned me into silence[11].

In less than twenty minutes a ship of three hundred thousand tons became a speck[12] on the horizon. When I turned away, Richard Parker was still looking in its direction. After a few seconds he turned away too and our gazes briefly met. My eyes expressed longing[13], hurt, anguish, loneliness. All he was aware of was that something stressful and momentous[14] had happened, something beyond the outer limits of his understanding. He did not see that it was salvation barely missed. He only saw that the alpha here, this odd, unpredictable tiger, had been very excited. He settled down to another nap[15]. His sole comment on the event was a cranky[16] meow.

"I love you!" The words burst out pure and unfettered[17], infinite. The feeling flooded my chest[18]. "Truly I do. I love you, Richard Parker. If I didn't have you now, I don't know what I would do. I don't think I would make it. No, I wouldn't. I would die of hopelessness. Don't give up[19], Richard Parker, don't give up. I'll get you to land, I promise, I promise!"

1. en train de languir dans les douves
2. j'ai mal visé
3. dépasser les fortifications
4. de toutes mes forces
5. le plus fort que je pouvais
6. en vain
7. hélices
8. est passé dans un grand bouillonnement
9. tanguant dans son sillage d'écume
10. terrifiants
11. m'ont abasourdi et réduit au silence
12. petite tache
13. de la nostalgie
14. capital
15. faire une nouvelle sieste
16. grognon
17. sans entraves
18. m'ont envahi la poitrine
19. N'abandonne pas

CHAPTER 87

One of my favourite methods of escape[1] was what amounts to[2] gentle asphyxiation[3]. I used a piece of cloth that I cut from the remnants of a blanket. I called it my dream rag[4]. I wet it with sea water so that it was soaked[5] but not dripping[6]. I lay comfortably on the tarpaulin and I placed the dream rag on my face, fitting it to my features[7]. I would fall into a daze[8], not difficult for someone in such an advanced state of lethargy to begin with. But the dream rag gave a special quality to my daze. It must have been the way it restricted my air intake[9]. I would be visited by the most extraordinary dreams, trances, visions, thoughts, sensations, remembrances[10]. And time would be gobbled up[11]. When a twitch[12] or a gasp[13] disturbed me and the rag fell away, I'd come to full consciousness[14], delighted to find that time had slipped by[15]. The dryness of the rag was part proof[16]. But more than that was the feeling that things were different, that the present moment was different from the previous present moment.

CHAPTER 88

One day we came upon trash[17]. First the water glistened with patches of oil[18]. Coming up soon after was the domestic and industrial waste[19]: mainly plastic refuse[20] in a variety of forms and colours, but also pieces of lumber[21], beer cans, wine bottles, tatters of cloth[22], bits of rope and, surrounding it all, yellow foam[23]. We advanced into it. I looked to see if there was anything that might be of use to us. I picked out an empty corked[1] wine bottle. The lifeboat bumped into[2] a refrigerator that had lost its motor. It floated with its door to the sky. I reached out, grabbed the handle and lifted the door open. A smell leapt out so pungent and disgusting[3] that it seemed to colour the air. Hand to my mouth, I looked in. There were stains, dark juices, a quantity of completely rotten[4] vegetables, milk so curdled[5] and infected it was a greenish jelly[6], and the quartered remains[7] of a dead animal in such an advanced state of black putrefaction that I couldn't identify it. Judging by its size I think that it was lamb[8]. In the closed, humid confines of the refrigerator, the smell had had the time to develop, to ferment, to grow bitter and angry. It assaulted my senses[9] with a pent-up[10] rage that made my head reel[11], my stomach churn[12] and my legs wobble[13]. Luckily, the sea quickly filled the horrid hole and the thing sank beneath the surface. The space left vacant by the departed refrigerator was filled by other trash.

We left the trash behind. For a long time, when the wind came from that direction, I could still smell it. It took the sea a day to wash off the oily smears[14] from the sides of the lifeboat.

I put a message in the bottle: "Japanese-owned cargo ship *Tsimtsum*, flying Panamanian flag[15], sank July 2nd, 1977, in Pacific, four days out of Manila[16]. Am in lifeboat. Pi Patel my name. Have some food, some water, but Bengal tiger a serious problem. Please advise family[17] in Winnipeg, Canada. Any help very much appreciated. Thank you." I corked[18] the bottle and covered the cork with a piece of plastic. I tied the plastic to the neck of the bottle with nylon string, knotting it tightly. I launched the bottle into the water.

1. fermée avec un bouchon de liège
2. a heurté
3. âcre et répugnante
4. pourris
5. qui avait tellement tourné
6. gelée verdâtre
7. les restes écartelés
8. un mouton
9. Elle m'a attaqué les sens
10. contenue
11. qui m'a fait tourner la tête
12. m'a retourné l'estomac
13. m'a coupé les jambes
14. taches
15. au drapeau du Panama
16. quatre jours après son départ de Manille
17. Merci d'en informer ma famille
18. J'ai refermé

CHAPTER 89

Everything suffered. Everything became sun-bleached[1] and weather-beaten[2]. The lifeboat, the raft until it was lost, the tarpaulin, the stills, the rain catchers, the plastic bags, the lines, the blankets, the net—all became worn[3], stretched[4], slack[5], cracked[6], dried, rotted, torn, discoloured. What was orange became whitish orange. What was smooth[7] became rough[8]. What was rough became smooth. What was sharp[9] became blunt[10]. What was whole[11] became tattered[12]. Rubbing[13] fish skins and turtle fat on things, as I did, greasing them a little[14], made no difference. The salt went on eating everything with its million hungry mouths. As for the sun, it roasted[15] everything. It kept Richard Parker in partial subjugation[16]. It picked skeletons clean[17] and fired them to a gleaming white[18]. It burned off[19] my clothes and would have burned off my skin, dark though it was[20], had I not protected it beneath blankets and propped-up turtle shells. When the heat was unbearable I took a bucket and poured sea water on myself; sometimes the water was so warm it felt like syrup. The sun also took care of all smells. I don't remember any smells. Or only the smell of the spent hand-flare shells. They smelled like cumin, did I mention that? I don't even remember what Richard Parker smelled like.

We perished away.[21] It happened slowly, so that I didn't notice it all the time. But I noticed it regularly. We were two emaciated mammals[22], parched[23] and starving. Richard Parker's fur lost its lustre[24], and some of it even fell away from his shoulders and haunches[25]. He lost a lot of weight, became a skeleton in an oversized bag of faded fur[26]. I, too, withered away[1], the moistness sucked out of me[2], my bones showing plainly[3] through my thin flesh.

I began to imitate Richard Parker in sleeping an incredible number of hours. It wasn't proper sleep, but a state of semi-consciousness[4] in which daydreams[5] and reality were nearly indistinguishable. I made much use of my dream rag.

These are the last pages of my diary:

Today saw a shark bigger than any I've seen till now. A primeval[6] monster twenty feet long[7]. Striped.[8] A tiger shark—very dangerous. Circled us.[9] Feared it would attack. Have survived one tiger; thought I would die at the hands of another. Did not attack. Floated away. Cloudy weather, but nothing.

No rain. Only morning greyness[10]. Dolphins. Tried to gaff one. Found I could not stand. R. P. weak and ill-tempered. Am so weak, if he attacks I won't be able to defend myself. Simply do not have the energy to blow whistle.

Calm and burning hot[11] day. Sun beating without mercy. Feel my brains are boiling inside my head. Feel horrid.[12]

Prostrate[13] body and soul. Will die soon. R. P. breathing but not moving. Will die too. Will not kill me.

Salvation. An hour of heavy, delicious, beautiful rain. Filled mouth, filled bags and cans, filled body till it could not take another drop. Let myself be soaked to rinse off salt. Crawled over[14] to see R. P. Not reacting. Body curled[15], tail flat. Coat clumpy with wetness.[16] Smaller when wet. Bony.[17]

---

1. je dépérissais
2. je me desséchais
3. se voyaient nettement
4. demi-conscience
5. les rêves
6. primitif
7. de 6 m de long
8. Rayé.
9. Il a fait des cercles autour de nous.
10. grisaille
11. caniculaire
12. Je me sens horriblement mal.
13. Je suis prostré
14. Je suis allé à quatre pattes de l'autre côté du bateau
15. en boule
16. Son pelage trempé faisait des touffes.
17. Osseux.

Touched him for first time ever. To see if dead. Not. Body still warm. Amazing to touch him. Even in this condition, firm, muscular, alive. Touched him and fur shuddered as if I were a gnat[1]. At length[2], head half in water stirred. Better to drink than to drown. Better sign still: tail jumped. Threw piece of turtle meat in front of nose. Nothing. At last half rose[3]—to drink. Drank and drank. Ate. Did not rise fully. Spent a good hour licking himself all over[4]. Slept.

It's no use.[5] Today I die.

I will die today.

I die.

This was my last entry. I went on from there, endured[6], but without noting it. Do you see these invisible spirals on the margins of the page? I thought I would run out of paper[7]. It was the pens that ran out.[8]

CHAPTER 90

I said, "Richard Parker, is something wrong? Have you gone blind?[9]" as I waved[10] my hand in his face.

For[11] a day or two he had been rubbing his eyes[12] and meowing disconsolately, but I thought nothing of it[13]. Aches and pains were the only part of our diet that was abundant. I caught a dorado. We hadn't eaten anything in three days. A turtle had come up to the lifeboat the day before, but I had been too weak to pull it aboard. I cut the fish in two halves. Richard Parker was looking my way.

1. moucheron
2. Finalement
3. il s'est levé à moitié
4. à se lécher le corps entier
5. Ça ne sert à rien.
6. j'ai souffert
7. que j'allais manquer de papier
8. C'est de stylos que j'ai manqué.
9. Es-tu devenu aveugle ?
10. en agitant
11. Depuis
12. il se frottait les yeux
13. je ne m'en étais pas préoccupé

294

I threw him his share[1]. I expected him to catch it in his mouth smartly[2]. It crashed into his blank[3] face. He bent down. After sniffing left and right, he found the fish and began eating it. We were slow eaters[4] now.

I peered into[5] his eyes. They looked no different from any other day. Perhaps there was a little more discharge[6] in the inner corners, but it was nothing dramatic, certainly not as dramatic as his overall[7] appearance. The ordeal had reduced us to skin and bones.

I realized that I had my answer in the very act of looking. I was staring into his eyes as if I were an eye doctor[8], while he was looking back vacantly[9]. Only a blind wild cat would fail to react to such a stare.

I felt pity for Richard Parker. Our end was approaching.

The next day I started feeling a stinging[10] in my eyes. I rubbed and rubbed, but the itch[11] wouldn't go away. The very opposite: it got worse, and unlike Richard Parker, my eyes started to ooze pus[12]. Then darkness came, blink as I might[13]. At first it was right in front of me, a black spot[14] at the centre of everything. It spread into a blotch[15] that reached to the edges[16] of my vision. All I saw of the sun the next morning was a crack[17] of light at the top of my left eye, like a small window too high up. By noon[18], everything was pitch-black.

I clung to life. I was weakly frantic[19]. The heat was infernal. I had so little strength I could no longer stand. My lips were hard and cracked. My mouth was dry and pasty, coated with a glutinous[20] saliva as foul to taste as it was to smell[21]. My skin was burnt. My shrivelled[22] muscles ached[23]. My limbs, especially my feet, were swollen and a

1. sa part
2. habilement
3. sans expression
4. Nous mangions lentement
5. J'ai scruté
6. sécrétions
7. générale
8. ophtalmologiste
9. d'un air absent
10. picotement
11. démangeaison
12. se sont mis à suinter du pus
13. cligner des yeux n'y changeait rien
14. point
15. C'est devenu une tache
16. qui s'étendait jusqu'aux limites
17. trait
18. À midi
19. dans tous mes états
20. gluante
21. dont le goût était aussi répugnant que l'odeur
22. rabougris
23. me faisaient mal

295

constant source of pain. I was hungry and once again there was no food. As for water, Richard Parker was taking so much that I was down to five spoonfuls[1] a day. But this physical suffering was nothing compared to the moral torture I was about to endure. I would rate[2] the day I went blind as the day my extreme suffering began. I could not tell you when exactly in the journey it happened. Time, as I said before, became irrelevant[3]. It must have been sometime between the hundredth and the two-hundredth day. I was certain I would not last another one.

By the next morning I had lost all fear of death, and I resolved to die[4].

I came to the sad conclusion that I could no longer take care of Richard Parker. I had failed as a[5] zookeeper. I was more affected by his imminent demise[6] than I was by my own. But truly, broken down[7] and wasted away[8] as I was, I could do no more for him.

Nature was sinking fast. I could feel a fatal weakness creeping up on me[9]. I would be dead by the afternoon. To make my going more comfortable I decided to put off[10] a little the intolerable thirst I had been living with for so long. I gulped down[11] as much water as I could take. If only I could have had a last bite to eat[12]. But it seemed that was not to be. I set myself against the rolled-up edge of the tarpaulin in the middle of the boat. I closed my eyes and waited for my breath to leave my body. I muttered, "Goodbye, Richard Parker. I'm sorry for having failed you[13]. I did my best. Farewell.[14] Dear Father, dear Mother, dear Ravi, greetings[15]. Your loving son and brother is coming to meet you. Not an hour has gone by that I haven't thought of you. The moment I see you will be the happiest of my

1. cuillerées

2. Je considère

3. n'avait plus d'importance

4. j'étais résolu à mourir

5. J'avais échoué en tant que

6. mort

7. déprimé

8. décharné

9. me gagner

10. apaiser

11. J'ai avalé goulûment

12. un dernier morceau à manger

13. de t'avoir déçu

14. Adieu.

15. salut à tous

life. And now I leave matters in the hands of God, who is love and whom I love."

I heard the words, "Is someone there?"

It's astonishing[1] what you hear when you're alone in the blackness of your dying mind. A sound without shape or colour sounds strange. To be blind is to hear otherwise.

The words came again, "Is someone there?"

I concluded that I had gone mad. Sad but true. Misery loves company[2], and madness calls it forth[3].

"Is someone there?" came the voice again, insistent.

The clarity of my insanity was astonishing. The voice had its very own timbre, with a heavy, weary rasp[4]. I decided to play along[5].

"Of course someone's there", I replied. "There's always some *one* there. Who would be asking the question otherwise?"

"I was hoping there would be someone *else*."

"What do you mean, someone *else*? Do you realize where you are? If you're not happy with this figment of your fancy[6], pick another one[7]. There are plenty of fancies[8] to pick from[9]."

Hmmm. Figment. *Fig*-ment. Wouldn't a fig[10] be good?

"So there's no one, is there?"

"Shush[11]... I'm dreaming of figs."

"Figs! Do you have a fig? Please can I have a piece[12]? I beg you.[13] Only a little piece. I'm starving."

"I don't have just one fig. I have a whole figment."

"A whole figment[14] of figs! Oh please, can I have some? I..."

The voice, or whatever effect of wind and waves it was, faded[15].

"They're plump[16] and heavy and fragrant[17]", I continued. "The branches of the tree are bent over[18],

1. étonnant

2. La consolation des malheureux est d'avoir des semblables

3. les invoquent

4. elle était fortement éraillée

5. jouer le jeu

6. ce fruit de votre imagination

7. prenez-en un autre

8. fantasmes

9. parmi lesquels vous pouvez choisir

10. figue

11. Chut

12. je peux en avoir une

13. Je vous en prie.

14. [Jeu sur la sonorité de « figment », « création de l'imagination »]

15. s'est éteinte

16. charnues

17. parfumées

18. ploient

1. sous le poids des figues

2. [plat à base de riz et légumineuses]

3. du riz au yaourt

4. du sambar épicé au tamarin

5. J'ai presque fini.

6. [palmier]

7. des légumes braisés

8. du chou frit

9. soupe

10. des aubergines farcies frites

11. un kootu à la noix de coco et à l'igname

12. à la menthe

13. des piments verts marinés

14. des groseilles à maquereau dans du vinaigre

15. [différents types de pains indiens]

16. au yaourt et au gombo

17. [sucre non raffiné]

18. des caramels à la cacahouète

they are so weighed down with figs[1]. There must be over three hundred figs in that tree."

Silence.

The voice came back again. "Let's talk about food..."

"What a good idea."

"What would you have to eat if you could have anything you wanted?"

"Excellent question. I would have a magnificent buffet. I would start with rice and sambar. There would be black gram dhal rice[2] and curd rice[3] and—"

"I would have—"

"I'm not finished. And with my rice I would have spicy tamarind sambar[4] and small onion sambar and—"

"Anything else?"

"I'm getting there.[5] I'd also have mixed vegetable sagu[6] and vegetable korma[7] and potato masala and cabbage vadai[8] and masala dosai and spicy lentil rasam[9] and—"

"I see."

"Wait. And stuffed eggplant poriyal[10] and coconut yam kootu[11] and rice idli and curd vadai and vegetable bajji and—"

"It sounds very—"

"Have I mentioned the chutneys yet? Coconut chutney and mint[12] chutney and green chilli pickle[13] and gooseberry pickle[14], all served with the usual nans, popadoms, parathas and puris[15], of course."

"Sounds—"

"The salads! Mango curd salad and okra curd[16] salad and plain fresh cucumber salad. And for dessert, almond payasam and milk payasam and jaggery[17] pancake and peanut toffee[18] and coconut

298

burfi[1] and vanilla ice cream with hot, thick chocolate sauce."

"Is that it?"

"I'd finish this snack[2] with a ten-litre glass of fresh, clean, cool, chilled[3] water and a coffee."

"It sounds very good."

"It does."

"Tell me, what is coconut yam kootu?"

"Nothing short of heaven[4], that's what[5]. To make it you need yams, grated[6] coconut, green plantains[7], chilli powder[8], ground[9] black pepper, ground turmeric[10], cumin seeds[11], brown mustard seeds and some coconut oil. You sauté[12] the coconut until it's golden brown—"

"May I make a suggestion?"

"What?"

"Instead of coconut yam kootu, why not boiled beef tongue with a mustard sauce?"

"That sounds non-veg.[13]"

"It is. And then tripe."

"Tripe? You've eaten the poor animal's tongue and now you want to eat its *stomach*?"

"Yes! I dream of *tripes à la mode de Caen*—warm—with sweetbread[14]."

"Sweetbread? That sounds better. What is sweetbread?"

"Sweetbread is made from the pancreas of a calf[15]."

"The pancreas!"

"Braised and with a mushroom[16] sauce, it's simply delicious."

Where were these disgusting, sacrilegious recipes coming from? Was I so far gone that I was contemplating setting upon[17] *a cow and her young*[18]? What horrible crosswind[19] was I caught in? Had the lifeboat drifted back into that floating trash?

1. lait concentré à la noix de coco

2. en-cas

3. frappée

4. C'est tout bonnement le paradis

5. voilà tout

6. râpée

7. des bananes plantains

8. du piment en poudre

9. moulu

10. curcuma

11. graines

12. Vous faites revenir

13. Ça a l'air non végétarien.

14. du ris

15. veau

16. aux champignons

17. j'envisageais de me jeter sur

18. son petit

19. vent de travers

"What will be the next affront?"

"Calf's brains in a brown butter[1] sauce!"

"Back to the head[2], are we?"

"Brain soufflé!"

"I'm feeling sick.[3] Is there anything you *won't* eat?"

"What I would give for oxtail soup[4]. For roast suckling pig[5] stuffed with rice, sausages, apricots and raisins[6]. For veal kidney[7] in a butter, mustard and parsley[8] sauce. For a marinated rabbit stewed[9] in red wine. For chicken liver sausages. For pork and liver pâté with veal. For frogs[10]. Ah, give me frogs, give me frogs!"

"I'm barely holding on.[11]"

The voice faded. I was trembling with nausea. Madness in the mind was one thing, but it was not fair[12] that it should go to the stomach.

Understanding suddenly dawned on me.[13]

"Would you eat bleeding raw beef[14]?" I asked.

"Of course! I love tartar steak."

"Would you eat the congealed[15] blood of a dead pig?"

"Every day, with apple sauce!"

"Would you eat *anything* from an animal, the last remains?"

"Scrapple[16] and sausage! I'd have a heaping plate[17]!"

"How about a carrot? Would you eat a plain, raw carrot?"

There was no answer.

"Did you not hear me? Would you eat a carrot?"

"I heard you. To be honest, if I had the choice, I wouldn't. I don't have much of a stomach for[18] that kind of food. I find it quite distasteful[19]."

I laughed. I knew it. I wasn't hearing voices. I hadn't gone mad. It was Richard Parker who was

1. au beurre brun
2. Encore la tête
3. J'ai la nausée.
4. soupe de queue de bœuf
5. du cochon de lait rôti
6. de raisins secs
7. des rognons de veau
8. au persil
9. mijoté
10. des grenouilles
11. Je n'en peux plus.
12. juste
13. J'ai soudain compris.
14. du bœuf cru saignant
15. gélatineux
16. [plat à base d'abats de porc]
17. une pleine assiette
18. Je n'aime pas trop
19. assez répugnant

speaking to me! The carnivorous rascal[1]. All this time together and he had chosen an hour before we were to die to pipe up[2]. I was elated[3] to be on speaking terms[4] with a tiger. Immediately I was filled with a vulgar curiosity, the sort that movie stars suffer from at the hands of their fans.

"I'm curious, tell me—have you ever killed a man?"

I doubted it. Man-eaters among animals are as rare as murderers[5] among men, and Richard Parker was caught while still a cub. But who's to say that his mother, before she was nabbed[6] by Thirsty, hadn't caught a human being?

"What a question", replied Richard Parker.

"Seems reasonable."

"It does?"

"Yes."

"Why?"

"You have the reputation that you have."

"I do?[7]"

"Of course. Are you blind to that fact?[8]"

"I am."

"Well, let me make clear what you evidently can't see: you have that reputation. So, have you ever killed a man?"

Silence.

"Well? Answer me."

"Yes."

"Oh! It sends shivers down my spine.[9] How many?"

"Two."

"You've killed two men?"

"No. A man and a woman."

"At the same time?"

"No. The man first, the woman second."

1. gredin

2. l'ouvrir

3. J'exultais

4. de pouvoir parler

5. les meurtriers

6. coincée

7. Vraiment ?

8. Tu n'es pas au courant ?

9. Ça me donne des frissons.

301

1. Je parie

"You monster! I bet[1] you thought it was great fun. You must have found their cries and their struggles quite entertaining[2]."

2. très distrayants

"Not really."

"Were they good?"

"Were they *good*?"

3. Ne fais pas l'imbécile.

"Yes. Don't be so obtuse.[3] Did they *taste* good?"

"No, they didn't taste good."

4. que ce n'est pas un goût inné

"I thought so. I've heard it's an acquired taste[4] in animals. So why did you kill them?"

5. Par nécessité.

"Need.[5]"

"The need of a monster. Any regrets?"

"It was them or me."

"That is need expressed in all its amoral simplicity. But any regrets now?"

6. l'acte d'un instant

"It was the doing of a moment[6]. It was circumstance."

"Instinct, it's called instinct. Still, answer the question, any regrets now?"

"I don't think about it."

"The very definition of an animal. That's all you are."

"And what are you?"

"A human being, I'll have you know[7]."

7. note-le bien dans ta petite cervelle

"What boastful pride.[8]"

"It's the plain truth[9]."

8. Quel orgueil, quelle vantardise.

"So, you would throw the first stone, would you?"

"Have you ever had oothappam?"

9. la stricte vérité

"No, I haven't. But tell me about it. What is oothappam?"

"It is *so* good."

10. des restes de pâte à crêpes

"Sounds delicious. Tell me more."

11. une recette à base de restes

"Oothappam is often made with leftover batter[10], but rarely has a culinary afterthought[11] been so memorable."

"I can already taste it."

I fell asleep. Or, rather, into a state of dying delirium.

But something was niggling at me[1]. I couldn't say what. Whatever it was, it was disturbing my dying[2]. I came to.[3] I knew what it was that was bothering me[4].

"Excuse me?"

"Yes?" came Richard Parker's voice faintly[5].

"Why do you have an accent?"

"I don't. It is you who has an accent."

"No, I don't. You pronounce *the* 'ze'."

"I pronounce *ze* 'ze', as it should be. You speak with warm marbles[6] in your mouth. You have an Indian accent."

"You speak as if your tongue were a saw[7] and English words were made of wood. You have a French accent."

It was utterly incongruous[8]. Richard Parker was born[9] in Bangladesh and raised[10] in Tamil Nadu, so why should he have a French accent? Granted, Pondicherry was once[11] a French colony, but no one would have me believe that some of the zoo animals had frequented the Alliance Française on rue Dumas.

It was very perplexing[12]. I fell into a fog[13] again.

I woke up with a gasp[14]. Someone was there! This voice coming to my ears was neither a wind with an accent nor an animal speaking up. It was someone *else*! My heart beat fiercely[15], making one last go[16] at pushing some blood[17] through my worn-out[18] system. My mind made a final attempt[19] at being lucid.

"Only an echo, I fear", I heard, barely audibly.

"Wait, I'm here!" I shouted.

"An echo at sea…"

"No, it's me!"

Glosses (margin):

1. me tracassait
2. m'empêchait de mourir tranquillement
3. J'ai retrouvé mes esprits.
4. m'ennuyait
5. faiblement
6. des billes
7. scie
8. totalement incongru
9. est né
10. a grandi
11. autrefois
12. déconcertant
13. Je me suis retrouvé dans le brouillard
14. le souffle coupé
15. à toute allure
16. tentative
17. pour faire circuler du sang
18. épuisé
19. essai

"That this would end![1]"

"My friend!"

"I'm wasting away...[2]"

"Stay, stay!"

I could barely hear him.

I shrieked.

He shrieked back[3].

It was too much. I would go mad.

I had an idea.

"MY NAME", I roared to the elements with my last breath[4], "IS PISCINE MOLITOR PATEL." How could an echo create a name? "Do you hear me? I am Piscine Molitor Patel, known to all as Pi Patel!"

"What? Is someone there?"

"Yes, someone's there!"

"What! Can it be true? Please, do you have any food? Anything at all.[5] I have no food left. I haven't eaten anything in days[6]. I must have something. I'll be grateful for whatever you can spare[7]. I beg you."

"But I have no food either", I answered, dismayed[8]. "I haven't eaten anything in days myself. I was hoping *you* would have food. Do you have water? My supplies are very low.[9]"

"No, I don't. You have no food at all? Nothing?"

"No, nothing."

There was silence, a heavy silence.

"Where are you?" I asked.

"I'm here", he replied wearily.

"But where is that? I can't see you."

"Why can't you see me?"

"I've gone blind."

"What?" he exclaimed.

"I've gone blind. My eyes see nothing but darkness. I blink for nothing[10]. These last two days, if my skin can be trusted[11] to measure time. It only can tell me if it's day or night."

I heard a terrible wail[1].

"What? What is it, my friend?" I asked.

He kept wailing.[2]

"Please answer me. What is it? I'm blind and we have no food and water, but we have each other[3]. That is something. Something precious. So what is it, my dear brother?"

"I too am blind!"

"What?"

"I too blink for nothing, as you say."

He wailed again. I was struck dumb.[4] I had met another blind man on another lifeboat in the Pacific!

"But how could you be blind?" I mumbled.

"Probably for the same reason you are. The result of poor hygiene[5] on a starving body at the end of its tether[6]."

We both broke down.[7] He wailed and I sobbed. It was too much, truly it was too much.

"I have a story", I said, after a while.

"A story?"

"Yes."

"Of what use is a story? I'm hungry."

"It's a story about food."

"Words have no calories."

"Seek[8] food where food is to be found."

"That's an idea."

Silence. A famishing[9] silence.

"Where are you?" he asked.

"Here. And you?"

"Here."

I heard a splashing sound[10] as an oar dipped[11] into water. I reached for[12] one of the oars I had salvaged[13] from the wrecked raft. It was so heavy. I felt with my hands and found the closest oarlock. I dropped the oar in it. I pulled on the handle. I had no strength. But I rowed[14] as best I could[15].

1. gémissement

2. Il a continué de gémir.

3. nous sommes deux

4. J'en suis resté muet de surprise.

5. une mauvaise hygiène

6. au bout du rouleau

7. Nous nous sommes tous les deux effondrés.

8. Il faut chercher

9. affamant

10. des clapotis

11. a plongé

12. J'ai attrapé

13. que j'avais récupérée

14. j'ai ramé

15. du mieux que j'ai pu

1. J'aimerais
entendre

2. Il était une
fois

3. l'a trouvée

4. C'est
époustouflant !

5. a détourné
mon attention

6. Du
dentifrice ?

7. si vous voulez

8. faire des
échanges

"Let's hear[1] your story", he said, panting.

"Once upon a time there was[2] a banana and it grew. It grew until it was large, firm, yellow and fragrant. Then it fell to the ground and someone came upon it[3] and ate it."

He stopped rowing. "What a beautiful story!"

"Thank you."

"I have tears in my eyes."

"I have another element", I said.

"What is it?"

"The banana fell to the ground and someone came upon it and ate it—and afterwards that person *felt better*."

"It takes the breath away![4]" he exclaimed.

"Thank you."

A pause.

"But you don't have any bananas?"

"No. An orang-utan distracted me[5]."

"A what?"

"It's a long story."

"Any toothpaste?[6]"

"No."

"Delicious on fish. Any cigarettes?"

"I ate them already."

"You *ate* them?"

"I still have the filters. You can have them if you like[7]."

"The filters? What would I do with cigarette filters without the tobacco? How could you *eat* cigarettes?"

"What should I have done with them? I don't smoke."

"You should have kept them for trading[8]."

"Trading? With whom?"

"With me!"

"My brother, when I ate them I was alone in a lifeboat in the middle of the Pacific."

306

"So?"

"So, the chance of meeting someone in the middle of the Pacific with whom to trade my cigarettes did not strike me as an obvious prospect[1]."

"You have to plan ahead[2], you stupid boy! Now you have nothing to trade."

"But even if I had something to trade, what would I trade it for[3]? What do you have that I would want?"

"I have a boot", he said.

"A boot?"

"Yes, a fine leather boot[4]."

"What would I do with a leather boot in a lifeboat in the middle of the Pacific? Do you think I go for hikes[5] in my spare time[6]?"

"You could eat it!"

"Eat a boot? What an idea."

"You eat cigarettes—why not a boot?"

"The idea is disgusting. Whose boot, by the way?"

"How should I know?"

"You're suggesting I eat a complete stranger's boot?"

"What difference does it make?"

"I'm flabbergasted[7]. A boot. Putting aside the fact that I am a Hindu and we Hindus consider cows sacred, eating a leather boot conjures to my mind eating all the filth[8] that a foot might exude[9] in addition to all the filth it might step in while shod[10]."

"So no boot for you."

"Let's see it first."

"No."

"What? Do you expect me to trade something with you sight unseen[11]?"

"We're both blind, may I remind you[12]."

"Describe this boot to me, then! What kind of a pitiful salesman are you?[13] No wonder[14] you're starved for customers[15]."

1. ne m'a pas semblé une perspective probable

2. prévoir à l'avance

3. contre quoi pourrais-je l'échanger

4. une botte en cuir fin

5. je fais des randonnées

6. pendant mon temps libre

7. sidéré

8. saleté

9. peut produire

10. portée

11. sans l'avoir vu

12. je vous rappelle

13. Quel mauvais commerçant vous faites !

14. Pas étonnant

15. que vous manquiez de clients

"That's right. I am."

"Well, the boot?"

"It's a leather boot."

"What *kind* of leather boot?"

"The regular kind.[1]"

"Which means?"

"A boot with a shoelace and eyelets[2] and a tongue[3]. With an inner sole. The regular kind."

"What colour?"

"Black."

"In what condition?[4]"

"Worn. The leather soft and supple, lovely to the touch[5]."

"And the smell?"

"Of warm, fragrant leather."

"I must admit—I must admit—it sounds tempting[6]!"

"You can forget about it."

"Why?"

Silence.

"Will you not answer, my brother?"

"There's no boot."

"No boot?"

"No."

"That makes me sad."

"I ate it."

"You ate the boot?"

"Yes."

"Was it good?"

"No. Were the cigarettes good?"

"No. I couldn't finish them."

"I couldn't finish the boot."

"Once upon a time there was a banana and it grew. It grew until it was large, firm, yellow and fragrant. Then it fell to the ground and someone

1. *Une botte normale.*

2. *des œillets*

3. *languette*

4. *Dans quel état ?*

5. *très agréable à toucher*

6. *c'est tentant*

came upon it and ate it and afterwards that person felt better."

"I'm sorry. I'm sorry for all I've said and done. I'm a worthless person[1]", he burst out.

"What do you mean? You are the most precious, wonderful person on earth. Come, my brother, let us be together and feast on[2] each other's company."

"Yes!"

The Pacific is no place for rowers[3], especially when they are weak and blind, when their lifeboats are large and unwieldy[4], and when the wind is not cooperating. He was close by; he was far away. He was to my left; he was to my right. He was ahead of me; he was behind me. But at last we managed it[5]. Our boats touched with a bump[6] even sweeter-sounding than[7] a turtle's. He threw me a rope and I tethered[8] his boat to mine. I opened my arms to embrace him[9] and to be embraced by him. My eyes were brimming[10] with tears and I was smiling. He was directly in front of me, a presence glowing[11] through my blindness.

"My sweet brother", I whispered.

"I am here", he replied.

I heard a faint growl.

"Brother, there's something I forgot to mention."

He landed upon me heavily. We fell half onto the tarpaulin, half onto the middle bench. His hands reached for my throat[12].

"Brother", I gasped through his overeager[13] embrace[14], "my heart is with you, but I must urgently suggest we repair to another part of my humble ship."

"You're damn right[15] your heart is with me!" he said. "And your liver and your flesh!"

1. un scélérat

2. régalons-nous de

3. des rameurs

4. difficiles à manier

5. nous avons réussi

6. se sont heurtés

7. en faisant un bruit encore plus doux que

8. j'ai attaché

9. le prendre dans mes bras

10. débordaient

11. qui rayonnait

12. se sont tendues vers ma gorge

13. trop empressée

14. étreinte

15. Tu as sacrément raison

I could feel him moving off the tarpaulin onto the middle bench and, fatally, bringing a foot down to the floor of the boat.

"No, no, my brother! Don't! We're not—"

I tried to hold him back[1]. Alas, it was too late. Before I could say the word *alone*, I was alone again. I heard the merest clicking of claws[2] against the bottom of the boat, no more than the sound of a pair of spectacles[3] falling to the floor, and the next moment my dear brother shrieked in my face like I've never heard a man shriek before. He let go of me[4].

This was the terrible cost of Richard Parker. He gave me a life, my own, but at the expense of taking one. He ripped the flesh[5] off the man's frame[6] and cracked his bones. The smell of blood filled my nose. Something in me died then that has never come back to life.

CHAPTER 91

I climbed aboard my brother's boat. With my hands I explored it. I found he had lied to me. He had a little turtle meat, a dorado head, and even—a supreme treat[7]—some biscuit crumbs[8]. And he had water. It all went into my mouth. I returned to my boat and released his[9].

Crying as I had done did my eyes some good. The small window at the top left of my vision opened a crack[10]. I rinsed my eyes with sea water. With every rinsing[11], the window opened further[12]. My vision came back within two days[13].

I saw such a vision that I nearly wished I had remained blind[14]. His butchered, dismembered[15] body lay on the floor of the boat. Richard Parker

1. le retenir
2. un petit bruit de griffes
3. lunettes
4. m'a lâché
5. Il a arraché la chair de l'homme
6. de son squelette
7. régal suprême
8. miettes
9. j'ai détaché le sien
10. s'est un peu ouverte
11. rinçage
12. s'ouvrait davantage
13. en l'espace de deux jours
14. j'ai failli regretter d'avoir retrouvé la vue
15. démembré

had amply supped on him[1], including on his face, so that I never saw who my brother was. His eviscerated torso, with its broken ribs[2] curving up[3] like the frame[4] of a ship, looked like a miniature version of the lifeboat, such was its blood-drenched[5] and horrifying state.

I will confess that I caught one of his arms with the gaff and used his flesh as bait. I will further confess that, driven by[6] the extremity of my need[7] and the madness to which it pushed me, I ate some of his flesh. I mean small pieces, little strips that I meant for the gaff's hook that, when dried by the sun, looked like ordinary animal flesh. They slipped[8] into my mouth nearly unnoticed[9]. You must understand, my suffering was unremitting[10] and he was already dead. I stopped as soon as I caught a fish.

I pray for his soul every day.

CHAPTER 92

I made an exceptional botanical discovery. But there will be many who disbelieve[11] the following episode. Still[12], I give it to you now because it's part of the story and it happened to me.

I was on my side. It was an hour or two past noon on a day of quiet sunshine and gentle breeze. I had slept a short while, a diluted[13] sleep that had brought no rest and no dreams. I turned over to my other side, expending[14] as little energy as possible in doing so. I opened my eyes.

In the near distance I saw trees. I did not react. I was certain it was an illusion that a few blinks[15] would make disappear.

1. l'avait en grande partie dévoré pour son souper

2. côtes

3. incurvées

4. structure

5. couvert de sang

6. poussé par

7. mon complet dénuement

8. Elles ont disparu

9. pratiquement sans que je m'en rende compte

10. je souffrais sans relâche

11. ne croiront pas à

12. Malgré tout

13. léger

14. dépensant

15. clignements des yeux

The trees remained. In fact, they grew to be a forest. They were part of a low-lying island[1]. I pushed myself up. I continued to disbelieve my eyes. But it was a thrill[2] to be deluded in such a high-quality way[3]. The trees were beautiful. They were like none I had ever seen before. They had a pale bark[4], and equally distributed branches that carried an amazing[5] profusion of leaves. These leaves were brilliantly green, a green so bright and emerald that, next to it, vegetation during the monsoons was drab olive[6].

I blinked deliberately, expecting my eyelids to act like lumberjacks[7]. But the trees would not fall.

I looked down. I was both satisfied and disappointed with what I saw. The island had no soil[8]. Not that the trees stood in water. Rather, they stood in what appeared to be a dense mass of vegetation, as sparkling[9] green as the leaves. Who had ever heard of land with no soil? With trees growing out of pure vegetation? I felt satisfaction because such a geology confirmed that I was right, that this island was a chimera, a play of the mind[10]. By the same token[11] I felt disappointment[12] because an island, any island, however strange[13], would have been very good to come upon.

Since the trees continued to stand, I continued to look. To take in green, after so much blue, was like music to[14] my eyes. Green is a lovely colour. It is the colour of Islam. It is my favourite colour.

The current gently pushed the lifeboat closer to the illusion. Its shore[15] could not be called a beach[16], there being[17] neither sand nor pebbles[18], and there was no pounding of surf[19] either, since the waves that fell upon the island simply vanished into its porosity. From a ridge[20] some three hundred yards inland[21], the island sloped to[22] the sea and, forty or so yards into it[1], fell off precipitously[2], disappearing from sight into the depths of the Pacific, surely the smallest continental shelf[3] on record[4].

I was getting used to the mental delusion[5]. To make it last I refrained from putting a strain on it[6]; when the lifeboat nudged[7] the island, I did not move, only continued to dream. The fabric of the island seemed to be[8] an intricate, tightly webbed mass[9] of tube-shaped seaweed[10], in diameter a little thicker than two fingers. What a fanciful[11] island, I thought.

After some minutes I crept up[12] to the side of the boat. "Look for green", said the survival manual. Well, this was green. In fact, it was chlorophyll heaven. A green to outshine[13] food colouring[14] and flashing neon lights[15]. A green to get drunk on[16]. "Ultimately, a foot is the only good judge of land", pursued the manual. The island was within reach of a foot[17]. To judge—and be disappointed—or not to judge, that was the question.

I decided to judge. I looked about to see if there were sharks. There were none. I turned on my stomach[18], and holding on to the tarpaulin, I slowly brought a leg down. My foot entered the sea. It was pleasingly cool. The island lay just a little further down[19], shimmering[20] in the water. I stretched. I expected[21] the bubble of illusion to burst[22] at any second.

It did not. My foot sank into clear water and met the rubbery resistance of something flexible but solid. I put more weight down.[23] The illusion would not give. I put my full weight on my foot. Still I did not sink. Still I did not believe.

Finally, it was my nose that was the judge of land. It came to my olfactory sense, full and fresh, overwhelming[24]: the smell of vegetation. I gasped. After

1. après près de 35 m
2. descendait à pic
3. plateau
4. répertorié
5. ce mirage
6. j'ai essayé de ne pas le faire disparaître
7. a doucement touché
8. L'île semblait constituée de
9. un enchevêtrement complexe et inextricable
10. d'algues en forme de tubes
11. fantasque
12. je me suis approché
13. à faire pâlir
14. les colorants alimentaires
15. les lampes néon clignotantes
16. enivrant
17. suffisamment proche pour que je puisse y poser le pied
18. Je me suis mis sur le ventre
19. un peu plus bas
20. elle scintillait
21. Je m'attendais à ce que
22. éclate
23. J'ai appuyé avec plus de poids.
24. étourdissante

1. décolorées par l'eau de mer
2. relent
3. s'est disloqué
4. ai-je gémi
5. avancer en rampant
6. J'ai bredouillé
7. J'ai essayé
8. de me mettre debout
9. Ma tête saignait abondamment.
10. J'ai été pris d'un vertige aveuglant.
11. que j'allais m'évanouir
12. J'ai rétabli mon équilibre.
13. haleter
14. m'asseoir
15. verdure
16. apaisante
17. entremêlées
18. comestible
19. de croquant
20. J'ai tiré dessus.
21. Quelques-unes se sont détachées
22. Coupée en deux dans le sens de la largeur
23. parois
24. nette

months of nothing but salt-water-bleached[1] smells, this reek[2] of vegetable organic matter was intoxicating. It was then that I believed, and the only thing that sank was my mind; my thought process became disjointed[3]. My leg began to shake.

"My God! My God!" I whimpered[4].

I fell overboard.

The combined shock of solid land and cool water gave me the strength to pull myself forward[5] onto the island. I babbled[6] incoherent thanks to God and collapsed.

But I could not stay still. I was too excited. I attempted[7] to get to my feet[8]. Blood rushed away from my head.[9] The ground shook violently. A dizzying blindness overcame me.[10] I thought I would faint[11]. I steadied myself.[12] All I seemed able to do was pant[13]. I managed to sit up[14].

"Richard Parker! Land! Land! We are saved!" I shouted.

The smell of vegetation was extraordinarily strong. As for the greenness[15], it was so fresh and soothing[16] that strength and comfort seemed to be physically pouring into my system through my eyes.

What was this strange, tubular seaweed, so intricately entangled[17]? Was it edible[18]? It seemed to be a variety of marine algae, but quite rigid, far more so than normal algae. The feel of it in the hand was wet and as of something crunchy[19]. I pulled at it.[20] Strands of it broke off[21] without too much effort. In cross-section[22] it consisted of two concentric walls[23]: the wet, slightly rough outer wall, so vibrantly green, and an inner wall midway between the outer wall and the core of the algae. The division in the two tubes that resulted was very plain[24]: the centre tube was white in colour, while

314

the tube that surrounded it was decreasingly green[1] as it approached the inner wall. I brought a piece of the algae to my nose. Beyond the agreeable fragrance of the vegetable, it had a neutral smell. I licked it. My pulse quickened[2]. The algae was wet with fresh water.

I bit into it. My chops[3] were in for a shock[4]. The inner tube was bitterly salty[5]—but the outer was not only edible, it was delicious. My tongue began to tremble as if it were a finger flipping[6] through a dictionary, trying to find a long-forgotten[7] word. It found it, and my eyes closed with pleasure at hearing it: *sweet*. Not as in *good*, but as in *sugary*. Turtles and fish are many things, but they are never, ever sugary. The algae had a light sweetness that outdid in delight[8] even the sap of our maple trees[9] here in Canada. In consistency, the closest I can compare it to is water chestnuts[10].

Saliva forcefully oozed[11] through the dry pastiness of my mouth[12]. Making loud noises of pleasure, I tore at the algae around me. The inner and outer tubes separated cleanly and easily. I began stuffing[13] the sweet outer into my mouth. I went at it with both hands, force-feeding my mouth[14] and setting it to work harder and faster than it had in a very long time. I ate till there was a regular moat[15] around me.

A solitary tree stood about two hundred feet away[16]. It was the only tree downhill from the ridge, which seemed a very long way off[17]. I say *ridge*; the word perhaps gives an incorrect impression of how steep the rise from the shore was[18]. The island was low-lying, as I've said. The rise was gentle, to a height of perhaps fifty or sixty feet[19]. But in the state I was in, that height loomed[20] like a mountain. The tree was more inviting. I noticed

1. d'un vert de plus en plus pâle

2. s'est accéléré

3. mâchoires

4. ont reçu un choc

5. terriblement salé

6. qui feuilletait

7. oublié depuis longtemps

8. dont le goût délicieux surpassait

9. celui de la sève de nos érables

10. des châtaignes d'eau

11. montait abondamment

12. dans ma bouche sèche et pâteuse

13. Je me suis mis à fourrer

14. en me gavant

15. un véritable fossé

16. à environ 60 m

17. très loin

18. de l'inclinaison de la pente jusqu'au rivage

19. 15 à 18 m

20. se dressait

its patch of shade[1]. I tried to stand again. I managed to get to a squatting position[2] but as soon as I made to rise[3], my head spun[4] and I couldn't keep my balance. And even if I hadn't fallen over, my legs had no strength left in them. But my will was strong. I was determined to move forward. I crawled[5], dragged myself[6], weakly leapfrogged[7] to the tree.

I know I will never know a joy so vast as I experienced when I entered that tree's dappled, shimmering shade[8] and heard the dry, crisp[9] sound of the wind rustling its leaves[10]. The tree was not as large or as tall as the ones inland[11], and for being on the wrong side of the ridge, more exposed to the elements, it was a little scraggly[12] and not so uniformly developed as its mates[13]. But it was a tree, and a tree is a blessedly good thing to behold[14] when you've been lost at sea for a long, long time. I sang that tree's glory, its solid, unhurried[15] purity, its slow beauty. Oh, that I could be like it[16], rooted[17] to the ground but with my every hand raised up to God in praise[18]! I wept.

As my heart exalted[19] Allah, my mind began to take in information about Allah's works. The tree did indeed grow right out of[20] the algae, as I had seen from the lifeboat. There was not the least trace of soil. Either there was soil deeper down, or this species of tree was a remarkable instance of a commensal or a parasite. The trunk was about the width[21] of a man's chest. The bark was greyish green in colour, thin and smooth, and soft enough that I could mark it[22] with my fingernail[23]. The cordate[24] leaves were large and broad, and ended in a single point. The head of the tree had the lovely full roundness of a mango tree, but it was not a mango. I thought it smelled somewhat like a lote tree[25], but it wasn't a lote either. Nor a mangrove. Nor any other tree I had ever seen. All I know was that it was beautiful and green and lush with leaves[1].

I heard a growl. I turned. Richard Parker was observing me from the lifeboat. He was looking at the island, too. He seemed to want to come ashore[2] but was afraid. Finally, after much snarling and pacing[3], he leapt from the boat. I brought the orange whistle to my mouth. But he didn't have aggression on his mind. Simple balance was enough of a challenge[4]; he was as wobbly[5] on his feet as I was. When he advanced, he crawled close to the ground and with trembling limbs, like a newborn[6] cub. Giving me a wide berth[7], he made for the ridge and disappeared into the interior of the island.

I passed the day eating, resting, attempting to stand and, in a general way, bathing in bliss[8]. I felt nauseous when I exerted myself[9] too much. And I kept feeling that the ground was shifting beneath me[10] and that I was going to fall over, even when I was sitting still.

I started worrying about Richard Parker in the late afternoon. Now that the setting, the territory, had changed, I wasn't sure how he would take to me[11] if he came upon me.

Reluctantly, strictly for safety's sake[12], I crawled back to the lifeboat. However[13] Richard Parker took possession of the island, the bow and the tarpaulin remained my territory. I searched for something to moor the lifeboat to[14]. Evidently the algae covered the shore thickly, for it was all I could find. Finally, I resolved the problem by driving[15] an oar, handle first, deep into the algae and tethering the boat to it[16].

I crawled onto the tarpaulin. I was exhausted. My body was spent[17] from taking in[18] so much food,

1. avait beaucoup de feuilles

2. sur la rive

3. après avoir longtemps tourné en rond

4. était déjà assez difficile

5. chancelant

6. qui vient de naître

7. En m'évitant soigneusement

8. nageant dans le bonheur

9. je bougeais

10. le sol s'enfonçait sous moi

11. comment il se comporterait envers moi

12. pour une question de sécurité

13. Même si

14. à quoi amarrer le canot

15. en enfonçant

16. en y attachant le canot

17. épuisé

18. d'avoir avalé

1. qui résultait de

2. vaguement

3. m'a gagné

4. bas-ventre

5. déconcertant

6. je ne m'en suis pas préoccupé davantage

7. J'étais plié en deux de douleur

8. s'est mis en marche

9. le sommeil le plus réparateur

10. se sont régalés

11. j'ai creusé

12. trou

13. en milieu de matinée

14. il a fait un bond en arrière

15. il a griffé

16. d'un pas nettement plus assuré

17. appuyé

18. J'avais la tête qui tournait.

19. J'ai repoussé la végétation

20. s'est précipité vers moi

and there was the nervous tension arising from[1] my sudden change of fortunes. As the day ended, I hazily[2] remember hearing Richard Parker roaring in the distance, but sleep overcame me[3].

I awoke in the night with a strange, uncomfortable feeling in my lower belly[4]. I thought it was a cramp, that perhaps I had poisoned myself with the algae. I heard a noise. I looked. Richard Parker was aboard. He had returned while I was sleeping. He was meowing and licking the pads of his feet. I found his return puzzling[5] but thought no further about it[6]—the cramp was quickly getting worse. I was doubled over with pain[7], shaking with it, when a process, normal for most but long forgotten by me, set itself into motion[8]: defecation. It was very painful, but afterwards I fell into the deepest, most refreshing sleep[9] I had had since the night before the *Tsimtsum* sank.

When I woke up in the morning I felt much stronger. I crawled to the solitary tree in a vigorous way. My eyes feasted[10] once more upon it, as did my stomach on the algae. I had such a plentiful breakfast that I dug[11] a big hole[12].

Richard Parker once again hesitated for hours before jumping off the boat. When he did, mid-morning[13], as soon as he landed on the shore he jumped back[14] and half fell in the water and seemed very tense. He hissed and clawed[15] the air with a paw. It was curious. I had no idea what he was doing. His anxiety passed, and noticeably surer-footed[16] than the previous day, he disappeared another time over the ridge.

That day, leaning[17] against the tree, I stood. I felt dizzy.[18] The only way I could make the ground stop moving was to close my eyes and grip the tree. I pushed off[19] and tried to walk. I fell instantly. The ground rushed up to me[20] before I could move a foot. No harm done. The island, coated[1] with such tightly woven[2], rubbery vegetation, was an ideal place to relearn how to walk. I could fall any which way[3], it was impossible to hurt myself.

The next day, after another restful[4] night on the boat—to which, once again, Richard Parker had returned—I was able to walk. Falling half a dozen times, I managed to reach the tree. I could feel my strength increasing by the hour[5]. With the gaff I reached up and pulled down[6] a branch from the tree. I plucked off[7] some leaves. They were soft and unwaxed[8], but they tasted bitter. Richard Parker was attached to his den on the lifeboat—that was my explanation for why he had returned another night.

I saw him coming back that evening, as the sun was setting. I had retethered the lifeboat to the buried oar. I was at the bow, checking that the rope was properly secured[9] to the stem. He appeared all of a sudden[10]. At first I didn't recognize him. This magnificent animal bursting over the ridge at full gallop[11] couldn't possibly be the same listless, bedraggled[12] tiger who was my companion in misfortune[13]? But it was. It was Richard Parker and he was coming my way at high speed. He looked purposeful[14]. His powerful neck rose above his lowered head. His coat and his muscles shook at every step. I could hear the drumming[15] of his heavy body against the ground.

I have read that there are two fears that cannot be trained out of us[16]: the startle reaction[17] upon hearing an unexpected noise, and vertigo[18]. I would like to add a third, to wit[19], the rapid and direct approach of a known killer.

1. recouverte
2. si étroitement entrelacée
3. dans n'importe quelle direction
4. reposante
5. d'heure en heure
6. j'ai tiré vers moi
7. j'ai arraché
8. n'étaient pas recouvertes de cire
9. attachée
10. subitement
11. à toute allure
12. apathique et hirsute
13. d'infortune
14. déterminé
15. tambourinement
16. dont on ne peut pas se débarrasser
17. sursaut
18. le vertige
19. à savoir

I fumbled for the whistle.[1] When he was twenty-five feet[2] from the lifeboat I blew into the whistle with all my might. A piercing cry split the air.

It had the desired effect. Richard Parker braked[3]. But he clearly wanted to move forward again. I blew a second time. He started turning and hopping on the spot[4] in a most peculiar, deer-like way[5], snarling fiercely. I blew a third time. Every hair on him was raised[6]. His claws were full out[7]. He was in a state of extreme agitation. I feared that the defensive wall of my whistle blows was about to crumble[8] and that he would attack me.

Instead, Richard Parker did the most unexpected thing: he jumped into the sea. I was astounded. The very thing I thought he would never do, he did, and with might and resolve. He energetically paddled his way to[9] the stern of the lifeboat. I thought of blowing again, but instead opened the locker lid and sat down, retreating to the inner sanctum of my territory.

He surged onto the stern, quantities of water pouring off him[10], making my end of the boat pitch up[11]. He balanced on the gunnel and the stern bench for a moment, assessing me[12]. My heart grew faint. I did not think I would be able to blow into the whistle again. I looked at him blankly[13]. He flowed down to the floor of the lifeboat and disappeared under the tarpaulin. I could see parts of him from the edges of the locker lid. I threw myself upon the tarpaulin, out of his sight—but directly above him. I felt an overwhelming urge[14] to sprout wings[15] and fly off[16].

I calmed down. I reminded myself forcefully that this had been my situation for the last long while[17], to be living with a live tiger hot[18] beneath me.

As my breathing slowed down, sleep came to me.

---

1. J'ai cherché le sifflet à tâtons.

2. à 7,50 m

3. a ralenti

4. sauter sur place

5. d'une façon très étrange, comme un cerf

6. hérissés

7. sorties

8. était sur le point de s'effondrer

9. s'est dirigé à coups de pattes vers

10. il ruisselait d'eau

11. se soulever

12. en me jaugeant

13. l'air hagard

14. désir ardent

15. de me voir pousser des ailes

16. de m'envoler

17. depuis un bon bout de temps

18. juste

Sometime during the night I awoke and, my fear forgotten, looked over. He was dreaming: he was shaking and growling in his sleep. He was loud enough about it to have woken me up.

In the morning, as usual, he went over the ridge. I decided that as soon as I was strong enough I would go exploring the inland. It seemed quite large, if the shoreline[1] was any indication; left and right it stretched on with only a slight curve[2], showing the island to have a fair girth[3]. I spent the day walking—and falling—from the shore to the tree and back, in an attempt to restore my legs to health[4]. At every fall I had a full meal[5] of algae.

When Richard Parker returned as the day was ending, a little earlier than the previous day, I was expecting him. I sat tight[6] and did not blow the whistle. He came to the water's edge and in one mighty leap[7] reached the side of the lifeboat. He entered his territory without intruding into mine, only causing the boat to lurch[8] to one side. His return to form was quite terrifying.

The next morning, after giving Richard Parker plenty of advance, I set off[9] to explore the island. I walked up to the ridge. I reached it easily, proudly[10] moving one foot ahead of the other in a gait[11] that was spirited[12] if still[13] a little awkward[14]. Had my legs been weaker they would have given way[15] beneath me when I saw what I saw beyond the ridge.

To start with details, I saw that the whole island was covered with the algae, not just its edges. I saw a great green plateau with a green forest in its centre. I saw all around this forest hundreds of evenly scattered, identically sized ponds[16] with trees sparsely distributed[17] in a uniform way between them, the whole arrangement giving the unmistakable impression[18] of following a design.

1. rive
2. en s'incurvant à peine
3. une circonférence assez importante
4. pour essayer de redonner de la force à mes jambes
5. j'avais mon compte
6. Je suis resté assis sans bouger
7. un énorme bond
8. faisant seulement pencher le canot
9. je me suis mis en route
10. fièrement
11. d'un pas
12. vif
13. bien que
14. maladroit
15. se seraient dérobées
16. étangs de même taille, régulièrement espacés
17. quelques arbres répartis
18. donnant clairement l'impression

But it was the meerkats[1] that impressed themselves most indelibly[2] on my mind. I saw in one look what I would conservatively estimate[3] to be hundreds of thousands of meerkats. The landscape was covered in meerkats. And when I appeared, it seamed that all of them turned to me, astonished, like chickens in a farmyard[4], and stood up.

We didn't have any meerkats in our zoo. But I had read about them. They were in the books and in the literature. A meerkat is a small South African mammal related to the mongoose[5]; in other words, a carnivorous burrower[6], a foot long[7] and weighing two pounds when mature[8], slender[9] and weasel-like in build[10], with a pointed snout[11], eyes sitting squarely[12] at the front of its face, short legs, paws with four toes and long, non-retractile claws, and an eight-inch[13] tail. Its fur is light brown to grey in colour with black or brown bands on its back, while the tip of its tail, its ears and the characteristic circles around its eyes are black. It is an agile and keen-sighted[14] creature, diurnal and social in habits, and feeding in its native range[15]—the Kalahari Desert of southern Africa—on, among other things, scorpions, to whose venom[16] it is completely immune[17]. When it is on the lookout[18], the meerkat has the peculiarity of standing perfectly upright[19] on the tips of its back legs, balancing itself tripod-like[20] with its tail. Often a group of meerkats will take the stance[21] collectively, standing in a huddle[22] and gazing in the same direction, looking like commuters[23] waiting for a bus. The earnest[24] expression on their faces, and the way their front paws hang before them, make them look either like children self-consciously[25] posing for a photographer or patients in a doctor's office stripped naked[26] and demurely[27] trying to cover their genitals.

That is what I beheld in one glance[1], hundreds of thousands of meerkats—more, a million—turning to me and standing at attention[2], as if saying, "Yes, sir?" Mind you[3], a standing meerkat reaches up eighteen inches at most[4], so it was not the height[5] of these creatures that was so breathtaking[6] as their unlimited multitude. I stood rooted to the spot, speechless[7]. If I set a million meerkats fleeing in terror the chaos would be indescribable. But their interest in me was short-lived[8]. After a few seconds, they went back to doing what they had been doing before I appeared, which was either nibbling at[9] the algae or staring into the ponds. To see so many beings bending down[10] at the same time reminded me of prayer time[11] in a mosque.

The creatures seemed to feel no fear. As I moved down from the ridge, none shied away[12] or showed the least tension at my presence. If I had wanted to, I could have touched one, even picked one up[13]. I did nothing of the sort. I simply walked into what was surely the largest colony of meerkats in the world, one of the strangest, most wonderful experiences of my life. There was a ceaseless noise in the air. It was their squeaking, chirping, twittering and barking. Such were their numbers and the vagaries of their excitement[14] that the noise came and went like a flock of birds[15], at times very loud, swirling[16] around me, then rapidly dying off[17] as the closest meerkats fell silent while others, further off, started up[18].

Were they not afraid of me because I should be afraid of them? The question crossed my mind[19]. But the answer—that they were harmless—was immediately apparent. To get close to a pond, around which they were densely packed[20], I had to nudge them away with my feet[21] so as not to step

1. d'un seul coup d'œil

2. au garde-à-vous

3. Cela étant

4. fait au plus 45 cm

5. taille

6. époustouflante

7. sans voix

8. éphémère

9. mordiller

10. se pencher

11. l'heure de la prière

12. ne s'est enfuie

13. j'aurais même pu en attraper une

14. leur imprévisible effervescence

15. une nuée d'oiseaux

16. tournoyant

17. disparaissant

18. recommençaient

19. m'a traversé l'esprit

20. entassées

21. les pousser du pied

on one[1]. They took to my barging[2] without any of-fence[3], making room for me[4] like a good-natured[5] crowd. I felt warm, furry[6] bodies against my ankles as I looked into a pond.

All the ponds had the same round shape and were about the same size—roughly forty feet[7] in diameter. I expected shallowness[8]. I saw nothing but deep, clear water. The ponds seemed bottom-less[9], in fact. And as far down as I could see, their sides consisted of green algae. Evidently the layer[10] atop the island was very substantial[11].

I could see nothing that accounted for[12] the meer-kats' fixed curiosity, and I might have given up on solving the mystery had squeaking and barking not erupted[13] at a pond nearby. Meerkats were jump-ing up and down in a state of great ferment[14]. Sud-denly, by the hundreds[15], they began *diving* into the pond. There was much pushing and shoving[16] as the meerkats behind vied to reach[17] the pond's edge. The frenzy was collective; even tiny meerkit-tens were making for the water, barely being held back by mothers and guardians[18]. I stared in dis-belief.[19] These were not standard Kalahari Desert meerkats. Standard Kalahari Desert meerkats do not behave like frogs. These meerkats were most definitely a subspecies that had specialized in a fas-cinating and surprising way.

I made for the pond, bringing my feet down gin-gerly[20], in time to see meerkats swimming—actu-ally swimming—and bringing to shore fish by the dozens, and not small fish either. Some were dora-dos that would have been unqualified feasts[21] on the lifeboat. They dwarfed the meerkats.[22] It was incomprehensible to me how meerkats could catch such fish.

It was as the meerkats were hauling[1] the fish out of the pond, displaying real feats of teamwork[2], that I noticed something curious: every fish, without exception, was already dead. Freshly dead.[3] The meerkats were bringing ashore dead fish they had not killed.

I kneeled[4] by the pond, pushing aside[5] several excited, wet meerkats. I touched the water. It was cooler than I'd expected. There was a current that was bringing colder water from below. I cupped a little water[6] in my hand and brought it to my mouth. I took a sip.

It was fresh water. This explained how the fish had died—for, of course, place a saltwater fish in fresh water and it will quickly become bloated[7] and die. But what were seafaring fish doing in a fresh-water pond? How had they got there?

I went to another pond, making my way through[8] the meerkats. It too was fresh. Another pond; the same. And again with a fourth pond.

They were all freshwater ponds. Where had such quantities of fresh water come from, I asked myself. The answer was obvious: from the algae. The algae naturally and continuously desalinated[9] sea water, which was why its core was salty[10] while its outer surface was wet with fresh water: it was oozing the fresh water out[11]. I did not ask myself why the algae did this, or how, or where the salt went. My mind stopped asking such questions. I simply laughed and jumped into a pond. I found it hard to stay at the surface of the water; I was still very weak, and I had little fat[12] on me to help me float. I held on to the edge of the pond. The effect of bathing in pure, clean, salt-free water was more than I can put into words[13]. After such a long time at sea, my skin was like a hide[14] and my hair was long,

1. tiraient
2. un formidable travail d'équipe
3. Ils venaient de mourir.
4. Je me suis agenouillé
5. repoussant
6. J'ai pris un peu d'eau
7. il gonflera rapidement
8. me faufilant à travers
9. dessalaient
10. elles étaient salées à l'intérieur
11. elle suintait l'eau fraîche
12. peu de graisse
13. inexprimable
14. du cuir

1. emmêlés
2. soyeux
3. ruban anti-mouches
4. rouillée
5. je me suis plongé dans l'eau
6. m'avait sali
7. comme un seul homme
8. Je suis sorti de l'eau
9. éradiquée
10. semant la mort et le chaos sur son passage
11. côte à côte
12. sautaient sur place
13. À mon tour !
14. à regarder les étangs
15. rôdait
16. avant de leur sauter dessus
17. passait à côté d'eux d'un pas traînant
18. cela leur était égal
19. Ils ne se laissaient pas décontenancer.
20. La docilité régnait.
21. refoulé
22. se déchaînait de plus belle
23. Il en avait vraiment besoin.

matted[1] and as silky[2] as a fly-catching strip[3]. I felt even my soul had been corroded[4] by salt. So, under the gaze of a thousand meerkats, I soaked[5], allowing fresh water to dissolve every salt crystal that had tainted me[6].

The meerkats looked away. They did it like one man[7], all of them turning in the same direction at exactly the same time. I pulled myself out[8] to see what it was. It was Richard Parker. He confirmed what I had suspected, that these meerkats had gone for so many generations without predators that any notion of flight distance, of flight, of plain fear, had been genetically weeded out[9] of them. He was moving through them, blazing a trail of murder and mayhem[10], devouring one meerkat after another, blood dripping from his mouth, and they, cheek to jowl[11] with a tiger, were jumping up and down on the spot[12], as if crying, "My turn![13] My turn! My turn!" I would see this scene time and again. Nothing distracted the meerkats from their little lives of pond staring[14] and algae nibbling. Whether Richard Parker skulked up[15] in masterly tiger fashion before landing upon them[16] in a thunder of roaring, or slouched by[17] indifferently, it was all the same to them[18]. They were not to be ruffled.[19] Meekness ruled.[20]

He killed beyond his need. He killed meerkats that he did not eat. In animals, the urge to kill is separate from the urge to eat. To go for so long without prey and suddenly to have so many—his pent-up[21] hunting instinct was lashing out with a vengeance[22].

He was far away. There was no danger to me. At least for the moment.

The next morning, after he had gone, I cleaned the lifeboat. It needed it badly.[23] I won't describe what the accumulation of human and animal skeletons, mixed in with innumerable fish and turtle remains, looked like. The whole foul, disgusting mess[1] went overboard. I didn't dare step[2] onto the floor of the boat for fear of leaving a tangible trace of my presence to Richard Parker, so the job had to be done with the gaff from the tarpaulin or from the side of the boat, standing in the water. What I could not clean up with the gaff—the smells and the smears[3]—I rinsed with buckets of water.

That night he entered his new, clean den without comment. In his jaws were a number of dead meerkats, which he ate during the night.

I spent the following days eating and drinking and bathing and observing the meerkats and walking and running and resting and growing stronger. My running became smooth and unselfconscious[4], a source of euphoria. My skin healed. My pains and aches left me. Put simply[5], I returned to life.

I explored the island. I tried to walk around it but gave up. I estimate that it was about six or seven miles[6] in diameter, which means a circumference of about twenty miles[7]. What I saw seemed to indicate that the shore was unvarying in its features[8]. The same blinding greenness throughout, the same ridge, the same incline from ridge to water, the same break[9] in the monotony: a scraggly tree here and there. Exploring the shore revealed one extraordinary thing: the algae, and therefore the island itself, varied in height and density[10] depending on the weather[11]. On very hot days, the algae's weave became tight and dense, and the island increased in height[12]; the climb to the ridge became steeper[13] and the ridge higher. It was not a quick process. Only a hot spell lasting several days[14] triggered it[15]. But it was unmistakable[16]. I believe it

1. Ce carnage infect et répugnant
2. Je n'ai pas osé poser le pied
3. traces
4. J'arrivais à courir de manière souple et naturelle
5. Autrement dit
6. elle faisait à peu près 10 km
7. un peu plus de 30 km
8. avait partout les mêmes caractéristiques
9. rupture
10. changeaient de hauteur et de densité
11. en fonction du temps
12. croissait en hauteur
13. abrupte
14. une canicule de plusieurs jours
15. avait cet effet
16. manifeste

had to do with water conservation, with exposing less of the algae's surface to the sun's rays.

The converse[1] phenomenon—the loosening[2] of the island—was faster, more dramatic, and the reasons for it more evident. At such times the ridge came down, and the continental shelf, so to speak, stretched out[3], and the algae along the shore became so slack[4] that I tended to catch my feet in it[5]. This loosening was brought on by overcast weather and, faster still, by heavy seas[6].

I lived through a major storm while on the island, and after the experience, I would have trusted staying on it[7] during the worst hurricane[8]. It was an awe-inspiring spectacle to sit in a tree and see giant waves charging the island, seemingly preparing to ride up[9] the ridge and unleash bedlam and chaos[10]—only to see each one melt away[11] as if it had come upon quicksand[12]. In this respect, the island was Gandhian: it resisted by not resisting. Every wave vanished into the island without a clash[13], with only a little frothing and foaming[14]. A tremor shaking the ground and ripples wrinkling[15] the surface of the ponds were the only indications that some great force was passing through. And pass through it did: in the lee of the island[16], considerably diminished, waves emerged and went on their way. It was the strangest sight, that, to see waves *leaving* a shoreline[17]. The storm, and the resulting minor earthquakes[18], did not perturb the meerkats in the least.[19] They went about their business[20] as if the elements did not exist.

Harder to understand was the island's complete desolation. I never saw such a stripped-down[21] ecology. The air of the place carried no flies[22], no butterflies[23], no bees[24], no insects of any kind. The trees sheltered no birds. The plains hid no rodents, no grubs, no worms[1], no snakes, no scorpions; they gave rise to no other trees, no shrubs[2], no grasses, no flowers. The ponds harboured no[3] freshwater fish[4]. The seashore teemed with no weeds[5], no crabs, no crayfish[6], no coral, no pebbles, no rocks. With the single, notable exception of the meerkats, there was not the least foreign matter[7] on the island, organic or inorganic. It was nothing but shining green algae and shining green trees.

The trees were not parasites. I discovered this one day when I ate so much algae at the base of a small tree that I exposed its roots. I saw that the roots did not go their own independent way into the algae, but rather joined it[8], became it. Which meant that these trees either lived in a symbiotic relationship with the algae, in a giving-and-taking[9] that was to their mutual advantage, or, simpler still, were an integral part of the algae. I would guess that the latter was the case because the trees did not seem to bear flowers or fruit. I doubt that an independent organism, however intimate the symbiosis it has entered upon[10], would give up on[11] so essential a part of life as reproduction. The leaves' appetite for the sun, as testified by[12] their abundance, their breadth and their super-chlorophyll greenness, made me suspect that the trees had primarily an energy-gathering function. But this is conjecture.

There is one last observation I would like to make. It is based on intuition rather than hard evidence[13]. It is this: that the island was not an island in the conventional sense of the term—that is, a small landmass[14] rooted to the floor of the ocean—but was rather a free-floating[15] organism, a ball of algae of leviathan[16] proportions. And it is my hunch[17] that the ponds reached down to the sides of this huge, buoyant mass and opened onto

1. pas de larves, pas de vers

2. pas d'arbustes

3. ne contenaient pas de

4. poissons d'eau douce

5. ne regorgeait pas d'herbes

6. écrevisses

7. pas le moindre corps étranger

8. les rejoignaient

9. en faisant des échanges

10. même en symbiose étroite

11. renoncerait à

12. dont témoignaient

13. des preuves matérielles

14. masse de terre

15. qui flottait librement

16. colossales

17. intuition

the ocean, which explained the otherwise inexplicable presence in them of dorados and other fish of the open seas.

It would all bear much further study[1], but unfortunately I lost the algae that I took away.

Just as I returned to life, so did Richard Parker. By dint of stuffing himself with[2] meerkats, his weight went up, his fur began to glisten[3] again, and he returned to his healthy look of old[4]. He kept up his habit of returning to the lifeboat at the end of every day. I always made sure I was there before him, copiously marking my territory with urine so that he didn't forget who was who and what was whose[5]. But he left at first light and roamed further afield than I did[6]; the island being the same all over[7], I generally stayed within one area. I saw very little of him[8] during the day. And I grew nervous. I saw how he raked[9] the trees with his forepaws— great deep gouges[10] in the trunks, they were. And I began to hear his hoarse[11] roaring, that *aaonh* cry as rich as gold or honey[12] and as spine-chilling as[13] the depths of an unsafe[14] mine or a thousand angry bees. That he was searching for a female was not in itself what troubled me; it was that it meant he was comfortable enough on the island to be thinking about producing young. I worried that in this new condition he might not tolerate another male in his territory, his night territory in particular, especially if his insistent cries went unanswered[15], as surely they would[16].

One day I was on a walk in the forest. I was walking vigorously, caught up in my own thoughts. I passed a tree—and practically ran into[17] Richard Parker. Both of us were startled. He hissed and reared up on his hind legs, towering over me[18], his great paws ready to swat me down[19]. I stood

---

1. Cela mériterait une étude plus approfondie

2. À force de s'empiffrer de

3. briller

4. d'autrefois

5. à qui appartenait quoi

6. s'aventurait plus loin que moi

7. partout pareille

8. Je ne le voyais guère

9. griffait

10. sillons

11. rauque

12. miel

13. qui vous glaçait le sang autant que

14. dangereuse

15. ne recevaient pas de réponse

16. ce qui serait sûrement le cas

17. je me suis retrouvé quasiment nez à nez avec

18. me surplombant

19. me frapper

---

frozen to the spot, paralyzed with fear and shock. He dropped back on all fours[1] and moved away. When he had gone three, four paces, he turned and reared up again, growling this time. I continued to stand like a statue. He went another few paces and repeated the threat a third time. Satisfied that I was not a menace, he ambled off[2]. As soon as I had caught my breath and stopped trembling, I brought the whistle to my mouth and started running after him. He had already gone a good distance, but he was still within sight[3]. My running was powerful.[4] He turned, saw me, crouched—and then bolted[5]. I blew into the whistle as hard as I could, wishing that its sound would travel as far and wide as[6] the cry of a lonely tiger.

That night, as he was resting two feet beneath me, I came to the conclusion that I had to step into the circus ring again.

The major difficulty in training animals is that they operate either by instinct or by rote[7]. The short-cut[8] of intelligence to make new associations that are not instinctive is minimally available. Therefore, imprinting[9] in an animal's mind the artificial connection that if it does a certain action, say[10], roll over[11], it will get a treat can be achieved only by mind-numbing[12] repetition. It is a slow process that depends as much on luck as on hard work, all the more so[13] when the animal is an adult. I blew into the whistle till my lungs hurt. I pounded[14] my chest till it was covered with bruises. I shouted "Hep! Hep! Hep!"—my tiger-language command to say "Do!"—thousands of times. I tossed hundreds of meerkat morsels[15] at him that I would gladly have eaten myself. The training of tigers is no easy feat[16]. They are considerably less flexible in their mental make-up[17] than other animals that are commonly

1. sur ses quatre pattes

2. il est parti tranquillement

3. je le voyais encore
4. Je courais vite.
5. il a déguerpi
6. aussi loin que

7. par conditionnement
8. raccourci

9. graver
10. disons
11. se rouler par terre
12. abrutissante
13. d'autant plus
14. Je me suis frappé

15. morceaux

16. difficile
17. structures mentales

trained in circuses and zoos—sea lions and chimpanzees, for example. But I don't want to take too much credit[1] for what I managed to do with Richard Parker. My good fortune, the fortune that saved my life, was that he was not only a young adult but a pliable[2] young adult, an omega animal. I was afraid that conditions on the island might play against me, that with such an abundance of food and water and so much space he might become relaxed and confident[3], less open to my influence. But he remained tense. I knew him well enough to sense it. At night in the lifeboat he was unsettled[4] and noisy. I assigned[5] this tension to the new environment of the island; any change, even positive, will make an animal tense. Whatever the cause, the strain he was under[6] meant that he continued to show a readiness to oblige[7]; more, that he felt a need[8] to oblige.

I trained him to jump through a hoop[9] I made with thin branches. It was a simple routine of four jumps. Each one earned him[10] part of a meerkat. As he lumbered[11] towards me, I first held the hoop at the end of my left arm, some three feet off the ground[12]. When he had leapt through it, and as he finished his run, I took hold of the hoop with my right hand and, my back to him[13], commanded him[14] to return and leap through it again. For the third jump I knelt on the ground and held the hoop over my head. It was a nerve-racking[15] experience to see him come my way. I never lost the fear that he would not jump but attack me. Thankfully, he jumped every time. After which I got up and tossed the hoop so that it rolled like a wheel[16]. Richard Parker was supposed to follow it and go through it one last time before it fell over[17]. He was never very good at this last part of the act, either because I failed to throw the hoop properly or because he

1. m'attribuer trop de mérite

2. docile

3. confiant
4. perturbé

5. J'attribuais

6. la tension à laquelle il était soumis

7. se montrer prêt à m'obéir

8. il avait besoin

9. cerceau

10. lui valait

11. il marchait pesamment

12. à un peu moins d'un mètre du sol

13. en lui tournant le dos

14. je lui ordonnais

15. éprouvante pour les nerfs

16. roue

17. avant qu'il ne tombe

clumsily[1] ran into it. But at least he followed it, which meant he got away from me[2]. He was always filled with amazement[3] when the hoop fell over. He would look at it intently, as if it were some great fellow animal he had been running with that had collapsed unexpectedly. He would stay next to it, sniffing it. I would throw him his last treat and move away.

Eventually I quit[4] the boat. It seemed absurd to spend my nights in such cramped quarters[5] with an animal who was becoming roomy in his needs[6], when I could have an entire island. I decided the safe thing to do would be to sleep in a tree. Richard Parker's nocturnal practice of sleeping in the lifeboat was never a law in my mind. It would not be a good idea for me to be outside my territory, sleeping and defenceless on the ground, the one time he decided to go for a midnight stroll[7].

So one day I left the boat with the net, a rope and some blankets. I sought out a handsome tree on the edge of the forest and threw the rope over the lowest branch. My fitness was such that I had no problem pulling myself up by my arms[8] and climbing the tree. I found two solid branches that were level[9] and close together, and I tied the net to them. I returned at the end of the day.

I had just finished folding the blankets to make my mattress when I detected a commotion[10] among the meerkats. I looked. I pushed aside branches[11] to see better. I looked in every direction and as far as the horizon. It was unmistakable. The meerkats were abandoning the ponds—indeed, the whole plain—and rapidly making for the forest. An entire nation of meerkats was on the move[12], their backs arched[13] and their feet a blur[14]. I was wondering what further surprise[15] these animals held in store

1. maladroitement
2. il s'éloignait de moi
3. frappé de stupeur
4. J'ai fini par quitter
5. dans un espace aussi restreint
6. commençait à avoir besoin de place
7. faire une balade de minuit
8. pour grimper à la corde avec les bras
9. au même niveau
10. agitation
11. J'ai poussé des branches
12. se déplaçait
13. courbés
14. courant à toute vitesse
15. quelle autre surprise

1. me
réservaient

2. impitoyable-
ment

3. indigné

4. en haut d'un
arbre

5. injuste

6. Ils ne me
voulaient aucun
mal.

7. chargé

8. Ils se sont
même emparés
de

9. devenait
marron

10. une foule
d'entre eux
galopaient

11. pour envahir
des arbres non
occupés

12. un troupeau
d'éléphants en
fuite

13. déserte

14. couchette

15. dortoir
bondé

16. nous réserve
d'incroyables
surprises

17. J'ai joué des
coudes

18. Ils se sont
blottis contre
moi.

19. Pas un
centimètre carré

for me[1] when I noticed with consternation that the ones from the pond closest to me had surrounded my tree and were climbing up the trunk. The trunk was disappearing under a wave of determined meerkats. I thought they were coming to attack me, that here was the reason why Richard Parker slept in the lifeboat: during the day the meerkats were docile and harmless, but at night, under their collective weight, they crushed their enemies ruthlessly[2]. I was both afraid and indignant[3]. To survive for so long in a lifeboat with a 450-pound Bengal tiger only to die up a tree[4] at the hands of two-pound meerkats struck me as a tragedy too unfair[5] and too ridiculous to bear.

They meant me no harm.[6] They climbed up to me, over me, about me—and past me. They settled upon every branch in the tree. It became *laden*[7] with them. They even took over[8] my bed. And the same as far as the eye could see. They were climbing every tree in sight. The entire forest was turning brown[9], an autumn that came in a few minutes. Collectively, as they scampered by in droves[10] to claim empty trees[11] deeper into the forest, they made more noise than a stampeding herd of elephants[12].

The plain, meanwhile, was becoming bare[13] and depopulated.

From a bunk bed[14] with a tiger to an overcrowded dormitory[15] with meerkats—will I be believed when I say that life can take the most surprising turns[16]? I jostled[17] with meerkats so that I could have a place in my own bed. They snuggled up to me.[18] Not a square inch of space[19] was left free.

They settled down and stopped squeaking and chirping. Silence came to the tree. We fell asleep.

I woke up at dawn covered from head to toe in a living fur blanket[1]. Some meerkittens had discovered the warmer parts of my body. I had a tight, sweaty[2] collar of them around my neck—and it must have been their mother who had settled herself so contentedly on the side of my head—while others had wedged themselves[3] in my groin area[4].

They left the tree as briskly[5] and as unceremoniously as they had invaded it. It was the same with every tree around. The plain grew thick with[6] meerkats, and the noises of their day started filling the air. The tree looked empty. And I felt empty, a little. I had liked the experience of sleeping with the meerkats.

I began to sleep in the tree every night. I emptied the lifeboat of useful items and made myself a nice treetop[7] bedroom. I got used to the unintentional scratches[8] I received from meerkats climbing over me. My only complaint would be that animals higher up occasionally relieved themselves on me.

One night the meerkats woke me up. They were chattering and shaking. I sat up[9] and looked in the direction they were looking. The sky was cloudless and the moon full. The land was robbed of its colour[10]. Everything glowed[11] strangely in shades of black, grey and white. It was the pond. Silver shapes were moving in it, emerging from below and breaking the black surface of the water.

Fish. Dead fish. They were floating up[12] from deep down. The pond—remember, forty feet across—was filling up with all kinds of dead fish until its surface was no longer black but silver. And from the way the surface kept on being disturbed[13], it was evident that more dead fish were coming up.

By the time a dead shark quietly appeared, the meerkats were in a fury of excitement[14], shriek-

1. couverture vivante en fourrure	
2. trempé de sueur	
3. s'étaient calés	
4. aine	
5. brusquement	
6. a été recouverte de	
7. au sommet d'un arbre	
8. égratignures involontaires	
9. Je me suis assis	
10. avait perdu ses couleurs	
11. luisait	
12. Ils remontaient à la surface	
13. continuait à se troubler	
14. complètement surexcités	

ing like tropical birds. The hysteria spread to the neighbouring trees. It was deafening[1]. I wondered whether I was about to see the sight of fish being hauled up trees[2].

Not a single meerkat went down to the pond. None even made the first motions of going down[3]. They did no more than loudly express their frustration.

I found the sight[4] sinister. There was something disturbing about all those dead fish.

I lay down again and fought to go back to sleep over the meerkats' racket[5]. At first light I was stirred from my slumber[6] by the hullabaloo[7] they made trooping down the tree[8]. Yawning and stretching, I looked down at the pond that had been the source of such fire and fluster[9] the previous night.

It was empty. Or nearly. But it wasn't the work of the meerkats. They were just now diving in to get what was left.

The fish had disappeared. I was confounded[10]. Was I looking at the wrong pond? No, for sure[11] it was that one. Was I certain it was not the meerkats that had emptied it? Absolutely. I could hardly see them heaving an entire shark out of water, let alone carrying it on their backs and disappearing with it. Could it be Richard Parker? Possibly in part, but not an entire pond in one night.

It was a complete mystery. No amount of staring into the pond[12] and at its deep green walls could explain to me[13] what had happened to the fish. The next night I looked, but no new fish came into the pond.

The answer to the mystery came sometime later, from deep within the forest.

The trees were larger in the centre of the forest and closely set[14]. It remained clear below, there being no underbrush[15] of any kind, but overhead the canopy[1] was so dense that the sky was quite blocked off[2], or, another way of putting it, the sky was solidly green. The trees were so near one another that their branches grew into each other's spaces; they touched and twisted[3] around each other so that it was hard to tell where one tree ended and the next began. I noted that they had clean, smooth trunks, with none of the countless tiny marks on their bark made by climbing meerkats. I easily guessed the reason why[4]: the meerkats could travel from one tree to another without the need to climb up and down[5]. I found, as proof of this, many trees on the perimeter of the heart of the forest whose bark had been practically shredded[6]. These trees were without a doubt the gates[7] into a meerkat arboreal city[8] with more bustle in it[9] than Calcutta.

It was here that I found the tree. It wasn't the largest in the forest, or in its dead centre[10], or remarkable in any other way. It had good level branches, that's all. It would have made an excellent spot from which to see the sky or take in[11] the meerkats' nightlife.

I can tell you exactly what day I came upon the tree: it was the day before I left the island.

I noticed the tree because it seemed to have fruit. Whereas elsewhere the forest canopy was uniformly green, these fruit stood out[12] black against green. The branches holding them were twisted in odd ways[13]. I looked intently. An entire island covered in barren[14] trees—but for one[15]. And not even all of one. The fruit grew from only one small part of the tree. I thought that perhaps I had come upon the forest equivalent of a queen bee[16], and I wondered whether this algae would ever cease to amaze me[17] with its botanical strangeness.

1. la voûte végétale

2. presque invisible

3. s'enroulaient

4. J'ai facilement deviné pourquoi

5. monter et descendre

6. déchiquetée

7. portes d'entrée

8. une ville arboricole peuplée de suricates

9. plus animée

10. le plus central

11. observer

12. se détachaient

13. bizarrement tordues

14. stériles

15. à l'exception d'un seul

16. la reine des abeilles

17. arrêterait un jour de me surprendre

I wanted to try the fruit, but the tree was too high. So I returned with a rope. If the algae was delicious, what would its fruit be like?

I looped[1] the rope around the lowest limb[2] of the tree and, bough by bough, branch by branch[3], made my way to the small, precious orchard[4].

Up close[5] the fruit were dull green. They were about the size and shape of oranges. Each was at the centre of a number of twigs that were tightly curled[6] around it—to protect it, I supposed. As I got closer, I could see another purpose to these curled twigs: support. The fruit had not one stem[7], but dozens. Their surfaces were studded[8] with stems that connected them to the surrounding twigs. These fruit must surely be heavy and juicy[9], I thought. I got close.[10]

I reached with a hand and took hold of one. I was disappointed at how light it felt. It weighed hardly anything.[11] I pulled at it, plucking it from[12] all its stems.

I made myself comfortable on a sturdy[13] branch, my back to the trunk of the tree. Above me stood a shifting roof[14] of green leaves that let in[15] shafts of sunlight[16]. All round, for as far as I could see, hanging in the air, were the twisting and turning roads[17] of a great suspended city. A pleasant breeze ran through the trees. I was keenly[18] curious. I examined the fruit.

Ah, how I wish that moment had never been! But for it[19] I might have lived for years—why, for the rest of my life—on that island. Nothing, I thought, could ever push me to return to the lifeboat and to the suffering and deprivation[20] I had endured on it—nothing! What reason could I have to leave the island? Were my physical needs not met[21] here? Was there not more fresh water than I could drink in all

---

1. J'ai enroulé
2. la branche la plus basse
3. branche après branche
4. verger
5. De près
6. brindilles étroitement entortillées
7. queue
8. constellée
9. juteux
10. Je me suis rapproché.
11. Il ne pesait presque rien.
12. lui arrachant
13. solide
14. un toit mouvant
15. laissait passer
16. des rayons de soleil
17. les routes entrelacées
18. extrêmement
19. Sans cela
20. dénuement
21. satisfaits

my lifetime? More algae than I could eat? And when I yearned for variety[1], more meerkats and fish than I could ever desire? If the island floated and moved, might it not move in the right direction? Might it not turn out to be a vegetable ship that brought me to land? In the meantime, did I not have these delightful[2] meerkats to keep me company? And wasn't Richard Parker still in need of improving his fourth jump? The thought of leaving the island had not crossed my mind[3] once since I had arrived. It had been many weeks now—I couldn't say how many exactly—and they would stretch on[4]. I was certain about that.

How wrong I was.[5]

If that fruit had a seed[6], it was the seed of my departure.

The fruit was not a fruit. It was a dense accumulation of leaves glued[7] together in a ball. The dozens of stems were dozens of leaf stems. Each stem that I pulled caused a leaf to peel off[8].

After a few layers I came to leaves that had lost their stems and were flatly glued to the ball. I used my fingernails to catch their edges and pull them off[9]. Sheath[10] after sheath of leaf lifted, like the skins off an onion[11]. I could simply have ripped the "fruit" apart[12]—I still call it that for lack[13] of a better word—but I chose to satisfy my curiosity in a measured way.

It shrunk from[14] the size of an orange to that of a mandarin. My lap[15] and the branches below were covered with thin, soft leaf peelings[16].

It was now the size of a rambutan[17].

I still get shivers in my spine[18] when I think of it. The size of a cherry[19].

And then it came to light[20], an unspeakable[21] pearl at the heart of a green oyster[22].

1. quand j'avais envie d'un peu de changement
2. charmants
3. ne m'avait pas traversé l'esprit
4. les semaines allaient se multiplier
5. J'avais bien tort.
6. graine
7. collées
8. faisait se décoller une feuille
9. les détacher
10. Épaisseur
11. comme on enlève les peaux d'un oignon
12. J'aurais pu ouvrir le « fruit » d'un seul coup
13. par manque
14. Il est passé de
15. Mes genoux
16. morceaux de feuilles
17. ramboutan [ou litchi chevelu]
18. J'en frissonne encore
19. cerise
20. elle est apparue
21. innommable
22. huître

A human tooth.

A molar, to be exact. The surface stained green[1] and finely pierced with holes.

The feeling of horror came slowly. I had time to pick at the other fruit[2].

Each contained a tooth.

One a canine.

Another a premolar.

Here an incisor[3].

There another molar.

Thirty-two teeth. A complete human set.[4] Not one tooth missing.

Understanding dawned upon me.[5]

I did not scream. I think only in movies is horror vocal[6]. I simply shuddered and left the tree.

I spent the day in turmoil[7], weighing[8] my options. They were all bad.

That night, in bed in my usual tree, I tested my conclusion. I took hold of a meerkat and dropped it[9] from the branch.

It squeaked as it fell through the air. When it touched the ground, it instantly made for the tree.

With typical innocence it returned to the spot right next to me. There it began to lick its paws vigorously. It seemed much discomforted[10]. It panted heavily.[11]

I could have left it at that.[12] But I wanted to know for myself[13]. I climbed down and took hold of the rope. I had made knots in it to make my climbing easier[14]. When I was at the bottom of the tree, I brought my feet to within an inch[15] of the ground. I hesitated.

I let go.[16]

At first I felt nothing. Suddenly a searing pain[17] shot up through my feet. I shrieked. I thought I would fall over. I managed to take hold of the

1. tachée de vert

2. peler les autres fruits

3. incisive

4. Une denture humaine complète.

5. J'ai commencé à comprendre.

6. c'est seulement dans les films que l'on pousse des cris d'horreur

7. en proie à un grand désarroi

8. à considérer

9. je l'ai lâché

10. très mal à l'aise

11. Il haletait fortement.

12. J'aurais pu en rester là.

13. m'en rendre compte par moi-même

14. pouvoir monter plus facilement

15. à quelques centimètres

16. J'ai lâché la corde.

17. douleur fulgurante

rope and pull myself off the ground[1]. I frantically rubbed the soles of my feet against the tree trunk. It helped, but not enough. I climbed back to my branch. I soaked my feet in the bucket of water next to my bed. I wiped my feet[2] with leaves. I took the knife and killed two meerkats and tried to soothe[3] the pain with their blood and innards[4]. Still my feet burned. They burned all night. I couldn't sleep for[5] it, and from the anxiety.

The island was carnivorous. This explained the disappearance of the fish[6] in the pond. The island attracted saltwater fish into its subterranean[7] tunnels—how, I don't know; perhaps fish ate the algae as gluttonously as I did[8]. They became trapped.[9] Did they lose their way?[10] Did the openings onto the sea close off? Did the water change salinity so subtly[11] that it was too late by the time the fish realized it? Whatever the case[12], they found themselves trapped in fresh water and died. Some floated up to the surface of the ponds, the scraps[13] that fed the meerkats. At night, by some chemical process unknown to me but obviously inhibited by sunlight, the predatory algae turned highly acidic[14] and the ponds became vats[15] of acid that digested the fish. This was why Richard Parker returned to the boat every night. This was why the meerkats slept in the trees. This was why I had never seen anything but algae on the island.

And this explained the teeth. Some poor lost soul had arrived on these terrible shores before me. How much time had he—or was it she?— spent here? Weeks? Months? *Years*? How many forlorn[16] hours in the arboreal city with only meerkats for company? How many dreams of a happy life dashed[17]? How much hope come to nothing[18]? How much stored-up[19] conversation that died un-

1. me soulever au-dessus du sol

2. Je me suis essuyé les pieds

3. soulager

4. entrailles

5. à cause de

6. pourquoi les poissons disparaissaient

7. souterrains

8. aussi goulûment que moi

9. Ils se retrouvaient pris au piège.

10. Est-ce qu'ils se perdaient ?

11. subtilement

12. Quoi qu'il en soit

13. bribes

14. devenaient fortement acides

15. des bacs

16. mélancoliques

17. détruits

18. anéantis

19. stockées

said? How much loneliness endured? How much hopelessness taken on? And after all that, what of it? What to show for it?[1]

Nothing but some enamel[2], like small change[3] in a pocket. The person must have died in the tree. Was it illness[4]? Injury?[5] Depression? How long does it take for a broken[6] spirit to kill a body that has food, water and shelter? The trees were carnivorous too, but at a much lower level of acidity, safe enough to stay in for the night while the rest of the island seethed[7]. But once the person had died and stopped moving, the tree must have slowly wrapped itself around the body and digested it, the very bones leached of nutrients[8] until they vanished. In time, even the teeth would have disappeared.

I looked around at the algae. Bitterness welled up in me.[9] The radiant[10] promise it offered during the day was replaced in my heart by all the treachery it delivered at night.

I muttered, "Nothing but teeth left! TEETH!"

By the time morning came, my grim[11] decision was taken. I preferred to set off and perish[12] in search of my own kind[13] than to live a lonely half-life of physical comfort and spiritual death on this murderous island. I filled my stores[14] with fresh water and I drank like a camel[15]. I ate algae throughout the day until my stomach could take no more. I killed and skinned as many meerkats as would fit in[16] the locker and on the floor of the lifeboat. I reaped[17] dead fish from the ponds. With the hatchet I hacked off[18] a large mass of algae and worked a rope through it[19], which I tied to the boat.

I could not abandon Richard Parker. To leave him would mean to kill him. He would not survive the first night. Alone in my lifeboat at sunset I would know that he was burning alive. Or that he had thrown himself in the sea, where he would drown. I waited for his return. I knew he would not be late.

When he was aboard, I pushed us off[1]. For a few hours the currents kept us near the island. The noises of the sea bothered me. And I was no longer used to the rocking motions of the boat. The night went by slowly.

In the morning the island was gone, as was the mass of algae we had been towing[2]. As soon as night had fallen, the algae had dissolved the rope with its acid.

The sea was heavy, the sky grey.

CHAPTER 93

I grew weary of my situation, as pointless[3] as the weather. But life would not leave me. The rest of this story is nothing but grief, ache and endurance. High calls low[4] and low calls high. I tell you, if you were in such dire straits as I was[5], you too would elevate your thoughts. The lower you are[6], the higher your mind will want to soar[7]. It was natural that, bereft[8] and desperate as I was, in the throes[9] of unremitting[10] suffering, I should turn to God.

CHAPTER 94

When we reached land, Mexico to be exact, I was so weak I barely had the strength to be happy about it. We had great difficulty landing.[11] The lifeboat nearly capsized[12] in the surf[13]. I streamed the sea anchors—what was left of them—full open to

1. j'ai poussé le canot vers le large

2. que nous avions remorquée

3. dépourvue de sens

4. Le haut appelle le bas

5. une situation aussi désespérée que celle dans laquelle j'étais

6. Plus vous sombrez

7. s'élever

8. seul

9. affres

10. implacable

11. Nous avons eu beaucoup de mal à accoster.

12. a failli chavirer

13. les vagues

1. nous étions
au sommet
d'une vague

2. nous avons
surfé

3. qui
s'effondraient

4. a échoué
dans le sable en
sifflant

5. 60 cm

6. plein de vie

7. un arc-en-
ciel éphémère et
poilu

8. sauts

9. laissant leur
empreinte dans

10. a fait demi-
tour

11. une centaine
de mètres

12. démarche

13. maladroite

14. manquait de
coordination

15. aplatir

16. Je suis allé
péniblement
jusqu'à la rive

keep us perpendicular to the waves, and I tripped them as soon as we began riding a crest[1]. In this way, streaming and tripping the anchors, we surfed in[2] to shore. It was dangerous. But we caught one wave at just the right point and it carried us a great distance, past the high, collapsing[3] walls of water. I tripped the anchors a last time and we were pushed in the rest of the way. The boat hissed to a halt against the sand[4].

I let myself down the side. I was afraid to let go, afraid that so close to deliverance, in two feet[5] of water, I would drown. I looked ahead to see how far I had to go. The glance gave me one of my last images of Richard Parker, for at that precise moment he jumped over me. I saw his body, so immeasurably vital[6], stretched in the air above me, a fleeting, furred rainbow[7]. He landed in the water, his back legs splayed, his tail high, and from there, in a few hops[8], he reached the beach. He went to the left, his paws gouging[9] the wet sand, but changed his mind and spun around[10]. He passed directly in front of me on his way to the right. He didn't look at me. He ran a hundred yards or so[11] along the shore before turning in. His gait[12] was clumsy[13] and uncoordinated[14]. He fell several times. At the edge of the jungle, he stopped. I was certain he would turn my way. He would look at me. He would flatten[15] his ears. He would growl. In some such way, he would conclude our relationship. He did nothing of the sort. He only looked fixedly into the jungle. Then Richard Parker, companion of my torment, awful, fierce thing that kept me alive, moved forward and disappeared forever from my life.

I struggled to shore[16] and fell upon the sand. I looked about. I was truly alone, orphaned not only of my family, but now of Richard Parker, and nearly, I thought, of God. Of course, I wasn't. This beach, so soft, firm and vast, was like the cheek[1] of God, and somewhere two eyes were glittering with pleasure[2] and a mouth was smiling at having me there.

After some hours a member of my own species found me. He left and returned with a group. They were six or seven. They came up to me with their hands covering their noses and mouths. I wondered what was wrong with them. They spoke to me in a strange tongue. They pulled the lifeboat onto the sand. They carried me away.[3] The one piece of turtle meat I had brought from the boat they wrenched from my hand[4] and threw away.

I wept like a child. It was not because I was overcome[5] at having survived my ordeal, though I was[6]. Nor was it the presence of my brothers and sisters, though that too was very moving. I was weeping because Richard Parker had left me so unceremoniously[7]. What a terrible thing it is to botch a farewell[8]. I am a person who believes in form, in the harmony of order. Where we can, we must give things a meaningful shape. For example—I wonder—could you tell my jumbled[9] story in exactly one hundred chapters, not one more, not one less? I'll tell you, that's one thing I hate about my nickname, the way that number runs on forever[10]. It's important in life to conclude things properly. Only then can you let go[11]. Otherwise you are left with words you should have said but never did, and your heart is heavy with remorse[12]. That bungled goodbye[13] hurts me to this day[14]. I wish so much that I'd had one last look at him[15] in the lifeboat, that I'd provoked him a little, so that I was on his mind[16]. I wish I had said to him[17] then—yes, I know, to a tiger, but still—I wish I had said, "Richard Parker, it's

1. joue
2. brillaient de plaisir
3. Ils m'ont emmené avec eux.
4. ils me l'ont arraché de la main
5. bouleversé
6. même si je l'étais
7. avec aussi peu de cérémonie
8. rater des adieux
9. embrouillée
10. continue à l'infini
11. passer à autre chose
12. plein de remords
13. Cet au revoir gâché
14. encore aujourd'hui
15. J'aimerais tant l'avoir regardé une dernière fois
16. pour qu'il ne m'oublie pas
17. Je regrette de ne pas lui avoir dit

1. Je te dois
2. solennellement
3. limitée
4. J'espère que tout se passera bien pour toi là-bas.
5. Fais attention aux êtres humains.
6. m'ont frotté
7. que j'avais naturellement la peau foncée
8. Elles ont hoché la tête
9. me dépecer vivant
10. bouleversé
11. des infirmières
12. se sont occupés de moi
13. les autorités
14. couloir
15. adresser mes plus sincères remerciements

over. We have survived. Can you believe it? I owe you[1] more gratitude than I can express. I couldn't have done it without you. I would like to say it formally[2]: Richard Parker, thank you. Thank you for saving my life. And now go where you must. You have known the confined[3] freedom of a zoo most of your life; now you will know the free confinement of a jungle. I wish you all the best with it.[4] Watch out for Man.[5] He is not your friend. But I hope you will remember me as a friend. I will never forget you, that is certain. You will always be with me, in my heart. What is that hiss? Ah, our boat has touched sand. So farewell, Richard Parker, farewell. God be with you."

The people who found me took me to their village, and there some women gave me a bath and scrubbed me[6] so hard that I wondered if they realized I was naturally brown-skinned[7] and not a very dirty white boy. I tried to explain. They nodded[8] and smiled and kept on scrubbing me as if I were the deck of a ship. I thought they were going to skin me alive[9]. But they gave me food. Delicious food. Once I started eating, I couldn't stop. I thought I would never stop being hungry.

The next day a police car came and brought me to a hospital, and there my story ends.

I was overwhelmed[10] by the generosity of those who rescued me. Poor people gave me clothes and food. Doctors and nurses[11] cared for me[12] as if I were a premature baby. Mexican and Canadian officials[13] opened all doors for me so that from the beach in Mexico to the home of my foster mother to the classrooms of the University of Toronto, there was only one long, easy corridor[14] I had to walk down. To all these people I would like to extend my heartfelt thanks[15].

PART THREE

*Benito Juárez Infirmary,
Tomatlán, Mexico*

CHAPTER 95

Mr. Tomohiro Okamoto, of the Maritime Department[1] in the Japanese Ministry of Transport, now retired[2], told me that he and his junior colleague[3] at the time, Mr. Atsuro Chiba, were in Long Beach, California— the American western seaboard's main container port[4], near L.A.[5]—on unrelated business[6] when they were advised[7] that a lone survivor[8] of the Japanese ship Tsimtsum, *which had vanished without a trace in Pacific international waters several months before, was reported to have landed[9] near the small town of Tomatlán, on the coast of Mexico. They were instructed by their department to go down to contact the survivor and see if any light could be shed on[10] the fate of the ship. They bought a map of Mexico and looked to see where Tomatlán was. Unfortunately for them, a fold of the map crossed Baja California[11] over a small coastal[12] town named Tomatán, printed in small letters[13]. Mr. Okamoto was convinced he read Tomatlán. Since it was less than halfway down Baja California[14], he decided the fastest way to get there would be to drive[15].*

They set off in their rented car[16]. When they got to Tomatán, eight hundred kilometres south of Long Beach, and saw that it was not Tomatlán, Mr. Okamoto decided that they would continue to Santa Rosalia, two hundred kilometres further south, and catch the ferry across the Gulf of California to Guaymas. The ferry was late and slow. And from Guaymas it was another thirteen hundred kilometres to Tomatlán. The roads were bad. They had a flat tire.[17] Their

1. *du service des affaires maritimes*

2. *à la retraite*

3. *assistant*

4. *le plus grand port à conteneurs de la côte ouest américaine*

5. *Los Angeles*

6. *pour une autre raison*

7. *on les a informés*

8. *l'unique survivant*

9. *aurait accosté*

10. *on pouvait apporter une quelconque lumière sur*

11. *un pli de la carte traversait la péninsule de Basse-Californie au Mexique*

12. *côtière*

13. *dont le nom était écrit en petits caractères*

14. *la ville se situait dans la première moitié de la péninsule*

15. *y aller en voiture*

16. *voiture de location*

17. *Un de leurs pneus a crevé.*

car broke down[1] and the mechanic[2] who fixed it[3] surreptitiously cannibalized the motor of parts[4], putting in used parts instead[5], for the replacement of which they had to pay the rental company[6] and which resulted in the car breaking down a second time, on their way back[7]. The second mechanic overcharged them[8]. Mr. Okamoto admitted to me[9] that they were very tired when they arrived at the Benito Juárez Infirmary[10] in Tomatlán, which is not at all in Baja California but a hundred kilometres south of Puerto Vallarta, in the state of Jalisco, nearly level with[11] Mexico City. They had been travelling non-stop for forty-one hours. "We work hard", Mr. Okamoto wrote.

He and Mr. Chiba spoke with Piscine Molitor Patel, in English, for close to three hours, taping[12] the conversation. What follows are excerpts[13] from the verbatim transcript[14]. I am grateful to Mr. Okamoto for having made available to me[15] a copy of the tape[16] and of his final report. For the sake of clarity[17] I have indicated who is speaking when it is not immediately apparent. Portions printed in a different font[18] were spoken in Japanese, which I had translated[19].

CHAPTER 96

"Hello, Mr. Patel. My name is Tomohiro Okamoto. I am from the Maritime Department in the Japanese Ministry of Transport. This is my assistant, Atsuro Chiba. We have come to see you about the sinking[20] of the ship *Tsimtsum*, of which you were a passenger. Would it be possible to talk to you now?"

"Yes, of course."

"Thank you. It is very kind of you. Now, **Atsuro-kun**[1], **you're new at this**[2], **so pay attention and seek to learn**[3]."

"**Yes, Okamoto-san**[4]."

"**Is the tape recorder**[5] **on?**"

"**Yes it is.**"

"**Good. Oh, I'm so tired! For the record**[6], **today is February 19th, 1978. Case file number**[7] **250663, concerning the disappearance**[8] **of the cargo ship Tsimtsum.** Are you comfortable[9], Mr. Patel?"

"Yes, I am. Thank you. And you?"

"We are very comfortable."

"You've come all the way from Tokyo?"

"We were in Long Beach, California. We drove down.[10]"

"Did you have a good trip?[11]"

"We had a wonderful trip. It was a beautiful drive[12]."

"I had a terrible trip."

"Yes, we spoke to the police before coming here and we saw the lifeboat."

"I'm a little hungry."

"Would you like a cookie?"

"Oh, yes!"

"Here you go.[13]"

"Thank you!"

"You're welcome.[14] It's only a cookie. Now, Mr. Patel, we were wondering[15] if you could tell us what happened to you, with as much detail as possible."

"Yes. I'd be happy to.[16]"

CHAPTER 97

The story.

1. [suffixe utilisé en japonais pour s'adresser à quelqu'un de plus jeune]

2. c'est la première fois que vous faites ça

3. efforcez-vous d'apprendre

4. [suffixe équivalent ici à « Monsieur »]

5. magnétophone

6. Pour information

7. Dossier numéro

8. disparition

9. à l'aise

10. Nous sommes descendus en voiture.

11. Vous avez fait bon voyage ?

12. trajet

13. Tenez.

14. Je vous en prie.

15. nous nous demandions

16. volontiers

CHAPTER 98

Mr. Okamoto: "Very interesting."

Mr. Chiba: "What a story."

"He thinks we're fools.[1] Mr. Patel, we'll take a little break[2] and then we'll come back, yes?"

"That's fine.[3] I'd like another cookie."

"Yes, of course."

Mr. Chiba: "*He's already had plenty and most he hasn't even eaten. They're right there beneath his bedsheet[4].*"

"*Just give him another one. We have to humour him.[5]* We'll be back in a few minutes."

1. Il nous prend pour des imbéciles.

2. nous allons faire une petite pause

3. D'accord.

4. drap

5. Il ne faut pas le contrarier.

CHAPTER 99

Mr. Okamoto: "Mr. Patel, we don't believe your story."

"Sorry—these cookies are good but they tend to crumble[6]. I'm amazed. Why not?"

"It doesn't hold up.[7]"

"What do you mean?"

"Bananas don't float."

"I'm sorry?"

"You said the orang-utan came floating on an island of bananas."

"That's right."

"Bananas don't float."

"Yes, they do."

"They're too heavy."

"No, they're not. Here[8], try for yourself[9]. I have two bananas right here."

Mr. Chiba: "*Where did those come from? What else does he have under his bedsheet?*"

6. faire des miettes

7. Ça ne tient pas.

8. Allez-y

9. essayez vous-même

352

Mr. Okamoto: "**Damn it.**[1] No, that's all right."

"There's a sink[2] over there."

"That's fine.[3]"

"I insist. Fill that sink with water, drop these bananas in, and we'll see who's right[4]."

"We'd like to move on[5]."

"I absolutely insist."

[Silence]

Mr. Chiba: "**What do we do?**"

Mr. Okamoto: "**I feel this is going to be another very long day.**"

[Sound of a chair being pushed back[6]. Distant sound of water gushing out of a tap[7]]

Pi Patel: "What's happening? I can't see from here."

Mr. Okamoto [distantly]: "I'm filling the sink."

"Have you put the bananas in yet?"

[Distantly] "No."

"And now?"

[Distantly] "They're in."

"And?"

[Silence]

Mr. Chiba: "**Are they floating?**"

[Distantly] "**They're floating.**"

"So, are they floating?"

[Distantly] "They're floating."

"What did I tell you?"

Mr. Okamoto: "Yes, yes. But it would take a lot of bananas to hold up[8] an orang-utan."

"It did. There was close to a ton. It still makes me sick[9] when I think of all those bananas floating away[10] and going to waste[11] when they were mine for the picking[12]."

"It's a pity.[13] Now, about—"

"Could I have my bananas back, please?"

Mr. Chiba: "**I'll get them.**"

1. Bon sang.
2. lavabo
3. C'est bon.
4. qui a raison
5. passer à autre chose
6. que l'on pousse
7. qui jaillit d'un robinet
8. faire flotter
9. Ça me rend encore malade
10. partant à la dérive
11. gaspillées
12. j'aurais pu les ramasser
13. C'est dommage.

[Sound of a chair being pushed back]

[Distantly] "**Look at that. They really do float.**"

Mr. Okamoto: "What about this algae island you say you came upon?"

Mr. Chiba: "Here are[1] your bananas."

Pi Patel: "Thank you. Yes?"

"I'm sorry to say it so bluntly[2], we don't mean to[3] hurt your feelings[4], but you don't really expect us to believe you, do you? Carnivorous trees? A fish-eating[5] algae that produces fresh water? Tree-dwelling[6] aquatic rodents? These things don't exist."

"Only because you've never seen them."

"That's right. We believe what we see."

"So did Columbus. What do you do when you're in the dark?"

"Your island is botanically impossible."

"Said the fly just before landing in the Venus flytrap[7]."

"Why has no one else come upon it?"

"It's a big ocean crossed by busy ships. I went slowly, observing much."

"No scientist[8] would believe you."

"These would be the same who dismissed Copernicus[9] and Darwin. Have scientists finished coming upon[10] new plants? In the Amazon basin[11], for example?"

"Not plants that contradict the laws of nature."

"Which you know through and through[12]?"

"Well enough to know[13] the possible from the impossible."

Mr. Chiba: "I have an uncle who knows a lot about botany. He lives in the country near Hita-Gun. He's a bonsai master."

Pi Patel: "A what?"

"A bonsai master. You know, bonsai are little trees."

---

1. Voilà
2. crûment
3. nous ne voulons pas
4. vous blesser
5. qui mange des poissons
6. qui habitent dans les arbres
7. dionée attrape-mouche
8. scientifique
9. Copernic
10. Les scientifiques ont-ils fini de découvrir
11. le bassin de l'Amazone
12. parfaitement
13. distinguer

354

"You mean shrubs[1]."

"No, I mean trees. Bonsai are little trees. They are less than two feet tall.[2] You can carry them in your arms. They can be very old. My uncle has one that is over three hundred years old."

"Three-hundred-year-old trees that are two feet tall that you can carry in your arms?"

"Yes. They're very delicate[3]. They need a lot of attention."

"Whoever heard[4] of such trees? They're botanically impossible."

"But I assure you they exist, Mr. Patel. My uncle—"

"I believe what I see."

Mr. Okamoto: "Just a moment, please. **Atsuro, with all due respect for[5] your uncle who lives in the country near Hita-Gun, we're not here to talk idly about botany[6].**"

"**I'm just trying to help.**"

"**Do your uncle's bonsai eat meat?**"

"**I don't think so.**"

"**Have you ever been bitten by one of his bonsai?**"

"**No.**"

"**In that case, your uncle's bonsai are not helping us.** Where were we?"

Pi Patel: "With the tall, full-sized[7] trees firmly rooted to the ground I was telling you about."

"Let us put them aside[8] for now."

"It might be hard. I never tried pulling them out[9] and carrying them."

"You're a funny man, Mr. Patel. Ha! Ha! Ha!"

Pi Patel: "Ha! Ha! Ha!"

Mr. Chiba: "Ha! Ha! Ha! **It wasn't that funny[10].**"

Mr. Okamoto: "**Just keep laughing.[11]** Ha! Ha! Ha!"

Mr. Chiba: "Ha! Ha! Ha!"

---

1. arbustes
2. Ils font moins de 60 cm.
3. fragiles
4. Qui n'a jamais entendu parler
5. avec tout le respect dû à
6. parler de botanique pour passer le temps
7. grands
8. Mettons-les de côté
9. Je n'ai jamais essayé de les déraciner
10. si drôle que ça
11. Continuez à rire.

Mr. Okamoto: "Now about the tiger, we're not sure about it either."

"What do you mean?"

"We have difficulty believing it."

"It's an incredible story."

"Precisely."

"I don't know how I survived."

1. difficile

"Clearly it was a strain[1]."

"I'll have another cookie."

"There are none left."

"What's in that bag?"

"Nothing."

"Can I see?"

2. On peut dire adieu à notre repas de midi.

Mr. Chiba: "**There goes our lunch.**[2]"

Mr. Okamoto: "Getting back[3] to the tiger ..."

3. Revenons

4. problème

Pi Patel: "Terrible business[4]. Delicious sandwiches."

Mr. Okamoto: "Yes, they look good."

Mr. Chiba: "**I'm hungry.**"

5. dans la nature

6. à présent

"Not a trace of it has been found. That's a bit hard to believe, isn't it? There are no tigers in the Americas. If there were a wild tiger out there[5], don't you think the police would have heard about it by now[6]?"

"I should tell you about the black panther that escaped from the Zurich Zoo in the middle of winter."

"Mr. Patel, a tiger is an incredibly dangerous wild animal. How could you survive in a lifeboat with one? It's—"

7. menaçante

8. des siècles

9. apaiser

10. surmonter

11. je ne crois pas qu'ils y arriveront un jour

"What you don't realize is that we are a strange and forbidding[7] species to wild animals. We fill them with fear. They avoid us as much as possible. It took centuries[8] to still[9] the fear in some pliable animals—*domestication* it's called—but most cannot get over[10] their fear, and I doubt they ever will[11]. When wild animals fight us, it is out of sheer desperation[1]. They fight when they feel they have no other way out[2]. It's a very last resort.[3]"

"*In a lifeboat?* Come on, Mr. Patel, it's just too hard to believe!"

"Hard to believe? What do you know about hard to believe? You want hard to believe? I'll give you hard to believe. It's a closely held[4] secret among Indian zookeepers that in 1971 Bara the polar bear[5] escaped from the Calcutta Zoo. She was never heard from again, not by police or hunters or poachers[6] or anyone else. We suspect she's living freely on the banks of the Hugli River. Beware[7] if you go to Calcutta, my good sirs: if you have sushi on the breath you may pay a high price! If you took the city of Tokyo and turned it upside down and shook it, you'd be amazed at all the animals that would fall out: badgers[8], wolves[9], boa constrictors, Komodo dragons, crocodiles, ostriches, baboons, capybaras[10], wild boars, leopards, manatees[11], ruminants in untold numbers[12]. There is no doubt in my mind that feral[13] giraffes and feral hippos have been living in Tokyo for generations without being seen by a soul[14]. You should compare one day the things that stick to the soles[15] of your shoes as you walk down the street with what you see lying at the bottom of the cages in the Tokyo Zoo—then look up[16]! And you expect to find a tiger in a Mexican jungle! It's laughable, just plain laughable[17]. Ha! Ha! Ha!"

"There may very well be feral giraffes and feral hippos living in Tokyo and a polar bear living freely in Calcutta. We just don't believe there was a tiger living in your lifeboat."

"The arrogance of big-city folk[18]! You grant your metropolises[19] all the animals of Eden, but you deny[20] my hamlet[21] the merest[22] Bengal tiger!"

"Mr. Patel, please calm down."

---

1. par pur désespoir
2. il n'y a pas d'autre issue
3. Ils le font en dernier recours.
4. soigneusement gardé
5. ours polaire
6. des braconniers
7. Attention
8. des blaireaux
9. des loups
10. cabiais
11. des lamantins
12. un nombre incalculable de ruminants
13. sauvages
14. par quiconque
15. collent aux semelles
16. levez les yeux
17. parfaitement ridicule
18. des habitants des grandes villes
19. Vous dotez vos métropoles de
20. vous refusez
21. à mon hameau
22. un seul

1. vous butez sur une simple question de crédibilité
2. Ne vous avisez pas de me brimer
3. politesse
4. Moi aussi !
5. des vêtements
6. boîte à outils
7. Rien n'est plus utile que
8. pour garder les tigres à distance
9. de jeter
10. l'eau du bain
11. des cimeterres
12. ne vous rendez-vous pas utile
13. un coriace
14. Une barre chocolatée !
15. Comme s'il ne nous avait pas volé
16. [un assortiment de beignets japonais]
17. Nous perdons de vue l'objectif
18. enquête

"If you stumble at mere believability[1], what are you living for? Isn't love hard to believe?"

"Mr. Patel—"

"Don't you bully me[2] with your politeness[3]! Love is hard to believe, ask any lover. Life is hard to believe, ask any scientist. God is hard to believe, ask any believer. What is your problem with hard to believe?"

"We're just being reasonable."

"So am I![4] I applied my reason at every moment. Reason is excellent for getting food, clothing[5] and shelter. Reason is the very best tool kit[6]. Nothing beats[7] reason for keeping tigers away[8]. But be excessively reasonable and you risk throwing out[9] the universe with the bathwater[10]."

"Calm down, Mr. Patel, calm down."

Mr. Chiba: "*The bathwater? Why is he talking about bathwater?*"

"How can I be calm? You should have seen Richard Parker!"

"Yes, yes."

"Huge. Teeth like this! Claws like scimitars[11]!"

Mr. Chiba: "*What are scimitars?*"

Mr. Okamoto: "*Chiba-san, instead of asking stupid vocabulary questions, why don't you make yourself useful[12]? This boy is a tough nut to crack[13]. Do something!*"

Mr. Chiba: "Look! A chocolate bar![14]"

Pi Patel: "Wonderful!"

[Long silence]

Mr. Okamoto: "*Like he hasn't already stolen[15] our whole lunch. Soon he'll be demanding tempura[16].*"

[Long silence]

Mr. Okamoto: "We are losing sight of the point[17] of this investigation[18]. We are here because of the sinking of a cargo ship. You are the sole survivor.

358

And you were only a passenger. You bear no responsibility for[1] what happened. We—"

"Chocolate is so good!"

"We are not seeking to lay criminal charges.[2] You are an innocent victim of a tragedy at sea. We are only trying to determine why and how the *Tsimtsum* sank. We thought you might help us, Mr. Patel."

[Silence]

"Mr. Patel?"

[Silence]

Pi Patel: "Tigers exist, lifeboats exist, oceans exist. Because the three have never come together in your narrow[3], limited experience, you refuse to believe that they might. Yet the plain fact[4] is that the *Tsimtsum* brought them together and then sank."

[Silence]

Mr. Okamoto: "What about this Frenchman?"

"What about him?"

"Two blind people in two separate lifeboats meeting up in the Pacific—the coincidence seems a little far-fetched[5], no?"

"It certainly does."

"We find it very unlikely[6]."

"So is winning the lottery[7], yet someone always wins."

"We find it *extremely* hard to believe."

"So did I."

"**I knew we should have taken the day off**[8]. You talked about food?"

"We did."

"He knew a lot about food."

"If you can call it food."

"The cook on the *Tsimtsum* was a Frenchman."

"There are Frenchmen all over the world."

"Maybe the Frenchman you met was the cook."

1. Vous n'êtes pas responsable de

2. Nous ne voulons pas porter plainte.

3. étroite

4. la simple vérité

5. tirée par les cheveux

6. très improbable

7. Gagner à la loterie l'est aussi

8. un jour de congé

"Maybe. How should I know? I never saw him. I was blind. Then Richard Parker ate him alive."

"How convenient.[1]"

"Not at all. It was horrific and it stank[2]. By the way[3], how do you explain the meerkat bones in the lifeboat?"

"Yes, the bones of a small animal were—"

"More than one!"

"—of *some* small animals were found in the lifeboat. They must have come from the ship."

"We had no meerkats at the zoo."

"We have no proof they were meerkat bones."

Mr. Chiba: "Maybe they were banana bones! Ha! Ha! Ha! Ha! Ha!"

"**Atsuro, shut up[4]!**"

"**I'm very sorry, Okamoto-san. It's the fatigue.**"

"**You're bringing our service into disrepute![5]**"

"**Very sorry, Okamoto-san.**"

Mr. Okamoto: "They could be bones from another small animal."

"They were meerkats."

"They could be mongooses."

"The mongooses at the zoo didn't sell[6]. They stayed in India."

"They could be shipboard pests[7], like rats. Mongooses are common in India."

"Mongooses as shipboard pests?"

"Why not?"

"Who swam in the stormy[8] Pacific, several of them, to the lifeboat? That's a little hard to believe, wouldn't you say?"

"Less hard to believe than some of the things we've heard in the last two hours. Perhaps the mongooses were already aboard the lifeboat, like the rat you mentioned."

"Simply amazing the number of animals in that lifeboat."

"Simply amazing."

"A real jungle."

"Yes."

"Those bones are meerkat bones. Have them checked[1] by an expert."

"There weren't that many left[2]. And there were no heads."

"I used them as bait."

"It's doubtful an expert[3] could tell whether they were meerkat bones or mongoose bones."

"Find yourself a forensic[4] zoologist."

"All right, Mr. Patel! You win. We cannot explain the presence of meerkat bones, if that is what they are, in the lifeboat. But that is not our concern[5] here. We are here because a Japanese cargo ship owned by Oika Shipping Company, flying the Panamanian flag, sank in the Pacific."

"Something I never forget, not for a minute. I lost my whole family."

"We're sorry about that."

"Not as much as I am.[6]"

[Long silence]

Mr. Chiba: "**What do we do now?**"

Mr. Okamoto: "**I don't know.**"

[Long silence]

Pi Patel: "Would you like a cookie?"

Mr. Okamoto: "Yes, that would be nice. Thank you."

Mr. Chiba: "Thank you."

[Long silence]

Mr. Okamoto: "It's a nice day."

Pi Patel: "Yes. Sunny."

[Long silence]

Pi Patel: "Is this your first visit to Mexico?"

1. Faites-les analyser

2. il n'en restait pas tant que ça

3. Je doute qu'un expert

4. expert en matière juridique

5. ce qui nous intéresse

6. Pas autant que moi.

Mr. Okamoto: "Yes, it is."

"Mine too."

[Long silence]

Pi Patel: "So, you didn't like my story?"

Mr. Okamoto: "No, we liked it very much. Didn't we[1], Atsuro? We will remember it for a long, long time."

Mr. Chiba: "We will.[2]"

[Silence]

Mr. Okamoto: "But for the purposes of our investigation, we would like to know what really happened."

"What really happened?"

"Yes."

"So you want another story?"

"Uhh … no. We would like to know what really happened."

"Doesn't the telling of something[3] always become a story?"

"Uhh … Perhaps in English. In Japanese a story would have an element of *invention* in it. We don't want any invention. We want the 'straight facts[4]', as you say in English."

"Isn't telling about something—using words, English or Japanese—already something of an invention? Isn't just looking upon this world already something of an invention?"

"Uhh …"

"The world isn't just the way it is. It is how we understand it, no? And in understanding something, we bring something to it, no? Doesn't that make life a story?[5]"

"Ha! Ha! Ha! You are very intelligent, Mr. Patel."

Mr. Chiba: "**What is he talking about?**"

"**I have no idea.**"

Pi Patel: "You want words that reflect reality?"

1. *N'est-ce pas*

2. *Certainement.*

3. *le fait de raconter quelque chose*

4. *faits bruts*

5. *Cela ne fait-il pas de la vie une histoire ?*

"Yes."

"Words that do not contradict[1] reality?"

"Exactly."

"But tigers don't contradict reality."

"Oh please, no more tigers."

"I know what you want. You want a story that won't surprise you. That will confirm what you already know. That won't make you see higher or further or differently. You want a flat story. An immobile story. You want dry, yeastless[2] factuality."

"Uhh …" "You want a story without animals."

"Yes!"

"Without tigers or orang-utans."

"That's right."

"Without hyenas or zebras."

"Without them."

"Without meerkats or mongooses."

"We don't want them."

"Without giraffes or hippopotamuses."

"We will plug our ears[3] with our fingers!"

"So I'm right. You want a story without animals."

"We want a story without animals that will explain the sinking of the *Tsimtsum*."

"Give me a minute, please."

"Of course. **I think we're finally getting somewhere**[4]. **Let's hope**[5] **he speaks some sense**[6]."

[Long silence]

"Here's[7] another story."

"Good."

"The ship sank. It made a sound like a monstrous metallic burp. Things bubbled at the surface and then vanished. I found myself kicking water[8] in the Pacific Ocean. I swam for the lifeboat. It was the hardest swim of my life. I didn't seem to be moving. I kept swallowing water. I was very cold. I was rapidly losing strength. I wouldn't have made it if[9]

1. ne contredisent pas

2. sans levure

3. Nous nous boucherons les oreilles

4. nous nous rapprochons du but

5. Espérons

6. qu'il va dire quelque chose de sensé

7. Voilà

8. en train de nager

9. Je n'aurais pas réussi si

the cook hadn't thrown me a lifebuoy and pulled me in. I climbed aboard and collapsed.

"Four of us survived. Mother held on to some bananas and made it to the lifeboat. The cook was already aboard, as was the sailor[1].

"He ate the flies. The cook, that is.[2] We hadn't been in the lifeboat a full day; we had food and water to last us for weeks; we had fishing gear and solar stills; we had no reason to believe that we wouldn't be rescued soon. Yet there he was, swinging his arms[3] and catching flies and eating them greedily[4]. Right away he was in a holy terror of hunger[5]. He was calling us idiots and fools for not joining him in the feast. We were offended[6] and disgusted, but we didn't show it. We were very polite about it. He was a stranger and a foreigner. Mother smiled and shook her head and raised her hand in refusal[7]. He was a disgusting man. His mouth had the discrimination of a garbage heap[8]. He also ate the rat. He cut it up[9] and dried it in the sun. I— I'll be honest—I had a small piece, very small, behind Mother's back. I was so hungry. He was such a brute, that cook, ill-tempered[10] and hypocritical.

"The sailor was young. Actually, he was older than me, probably in his early twenties[11], but he broke his leg jumping from the ship and his suffering made him a child. He was beautiful. He had no facial hair at all[12] and a clear, shining complexion[13]. His features—the broad face, the flattened[14] nose, the narrow, pleated eyes[15]—looked so elegant. I thought he looked like a Chinese emperor. His suffering was terrible. He spoke no English, not a single word, not *yes* or *no*, *hello* or *thank you*. He spoke only Chinese. We couldn't understand a word he said. He must have felt very lonely. When he wept, Mother held his head in her lap[16] and I held his

1. ainsi que le marin
2. Le cuisinier.

3. battant des bras
4. goulûment
5. il avait terriblement peur d'avoir faim
6. outrés
7. en signe de refus
8. n'était pas plus sélective qu'un tas d'ordures
9. Il l'a coupé en morceaux
10. grincheux
11. il devait avoir dans les vingt ans
12. Son visage était imberbe
13. teint
14. aplati
15. ses yeux bridés

16. sur ses genoux

364

hand. It was very, very sad. He suffered and we couldn't do anything about it.

"His right leg was badly broken at the thigh[1]. The bone stuck out of[2] his flesh. He screamed with pain. We set[3] his leg as best we could and we made sure he was eating and drinking. But his leg became infected. Though we drained it of pus[4] every day, it got worse[5]. His foot became black and bloated[6].

"It was the cook's idea. He was a brute. He dominated us. He whispered that the blackness would spread[7] and that he would survive only if his leg were amputated. Since the bone was broken at the thigh, it would involve no more than[8] cutting through flesh and setting a tourniquet[9]. I can still hear his evil whisper[10]. He would do the job to save the sailor's life, he said, but we would have to hold him. Surprise would be the only anaesthetic[11]. We fell upon him. Mother and I held his arms while the cook sat on his good leg. The sailor writhed[12] and screamed. His chest rose and fell. The cook worked the knife quickly[13]. The leg fell off. Immediately Mother and I let go and moved away. We thought that if the restraint was ended[14], so would his struggling[15]. We thought he would lie[16] calmly. He didn't. He sat up instantly. His screams were all the worse[17] for being unintelligible[18]. He screamed and we stared, transfixed[19]. There was blood everywhere. Worse, there was the contrast between the frantic activity of the poor sailor and the gentle repose of his leg at the bottom of the boat. He kept looking at the limb, as if imploring it to return. At last he fell back[20]. We hurried into action. The cook folded some skin over the bone. We wrapped the stump[21] in a piece of cloth and we tied a rope above the wound to stop the bleeding. We laid him as comfortably as we could on a mattress of

1. au niveau de la cuisse
2. sortait de
3. Nous avons remis
4. Même si nous évacuions le pus
5. l'infection s'est aggravée
6. a enflé
7. allait s'étendre
8. il suffisait de
9. faire un garrot
10. son chuchotement diabolique
11. anesthésiant
12. s'est débattu
13. a rapidement fait usage du couteau
14. si nous arrêtions de le tenir
15. il arrêterait de se débattre
16. qu'il s'allongerait
17. d'autant plus insupportables
18. que nous ne les comprenions pas
19. paralysés
20. il s'est laissé retomber en arrière
21. moignon

life jackets and kept him warm. I thought it was all for nothing. I couldn't believe a human being could survive so much pain, so much butchery. Throughout the evening and night he moaned, and his breathing was harsh and uneven[1]. He had fits of agitated delirium[2]. I expected him to die during the night.

"He clung to life. At dawn he was still alive. He went in and out of consciousness.[3] Mother gave him water. I caught sight of[4] the amputated leg. It cut my breath short.[5] In the commotion[6] it had been shoved aside[7] and forgotten in the dark. It had seeped a liquid[8] and looked thinner. I took a life jacket and used it as a glove[9]. I picked the leg up.

"'What are you doing?' asked the cook.

"'I'm going to throw it overboard,' I replied.

"'Don't be an idiot. We'll use it as bait. That was the whole point.[10]'

"He seemed to regret his last words even as they were coming out, for his voice faded quickly[11]. He turned away.

"'The *whole point*?' Mother asked. 'What do you mean by that?[12]'

"He pretended to be busy.

"Mother's voice rose. 'Are you telling us that we cut this poor boy's leg off not to save his life but to get *fishing bait*?'

"Silence from the brute.

"'Answer me!' shouted Mother.

"Like a cornered[13] beast he lifted his eyes and glared at her[14]. 'Our supplies are running out[15],' he snarled. 'We need more food or we'll die.'

"Mother returned his glare. 'Our supplies are *not* running out! We have plenty of food and water. We have package upon package[16] of biscuits to tide us over[17] till our rescue.' She took hold of the plas-

---

1. rauque et irrégulière

2. des crises de délire

3. Il perdait régulièrement conscience.

4. J'ai aperçu

5. J'en ai eu le souffle coupé.

6. tumulte

7. elle avait été poussée sur le côté

8. Un liquide s'en était écoulé

9. gant

10. C'était le but.

11. s'est évanouie

12. Qu'est-ce que vous voulez dire par là ?

13. acculée

14. lui a lancé un regard furieux

15. Nos provisions s'épuisent

16. plein de paquets

17. nous permettre de tenir

tic container[1] in which we put the open rations of biscuits. It was unexpectedly light in her hands. The few crumbs in it rattled. 'What!' She opened it. 'Where are the biscuits? The container was full last night!'

"The cook looked away. As did I.[2]

"'You selfish[3] monster!' screamed Mother. 'The only reason we're running out of food[4] is because you're gorging yourself on it[5]!'

"'He had some too,' he said, nodding my way[6].

"Mother's eyes turned to me. My heart sank.

"'Piscine, is that true?'

"'It was night, Mother. I was half asleep and I was so hungry. He gave me a biscuit. I ate it without thinking …'

"'Only one, was it?' sneered[7] the cook.

"It was Mother's turn to look away. The anger seemed to go out of her. Without saying another word she went back to nursing[8] the sailor.

"I wished for her anger.[9] I wished for her to punish me. Only not this silence. I made to arrange[10] some life jackets for the sailor's comfort so that I could be next to her. I whispered, 'I'm sorry, Mother, I'm sorry.' My eyes were brimming with[11] tears. When I brought them up, I saw that hers were too. But she didn't look at me. Her eyes were gazing upon some memory in mid-air.

"'We're all alone, Piscine, all alone,' she said, in a tone that broke every hope in my body. I never felt so lonely in all my life as I did at that moment. We had been in the lifeboat two weeks already and it was taking its toll on us[12]. It was getting harder to believe that Father and Ravi had survived.

"When we turned around, the cook was holding the leg by the ankle over the water to drain it[13]. Mother brought her hand over the sailor's eyes.

---

1. récipient
2. Moi aussi.
3. égoïste
4. nous manquons de nourriture
5. vous vous empiffrez
6. en faisant un mouvement de la tête dans ma direction
7. a ricané
8. elle est retournée soigner
9. J'aurais voulu qu'elle soit en colère contre moi.
10. Je suis allé installer
11. noyés de
12. nous commencions à mesurer l'étendue des dégâts
13. l'assécher

"He died quietly, the life drained out of him[1] like the liquid from his leg. The cook promptly butchered him. The leg had made for poor bait[2]. The dead flesh was too decayed[3] to hold on to the fishing hook; it simply dissolved in the water. Nothing went to waste[4] with this monster. He cut up everything, including the sailor's skin and every inch of his intestines. He even prepared his genitals. When he had finished with his torso, he moved on to his arms and shoulders and to his legs. Mother and I rocked[5] with pain and horror. Mother shrieked at the cook, 'How can you do this, you monster? Where is your humanity? Have you no decency? What did the poor boy do to you? You monster! You monster!' The cook replied with unbelievable vulgarity.

"'At least cover his face, for God's sake[6]!' cried my mother. It was unbearable to have that beautiful face, so noble and serene, connected to such a sight below. The cook threw himself upon the sailor's head and before our very eyes scalped him and pulled off his face[7]. Mother and I vomited.

"When he had finished, he threw the butchered carcass overboard. Shortly after, strips of flesh and pieces of organs were lying to dry in the sun all over the boat. We recoiled in horror. We tried not to look at them. The smell would not go away.

"The next time the cook was close by, Mother slapped him in the face[8], a full hard slap that punctuated the air with a sharp crack. It was something shocking coming from my mother. And it was heroic. It was an act of outrage and pity and grief and bravery[9]. It was done in memory of that poor sailor. It was to salvage his dignity.

"I was stunned[10]. So was the cook. He stood without moving or saying a word as Mother looked him straight in the face[1]. I noticed how he did not meet her eyes.

"We retreated to our private spaces. I stayed close to her. I was filled with a mix of rapt admiration and abject fear.

"Mother kept an eye on him[2]. Two days later she saw him do it. He tried to be discreet, but she saw him bring his hand to his mouth. She shouted, 'I saw you! You just ate a piece! You said it was for bait! I knew it. You monster! You animal! How could you? He's *human*! He's your own kind!' If she had expected him to be mortified, to spit it out[3] and break down and apologize[4], she was wrong. He kept chewing.[5] In fact, he lifted his head up and quite openly put the rest of the strip in his mouth. 'Tastes like pork,' he muttered. Mother expressed her indignation and disgust by violently turning away. He ate another strip. 'I feel stronger already,' he muttered. He concentrated on his fishing.

"We each had our end of the lifeboat. It's amazing how willpower[6] can build walls. Whole days went by[7] as if he weren't there.

"But we couldn't ignore him entirely. He was a brute, but a practical[8] brute. He was good with his hands[9] and he knew the sea. He was full of good ideas. He was the one who thought of building a raft to help with the fishing. If we survived any time at all, it was thanks to him. I helped him as best I could. He was very short-tempered[10], always shouting at me and insulting me.

"Mother and I didn't eat any of the sailor's body, not the smallest morsel, despite the cost in weakness to us, but we did start to eat what the cook caught from the sea. My mother, a lifelong[11] vegetarian, brought herself to[12] eat raw fish and raw turtle. She had a very hard time of it.[13] She never got

1. droit dans les yeux

2. l'a gardé à l'œil

3. à ce qu'il recrache le morceau

4. s'excuse

5. Il a continué à mâcher.

6. la volonté

7. sont passés

8. pragmatique

9. habile de ses mains

10. irritable

11. depuis toujours

12. s'est forcée à

13. Elle a eu beaucoup de mal à le faire.

over[1] her revulsion[2]. It came easier to me. I found hunger improved the taste of everything.

"When your life has been given a reprieve[3], it's impossible not to feel some warmth for the one to whom you owe that reprieve. It was very exciting when the cook hauled aboard a turtle or caught a great big dorado. It made us smile broadly and there was a glow in our chests[4] that lasted for hours. Mother and the cook talked in a civil way[5], even joked[6]. During some spectacular sunsets, life on the boat was nearly good. At such times I looked at him with—yes—with tenderness. With love. I imagined that we were fast friends. He was a coarse[7] man even when he was in a good mood, but we pretended not to notice it, even to ourselves. He said that we would come upon an island. That was our main hope. We exhausted our eyes scanning[8] the horizon for an island that never came. That's when he stole[9] food and water.

"The flat and endless Pacific rose[10] like a great wall around us. I never thought we would get around it[11].

"He killed her. The cook killed my mother. We were starving. I was weak. I couldn't hold on to a turtle. Because of me we lost it. He hit me. Mother hit him. He hit her back. She turned to me and said, 'Go!' pushing me towards the raft. I jumped for it. I thought she was coming with me. I landed in the water. I scrambled aboard[12] the raft. They were fighting. I did nothing but watch. My mother was fighting an adult man. He was mean[13] and muscular. He caught her by the wrist and twisted it. She shrieked and fell. He moved over her. The knife appeared. He raised it in the air. It came down. Next it was up—it was red. It went up and down repeatedly. I couldn't see her. She was at the bottom

---

1. Elle n'a jamais surmonté
2. dégoût
3. sursis

4. une douce chaleur se répandait dans nos poitrines
5. de façon courtoise
6. ils faisaient même des plaisanteries
7. grossier

8. à scruter
9. C'est à ce moment qu'il volait
10. se dressait
11. que nous pourrions le contourner

12. Je suis grimpé tant bien que mal sur
13. méchant

of the boat. I saw only him. He stopped. He raised his head and looked at me. He hurled something[1] my way[2]. A line of blood struck me across the face. No whip[3] could have inflicted a more painful lash[4]. I held my mother's head in my hands. I let it go. It sank in a cloud of blood, her tress trailing[5] like a tail. Fish spiralled down towards it[6] until a shark's long grey shadow cut across its path[7] and it vanished. I looked up. I couldn't see him. He was hiding at the bottom of the boat. He appeared when he threw my mother's body overboard. His mouth was red. The water boiled with fish.

"I spent the rest of that day and the night on the raft, looking at him. We didn't speak a word. He could have cut the raft loose.[8] But he didn't. He kept me around, like a bad conscience.

"In the morning, in plain sight of him, I pulled on the rope and boarded[9] the lifeboat. I was very weak. He said nothing. I kept my peace.[10] He caught a turtle. He gave me its blood. He butchered it and laid its best parts for me on the middle bench. I ate.

"Then we fought and I killed him. He had no expression on his face, neither of despair nor of anger, neither of fear nor of pain. He gave up. He let himself be killed, though it was still a struggle. He knew he had gone too far, even by his bestial standards[11]. He had gone too far and now he didn't want to go on living any more. But he never said 'I'm sorry.' Why do we cling to our evil ways[12]?

"The knife was all along in plain view on the bench. We both knew it. He could have had it in his hands from the start. He was the one who put it there. I picked it up. I stabbed him[13] in the stomach. He grimaced but remained standing. I pulled the knife out and stabbed him again. Blood was pouring out.[14] Still he didn't fall over. Looking me

1. Il a jeté quelque chose

2. dans ma direction

3. fouet

4. coup

5. suivant

6. l'ont suivie vers le fond en tournant

7. se mette en travers de son chemin

8. Il aurait pu détacher le radeau d'un coup de couteau.

9. je suis monté sur

10. Je suis resté silencieux.

11. selon ses critères bestiaux

12. instincts barbares

13. Je l'ai poignardé

14. Le sang coulait abondamment.

in the eyes, he lifted his head ever so slightly[1]. Did he mean something by this? I took it that he did. I stabbed him in the throat, next to the Adam's apple[2]. He dropped like a stone. And died. He didn't say anything. He had no last words. He only coughed up[3] blood. A knife has a horrible dynamic power; once in motion, it's hard to stop. I stabbed him repeatedly. His blood soothed[4] my chapped[5] hands. His heart was a struggle[6]—all those tubes that connected it. I managed to get it out. It tasted delicious, far better than turtle. I ate his liver. I cut off great pieces of his flesh.

"He was such an evil man. Worse still, he met evil in me—selfishness[7], anger, ruthlessness[8]. I must live with that.

"Solitude began. I turned to God. I survived."

[Long silence]

"Is that better? Are there any parts you find hard to believe? Anything you'd like me to change?"

Mr. Chiba: "What a horrible story."

[Long silence]

Mr. Okamoto: "Both the zebra and the Taiwanese sailor broke a leg[9], did you notice that?"

"No, I didn't."

"And the hyena bit off[10] the zebra's leg just as the cook cut off the sailor's."

"Ohhh, Okamoto-san, you see a lot."

"The blind Frenchman they met in the other lifeboat—didn't he admit to killing[11] a man and a woman?"

"Yes, he did."

"The cook killed the sailor and his mother"

"Very impressive."

"His stories match[12]."

Marginal notes:
1. il a à peine levé la tête
2. la pomme d'Adam
3. Il a seulement craché
4. a apaisé
5. desséchées
6. a été difficile à arracher
7. l'égoïsme
8. la cruauté
9. se sont cassé une jambe
10. a arraché
11. n'a-t-il pas admis avoir tué
12. se correspondent

372

"**So the Taiwanese sailor is the zebra, his mother is the orang-utan, the cook is ... the hyena— which means he's the tiger!**"

"**Yes. The tiger killed the hyena—and the blind Frenchman—just as he killed the cook.**"

Pi Patel: "Do you have another chocolate bar?"

Mr. Chiba: "Right away![1]"

"Thank you."

Mr. Chiba: "**But what does it mean, Okamoto-san?**"

"**I have no idea.**"

"**And what about[2] the island? Who are the meerkats?**"

"**I don't know.**"

"**And those teeth? Whose teeth were those[3] in the tree?**"

"**I don't know. I'm not inside this boy's head.**"

[Long silence]

Mr. Okamoto: "Please excuse me for asking, but did the cook say anything about the sinking of the *Tsimtsum*?"

"In this other story?"

"Yes."

"He didn't."

"He made no mention of anything leading up to[4] the early morning of July 2nd that might explain what happened?"

"No."

"Nothing of a nature mechanical or structural?"

"No."

"Nothing about other ships or objects at sea?"

"No."

"He could not explain the sinking of the *Tsimtsum* at all?"

"No"

"Could he say why it didn't send out a distress signal[5]?"

1. Tout de suite !

2. que penser de

3. À qui appartenaient les dents

4. dans la période précédent

5. un signal de détresse

"And if it had? In my experience, when a dingy, third-rate rust-bucket[1] sinks, unless it has the luck of carrying oil[2], lots of it, enough to kill entire eco-systems, no one cares[3] and no one hears about it. You're on your own.[4]"

"When Oika realized that something was wrong, it was too late. You were too far out[5] for air rescue[6]. Ships in the area were told to be on the lookout[7]. They reported seeing nothing."

"And while we're on the subject, the ship wasn't the only thing that was third-rate. The crew were a sullen, unfriendly lot[8], hard at work[9] when officers were around[10] but doing nothing when they weren't. They didn't speak a word of English and they were of no help to us. Some of them stank of alcohol[11] by mid-afternoon[12]. Who's to say what those idiots did? The officers—"

"What do you mean by that?"

"By what?"

"'Who's to say what those idiots did?'"

"I mean that maybe in a fit of drunken insanity[13] some of them released[14] the animals."

Mr. Chiba: "Who had the keys to the cages?"

"Father did."

Mr. Chiba: "So how could the crew open the cages if they didn't have the keys?"

"I don't know. They probably used crowbars[15]."

Mr. Chiba: "Why would they do that? Why would anyone want to release a dangerous wild animal from its cage?"

"I don't know. Can anyone fathom the workings of a drunken man's mind[16]? All I can tell you is what happened. The animals were out of their cages."

Mr. Okamoto: "Excuse me. You have doubts about the fitness[17] of the crew?"

"Grave doubts."

"Did you witness[1] any of the officers being under the influence of alcohol?"

"No."

"But you saw some of the crew being under the influence of alcohol?"

"Yes."

"Did the officers act in what seemed to you a competent and professional manner?"

"They had little to do with us.[2] They never came close to the animals."

"I mean in terms of running the ship[3]."

"How should I know? Do you think we had tea with them every day? They spoke English, but they were no better than the crew. They made us feel unwelcome[4] in the common room and hardly said a word to us during meals. They went on[5] in Japanese, as if we weren't there. We were just a lowly[6] Indian family with a bothersome cargo[7]. We ended up eating on our own[8] in Father and Mother's cabin. 'Adventure beckons[9]!' said Ravi. That's what made it tolerable, our sense of adventure. We spent most of our time shovelling excrement[10] and rinsing cages and giving feed while Father played the vet[11]. So long as[12] the animals were all right, we were all right. I don't know if the officers were competent."

"You said the ship was listing[13] to port?"

"Yes."

"And that there was an incline from bow to stern[14]?"

"Yes."

"So the ship sank stern first[15]?"

"Yes."

"Not bow first?"

"No."

"You are sure? There was a slope[16] from the front of the ship to the back?"

1. Avez-vous vu

2. Ils avaient très peu de contact avec nous.

3. en ce qui concerne la navigation du bateau

4. Ils nous ont fait comprendre que nous n'étions pas les bienvenus

5. Ils continuaient à parler

6. modeste

7. un chargement contrariant

8. Nous avons fini par manger seuls

9. interpelle

10. à enlever les excréments à la pelle

11. jouait au véto

12. Tant que

13. gîtait

14. une inclinaison de la proue vers la poupe

15. c'est l'arrière du bateau qui a sombré en premier

16. inclinaison

"Yes."

"Did the ship hit another ship?"

"I didn't see another ship."

"Did it hit any other object?"

"Not that I saw."

"Did it run aground?[1]"

"No, it sank out of sight[2]."

"You were not aware of mechanical problems after leaving Manila?"

"No."

"Did it appear to you that the ship was properly loaded[3]?"

"It was my first time on a ship. I don't know what a properly loaded ship should look like."

"You believe you heard an explosion?"

"Yes."

"Any other noises?"

"A thousand."

"I mean that might explain the sinking."

"No."

"You said the ship sank quickly."

"Yes."

"Can you estimate how long it took?"

"It's hard to say. Very quickly. I would think less than twenty minutes."

"And there was a lot of debris?"

"Yes."

"Was the ship struck by a freak wave[4]?"

"I don't think so."

"But there was a storm?"

"The sea looked rough to me. There was wind and rain."

"How high were the waves?"

"High. Twenty-five, thirty feet.[5]"

"That's quite modest, actually."

"Not when you're in a lifeboat."

1. S'est-il échoué ?
2. au large
3. chargé de façon appropriée
4. frappé par une vague géante
5. Elles faisaient 8 à 9 mètres.

"Yes, of course. But for a cargo ship."

"Maybe they were higher. I don't know. The weather was bad enough to scare me witless[1], that's all I know for sure."

1. me terroriser

"You said the weather improved quickly. The ship sank and right after it was a beautiful day, isn't that what you said?"

"Yes."

"Sounds like no more than a passing squall[2]."

"It sank the ship."

2. une simple rafale

"That's what we're wondering[3]."

"My whole family died."

3. ce qui nous étonne

"We're sorry about that."

"Not as much as I am."

"So what happened, Mr. Patel? We're puzzled[4]. Everything was normal and then ... ?"

4. perplexes

"Then normal sank."

"Why?"

"I don't know. You should be telling me[5]. You're the experts. Apply your science."

"We don't understand."

[Long silence]

Mr. Chiba: "**Now what?**"

5. pouvoir me le dire

Mr. Okamoto: "**We give up. The explanation[6] for the sinking of the Tsimtsum is at the bottom of the Pacific.**"

[Long silence]

Mr. Okamoto: "**Yes, that's it. Let's go.** Well, Mr. Patel, I think we have all we need. We thank you very much for your cooperation. You've been very, very helpful[7]."

6. explication

"You're welcome. But before you go, I'd like to ask you something."

"Yes?"

"The *Tsimtsum* sank on July 2nd, 1977."

"Yes."

7. utile

377

"And I arrived on the coast of Mexico, the sole human survivor of the *Tsimtsum*, on February 14th, 1978."

"That's right."

"I told you two stories that account for¹ the 227 days in between."

"Yes, you did."

"Neither explains the sinking of the *Tsimtsum*."

"That's right."

"Neither makes a factual difference to you.²"

"That's true."

"You can't prove which story is true and which is not. You must take my word for it.³"

"I guess so.⁴"

"In both stories the ship sinks, my entire family dies, and I suffer."

"Yes, that's true."

"So tell me, since it makes no factual difference to you and you can't prove the question either way⁵, which story do you prefer? Which is the better story, the story with animals or the story without animals?"

Mr. Okamoto: "That's an interesting question ..."

Mr. Chiba: "The story with animals."

Mr. Okamoto: "**Yes.** The story with animals is the better story."

Pi Patel: "Thank you. And so it goes with God⁶."

[Silence]

Mr. Okamoto: "You're welcome."

Mr. Chiba: "**What did he just say?**"

Mr. Okamoto: "**I don't know.**"

Mr. Chiba: "**Oh look — he's crying.**"

[Long silence]

Mr. Okamoto: "We'll be careful when we drive away. We don't want to run into⁷ Richard Parker."

1. qui expliquent ce qui s'est passé pendant

2. Elles ne changent rien pour vous sur le plan factuel.

3. Vous devez me croire sur parole.

4. J'imagine.

5. prouver que l'une ou l'autre est vraie

6. il en est de même pour Dieu

7. tomber sur

Pi Patel: "Don't worry, you won't. He's hiding somewhere you'll never find him."

Mr. Okamoto: "Thank you for taking the time to talk to us, Mr. Patel. We're grateful. And we're really very sorry about what happened to you."

"Thank you."

"What will you be doing now?[1]"

1. Qu'est-ce que vous allez faire maintenant ?

"I guess I'll go to Canada."

"Not back to India?"

"No. There's nothing there for me now. Only sad memories."

"Of course, you know you will be getting insurance money[2]."

2. vous allez être indemnisé

"Oh."

"Yes. Oika will be in touch with you[3]."

3. va vous contacter

[Silence]

Mr. Okamoto: "We should be going. We wish you all the best[4], Mr. Patel."

4. bonne chance pour l'avenir

Mr. Chiba: "Yes, all the best."

"Thank you."

Mr. Okamoto: "Goodbye."

Mr. Chiba: "Goodbye."

Pi Patel: "Would you like some cookies for the road?"

Mr. Okamoto: "That would be nice."

"Here, have three each."

"Thank you."

Mr. Chiba: "Thank you."

"You're welcome. Goodbye. God be with you, my brothers."

"Thank you. And with you too, Mr. Patel."

Mr. Chiba: "Goodbye."

Mr. Okamoto: "I'm starving. Let's go eat. You can turn that off[5]."

5. éteindre ça

CHAPTER 100

Mr. Okamoto, in his letter to me, recalled the interrogation[1] as having been "difficult and memorable." He remembered Piscine Molitor Patel as being "very thin, very tough, very bright[2]."

His report, in its essential part, ran as follows[3]:

Sole survivor could shed no light[4] on reasons for sinking of Tsimtsum. *Ship appears to have sunk very quickly, which would indicate a major hull breach[5]. Important quantity of debris would support[6] this theory. But precise reason of breach impossible to determine. No major weather disturbance[7] reported that day in quadrant. Survivor's assessment of weather[8] impressionistic and unreliable[9]. At most, weather a contributing factor. Cause was perhaps internal to ship. Survivor believes he heard an explosion, hinting at[10] a major engine problem, possibly the explosion of a boiler[11], but this is speculation. Ship twenty-nine years old (Erlandson and Skank Shipyards[12], Malmö, 1948), refitted[13] in 1970. Stress of weather combined with structural fatigue a possibility, but conjecture. No other ship mishap[14] reported in area[15] on that day, so ship-ship collision unlikely. Collision with debris a possibility, but unverifiable. Collision with a floating mine might explain explosion, but seems fanciful[16], besides highly unlikely as sinking started at stern, which in all likelihood[17] would mean that hull breach was at stern too. Survivor cast doubts[18] on fitness of crew but had nothing to say about officers. Oika Shipping Company claims[19] all cargo absolutely licit and not aware of[20] any officer or crew problems.*

Cause of sinking impossible to determine from available evidence[21]. Standard insurance claim pro-

cedure[1] for Oika. No further action required.[2] Recommend that case be closed.

As an aside[3], story of sole survivor, Mr. Piscine Molitor Patel, Indian citizen, is an astounding[4] story of courage and endurance in the face of extraordinarily difficult and tragic circumstances. In the experience of this investigator[5], his story is unparalleled[6] in the history of shipwrecks. Very few castaways can claim to have survived so long at sea as Mr. Patel, and none in the company of an adult Bengal tiger.

1. Déclaration de sinistre habituelle
2. Aucune autre mesure requise.
3. Par ailleurs
4. stupéfiante
5. enquêteur
6. n'a pas d'équivalent